MARKETIN
PUBLICITY CAMPAIGN

- National Media Appearances

- National Review Attention

- Multicity Author Tour

- Most Anticipated Book Lists

- Podcast Outreach

- Major Consumer Advertising Campaign

- Influencer Outreach and Social Promotion

- Early Reader Review Campaign

- Author Backlist Promotion

- Book Club Marketing

- Library and Academic Marketing Campaign

What We Can Know

A Novel

by Ian McEwan

ALFRED A. KNOPF  PUBLISHER, NEW YORK

■ ON SALE: 23 SEPTEMBER 2025

■ U.S.A.: $30.00 ■ PAGES: 320

FOR MORE INFORMATION OR TO INTERVIEW THE AUTHOR
Todd Doughty, tdoughty@penguinrandomhouse.com, 212-782-9796

THIS IS AN UNCORRECTED PROOF
It should not be quoted without comparison with the finished book.

What We Can Know

Also by Ian McEwan

What We Can Know

A Novel

Ian McEwan

Alfred A. Knopf
New York
2025

[CIP Data TK]
ISBN: 978-0-593-80472-8 (hardcover)
ISBN: 978-0-593-80473-5 (eBook)

penguinrandomhouse.com I aaknopf.com

Printed in the United States of America
[printing line or automated Scout code]

The authorized representative in the EU for product safety and compliance is Penguin Random House Ireland, Morrison Chambers, 32 Nassau Street, Dublin D02 YH68, Ireland, https://eu-contact.penguin.ie.

[dedication to come]

It concerns the kind of human truth, poised between fact and fiction, which a biographer can make as he tells the story of another's life, and thereby make it both his own (like a friendship) and the public's (like a betrayal). It asks what we can know, and what we can believe, and finally what we can love.

Richard Holmes, *Dr Johnson & Mr Savage* (1993)

PART ONE

PART ONE

1

On 20 May 2119 I took the overnight ferry from Port Marlborough and arrived in the late afternoon at the small quay near Maentwrog-under-Sea that serves the Bodleian Snowdonia Library. The spring day was warm and tranquil, and the journey had been smooth though, as everyone discovers, sleeping in a sitting position on a slatted wooden bench is an ordeal. I walked two miles up a picturesque track towards the water-and-gravity-powered funicular. Four library users joined me and we small-talked as we were carried a thousand feet up the mountain in the creaking polished oak carriage. I ate supper alone in the library canteen and afterwards phoned my friend and colleague, Rose Church, to let her know I had arrived safely. That night, I slept well in my cell of a bedroom. It did not bother me, as it had on my first visit, to share a bathroom with seven others.

After breakfast, one of the assistant archivists, Donald Drummond, showed me to my carrel. His domain included my period, 1990 to 2030, and he took a strong interest in my topic, the ineptly named Second Immortal Dinner and its famous lost poem, 'A Corona for Vivien' by Francis Blundy. It was useful to have someone fetching this and that from the stacks, but Drummond's well-intentioned manner, his habit of pausing mid-sentence after minor words like 'of' or 'the' while letting his mouth hang open, made me tense. I suspected that he was ferociously clever. He spoke too often of his fourteen-year-old niece, a maths prodigy. He wanted to pick my brains, which suggested he was writing something of his own. I made matters worse by being exaggeratedly pleasant to conceal my aversion.

As requested, he brought to my desk the twelve volumes of Vivien Blundy's journals from her archive, which, for reasons scholars have never resolved, once rested marsupially within her husband's. As soon as I was alone, I opened the airtight folder and found volume five. I turned to page thirty-two. I needed to see this again. 'Things are settled between Francis and me. I'm mostly happy here. An achievement.' She is referring to the tragic case of her first husband, Percy Greene, who suffered from Alzheimer's disease.

She believed Francis loved her and, though neither was young and he was ten years older, they had 'a decent sex life' and there was always plenty to talk about. Nowhere in the journals does she regret marrying the great poet, though he spent much time in his study. Elsewhere she writes, 'I wonder if I sometimes enjoy disliking him.' By volume seven they had been married nine years. Early on, she had kept herself 'sensible' researching her second book, which she abandoned. When she had her job at Oxford, she had published a scholarly biography of the poet John Clare, a reworking of her doctoral thesis. She had enjoyed teaching. Several years later, her situation prompted wonder among her friends. By her own successive decisions, she had ended up above a small valley in rural Gloucestershire, without paid work, four miles from the nearest village, in a cavernous barn with 7,000 books. She would never have guessed that she would abandon a career, a vocation even, to serve another's genius.

One early afternoon in October 2014, 'with a strong wind roaring in a tree beyond my window', Vivien Blundy was in her study, which was in a converted old dairy separate from the Barn. She was probably making a shopping list of ingredients for the meal she would cook the following day to celebrate her birthday. She would serve the dishes at a gathering to which eight friends had been invited. She would have already devised the placement. Later in the evening they would listen to her husband read a long new poem, which was to be her present. The shopping and cooking were not acts of self-effacement. Vivien had a generous nature, and she liked to please. She enjoyed producing a well-turned meal. An orderly household gave her satisfaction. Francis had never pressured her to become his secretary, never encouraged her to disengage from her career, though it clearly suited him. At each successive move, she had made decisions for her own good reasons, though they seemed weaker now. The process took years. She was once a don, a candidate for a professorship, then she was part-time, then an occasional lecturer at an American summer school and working on the second book until she accepted it was going nowhere. Abandoning it was a liberation. She always felt herself to be in control. But it surprised her how, in caring for her first husband, and then in the name of freedom, of disenchantment with the university administration or of delight in the poetry of Francis Blundy, she had emptied herself of ambition, salary, status and achievement.

Perhaps it was by default, a failure to make provision in time, that her journals ended up among the poet's papers in the Bodleian Library, Oxford, later Snowdonia. A long time ago, a librarian had sorted husband and wife into separate boxes placed side by side. I have paid close attention to Vivien's sporadic and sad references to her first husband, Percy, a violin maker whom she nursed tenderly and who died after a bad fall. Many entries are bafflingly mundane and fail to tell Blundy scholars and others what they most want to know concerning the evening of her birthday, the famous poem dedicated to her, and what happened to the special copy – the only copy – that was the gift Francis presented to her after reading it aloud.

We can assume that on the afternoon of her list-making, she drove eight miles to the market town of Cirencester to collect from the butcher 'five brace of prepared quail, unnaturally plump'. She would wrap them in bacon and roast them in red wine and herbs, along with ceps picked in the beechwoods of the Chiltern Hills and brought to the Barn by a friend. She also bought eight pounds of potatoes for the oven and, in the same greengrocer, three cauliflowers whose florets she would cook in a large paella pan with 'olive oil, garlic, chopped green

5

chillies, anchovies, cherry tomatoes, black pepper, thyme and breadcrumbs'. Those were the days.

On the way home, the single-track country lane was blocked by an oak sapling brought down by the October gales. In the Severn Estuary, winds had gusted at 105 miles an hour. She and another motorist, a farmer she vaguely knew, lifted the tree clear and 'set it down in the long grass tenderly, like a corpse, which I suppose it was'.

Among the homely details are sporadic intrusions, bleak, faint cries of honest feeling, generally overlooked by the Francis Blundy hounds. I turned to an example now, also in volume five. The handwriting tips forward and is smaller than the rest. The punctuation is freer. 'I've never hated him. Never! But.' You might try to guess at the truncated final sentence or gaze at the middle letter of 'but' as though it might swing open on its hinges to reveal a peephole through which you could see a disappointed heart, reduced by lost opportunities.

Beyond the recipes, gardening notes, mentions of their nephew Peter, Vivien makes frequent references to the weather as the Barn years passed. A succession of mild winters oppressed her. For three weeks in one February, the temperature did not fall below nine degrees. She couldn't remember when she last saw icicles hanging from a gutter. Even snow was unusual. She noted the premature appearance of daffodils, of her roses, of the apples and pears in a neighbour's orchard. She is relieved when the stream below bursts its banks and floods the meadows, 'just as it should'. Two years later she is indignant when she sees that its clear water has turned 'a disgusting milky green and smelled'. Run-off from the farms or a sewage discharge or both. Neither she nor Francis was what they called 'political people'. They would not have joined with the local environmental groups, or the anglers and ramblers to protest and campaign for change. It was enough to observe and make a journal entry. Vivien keeps a lookout for the 'usual hedgehogs' and is disappointed. She is outraged by the badger culls. The strong winds that now streak down the valley make her irritable. When a short heatwave in July

6

tops thirty-seven degrees, she writes that it is 'impossible to sleep at night'. These various anomalies were not gathered into a larger pattern of concern for a changing climate or degraded nature, though a word she uses about the heat – 'sinister' – suggests that she was beginning to take a larger view and was troubled.

The birthday was her fifty-fourth. Apart from the shopping, we know little of the preparations for the evening that would come to be known as the Second Immortal Dinner. The first, so named by its host, the painter Ben Haydon, took place at 22 Lisson Grove, London on 28 December 1817. Among the guests were William Wordsworth, John Keats and Charles Lamb. According to Haydon's account, written and no doubt polished up more than twenty years later, it was an evening of wit, profundity, laughter, sarcasm and goodwill. There was a fine account of it in a highly regarded book by P. Hughes-Hallett published in 2000. It is likely that Vivien started preparing the night before, perhaps by tidying and cleaning the dining room and fetching greenery from the garden to make a table decoration. A visitor to the Barn the year before wrote a description of her doing just that one Saturday evening ahead of a Sunday lunch. As she did most afternoons after four, Vivien would have attended to the poet's business – the letters and emails from scholars and fans, invitations to speak, good causes wanting Blundy's support, complicated summaries from his agent of anthology rights. Younger guests especially were surprised by the domestic arrangement whereby an educated, bookish woman took on so many tasks. Francis would no longer drive, so she took him everywhere he wanted to go. She cooked, she cleared away, she washed the dishes while Blundy worked, read, talked or dozed. She topped up the drinks for him and his visitors. In her mid-sixties, she was still mowing the lawn, in winter she brought in the logs. A woman friend said in an interview years later, 'It was medieval serfdom out at their place and after a while you got used to it. If you offered to help, Vivien cheerfully refused. Francis never stirred from his chair, never did a thing. I don't think it crossed his mind that the household, the meals or even the state of his underwear might have something to do with him. He was, after all, a genius.'

The friend who gathered the ceps heard that interview and wrote a light-hearted piece for the *Spectator*, a weekly political magazine. The men, the young poets, who came to sit at the master's feet, were quietly envious of Blundy's 'no-finger-lifted life. It was common among the generation that came of age in the 1950s and early 60s and, of course, in every generation before it, for the men, especially the writers, to sit back and dream while the women busied themselves around the house. No one complained or even noticed. Then, poor chaps, along came feminism's second wave in the early seventies, determined to sweep away such civilised arrangements.' The Blundys were genteel survivors from another age and, according to the writer: 'The awkward truth was, she was a good deal happier and physically fitter than he ever was. She was bound to outlive him.'

The records show that by 14 October the wind had dropped and the day was cloudless and warm. The thermometer on the north wall of the old dairy would later give a high point of twenty-three degrees. That morning, while Vivien was in the garden cutting late roses for the table, the postman appeared in his van and brought a heavy parcel which he kindly carried into the kitchen. It was addressed to Francis. She guessed what it was. She also guessed that someone had made a mistake and thought it was Francis's birthday, not hers. Before lunch she showed the package to Francis and removed the wrapping for him. It was a rectangular box in pale wood with a sliding lid, like an oversized pencil case. As she opened it, he groaned.

He believed he had everything he needed, and he did not need much. A gift not only represented clutter, it took up room in his thoughts as one more distracting obligation of gratitude, as an unwanted requirement to think of someone else, of their goodwill bearing down on him like a low cloud. Vivien generally wrote his thank-you letters, which he sometimes signed.

8

But this was different, a magnum of champagne from their nephew, Peter. He was in Pasadena, California at the Huntington Library for a conference on loop quantum gravity. No one understood what that was, despite Peter's patient explanations. Francis believed he had grasped what 'background independent' meant but had already forgotten. It was decent of Peter to tell them, one summer's evening when they sat out in the garden, that barely a hundred people in the world really understood LQG.

He or his mother had arranged for a wine shop in Oxford to select and send the bottle. Blundy was relieved. The champagne was not from some young poet wanting his work read. Vivien, irritated that her husband had not wished her a happy birthday, recorded this exchange.

He said, 'Better stick it in the fridge.'

'There won't be room. I'll put it in the ice bucket later. Or in the chest freezer. As long as I can remember.'

Francis probably took an apple from a bowl as he left the kitchen. He went along the passage to his study to write something down and make the final preparations of the birthday gift. The papers fill 135 document boxes. I hadn't called them up from the stacks on this visit, but I had already made notes on October 2014. Most of the entries concern ideas for poems, working notes and drafts, and thoughts on his own processes. References to other people are rare. Family dramas, personal relations never make it into his field of consideration. On the day of the Corona dinner, he clearly remembered something of Peter's descriptions. He was making notes towards his poem 'String'.

> Space and time are woven from minuscule loops into a fabric
> a trillion trillion times finer than silk. The loops are as small
> as physics allows things to be.

Over the page he acknowledges some of the serious players in the field.

Ashtekar, Rovelli, Smolin, like expensive brands of gin . . . Apparently, the field of speculation is 'the nature of the universe'. In which case it's also a matter for poetry. The impenetrable concepts don't need to be understood to be made to sing. Not necessary to know anything about the brain to enjoy a sonnet or a sunset. A black box! But if Wystan got his mind round physics, then who can't?

2

I saw Drummond heading my way. It was mid-morning and many had left their desks for acorn coffee in a communal room. As he came closer, I winced. The archivist must have thought I was in Snowdonia for a holiday.

He leaned over my partition. 'Tom. About the numbers.'

That again. 'Sorry. I completely forgot.'

In Vivien Blundy's last journal, in the right-hand corner of the final pages, are two late-twentieth-century eleven-digit mobile-phone numbers. In the hundred years since, despite extensive online directories, no one has discovered whose numbers they were, not that many have bothered. Drummond thought he and I could work on it together. I wasn't interested. It was most likely some local supplier, but on my last visit, I had said that I would take the sequence to our Communications Department. It was an empty promise, which I immediately forgot. I would be wasting my time. It was also depressing to visit what we in the humanities called 'the other side'. The Science and Technology buildings were vast and beautiful compared to ours.

'I've had an idea. Might interest you.'

'Of course, but not now Donald. Got to get on.'

'Quite. After dinner perhaps.'

I nodded. He did not appear offended as he left. I wondered if he was used to people turning him away. Suppressing my guilt, I went back to my long-ago world.

When public interest in the Blundy dinner began to spread, there was much righteous media scorn. The National Press Library in the Pennines holds a lot of it. It was not the poetry that fascinated people at first, it was the guest list. Most barely noticed or cared, but a minority took issue. They did not like the 'Barn set' – straight, white, an influential and comfortable literary elite drawn from the London–Oxford axis. Why, journalists and bloggers asked themselves, this preoccupation with a gathering of elderly, self-satisfied mediocrities? This was even worse than the long-forgotten Bloomsbury obsession. Twelve years after the event, an article in the *Telegraph*, a national newspaper, made a defence. It was a private party, with no social obligation to regulate its own composition. The Blundys invited mostly friends they had known for years and had known them before they published. Blundy ranked with Seamus Heaney as one of the greatest poets writing in English in the late twentieth and early twenty-first centuries. Granted, one of Blundy's friends was the novelist Mary Sheldrake, and another guest was his editor and brother-in-law Harry Kitchener. But two of the guests were gay, two were well under forty, none was rich or had political influence and half of those present had never published at all.

But this could not settle the matter. The evening may have once been a private affair, but it no longer was. The issue was not a lost birthday poem read after dinner, it was what the poem by its non-existence had become: a repository of dreams, of tortured nostalgia, futile retrospective anger and a focus of unhinged reverence; Blundy's choice of form, it was said, told all. A corona was an ornate anachronism in the twenty-first century. The poem, through no merit of its own but the folly of its admirers, had leapt its bounds to plunge into the mire of political economy, global history and suffering. Comparisons with the 'immortal dinner' of 1817, so the argument went, were baseless. Wit is largely the preserve of the agile-minded young. There was no one at the Blundys' that evening who could have matched Leigh Hunt or Keats, only four years from the end of his short life. No one in that well-appointed barn could have competed with Wordsworth for learning, memorised verse or force of personality.

And so the debate has limped on, and the fame of the Blundy evening has grown through the years as cities, landscapes and institutions have drowned or withered. But so much information, in countless strata of unimportant detail, has survived. It could bury us. Many scholars have suffocated under the weight of trivial facts. We know, for example, that Francis Blundy was fond of apples. He had a good supply each late summer and autumn from the generous neighbour with an orchard. There are three Blundy poems about apples, the best known of which is often anthologised. 'On Floral Street' is about a long life shrinking, gradually divesting itself of friends, family, possessions – and ultimately, meaning. The central image is of a street juggler Blundy saw once in an quarter known as Covent Garden. In place of balls or clubs tumbling in the air, there were apples. The juggler snatched a bite out of each as it descended, until there were barely visible pieces of rotating skin and flesh, memento mori circling above his head. As a finale, the juggler tossed the remnants up high into a vertical column, tilted back his head, opened his mouth wide like a welcoming god – then nothing remained but the performer's bow. So it went, a merry poem about death.

After he had walked away from his conversation with Vivien, Francis ate his apple as he sat at his desk and made the notes towards a first draft of 'String'. By his elbow was the gift, a large rectangle of vellum, bought from the only producer of treated calfskin in the country, William Cowley of Newport Pagnell. On it Blundy had written in minuscule handwriting and black, durable ink a fair copy of the long poem he had put through many drafts over the previous five months. There were about 2,500 words on a single expanse of beaten, softened skin. 'A dead animal has conferred novel sensuality on my words. Now they are alive.' Also on the desk was a length of green silk ribbon. He had promised himself in a notebook (dated 2013–14 in box number 110 in the Snowdonia archive) that he would destroy all his notes and drafts so that his gift would be uniquely precious. After he had read it aloud, he would roll up the vellum, secure it with the ribbon, make a short speech and present it to Vivien.

He thought the poem was among his best. He looked forward to reading it that evening among friends and he would not need to rehearse. He had given many readings of his work to audiences in dozens of countries during the previous forty years. People thought he read well. He didn't adopt the derided high-priest sing-song of Yeats or Eliot's bogus crooning, and he despised the shambling apologetic tone that was the current fashion. He liked to be dramatic. He could be urgent or humorous or scathing by turns. He was gratified to read somewhere that he appeared to have a hundred modes at his disposal. Like his contemporaries, James Fenton and Alice Oswald, he knew his poems by heart. To come away from the microphone, go to the edge of the stage, to look into the eyes and minds of his audience as his baritone words flowed between the expressive swoop of his hands, to *perform* – was what he liked.

For this birthday present – he rarely gave gifts, but this one was also for himself – he had chosen another kind of performance, a Renaissance (some say rococo) form, a sequence of sonnets governed by demanding rules of composition. The medium pleased him. Vellum has served well the Magna Carta (now in the Mendips Historical Collection) for nine centuries. His shrunken handwriting, which he could not read without his glasses, ended just before the bottom of the page, in the right-hand corner and had 'an ancient, permanent look'.

A corona was a formidable undertaking. It consisted of fifteen sonnets. The last line of each had to be repeated in the first line of the next. The fifteenth sonnet, the 'crown', must consist of the first lines of the preceding fourteen and make sense. Francis had chosen the Petrarchan sonnet form: two stanzas, the first of eight lines, the second of six. The rhyme scheme was the traditional ABBAABBA CDECDE. Simple enough. The task was to write a long poem – conventionally addressed to one honoured person – that flowed naturally and did not buckle under the constraints of the rules. Blundy believed he had succeeded. We know this from a triumphant entry in notebook 2014–15, box 111. 'Concede the fact. My fifteen are superior to John Donne's humble seven.'

He wrote, 'That morning I lifted the parchment from the desk and brought it close to my nose. No smell of blood or flesh. Only the faint memory of a boarding-school inkwell sunk into a lidded desk of gouged obscenities. I felt the friendly weight of the skin in two hands. I don't remember when I last felt so innocently, serenely, unambiguously pleased with myself.'

He would have been satisfied but not surprised to learn that a century later his 'Corona for Vivien' would still be discussed. Perhaps not satisfied if he had also been told that the one copy in existence vanished. As far as we know, his wife has been its only reader. He must have assumed that the poem was bound to leak out and be published, if not in his lifetime, then inevitably after his death.

During his lifetime, some critics compared Francis Blundy's poetry to T. S. Eliot's. It was a shallow comparison based on a strain in only a few of Blundy's poems that lamented, as Eliot had, a supposed rupture in civilisation between feeling and the intellect that could never be repaired. But there were other parallels. Both poets had a Vivien in their lives, however spelled, and, on the surface, a comfortable kind of English existence that masked turmoil and carelessness with the lives of others. *Of things ill done and done to others' harm.* They shared a dangerous fate that all writers should hope to avoid. It was expressed by one critic, a contemporary of Francis, who, writing about the popularity of literary biographies, regretted a trend towards a fascination with the life but not the work. The affairs and penury in the lives of poets, the drunken lost weekends, professional jealousies, status anxieties and crises of self-doubt relieve a wider readership from engaging with the poetry.

3

Blundy's Vivien, unlike Eliot's, was not mentally ill. She was in the kitchen peeling potatoes. That we know what kind of potatoes these were raises again the matter of information. Burden or deliverance. Last year a respected scholar pointed out, self-evidently, that Vivien and Francis Blundy are as remote from us in time as Oscar Wilde was from the Blundys. By the late Victorian era, letter-writing and journal-keeping were highly evolved, but as one reaches back through time, before the Penny Post, the evidence of daily life thins out. By the time you reach the beginning of the seventeenth century, you are reliant on a handful of well-off and well-connected individuals, often aristocratic, with leisure to record quotidian existence or the goings-on at the court. On the Barn's bookshelves were a dozen biographies of Shakespeare, and another thirty covering the lives of other Elizabethan and Jacobean writers. These books contrived to convey a fair degree of intimacy with their subjects. But Shakespeare's case can stand for the rest. We still know very little about him. The cultivation and examination of the self, as represented by the character of Hamlet – a revolutionary moment in world literature – had yet to be translated into a general habit of reflective journal-keeping. Handwritten letters tend to get lost. Though printing technology existed, there were no newspapers that took an interest in the lives and thoughts of mere playwrights. The author interview was a long way off. Traces of Shakespeare's existence are mostly to be found in public records. He bequeathed centuries of dispute. He was an atheist, no, a Catholic. He kept a much-loved second

16

'wife' in London. He travelled to Poland. He didn't write those plays.

However, our biographers, historians and critics, whose subjects were active from about 2000 onwards, are heirs to more than a century of what the Blundy era airily called 'the cloud', ever expanding like a giant summer cumulus, though, of course, it simply consisted of data-storage machines. We have inherited almost two centuries of still photography and film. Hundreds of Francis Blundy lectures, interviews and readings were recorded and remain available by way of the Nigerian internet. All his newspaper and magazine reviews and profiles exist in digital form. In 2004, when the Blundy phones became cameras, pictures of the Barn, its interior and the surrounding countryside proliferated. Neither he nor Vivien was active on social media accounts, but they sent thousands of digital messages during the later years of their lives. These track daily trivia, give an accurate record of friends and acquaintances, of poems completed, and trace the rise and dip of mood. They tell us of Vivien's sorrows and regrets and all she wanted to let her sister Rachel and close friends know about them. We too can watch the daily news that troubled her contemporaries, the diverting scandals, the ancient sporting triumphs. We know everything that passed between Francis and his agent, publishers and translators, accountant, doctor and solicitor. Even his and Vivien's browsing habits are now obtainable. Messages sent by end-to-end encryption have been laid bare. As our dean once said in a speech, we have robbed the past of its privacy.

From the mid-1980s, in the expectation, lavishly fulfilled, of selling his archive to a library, Francis kept copies of all letters sent and received. The Barn library was catalogued and put online. Husband and wife kept journals. We know their voices well, their clothes and their faces changing through time. The differences between their private and public selves are apparent. Scholars see, hear and know more of them, of their private thoughts, than we do of our closest friends.

Even so, there are obvious limits to our understanding. An

email or text rarely carries as much interesting subjective reflection as a thoughtful nineteenth- or twentieth-century letter. When Francis and Vivien stepped out of the Barn on a summer's morning and looked about at the rich and tangled growth along the valley, they were not so completely estranged from the kind of landscape Shakespeare knew whenever he rode westwards from London by way of Oxfordshire to the family home in Stratford. If the Blundys could ignore the far-off rumble of combustion engines when the wind blew in from the east, they could experience an environment essentially unchanged and described by an unbroken 500-year tradition of poetry. All around were the narrow country lanes, surfaced by then rather than muddy or dusty, but following the same ancient routes, overhung by the same kinds of trees. The wildflowers were largely replaced by nettles. Populations of birds, butterflies and small mammals were vastly reduced but in theory they could, with good management, have returned. Over the next hill might be a line of pylons or an industrial chicken farm. The peace could be wrecked by the whine of a chainsaw or the scream of a low-flying jet from the nearby military airbase, but on various points of the compass were the distant steeples and Norman towers of village churches almost a thousand years old, and across the landscape lay a jealously preserved latticework of old footpaths that ran through woods, across the last remaining meadows, alongside impure streams. They too, in theory, could have been rescued one day. As long as one stayed out of towns and cities, there was a continuity which must have shaped the understanding of a poet, and which is not available to us today. Too many absolute ruptures, cultural and physical, cut us off from Shakespeare. The Blundys and their contemporaries lived with a sense of proximity to him which they took for granted and which we can never recover by digital means.

Still, we know more about the twenty-first century than it knew about its own past. Specialists in literature pre-1990, like our university colleagues along the department corridor, know only as much about their writers of interest as scholars in

Blundy's time did. The wells, always meagre, were drunk dry long ago. For them, no new facts, only new angles. And still, they talk of their 500-year-old subjects, playwrights and poets, as if they knew them as neighbours. Up at our end, 'Literature in English 1990 to 2030', we have more facts and possibilities of interpretation than any of us could articulate in a dozen life-times. For the post-2030 crowd, which is most of the department, there's even more. If civilisation manages to scrape through the next century as it scraped through the last, then we'll need to find another hundred metres of corridor.

So, we know that 108 years ago, in 2014, the potato Vivien Blundy held in her hand to peel for supper on her birthday was of the Rooster variety. 'I prefer them for roasting,' she had writ-ten recently to her sister Rachel. We can assume that the matter of her husband's absent birthday greetings was settled over a light lunch.

The first guests, Graham and Mary Sheldrake, would be staying the night and they arrived in the late afternoon. The sky was still cloudless, and sunset that October day was not until six. In the orange glow of a low sun, the brick and timber Barn, the stone dairy and their surrounds should have looked glorious to the visitors from London. But they didn't. There was a crisis. According to Mary's emails, they rowed bitterly during the three-hour journey. It was banal enough. For almost a year, in the face of her persistent questions and accusations, Graham had denied having an affair. Now, recklessly, and enraged by the heavy, slow-moving traffic, he had become impatient with her and his own lies. She wanted to know so he told her. Take that! In fury, she announced the end of the marriage. They emerged from their car with a terrific slam-ming of doors. Graham stood a few paces away with his back to the Barn as if to take in the view, its brilliant autumnal glow, while he gathered himself for the unavoidable social moment, the friendly embraces, chatty questions about the journey, then tea and scones. Everything he did not want. Mary managed the transition with ease. She felt triumphantly released, as one

19

might after winning a tough game of chess. Like a dancer she flitted across the gravel towards the Blundys' front door. She too was having an affair, which Graham, so busy with his own, did not suspect. It was ideal. She could guiltlessly dissolve the marriage (she was prone to guilt) and, in time, live with Leonard, an architect. She would text him as soon as she was alone.

Graham, also a prolific emailer, still facing the blazing trees, was regretting his confession in the car. He had omitted to tell Mary that he had terminated his affair with June Thompson three months before. In his irritation, he had thought it would have sounded too much like an attempt at a reconciliation, which was bound to fail. He turned and thought his wife looked young at fifty-three, and pretty and light on her feet as she let out a whoop and wrapped her arms around Vivien's neck. Soon, he was embracing her too, and then his old friend Francis. After they had been shown their usual room and had unpacked and were strolling about the garden with Vivien, Graham grew increasingly suspicious of Mary's gaiety. He excused himself from the company and went indoors to the guest bedroom, where he found her handbag on the floor of a wardrobe. He reached for her phone. It took less than five minutes to come across Leonard. Before he could absorb the shock or return the phone to the bag, Mary had entered the bedroom.

But their story is less of a concern than their states of mind which, in turn, directed their separate responses to the birthday Corona. Mary Sheldrake was among the most successful novelists of her generation. Translated around the world, winner of all the usual prizes, almost a national treasure. Her writing was minimal, all descriptive colour stripped out, too cautious for any fictional tricks, false histories or false trails. Some found her 'too intellectual' and lamented the dryness of tone and absence of sex or love in her novels. Others delighted in such tales as that of the convoluted kidnapping where the victim turns perpetrator, a financial fraud by which all prosper and all are innocent, and famously, a popular kitchen device, a microwave, that evolves a form of malign consciousness.

20

Twenty years after her death she was still popular, after which, tastes or needs changed and she was forgotten and now she is known only to a handful of academic specialists. Her story of complicated bank theft was derived from Graham, a personal financial advisor who seemed to have few or no clients and no money of his own. His interests were wine, cooking and golf, a game which took up a lot of space and became impossible to justify once the sea invaded the land. The general assumption was that Mary paid for his pastimes.

They were a popular couple. In company there was a merriness and daring about them that literary people liked. G-and-M, as they were known, had a taste for unusual recreational drugs and often enlivened an evening with a psychotropic novelty, a micro-dose too new to be illegal, from a laboratory near Big Sur, California. Rumours still went about of an inventive sex life, even as the couple approached their sixties. It was believed by insiders that Mary kept her novels sexless to guard her privacy.

4

While Vivien took a phone call from one of the delayed guests and had tea with G-and-M, Francis was having a shower. He knew his own processes and outcomes well enough to be convinced he had written 'something exceptional, of beauty and resonance'. As he stood under an insufficient trickle, for the shower pump had failed,

> Certain lines ran through my thoughts like old-fashioned ticker tape. Then a voice was reading them in the light tenor of a young man, my younger self. If I didn't feel young, I could at least remember how it once felt.

Again, he played with the idea of publishing. Vivien would not object. But the intimacy and weight of the gift would be reduced.

His mad scheme was also bold. The Corona was addressed to her, profoundly addressed. He must remain true to his original plan, and so in a burst of self-praise, he indulged some thrilled contemplation of his achievement, of how its 210 lines had not been cramped by the demands of the form but had kept instead

> a warm conversational tone, also lyrical, wise, also loving, also playful. It loves the natural world more than I do. Good on flow of passing time, on nature, on murder of what she loves. Rhymes unforced. Rhythm, like melody by Purcell, nicely sprung against iambic ground.

He thought it was too good not to escape into the public realm one day. But he did not need to be the one to set it free, and there was no hurry.

He stood by the bedroom window drying his shivering body. Coming up the valley, partly hidden among the trees, was an old Renault with running boards, a car that always reminded him of Chicago gangster movies. Somewhere for a thug to stand with a machine gun. He glimpsed a white shirt-sleeved elbow protruding through the driver's open window. The car was moving slowly, barely ten miles per hour. Tony Spufford, a professor of botany, and John Bale, a vet, were taking in the valley's glorious russet light. They would surely love this poem. They would not understand it. But Vivien would.

He dressed quickly, took the rolled-up vellum from his desk and went into the sitting room. Vivien had gone back into the garden with Mary. Graham wasn't in sight. Francis watched through the sliding doors as the novelist stooped to examine the raised beds. At the sound of a voice calling, the two women turned to greet Tony and John. They all knew each other from their north Oxford years. Francis came away. He felt comfortable in his thoughts and would rather have done without company, even if it included old friends. But soon it would be six and time for a drink. Then he would feel differently. His arthritic right hand would not allow him to work a corkscrew, but with his thumbs he could ease the stopper off a bottle of gin, he could get out the flask, ice, lemon and tonic and fill the flask. He went into the dining room and slipped the scroll behind the mantel clock. We know from digital photographs that its faded yellow dial was supported by two cherubs. The pouting smile of one was distorted into a toothless grimace of pain by a crack in the polished wood. It had been like that for thirty years, while its companion had remained cheerful.

Fifteen minutes later they were in the kitchen except for Mary and Graham who were in their room. Those with good hearing may have heard raised voices. Vivien drained the parboiled potatoes and put the quail in the oven on a low heat. Tony and

John were watching Francis's method with their drinks. He had filled a two-litre vacuum flask with ice, one part gin and two parts cold tonic. He added lemon chunks to four of the ten tumblers lined up and poured. Plenty left for a second round and for the visitors yet to arrive. They were about to lift their glasses to Vivien when the G-and-Ms appeared, flushed and in need of a drink. They all lifted their glasses in a birthday toast. It was a strong mix, they agreed, and you could taste the herb-infused gin. When someone asked John Bale how his practice was doing, he told a story about an operation he had performed that morning on a little girl's tortoise. It was suffering from a stomach blockage. In the theatre he turned the creature on its back and held it steady.

'I was about to give the Saffan anaesthetic when the fellow brought his old head slowly out of his shell and gave me this long look. We stared at each other. You know, he looked so intelligent. Like ET. A million years old. He seemed to be saying, Am I about to die? Do you really know what you're doing? And I actually began to wonder if I did. I gave the injection and these leathery lids rolled down over his eyes. First incision, then it was straightforward. You know, the inside of a tortoise is a thing of beauty.'

According to Mary Sheldrake's journal, Francis invoked Larkin. 'The tortoise was right. "The anaesthetic from which none comes round."'

'The girl came with her dad after school to see the dozy patient in his cage. She cradled him in her arms and cried for joy. Just eight years old. Quite a scene.'

This detail caused Vivien to turn away to spread olive oil, salt and pepper over the potatoes.

The exchanges were recorded or invented by Vivien and Mary. Tony said, 'Until I met John, I didn't know they did surgery on reptiles. A while ago he did a snake with a broken back.'

'Grass snake, crushed spine. But she came through.'

After John had told how he had operated on the snake, Francis said, 'Who'd like another drink?'

'A few years back,' John Bale said, 'this old-school vet in

Buffalo, New York told me that tortoises don't feel pain. He'd pop his patient in the fridge the night before to make it sleepy and then set to.'

When Francis reached for the flask, Graham was the first to hold out his glass. He said, 'If you're an animal in our world you're better off with fur and big eyes.'

'Doesn't stop us slaughtering sheep.'

They heard a car pulling up outside and in the kitchen there was a sense of relief. Tortoise injection, crushed snake and slaughter had lowered the festive atmosphere. Mary could not dispel an image of John bent over his scalpel, slicing into a bleeding snake with extruding innards. Tyre marks on the patterned skin! She thought she would not be able to eat. Quietly, she asked for water.

Vivien suspected that something was upsetting Graham and Mary. Their voices were constricted or flat.

Together the company took their drinks outside to greet the Kitcheners, Harry and Jane, sister of Francis. They were both well built and tall. It was quite something, to watch them emerge from their car, unfolding themselves into the dusk and stretching their arms. Harold T. Kitchener was also a poet, not much read, for his work was difficult, with frequent allusions to Italian Renaissance painting and sculpture and Hindu gods. He was also Blundy's editor at one of the grand publishing houses and had become a fierce arbiter of contemporary poetry and a champion of his brother-in-law's work, about which he had written two books. Whether their friendship was independent of that fact or because of it was discussed among a younger generation of poets. But it hardly mattered. Where the Blundy oeuvre was concerned, Blundy shared Harry's high regard. Harry had agreed after much discussion to be his brother-in-law's biographer, but had recently changed his mind, for reasons unknown, and had not yet told Francis. Now the two men embraced, then Jane, a professional potter, took her turn, and when all the hugging was done – there were no strangers here – they went inside and Francis poured the welcoming drinks. The Kitcheners had some catching up to do, and there was still plenty for the last couple, who had been delayed because their baby would not settle.

The sun was down. With a clear sky, the temperature, so the records show, dropped within the hour to eleven degrees. My sources for the evening stretch across the entire company and are collated here. Email and social media traffic are held centrally these days, and easily accessed by those who work for an institution. Where necessary, I have added a few touches, but always within the bounds of the highly probable.

Vivien was on her way across the room to the fireplace but was intercepted by John and Tony, who were concerned by how much she took on and liked to tease her about it. While they got the fire going and brought in more logs from the shed outside, she went back to the kitchen to make a salad. Jane and Mary insisted on helping. As always, she resisted, then allowed them to lay the table. Francis, Graham and Harry, vaguely aware of work going on around them, protected their conversation by moving further away. Two years before, Sir 'Jimmy' Savile, a radio and TV personality, friend to the young and disadvantaged, supporter of charities, close to certain of the royals and the former prime minister, Mrs Thatcher, and knighted by the queen, had been revealed as a monster, a rapist, a serial abuser of children, even very ill children. There were rumours of necrophilia. A TV documentary had been repeated recently. A few months before, the Secretary of State for Health had given an apology in Parliament to those who had suffered abuse as children while staying in state-run hospitals and care homes.

Harry said, 'Do you remember people saying, "I always knew he was a wrong'un. I always thought there was something fishy about that bastard"? But where were they, when we needed them?'

'Savile hid in plain sight,' Graham said. 'Came on as a grotesque. Then look.'

Francis took their empty glasses. 'Another one? Can it

be true? How could he have sex with corpses in a morgue undetected?'

'Friends in low places.'

They laughed mournfully and at that moment there was a crash and a cry from Jane of 'Fuck!' across the kitchen. Mary had let slip from her wet hands a large salad bowl, one that Jane had thrown and painted ten years ago as a wedding present for her brother and Vivien. It had smashed and scattered across the flagstones. Now she and Mary were stooping to gather up the bits. Vivien was trying to soothe them both.

'It doesn't matter.'

'But that was bloody stupid. I'm so sorry. So *sorry*!'

'Really, it's OK.'

Jane said, 'I can do them another.'

'I'm so ashamed!'

'Mary, it's OK.'

When the larger pieces were on a newspaper in piles and Tony had finished with a brush and dustpan, Vivien and Jane embraced Mary, Savile was set aside, and all was well again as they drifted towards the fire.

5

A t the Bodleian I sometimes wonder if I'm suffering some mild form of dementia. If I look up from my papers and peep over the carrel's partition at the room and its silent scholars, I can believe that I'm in a dream, and that my waking reality is within the pages in my hands, that I'm at the Barn with these friends gathering for an evening to celebrate Vivien and hear a new Francis Blundy poem. I could have been there. I am there. I know all that they knew – and more, for I know some of their secrets and their futures, and the dates of their deaths. That they are both vivid and absent is painful. They can move me and touch me, but I cannot touch them. Sustained historical research is a dance with strangers I have come to love, and there are still two guests to arrive.

The baby, whose name was Todd, was eight months old and would not stop crying. He was being walked up and down the sitting room by his father, Chris Page. The fifteen-year-old babysitter, Jess, watched from the sofa. She had three younger siblings by her mother's second marriage and believed that she knew what to do, but that it would be impolite to say so. Todd's mother, Harriet, hurried in with a bottle of pink viscous fluid and a plastic spoon. There were murmured commands and a tussle around the baby's wide-open mouth as the screams grew louder. In the cramped living room of a small terraced house on Observatory Street, Oxford, the sound was overwhelming. The parents were distraught. Todd was their first child and their feelings of love for him were unexpectedly disorienting. Awareness of their incompetence and helplessness on display

before a young stranger had a numbing effect. They stood irres-
olutely in the centre of the room, somehow holding the baby
between them, and looked wounded as Todd reached for his
highest note yet. This was to be their first night out together
since the birth. Clearly, too soon.

At last Jess stood and raised her voice to offer to take a
turn. They handed Todd across. Softly singing a nursery song
in what sounded like fluent French, the babysitter walked out
of the room, and slowly up the stairs, then down, pausing
halfway, then up and, after five minutes, down again, this
time empty-handed. There was silence. She had put Todd in
his cot.

'On his back?' both parents said quickly.

Fifteen minutes later, Chris and Harriet were in their car,
heading north out of town. They would only be an hour late,
they kept telling each other.

'So don't race,' Harriet said.

They silently contemplated a collision and the course of
Todd's orphaned life. Chris was thirty years old. He and those
like him – this is from Vivien's journal – had recently come to
the attention of sociologists for defying the usual categories
and representing an interesting shift within the general population: reasonably well educated, but not to the heights, no fixed
careers, placed quality of life above income, shifted jobs often,
were not officially classified as skilled, read books and watched
art-house movies sometimes, followed music trends, travelled
well, were socially tolerant, not politically engaged, rarely
voted, used drugs without giving them much thought, had
little in the way of savings, enjoyed wide friendships. Chris left
school at sixteen, had talked his way into agricultural college
and left after a year. During the next six years he worked in a
warehouse, was an assistant stage manager in a rep theatre,
worked in a local-authority call centre, then in a racing-bike
shop, then trained to be a men's hairdresser and worked in one
of the new-wave barbers around Bloomsbury and Farringdon –
industrial light fittings, white-tiled walls, bare floorboards,

cutting-edge piped music. Two years later he moved on. He was good with his hands and worked for a friend who set up a shopfitting concern. After marrying Harriet, his girlfriend from schooldays, and they had moved to Oxford, into the house that Harriet's estate-agent parents had found for them, Chris built or fixed things for people, arranged things, delivered things, was a good carpenter, could bring in the right people, and was generally known around north and east Oxford and Jericho as a capable guy you could trust.

Still Vivien: Harriet was more mainstream. English degree from the University of Newcastle, a spell for a local newspaper there, then freelance in London, eventually writing profiles for magazines. She was known for dependability rather than brilliance. Francis Blundy had a reputation for being foul to journalists. Three writers had turned down a profile commission for a magazine called *Vanity Fair* before a desperate editor approached Harriet. No one knew that the poet was going through a period of self-doubt and was anxious about his standing and, untypically, keen to be liked by the young woman who arrived at the Barn with flowers and a box of chocolates. She was intelligent and beautiful, she talked sensibly about his work. Afterwards, Vivien walked her round the garden and liked her too. Harriet's article cast Francis Blundy as the rugged genius whose flinty exterior concealed a kindly heart, and as a profoundly sensitive, humorous and knowing figure now working at the unmatched heights of his art. The poet was content. Harriet and Chris were invited to lunch and it went well. But Francis couldn't quite place or understand the young man and his mild cockney accent. Seemed a bit dim and had never read a book. Only after Chris had repaired the Barn's leaking roof, increased the internet download speed, updated the poet's ancient computer and introduced him to an excellent physiotherapist willing to drive out from Oxford was he accepted. Vivien took to the couple. When Chris expressed an interest in physics, she arranged for the Pages to come to dinner with nephew Peter. She later became close to Harriet once she was pregnant. A daughter at last, a grandchild-substitute in prospect. The Pages asked the Blundys to be Todd's godparents.

Harriet and Chris were familiar enough at the Barn to let themselves in without knocking. As they entered the sitting room, the company stood. The gin and tonics were a memory now. Three empty wine bottles clustered on a nearby table. When the embraces were done – the couple was known to all – Vivien asked Harriet how it was going with poor Todd. Harriet answered that he was neither dead nor awake and everyone laughed agreeably and made space around the fire.

The subject was climate change, the mild term by which it was still known. That again. It was a major theme for Francis, and Harriet had tactfully excluded his opinions from her profile. He was, as someone had once said, a nuanced denier, but if opposed, a denier to his core. He had the knack in argument of making dissenting opinions appear like personal hostility. Most of his friends disagreed with him, and a few social occasions had been marred by raised voices. Now, when the issue came up, they tended to let him run on until the subject could be changed. They believed that the views of a poet made no difference to the earth's fate and it was never worth making old Blundy furious. He derived his analysis from the press – a former solicitor turned columnist, an Australian poet and critic, an ex-Chancellor of the Exchequer.

What was animating Francis now was a radio item that morning about a leak from the UN's intergovernmental panel. Its report was not due yet, but someone highly placed had divulged that alarm was spreading among the hundreds of contributing climate scientists. The community of nations was heading in the wrong direction at increasing speed. Here came the stultifying incantation: floods, droughts, typhoons and hurricanes, forest fires – increase in frequency noted; measurements across diverse scientific disciplines had confirmed accelerating ocean acidification, polar ice melt, glacier retreat, sea-level rises, land surface temperatures pushing upwards. Colossal migration, pandemics, resource wars and species extinction predicted – and so it went on. Francis was angrily unimpressed. Usefully, Harriet had transcribed her entire interview tape and kept the file. We can assume he made the same points that evening.

Interesting to note that in the mid-2030s, 'the Derangement', respectfully capitalised, came into general usage as shorthand for the usual list of global heating's consequences – a litany that wearied activists and sceptics alike. The term suggested not only madness but the vengeful fury of weather systems. There was also a hint at collective responsibility for our innate cognitive bias in favour of short-term comfort over long-term benefits. Humanity itself was deranged. The term did not stretch to include the related Metaphysical Gloom – the collapse of belief in a future, or more specifically, the fading of a belief in progress.

Blundy pressed on as the young couple found their seats and were given a drink. It was obvious to any fool that this was a gravy train. Hundreds of left-leaning so-called scientists and their bureaucratic masters needed to keep frightening us to maintain a flow of lucrative funding. Naturally, they skewed their data. For example, the ocean was not rising to envelop Tuvalu. The geology was clear. Tuvalu was sinking!

To adapt to a non-existent crisis, colossal wealth was being diverted from the world's poorest. Of course, there was warming, and humans were partly the cause. But it was slight, and it had become taboo to mention the benefits. Huge tracts of northern Canada and Russia would soon be able to grow grain and feed the world. What about breadfruit? Nutritious. Delicious. The trees were spreading north and south out of the tropics and just one plant could feed a family for a lifetime. Birds and butterflies of the Mediterranean were migrating north to England. The Northwest Passage would open to global trade. Fewer old people would die of flu in winter. We needed to understand that the earth was a self-regulating system. A fractional increase in atmospheric carbon dioxide would encourage faster plant growth and more carbon dioxide would be absorbed. Likewise, warming would generate more vapour, which would deflect the sun's radiation. The oceans were the perfect carbon sink. It all balanced out! Intellectuals of all kinds were professional pessimists and always had been. Even by their own standards, it should be clear to the green lobby that solar panels consumed more energy in their manufacture than they could ever generate. Slabs of glass and steel were despoiling the countryside for greedy profit. Offshore wind turbines were killing whales and seabirds. The end is nigh, was what these climate high priests loved to shout. But the end never came. It was fashionable nonsense! Life on earth, which included clever humans, was highly adaptable.

The company heard Francis out in silence. He paused, cleared his throat and concluded by saying brightly, as if all was settled between them, 'Let's have another drink. How about some red?'

John Bale got up to fetch the bottles he and Tony had brought. His alacrity was expressive of the general relief. Now they could move on, and Vivien's birthday would not be spoiled. While John filled the glasses, she went to the kitchen to check on the meal. It was a necessary respite, to distance herself from Francis, if only by thirty feet. The quail, the sliced ceps piled about them, the cauliflower with anchovies, and the roast potatoes were ready. The plates were warm. She had heard her husband's set piece too often, sometimes at breakfast. The guests' indulgent silence embarrassed her. Francis believed he had made an unanswerable case. At times like this, and she couldn't help it, she was irritated by his certitude, his entitlement, his capacity for repetition. A brilliant man, and such a fool.

We know from Mary Sheldrake's journal and from her correspondence that as Francis was speaking, she was beginning to take a loftier view of her row with Graham. Her three glasses had been helpful. There was a comic aspect, obviously. Both having affairs. He the liar, she the hypocrite. Then it was simple. Why fight? They should declare it to each other – they had an open marriage. The benefits heaped themselves before her like a pyramid of captured treasure. Banish the ugly and tedious business of parting. No perilous furniture share-out. No property sale, no packing up, no house move that would likely wreck the novel she was halfway through. No excruciating explanations to their sceptical grown-up children. She looked across at Graham where he sat to the right of Francis. The glow from a dimmed overhead reading light caught the fine contours of his elongated face. She was reminded that he could be gorgeous in a soppy way. They'd had many wild times. Two men in her life, her husband and Leonard. The wild nights could go on. What then of a threesome? She knew her architect, a decent upright sort, would not take to that or the latest derivative of Ecstasy. She would have to have them both – separately.

He suddenly lifted his head and their eyes met. It was a deep, penetrating exchange. His face was immobile, impossible to read. He simply looked at her. They may have held themselves there for five seconds. Or longer. Ten seconds? As she wryly noted later, she would have found the moment difficult to describe. There was nothing new to say about the mutual gaze of lovers after John Donne's twisted eye-beams threading eyes on a double string. The obscenities she and Graham had smeared over each other in the guest room across the narrow double bed had set them free. They were falling in love again.

Then, like a thrown switch, something happened, in her, not him. She doubted everything and had to look away. She was untethered and frightened. He had faced her with blank loathing, like the bullock-cart driver does the poet in the Lawrence poem 'Meeting Among the Mountains'. 'The brown eyes black with misery and hate.' She had read too much. Everything was like something else. That was what weakened her hold on the real. Idiocy, to have assumed that her kind of intense communion was also Graham's. She could no longer read him. He had given nothing away. Now he turned to talk to Francis, who smiled as he replied and placed a hand on Graham's forearm. If he had shared her heightened moment of joyous possibility, he would have been incapable of light remarks. But nor could murderous loathing precede small talk. So it was pure indifference she had seen. Perhaps. She was in a void. Flustered – a rare state for Mary – she took her empty glass and stood. The friends round the fire went on talking and did not hear her as she muttered through an uncleared throat that she was going to give Vivien a hand.

6

First-year students of literature or history who come to our department at the University of the South Downs have no interest in history. They prefer things that are new, like the latest toys and novelties of Nigerian pop culture. The few that make the effort are surprised to discover how approachable the past is, and how easy it is to understand the voices of historical figures. We like to tell them that their surprise should be all the greater. Writing in the late twentieth century, the poet James Fenton made the same point. Poetry and prose from the mid-sixteenth century onwards could be read without a dictionary. So, in Fenton's and Blundy's time there was already a continuous, 450-year tradition of comprehensible literature in English. That continuity, of course, stretches to include us. We on our sleepy overlooked archipelago-republic are the proud inheritors of that tradition. We introduce the students to Wyatt's most famous poem, 'They flee from me that sometime did me seek'. They have little trouble understanding that ageless refrain of low and high culture – she loved me, now she doesn't. Always a good moment then to introduce the kids to the pleasures of rhyme royal and the joys of the iambic pentameter. We teach the orthodoxy, as demanded by the dean, but no one really believes that iambs form the basic rhythm of natural spoken English – look at all the trochees in this sentence. By their stresses, even iambs are trochees. That's another matter – and there are three more.

Between the sixteenth and twentieth centuries there were, obviously, changes in diction. What's remarkable in our time is how minimally English has changed, despite the upheavals of wars, pandemics, nuclear exchanges, the catastrophic Inundation and the Derangement driving scores of millions northwards out of Africa into Europe. There is, as Adam Smith might have said, a great deal of ruin in a planet.

In our recent seminar series, 'Blundy and his Circle', the students were aroused from their stupor when they discovered how the various characters seemed so credible, and they came to know Blundy well, his voice, his moods and his changes over a lifetime. It was interesting to linger during one session on certain differences and similarities between now and then. All those about to sit down at table in the Barn that October evening in 2014 would live past their mid-sixties. Average life expectancy today is sixty-two. Then as now, cancer, heart disease and dementia were what did and do for most. The Blundys and their guests lived in what we would regard as a paradise. There were more flowers, trees, insects, birds and mammals in the wild, though all were beginning to vanish. The wines the Blundys' visitors drank were superior to ours, their food was certainly more delicious and varied and came from all over the world. The air they breathed was purer and less radioactive. Their medical services, though a cause of constant complaint, were better resourced and organised. They could have travelled from the Barn in any direction for hours on dry land. But scientists like nephew Peter would have known nothing of 'our' elegant and apparently poetic unified field theory, or of how to make cheap, edible protein from atmospheric carbon dioxide and cultivated soil bacteria. It would be a good while before nuclear fusion was a commonplace, at least in Nigeria.

We discussed with our students the causes of this constancy in the language. There are various theories as to why we are at a virtual standstill. The department prefers the view that the past, in print and on the internet, has such accumulated weight that it holds our utterances steady, even as it comes close to crushing us. What has happened in English is also observed in Arabic and Chinese. That the past teaches us how to speak and write is the emphatic version of this view. In English, approximately 30,000 classics of literature, television and film press in on us, with more to be rediscovered. Vastly more numerous are the barely lesser works. In literature and the performing arts, the modes of transmission have changed, but most works are in the business of expressing or investigating the human lot, and these are just the fictional domain. There are even more classics of documentary, history, nature and science writing, biography, politics, anthropology, on and on, a bottomless well of treasures. Then all the highly informative trash, as well as diplomatic traffic, legislation, trade agreements, pornography, legal business, instruction manuals, industrial regulations and, beyond those, billions if not trillions of ordinary everyday digital personal exchanges, of fads and viral wonders, scandals and abuses and the torrent of each day's news. It is hard now to regret that artificial intelligence did not add substantially to the pile before man-made disasters slowed its progress. The mighty past wears hard against the present, like oceans, wind and rain on limestone cliffs.

So, we know with pleasing immediacy, from routine messages of thanks to the Blundys, that the famous dinner of 2014 went well. The slow-roasted quail with ceps must have been a success. The note from Mary and Graham was more effusive than the rest. In the chilly guest room, mindful of the authentic but porous lath and plaster walls, they had spent a night of quiet bliss. Mary, telling all to her journal, wrote of 'the slowest, most languorous and silent sex conceivable'. She had been right first time. When their eyes met, Graham had been seized by rapture at the prospect of erotic liberation. It was, he told his wife, a swooning sensation that for a few seconds had rendered him deaf to other voices in the room. He had turned to speak to Francis to tame an uncomfortable erection.

We have a general sense of topics the company discussed while they ate. Jane Kitchener wrote about it to a close friend, also a potter. The other sources are Vivien and Harriet Page. The table was round, an encouragement to general conversation.

The Olympic Games of two years before in east London still shimmered in memory. They had enjoyed seeing Queen Elizabeth II appear to leap from a helicopter, and children en masse bouncing on hospital beds. The Russian annexation of Crimea in February came up, as it had before. The view round the table was almost unanimous, as far as one can tell, with Francis dissenting and Vivien remaining silent. Crimea had always been Russian. Didn't Pushkin go there to write? Surely, Ukraine was so vast it could afford this small triangle of land. It was hardly worth risking a Third World War to reclaim it. Francis insisted that the Russians should be forced to withdraw, otherwise they would be tempted to greater aggression. Eight years later, when Russia invaded Ukraine and a new chapter in European history began, the record shows that the other guests forgot their earlier views.

Just before they sat down to dinner, the anxious parents had phoned the babysitter again. All was well. From there, the conversation, like most, proceeded by a process of free association. After Todd, then child-raising and tiredness. Then tiredness and forgetfulness. Someone reminded the table of how, not long ago, the prime minister, a Mr Cameron, had accidentally left his eight-year-old daughter behind in a pub. Emerging from him, as from a matryoshka doll, a French president, M. Hollande, unpopular even among his supporters, within weeks of being elected. That was how it once was for the leader of a country that stood in constant readiness to storm the Bastille. From a foreign leader to an embassy, the Ecuadorian one in London, which had granted asylum to Julian Assange, an Australian who had leaked sensitive information online. A difficult man by all accounts, but his threatened extradition raised important issues of press freedom. Surely, Harry Kitchener said, he must be protected from a lifetime's solitary confinement in an American prison, a cruel and unusual punishment.

Francis typically dominated the table talk, but tonight, after the Crimea discussion, he was subdued. He was surprised how nervous he was. 'I kept in my sightline the dining-room clock. Just visible behind it was one end of the scroll. Whenever I looked, I felt my stomach tightening.' He was impressed by what he had achieved with his Corona, but its importance was also a burden. Would it, could it be understood? He thought 'it might need footnotes, sensible, helpful ones, unlike Eliot's at the end of *The Waste Land*'. He believed that this work equalled or surpassed Eliot's poem, and that was why he was so jittery. In the history of poetry, it could be a turning point. On first hearing, no one apart from Vivien and Harry would grasp his Corona's significance.

The conversation was interrupted by Harry Kitchener tapping the stem of his wine glass with his knife. He would make a short speech before proposing a toast, this time to Francis, who was to read a birthday poem. Harry had been described in a newspaper as 'the taste-making editor-dandy'. This probably meant no more than that he dressed well and, for a poetry editor, drove an expensive car. It was general knowledge that he was consistently unfaithful in his marriage. It was a mystery, so the gossip ran, that Jane put up with him so calmly. But she had thrown him out more than once. She took him back, it was assumed, because she wanted to keep the family together for the sake of their three children. Harry promoted his brother-in-law's poetry, but he was jealous of him too. The word was that the editor was always competing with his poet and always losing.

The evening presented a difficulty for Harry. For the past two years, he and Francis had been talking about the biography Harry would write. He had recently decided he 'was not the man for this', and he had not yet told Francis. There was bound to be an unpleasant scene. His guilt might explain why his speech was, in Vivien's record, 'over the top, fulsome to the point of satire'.

In an email to a friend, Harry described how uneasy he felt as the company fell silent and looked at him with pleased expectation. The Kitchener papers are with the University of Ardnamurchan at Roshven in north-west Scotland. These

40

days, it is a long and possibly dangerous journey and as far as I know, no English Blundy scholars have made it up there. Beyond the references he made in emails, we have no further access to Harry's thoughts about his speech or the poem that followed. It is possible that, as a dedicated editor, Harry spoke in good faith, or self-serving pride in 'his' author. According to Vivien, he described Francis as the best poet now writing in English ... standing at the summit of a great humanist tradition ... lyrical intensity, boundless irreverence, delightful humour ... returning poetry to the rhythms of everyday speech while achieving extraordinary density of meaning ... above all, the indispensable seer for our times who—

Suddenly, with a loud scrape of his chair, Blundy was on his feet and trembling, not in anger but excitement. His face was flushed. He stretched out a hand to prevent his friend from saying more.

'That's it. Thank you, Harry. But enough, enough! The evening is for Vivien.'

He strode to the marble mantelpiece and pulled out the scroll from behind the clock. He stood close to where Vivien sat. He gasped in irritation as he fumbled with the knotted ribbon. At last, he unrolled the vellum. He took deep slow breaths while he pulled his glasses from the breast pocket of his shirt, then he quickly scanned the first lines and closed his eyes. Calmer now, and looking round at them with a thin, distant smile, he began to read.

7

It was a rough passage home from the Bodleian, southward through the Irish Sea, and I was very sick. I paid extra for a miniature cabin. I lay there, repeatedly vomiting and gripping a rail with both hands for fear of being thrown against the adjacent wall. By recalling accounts of seasick sailors who jumped overboard, I persuaded myself that my bout was mild. We came at last through calmer waters of the old Severn Estuary then turned east towards Port Marlborough. It was midday when we tied up and the oppressive hum of the ferry's electric motors faded. Four hours late. I was unsteady on my feet as I made my way across the decks of two boats to reach solid ground.

I've always liked this port. Only eighty years old, it has an old-fashioned look, like a film set from an ancient movie packed with extras. On that day, the din of the quayside sounded merry, a carnival of jostling passengers, seamen, porters, fruit and snack vendors and a busker with a trumpet. In my state, the smell of grilled fish was disgusting. Moored against the quay, three and even four deep, was a jumble of sailing and electric boats and hybrids. A group of prosperous passengers stood with their trunks behind a velvet-roped enclosure waiting for their transfer to a larger ship, probably moored out on the Swindon straits. I've often dreamed of making an Atlantic crossing, if I ever had the funds. From what I'd heard, as soon as these passengers landed in America they would need to pay for the protection of a local warlord. The politics were complicated. Various armies and their offshoots were fighting to inherit the spirit and legitimacy of a glorious imperial past.

But that was not my concern. During my time in Snowdonia I had thought about Rose and was missing her. I used a card to free a hardwood-frame electric bike and set off to the south shore of Marlborough Island. My sickness soon passed, the strong winds had died and it was a delight to bowl along the unpaved lanes, past bare vineyards and through the occasional holm oak copse, twenty miles towards Ball Hill Quay. It was a ninety-minute ride, then a long wait for the last ferry across the Weald Sea to South Downs Harbour. From there, a two-mile walk to the university campus and my flat on the eleventh floor of the faculty building. I did not trouble to unpack. I went straight to bed.

A few years back we lived together for fifteen months until things went stale and we parted without drama. The university found me a one-room place in another building. Rose had a better formal education and is certainly richer than me. Or her parents were. The money she inherited embarrasses her and she prefers to live off the same meagre university salary as the rest of us. She is my brilliant young collaborator who knows more about the literature of 2000 to 2050 than anyone I know. My Blundy project has come to mean little to me without her. I need her good sense. But there has hung over us a question we prefer not to address. We had ceased to be lovers, but after I moved out we became good friends, determined not to let each other go. We had affairs, even talked about them, and colluded in the idea that it was a relief to be intimate, like siblings. It was as if we were waiting. We were close, and something would have to happen to force us apart or even closer.

We were taken on by the university when Rose was in her early twenties and I was thirty-two, thrown together to teach a course, 'The Politics and Literature of the Inundation'. It was hard work. These were surly second-year students, not the sparkiest bunch. Rose and I mapped out the sessions over a recess. Before covering the shifting global alliances, the resource wars and the literature that came out of the turmoil, we thought we should deal with the background in terms of nuclear war, the water cycle and the Derangement. We invited a couple of friendly specialists to address the group, one from Earth Sciences, the other a politics professor. In two hours the students offered no more than a grunt or a reluctant simple sentence. They did not want to know or think about a hostile sea. It bored them in advance. They lived on and among islands. So what? Fourteen young men and women were slumped around the table. They had grown up with the consequences, heard their grandparents go on about it. The past was peopled by idiots. Big deal. The matter was dead. The kids attended our course because it was compulsory. But they had moved on. What animated them in those days was a twenty-minute two-string bass guitar solo. Or possession of fashionable pale green and purple linen pants, worn low on the hips by both men and women and secured by a large tin buckle.

Rose and I met that evening for a post-mortem. We were inexperienced and took matters personally. It was as if we were teaching a dead language. No point asking the specialists back. Too embarrassing. We would get our minds round the material and do it ourselves. So at the next seminar we laid it out, we spoon-fed them a short history of sea levels. We spoke in cheery sing-song voices, as if addressing a pre-school class. We made jokes. We showed colourful animations, simple to understand. Twentieth and twenty-first centuries, sea-level rise two millimetres a year, mostly driven by anthropogenic (we explained the term) warming. Warmer water expands, adding to the rise. Freshwater lakes drained by human overuse, the water recycled as rain and snow back into the oceans – more rise. Melting ice, albedo effect explained – more warmth, more rise. But more significant, the nuclear politics of the mid-twenty-first century and the fatal concept of limited nuclear war, then a poorly engineered Russian intercontinental missile aimed at the southern United States exploding in the mid-Atlantic ocean, catastrophic tsunamis devastating Europe, West Africa and coastal North America, the suspicion that the mighty explosion was planned, the political pressure for revenge, further catastrophe before a

44

panicked peace was arranged. We spoke of the newly created inland seas, enlarged over time by increased rainfall. The land beneath them compressed and lowered, so they did not drain, but persisted like glacial lakes. Scores of vanished cities. (We showed old pictures of Glasgow, New York and Lagos.) The globalised economy and its distribution networks broken. Markets and communities became cellular and self-reliant, as in early medieval times. Those science and technology institutes, seed- and databanks, museums, libraries and universities not destroyed took to the hills and mountains. The knowledge base and collective memory were largely preserved, along with the internet, mostly maintained later by Nigeria, whose rise we also covered. Heavy industry and fossil-fuel use collapsed. So-called war-dust from Middle East battlefield nuclear exchanges rose to the upper atmosphere and average global temperatures dropped. By way of tsunamis, wars, starvation and disease, earth's population dropped below four billion around the time a shattered Germany was incorporated into Greater Russia. Amid the disasters, world literature produced its most beautiful laments, gorgeous nostalgia, eloquent fury – and those masterpieces, so we promised, we would study together.

Were all the kids asleep by the end, or just most of them? That night Rose and I went back to her place and got drunk. We were so young then, and in my despair I believed that I could not go on with my career. I'd find something else to do. Rose was of the same mind. But gallows humour rescued us.

At some point in the small hours she said, 'Tom, I think I'll walk down to the beach and hang myself by the lifeguard station.' She didn't move.

I said, 'Off you go then.'

And she said, 'Come with me.'

We laughed at ourselves and kissed and became lovers that night.

8

The varieties of silence are as numerous as those of speech or thought. Or of listening. After Francis had read the last word of the final line of the final sonnet of his Corona, there were ten distinct silences around the table. The poet's was the simplest. Francis reported in his journal 'a return to earth, to the present, to the self I had forgotten for twenty minutes'. He experienced a pleasant sensation of emptiness and exhaustion. He had nothing more to say, and he did not wish to hear anyone else. The matter was complete. While the room remained silent, he rolled up the vellum, looped the ribbon around and secured it with two neat bows. He may have had in mind lines from his early poem about a garrotting in the Spanish Civil War: 'with the transferred competence / of lifelong shoelace-tying . . .' He stepped around his wife's chair, stooped to kiss her and presented his gift.

She pressed it against her and whispered to him, 'Thank you. Thank you darling.'

As Francis walked stiffly towards his seat – he had a glass of champagne in mind – there was a sound, a suppressed sob. It came from Harriet as she lifted her hand from her wet face, half smiled at the others and began timidly to clap. With relief, the rest joined in, including Vivien, and the applause grew louder and there were murmurs of 'terrific' and 'beautiful'. Easier to applaud than to attempt something apt. To drink as they had, then listen to fifteen sonnets in Blundy's condensed style was a cruel demand. Helpless daydreaming was inevitable. But the sense of a serious historic occasion was not diminished. Everyone loved the poem. Much of what follows is drawn from journals, emails, various social media, a handful of letters and some reasoned supposition.

Harry Kitchener stood to lift the magnum and fill the poet's glass and went round the table. When all glasses were filled, Francis proposed a toast to Vivien. Then Harry proposed a toast to Francis and the Corona. The silence, instantly forgotten, had lasted as long as thirty seconds, according to an email Vivien wrote to her sister. Loudly toasting the poem – only Vivien and Harry knew it as a corona – was all anyone could think of. What had brought Harriet to tears, as she explained later to Chris as they headed home to relieve the babysitter, was the gorgeous music of the words and the evocation of companionable love, and love of teeming nature. 'So warm,' she said as she drove, 'so luscious and tender and wise. And so threatened with death. I felt it pouring all over me and I wanted to shout for joy and terror all at once. When it ended, I had to keep my big mouth shut.'

Chris nodded and said, 'Yeah.' Poetry had a lowering effect on him. Classical music too. Their cultural weight and solemnity and self-importance oppressed him. He suspected that people were subtly bullied into faking appreciation in order not to appear uneducated fools. Long ago he had proposed this to Harriet. She was so dismissive and irritated that he never mentioned it again. Among the craftsmen and women, marquee erectors and roadies he worked with, string quartets and sonnet sequences never came up. Stoically, he kept his suspicions to himself. But during the reading, his attention was briefly held by the poet's word 'proscenium'. It set Chris wondering how he would organise the transportation of some scenery flats from a children's theatre in east Oxford to a similar theatre outside Carlisle. It was a cost and logistical problem which he was determined to solve. Neither theatre had any money. The van he could get for almost nothing was too small for the flats. He could call in a favour and borrow a truck and drive it up north himself. He would pay for the petrol too. He knew that Harriet would approve. He did not notice the recitation ending or the silence that followed. What brought him back to the room was Harriet's little sob. He was happy to join in the applause and was the first to murmur 'beautiful'.

Graham Sheldrake had remained focussed for the first few minutes. He felt obliged as a house guest to give his host his full attention. Or the appearance of it. At the emergence of a rotund father-figure and then a certain significant phrase, something about a fracture, he started to wander. A crack now lay across his existence. If the marriage was over . . . or was it? Untracked minutes later he forced himself back and discovered he was lost. Francis was outside a church porch, when not long before, he had been contemplating a swim in a river with Vivien, if it was her. So . . . in which case, if the marriage was over, he was under no obligation to resume with June. She probably would not want him . . . manager at the golf club, a wonderful woman, but sort of . . . and Mary herself might like some kind of infor-mal, occasional . . . By the fire it had been hard to read her mood.

He came back at last to the dining table, into an alarming silence. It was over and they were sitting there like mannequins. For such a worldly, easy-living man, he had a refined sense of social obligation. He thought someone ought to say something, for the sake of an old friend. He and Vivien had gone to such trouble. The hospitality, as always, was splendid, and they were the only ones staying over. In desperation, Graham was close to saying he liked the bit about the church. But it may have been a house. Or a pub. There was also that crack, but in what? Not in a marriage. It might have been between sickness and health, or youth and age. When lovely Harriet started the applause, he could have leaned across the table to kiss her.

Many years before, Tony Spufford had published a guide to the wildflowers of Shakespeare's plays and poems. It was long out of print. The illustrations, though exquisite, were line drawings. In the bookshops there were now colourful books on the same subject at half the price. His was more scholarly, and botanists and Shakespeareans preferred his edition, but that made little difference to sales. In the Oxford house he shared with John, there were still a dozen copies on the shelves and Tony sometimes gave one, specially dedicated, to a botany colleague he admired. When Francis spoke of honeysuckle in his second sonnet, Tony thought of Shakespeare's 'over-canopied with luscious woodbine' and Clifton Darke's drawing. And then, as more meadow, woodland and riverbank plants appeared in the poem, some with beautiful and accurate descriptions, the professor suddenly remembered – Francis knew nothing about plants. Tony was a practised reader and knew to separate the implied narrator from the poet. Sometimes they overlapped and parted in the same poem, but could they diverge so wildly throughout and be emotionally honest? Once, in Tony's presence, Francis had called a dandelion a buttercup. When corrected he had muttered, 'Same difference.' When Vivien was away, the houseplants suffered. Some withered and died.

It was a trick then, impressive, probably legitimate. The poet wore a gorgeous mask. His apparent expertise was easily and rhythmically born, lightly folded into the lines with close observation and melodic grace. There was a clumsily symbolic Lord of Nature figure, set for destruction, but otherwise, these were songs of seductive complicity. But Tony could not free himself from an ungenerous thought. This was fraudulent, it was fakery. Francis had no love for the things his poem seemed to love. Or was this an aspect of the murderous destruction that seemed to permeate the poem? The professor knew all the flowers of the poem's first five sonnets, and he could never have conjured them so vividly. The poetry would have been easier to dismiss had there been coldness in Blundy's pretence, but it was fondly intimate with the living fabric. Better not to have known the poet personally. Like drifting clouds over a full moon, Tony's musings occluded sonnets six to fourteen. He listened to the fifteenth but could not be moved. When it ended, he sat in silence with the rest. The poem was accomplished, he was sure, but he could not eliminate a thread of dark feeling which he identified, as the applause began, as contempt. He clapped all the harder.

As soon as her brother began his reading and the social moment was in temporary suspension, Jane Kitchener tumbled inwards into self-reproach complicated by familiar sibling resentment. It was bad enough to have seen Mary drop the salad bowl she had made for Francis and Vivien, but her own shouted expletive shamed her. She knew that in this vaguely bohemian milieu no one minded, but *she* minded, and she thought her brother did too.

But Jane had deeper reasons for shame. She and her brother had a strict upbringing by the standards of the time. Their parents were observant High Anglicans. Francis, two years older, shrugged off the wasted hours of Sunday school and extra Bible classes more easily than Jane. In her mid-teens she had turned her back on the entirety of her parents' beliefs, but by late middle age had come to accept that she was shaped by her past and could do nothing about it. This was who she was. She did not believe, but she could not bear to read or listen to atheists, and crude expressions made her wince.

Jane entered the well-trodden labyrinth of fondness and resentment towards her brother, one she could never escape. The azure bowl she had made for him had been one of her best. It gleamed. Its faint lack of symmetry was its charm, its human touch. When she presented it before the wedding, he did not acknowledge it. Their childhoods together had been corrupted by imbalance. She had helped him with all that interested him – joining in to build his 'camps', collecting stones for his deafening polisher, pretending to be passionate about his favourite football team. But nothing of hers – music, running, clay modelling, wood carving – featured for him. He could not *see* what she did, or what she did with and for him. Even books, once her passion, were his in adult life. He had stolen them from her.

That she rejoiced in his talent and success was a continuation of their childhood pattern. He had never visited her studio, never asked about her work, did not read the article she sent him from a local paper about her exhibition. When Francis came to dinner, it was to talk to Harry about Francis's work. She resented being introduced to people as Francis Blundy's sister. Now Jane was expected to listen awestruck to his latest and join the adulation. This was the self-denying arrangement fixed in place since she was five years old.

She knew herself well. Her grudges surfaced because she had no choice – she loved her brother and longed for him to return her love. She had spoken to Harry about her feelings. He pretended not to understand. 'Just tell him how you feel!' But he quietly worshipped and resented Francis too.

At the dining table she drifted back into the reading. Unaccountably, an old man was lying face down in lush wet grass at the foot of a waterfall or was it a flight of stone steps? Jane was of a mind to stage her own form of rebellion. At last, the poem ended. During the silence she was determined not to speak. When Harry proposed a toast to Francis, she raised her glass to her lips, but she did not drink.

Francis was on his first sonnet and John Bale was thinking again about the snake and how touched he had been by the elderly couple who brought it to his practice at the end of a working day. They knew it was a grass snake and were not afraid to handle it. But when the woman went to lift it out of its cardboard box, John put his hand on hers to dissuade her. It was a spinal injury. It would be hazardous to move the patient. Though the creature was conscious, he thought that it would die and that he should wait for the couple to leave before putting it down. But as they said goodbye, they promised to be back the next day to see how their snake was doing. Such faith in him was touching. He cut away the sides of the box – he was unable to afford an assistant yet – and carried the snake on its cardboard tray into the operating theatre. It was a large barred grass snake, over three feet long, probably a female. The distinctive black and yellow collar and the black bars along its flanks were vivid under the theatre lights. Her eyes, black encircled by orange, seemed to be on him as he made his first inspection. The damage was in two places, both, fortunately, towards the tail, and not as bad as it looked. A bike, not a car. Snakes have an impressive capacity for axonal regrowth and neurogenesis from special cells in their spines. The immune system would kick the process into action. John administered an anaesthetic and sedative, phoned Tony to tell him he would be late home, scrubbed up and set to work with special cement, repairing what he could of the broken, feathery bones of the vertebrae, then stitching the wounds.

He worked for two hours, seized by a familiar passion, when rescuing a particular animal stood in for all that was important in his life: keeping his struggling practice together, maintaining his loving relationship with Tony – the best thing that had ever happened to him – and doing his best for his younger brother, who suffered from MS. The three elements of his existence were grafted into the body of a serpent, and therefore she had to be returned to full health. It drove him on, this mode of metaphorical thinking – and it often worked. The couple, Sam and Jackie Bryant, came the next day to check, and again a week later to take the patient home in a grass-lined aquarium, into their convalescent care. He wrote out instructions on diet and the rest. Earthworms would have to do. A month later they were back and together, vet and clients, drove after work to Wytham woods. He chose a quiet corner away from the main tracks, and not far from a pond. For ten minutes the snake lay still before sliding slowly into the undergrowth. When its tail vanished at last, the trio gave a cheer. On the way back, they stopped at a Thameside pub, the Trout, for a celebratory beer.

During drinks before dinner, it had bothered John when everyone had chuckled at the idea of his performing surgery on a snake. Reptiles had as good a claim on health as people did. When the poem ended and Francis was rolling up and securing the scroll, John returned to the couple, Sam and Jackie. He was a retired train driver, she a retired dental nurse. Now they volunteered a day a week at the practice. They fed the inpatient animals, tidied, cleaned, cut the grass and weeded the beds in the front garden. He and they had shared an intense concern, and it bound them. There was a lesson in this. If you could care for a damaged creature as biologically remote from you as a snake, then other closer human matters would fall into place. Startled by a sound, John joined in the applause.

As Francis reached the end of his third sonnet, Mary Sheldrake, who had immediately thrilled to the poem, reflected as she had before, that poetry, not the novel, was literature's indispensable form. The spoken or written poem was as old as literature, perhaps as old as speech, with roots in song, in the rhythms of daily life and the body's pulse, in the hunger to catch the passing moment and to glorify love. It was not a generous concession she was making, but an uneasy one. Poetry, it was said, was the senior service. She had sat with novelists on onstage panels and contributed to the usual extravagant claims for her art, but it was the poets who made the book of life. The novel was the froth of recent centuries. It had developed to meet the needs of intelligent, privileged women excluded from formal education and meaningful work. Indeed, 'work' was the word Jane Austen and others used to describe womanly hours of incessant and pointless embroidery as they chatted about their neighbours. And so, Mary insisted, the novel grew into the paradigm of higher gossip. Love, marriage, adultery, contested wills – the stuff of neighbourly fascination. It took modernism to shake the novel up (Mary had no regard for Tolstoy or George Eliot) and offer it higher aspirations and bolder claims.

Such thoughts often led Mary to turn on herself. She had crouched, but so gainfully, in modernism's long shadow, riding on the waves of Virginia Woolf's powerful wake. The Sheldrake style was so impenetrably bland that readers, academics included, mistook it for the hard gleam of postmodern profundity. Lulled by her public reception, she thoughtlessly deployed clichés, which were eagerly read through the prism of irony. The prose was empty of simile, metaphor or any extravagance of invention. She had turned her lack of a visual sense into a declared aesthetic. Her characters were not short of, but beyond, emotional complexity, their diction weirdly wooden, their motivation, or lack of it, unexplained. Her landscapes and urban settings were featureless. Taking no risks, she suspended her fictions above place and time, immune to any reasonable measure of their truth, sealed off against the mess of daily life.

She had suffered before from moments of self-loathing such as this one (Francis was on his ninth sonnet. A strange man resembling Falstaff had appeared) but she had pressed on with her writing as usual. She couldn't go on, but she went on. Who wouldn't? She was accepted as having written one masterpiece after another. The state would soon honour her as a dame. 'The sunshine of critical reception and readers' applause warm her fraudulent heart,' she wrote of herself in a notebook, in a style not her own. She had thought she couldn't change, that she didn't dare, but now she was going to. The poet's lines were flashing by her, but one sensual aside caught her attention. On a hot day, the couple, obviously Francis and Vivien, step out of the house barefoot onto the terrace to cross the lawn and respond keenly to the coolness of summer grass on their soles after the warmth of York stone. Mary was impressed by the rich invocation of a tactile and sensuous moment.

As Francis read, her admiration swelled. She would abandon the arid geometry of her fiction. The poet was reminding her, she wrote later, how good writing could be. She wanted his vitality and bright invention, but the spur was not only aesthetic. The recent turmoil, the thrill of momentous rupture, of breaking with Graham while wanting him, the possibilities of change and freedom in her life contributed to a sensation that rose through her, from the perineum to wherever in her brain these resolutions were located, a delicious, mad, tingling certitude. Later, at home, a sceptical inner voice told her that all she had in mind was an affair with this or that person, including her husband, and a possible furtive embrace with the amoral, easy-living ways of conventional fictional realism. Absolutely no need to have involved her perineum.

After Harry Kitchener's speech in praise of Francis had been forcefully interrupted by him, there was nothing for Harry to do but relax and sip the wine John and Tony had brought and watch as his brother-in-law fumbled with the tube, or whatever it was he had taken from behind the dining-room clock. There was a pencil and notebook by his glass. He liked to keep up with Blundy's work, but Harry was clearer than ever – he was pulling out of the biography. Francis was too controlling. He would want to see drafts of every chapter. The past would have to be sanitised. The slightest reservation about his work enraged him. It was madness to have considered signing up to years of trouble that was bound to spread through the family. Harry disliked confrontations. There would be an unpleasant scene, but he had his own ambitions and could hardly be expected to commit to a biography simply to avoid his brother-in-law's fury.

He recognised the corona form, having tried long ago to write one himself in seven stanzas. He had given up. We know his reactions from the letter, not an email, he wrote to Francis five days later. It survives in the Blundy archive. Harry's suave ironies drop away in favour of overstated praise. Pulling out of the biography might be rendered a little less stormy.

The opening sonnet, Kitchener announced, rings out like 'an Angelus bell', a summons to total concentration. It has a magnificent, assured tone of triumph – 'like the poker player behind his castle of chips, revealing at the end of play his royal flush'. Here, it is a set of promises: 'memory, mortality, the elusive nature of time, and of poetry itself. You caught it, Francis – the natural world in the symbol of a fertility figure. We love him even as we destroy him. Beauty and murder.' The assurances of religion are evoked, then fondly dismissed. Consciously, but fleetingly, 'you summon your spirit companions – the great poets, Donne and Herbert, Wordsworth and Keats, old hats made new', and then 'your bow to Wallace Stevens and "Credences of Summer". I've never forgotten how we used to quote it . . . "The physical pine, the metaphysical pine [. . .] Let's see it with the hottest fire of sight." ' Glancing but generous references. It wouldn't matter if other readers could not place them. 'The sinewy disruptions of the poem's iambic tread are Shakespearean, the Shakespeare of his late phase, when he was about to drown his book', and in all the poem's reflections, in the 'hallucinatory splendour of lush nature observed in miniature', there's the 'same valedictory quality, a farewell, but with regret and fondness – love for everything that lives, the ruin we inflict, as if we're watching the slow death of an old friend'.

Further on in this long letter Harry wrote, 'Francis, it's a glorious love poem, a hymn to Vivien.' How striking, Harry wrote, working from memory or his notes, were the lines evoking a swim the couple take together in a river, through a gorge. Could it be the River Wye before it joins the Severn, he wondered, or in France where they went once, the Tarn or the Hérault? Then he was 'entranced' by the lovers in the porch of a rural English church, about to be married, and no one there but the vicar, whose words from the King James Bible 'they love but do not own'. Harry had a sense of a 'face drifting upwards, formed from the dust of a billion torn petals. A persecuted man, the figure of Jesus perhaps, is being sacrificed.'

Then the couple as they grow older, love altered but still love in the face of an end from which they will not avert their gaze. 'They must accept what Eliot called *the gifts reserved for age*.' Fifteen sonnets, their ornate technical demands 'breezily met', and 'the last sonnet so magnificently and coherently summoning the rest, truly your crown'. In the gathering momentum of the poem's ending, Francis summoned not only Eliot but the grandeur of landscape from Wordsworth's *The Prelude* and MacCaig's songs to the Flow Country, both threatened, as if by Plath's lyrical despair. 'Your corona is a monument to a threatened biological civilisation. It's not only the poem's brilliance that strikes me, but its greatness.'

On the same day that he wrote his letter, Harry started an email which he did not complete or send. He stored the message in his drafts and must have forgotten it was there. 'In love? We must be mad. But I don't think we'. No salutation, no addressee.

9

The humanities are always in crisis. I no longer believe this is an institutional matter – it's in the nature of intellectual life, or of thought itself. Thinking is always in crisis. But we count ourselves a lucky generation. Together, science and technology (a technology largely devoted to the search for materials or their substitutes) devour most of the meagre feast, and we take the crumbs. But historically, these leftovers are almost sufficient, and we do not cost much anyway. Our major libraries and museums are relatively safe at their various elevations. Everything that ever flowed through the internet is now held centrally in Lagos and has been well catalogued. Advances in quantum computing and mathematics have cracked open all that was once encrypted. I'd like to shout down through a hole in the ceiling of time and advise the people of a hundred years ago: if you want your secrets kept, whisper them into the ear of your dearest, most trusted friend. Do not trust the keyboard and screen. If you do, we'll know everything.

Yes, for now we are safe. Some years ago, as a bunch of ambitious young academics with a project, we fought a battle which, seen through the rosy prism of success, we still love to celebrate. But how self-serving, the bitterness of the opposition, how depressed our spirits were sometimes. We called our dream '90–30' for short. Our plan was to set up a small department nestling in the folds of the Humanities Complex, along one of its shabby and interminable corridors. Our official title: 'The Literature and History Joint Programme in Postgraduate Studies, 1990 to 2030'. Immediately, our elders, the deans and professors, rejected our proposal. The period was too narrow! The great wars came before and after those forty years! The Inundation had not happened, the internet and the Derangement had hardly begun. The finest literature belonged to the 2050s and 60s as Mabel Fisk established her ascendance. The old professors were jealous, defending their own turfs, anxious to ensure that any extra funding came their way, not ours.

Among much else, they resented our youth, and they were right to. We would never have set this down in our submissions or even admitted it among ourselves, but it was precisely our youth that drew us to the period. What brilliant invention and bone-headed greed. What music, what tasteless art, what wild breaks and sense of humour: people flying 2,000 miles for a one-week holiday; buildings that touched the cloud base; razing ancient forests to make paper to wipe their backsides. But they also spelled out the human genome, invented the internet, made a start on AI and placed a beautiful golden telescope a million miles out in space. Then, of course, hardly worth repeating, they watched amazed as the decades sped by and the Derangement gathered pace, the weapons proliferated and they did little, even as they knew what was coming and what was needed. Such liberty and abandon, such fearful defiance. They were brilliant in their avarice, quarrelsome beyond imagining, ready to die for bad and good ideas alike. As science extended its domain, religious belief and conspiracy theories swelled. They were big and brave, superb scholars and scientists, musicians, actors and athletes, and they were idiots who were throwing it all away, even as their high culture lamented or roared in pain. We thrill in horror at their feistiness. They were loud, hungry, reckless and free, except for the hundreds of millions they left behind. We longed to study their literature and times with our students. We hoped the kids would share our passion for the furious energy of those times, and that they would throw off their own constraints and the timorous orthodoxies that hobble our institutions.

We had come a long way since our 'Politics and Literature of the Inundation'. We understood how the departments worked, and how to get round the professors. We knew how to teach. At last, we won through, and every year since it began, '90–30' has been oversubscribed. Other universities have followed us, with variants. Most take the view that 2030–90 at the Pennines Institute covers even greater tragedies and splendours. I never spoke about it while we were fighting our battles, but I intended to write a book about our period on its own terms, not describe it with historical or literary neutrality or through the misty lens of our own regrets. On that, I failed. The regrets were impossible to shift. My ambition, however vague, was to present the times as if I were living them. The sources were rich and diverse, the material was copious. It was while I was preparing the 'Francis Blundy and his Circle' seminars that a clearer plan took shape. I would let the poet himself be my vehicle, my vector. I would live with the Blundys, share with them that vital evening and recount the story, the journey through the decades of a lost poem. Where the source material did not exist, surely it was permissible to make educated guesses about the subjective states and lines of thought of people who had died a hundred years ago. Perhaps it was not. I had many changes of mind. Unprofessional to make things up, arid not to. I thought I was set free when a colleague suggested that the full title of our course pointed the way and granted permission. Let history and literature conjoin. Set out the facts, the story as told by the participants. When faced with the essential but undisclosed inner life, *invent within the confines of the probable*. I thanked him. However, in biography the price of invention is unease, then guilt, amplified in my case by Rose's scepticism. It was not my business, she insisted, to invent.

10

It was fortunate that the Corona reading sent Vivien to her journal the next day to consider her life beyond gardening, recipes, family news and all else she deployed to smother her formidable learning. The prose has a staccato quality, like so many stabs. When Francis presented her with the roll of vellum, she thanked him and called him 'darling' for the first time in a couple of years. She did so, she wrote, 'for the benefit of our guests'. But perhaps, after all, 'I do love him. Comfortable with it. Anyway, too late to go looking elsewhere.' She liked her life, her dairy and garden, her walks, the tranquillity, her friends, the spaciousness of the Barn. She noted that over the past year Francis had borrowed books and guides to butterflies, birds and wildflowers and left them scattered around the place. He had 'transmuted bland facts into sensual observation'. Later she wrote, 'Francis is trying to beat Heaney at his own game.' For a man and poet so 'startlingly unobservant', Francis had done 'a job on himself, or on the voice in his poem. That's his talent.' But as a poem addressed to her in celebration of their 'lifetime's love' (ten years, in fact) it was misleading. He was well known for disliking country walks. Away from his study, he regretted the wasted time. Why walk when he could write? She went 'happily alone' or, once or twice, with her nephew Peter.

It surprised her that Francis would want to imagine a life, evoked in such detail, in which they freely roamed, adoring nature's plenitude. That was an existence she would love. It was as if he was beguiling her with all that was missing from their marriage. 'Perhaps,' she wrote that next day, 'he's about to change his ways.' But 'float down a river together on strong currents through a gorge? He could barely swim.' On a summer's evening, he might lower himself into their neighbour's pool to cool off, gin and tonic in hand. He feared rivers because of Weil's disease caused, so he claimed, by liver-destroying bacterial swarms that flourished in the urine of water rats. Vivien and Francis had married in a London registry office, not a rural church as she had argued for at the time. He had never expressed interest in the King James Bible. He was contemptuous of religion and its sacred texts. A poem was a fiction, but this one was addressed to her, and no reader could doubt that as the poet's life companion, she was the subject.

Her first husband Percy had been 'a different species of man'. He learned his birds from his mother, a gifted amateur ornithologist. Vivien learned her wildflowers at school. Before his illness they sometimes covered twenty miles on a long summer's day, making discoveries and teaching each other what they knew. They once swam and drifted two miles down the Cherwell, then in spate, and ran back in wet swimsuits, barefoot along the footpaths. It troubled her that she was no longer able to see Percy vividly from 'the primary source of memory'. Over the years he had receded into the photographs she kept in a walnut box he made for her one Christmas. In a drawer in her study wrapped in a tablecloth was the violin Percy had built for the sheer pleasure in his craft – a copy of a famous old model. His physical presence, once so powerful, left no record but clichés like the one she had once found in a Mary Sheldrake novel, 'a great bear of a man'. He was big, bearded, cheerful, competent, reliably affectionate, loudly sociable, not the shape of a man you would associate with the delicacy of a violin maker. He worked from a shed in their Headington garden. Among chamber groups his reputation was growing. There was a significant leap in his income when he met a member of the famous group Radiohead, and designed and built for him an electric guitar. A friendly sound engineer from

Oxford Brookes University helped Percy with the electronics. More orders came in for guitars, but he turned them down. His passion was for violins.

According to Vivien's journal, they had been married four years when he suffered a serious lapse of memory. In a 'spooky episode', a few hours went missing from his life. The general medical view was that such lapses were common and harmless. Vivien was not convinced. The following year, a consultant neurologist showed her and Percy on a computer screen the results of a scan. There was the compromised brain tissue. The diagnosis was clear, and his future was set – Alzheimer's, a case of early onset. He was forty-three. In retrospect it was not clear which time was worse, when he lived in anguish about his future and discussed suicide with her, or when he crossed the line into vacancy and no longer understood what was happening. The second stage was by far the longer. He reached a 'dreary plateau'. For a long while he ceased to decline. Later he wandered at night. He was brought home by cheerful local volunteers in hi-viz jackets who went out with torches, phones and pet dogs to search for lost children and the demented. Vivien became more vigilant and at last accepted that she would have to take leave from teaching.

In their small house she began to doubt her own sanity. In eighteen months Percy had transformed from a happy, intelligent and worldly husband who loved and cared for her, into 'a childish dope' with incessant repeated questions, 'meaningless frets and total dependence'. She hated herself for thinking this way. Her duty was to respect and maintain his dignity. She knew she shouldn't be using a word like 'dope'. But it was hard. Every few minutes he nagged her with the same question. For days it might be, 'What time is it?' Then shifting to, 'When are they coming?' If she asked, 'Who's coming?' he would say, 'I don't know.' He would wake her in the night to ask her the time. During the long day he followed her about the house. 'What are you doing?' And sometimes, without affect, 'Why are you crying?'

Because he was wakeful at night, he sometimes dozed in his chair in the afternoons. Then she would phone or email her sister, Rachel, her vital resource. In one message Vivien wrote

What's so weird as well as pitiful is that he looks like he always did, like his real self. As long as he's not saying anything. He gets up, washes, sometimes even trims his beard. He puts on the clothes I set out for him. At breakfast he's in his usual place, drinking coffee. I glance across at his lovely big face and I think it's all been a bad dream. In a minute he'll get up and kiss me. He'll go out to his workshop to start on a commission. He looks at me and I imagine a gleam of mischief. He's been pretending all along. It's been a joke in bad taste. He was testing my love. Then he says, 'When are they coming?' When I fail to answer, he asks again. I go into the kitchen and start on the dishes. I know he'll follow me in and ask, 'What are you doing?' It's only seven thirty and there's a whole day ahead. Nowhere to escape to, for me or for him. If I take him for a walk, he'll ask, 'Where are we going?' If I tell him, he'll forget and ask me again. But then he holds my hand and gives it a squeeze and I know I love him. I can never put him in a home. We're both prisoners here.

Her sister came to sit with Percy to give Vivien a few hours to herself. The first time Vivien stepped out of the house alone into the back garden, passed his unused shed and opened the gate onto the gravel lane outside, she 'almost fainted with guilty joy'. The track ran along the backs of the Edwardian terrace and where it ended at the rotted remains of a stile, before a vast field of cereal crops, was an old chalk pit filled with rubbish and a copse of horse chestnut trees. They had 'somehow escaped the farmer's mad chainsaw'. A path formed by tractor wheels took her across the field under the 'dipped and humming cables of giant striding pylons'. It was 'a defiantly unlovely landscape of chemical farming'. But this 'lifeless immensity, scraped clean of hedgerows and trees' gave her a large sky, and 'the iron lid on my spirits was lifted for a while'.

Rachel came as often as she could, despite her own health problems. Vivien always took the same walk. To take any other route, by going out of the front door, would be dull, taking her down the suburban streets she walked most days to reach the local shops. When she returned from her solitary stroll, it became a reassuring routine to call out to Percy and Rachel that she was home. During that time, 2000 to 2002, Percy's mental shrinking proceeded imperceptibly. Vivien was desperate. She loved him and lived in 'constant grief'. This Percy was not the one she married, not the one who had 'brought me such joy and freedom'.

Rachel often brought her eldest, Peter, with her. Vivien adored her nephew. He was eleven years old, beginning to be a lanky boy, with an endearing shy manner and graceful movements. His dark brown hair grew thickly over his ears. He would not speak unless prompted, and then his manner was intimate and gave the impression of a rich inner life. What also struck Vivien were his eyes, clear, also deep brown and, whatever his mood, always merry. He did withdraw sometimes, not into sulkiness, but into a curious diffidence, as if he did not wish to be impolite and tell his aunt he had drifted far off to a place he could not describe, even to himself. She felt protective of him, worried that his tenderness and delicacy would not survive the demands of the school football pitch and the crude jostling competitiveness of male adolescence.

Peter and Percy always got on well. Before the illness they spent hours together in the workshop, where Percy, with good-humoured patience, cast the boy as his indispensable assistant, a natural luthier, he would say. Peter was a quick learner, with focussed curiosity about how things worked – machines, weather, animals, the cosmos. He was drawn to the fine electric polisher and miniature clamps ranged along the shed's workbench. In a solemn ritual on entry, he would tie on one of his uncle's enormous brown aprons, fix the specially adjusted goggles over his eyes, and work on a scrap of discarded seasoned rosewood that Percy had kept for him. He had the knack of treating his nephew as an adult with whom he was on easy terms, showed him some chords on the banjo and let him hold the special violin he was building – not a commission, but a personal project to recreate in maple and spruce the famous 'Vieuxtemps Guarneri' violin of 1741. Vivien once watched Percy and Peter coming up the garden path from the shed for their lunch, hand in hand, talking intently, and she felt 'a stab of love for them both that was almost like pain. The child we never had.'

It would have been actual pain had she known what lay ahead. When Percy began to unravel, Peter's visits dropped away, but that was Rachel's decision, not the boy's. When he did come and found the shed locked up, his uncle changed and the Guarnari violin forgotten, Peter adapted instantly. He and Percy remained close. It may have been that a more child-like quality in his uncle drew them even closer. Percy did not trouble Peter with repeated questions. Instead, they had inconsequential exchanges in low voices that could last an hour. Vivien overheard and wrote down the following.

> Percy: You don't know what makes the wind blow.
> Peter: Warm air is rising somewhere else.
> Percy: But what about the badgers?
> Peter: They're underground in their setts, Uncle Percy.
> Percy: Air up, rabbits down.
> Peter: You mean badgers.
> Percy: What about them?

Rose knows Vivien's journals almost as well as I do, and she knows the literature and social history of the period better than anyone. She reads the first drafts of my chapters as I complete them and our conversations often turn around the same issue. She is impatient of what I regard as an essential freedom to speculate, infer, make educated guesses and animate circumstance and states of mind with the reasonable projection of a common humanity unchanged across the intervening century. The alternative, I tell her, would be a numbing series of agnostic shrugs. The dead hand of academic neutrality would cause these characters to wither. I tell her that my duty is to *vitality*, to convey the experience of lived and felt life, to what it was to live in a certain time, however remote. Rose replies that my only duty is to the truth. Misquoting – not St Augustine as I thought, but the great twentieth-century philosopher, Wittgenstein – she says, whereof you do not know, thereof you must be silent. Otherwise, she adds, own up each time you make an educated guess. Our positions have become entrenched, but I think our exchanges are good-humoured, or at least we don't raise our voices.

Our first conversation fixed the pattern for the rest. Rose said, 'It could be missing from my notes, but Vivien doesn't mention in the journal what she cooked on the big night.'

'Quail with mushrooms was one of her special dishes. Blundy was very keen on it.'

'But you can't know. So you don't know what she shopped for.'

I said, 'Highly likely she bought cauliflower, another favourite.'

Rose kept at it. 'You don't even know she went shopping.'

'She must have been. Remember that tree blocking the road as she drove back.'

'Ah yes. Tree, or was it just a branch?'

I did not reply. Rose pressed on. 'That reading Blundy gave at the Sheldonian, Tom. Was it videoed?'

'No. But I've watched dozens of his other events.'

Before one respite afternoon and evening in January, Vivien knew that it was not a big sky she needed but stimulation. At the end of a lengthy goodbye, a complicated disentanglement, during which she almost changed her mind, she kissed Rachel and Percy and walked fast to her nearest bus stop. Soon she was standing across the street from Christopher Wren's Sheldonian Theatre. It was forty minutes until the event and already a queue was forming. Over to her left was the King's Arms, where she sometimes used to meet her students. Blackwell's bookshop was at her back, Hertford and New College minutes away. The epicentre of her professional career. She was eight months into an unpaid year's sabbatical. Around was the life she had left behind. She crossed the road to join the line and stood numbly waiting, speaking to no one. She had forgotten how to be with talkative strangers.

She was among the first fifty or so to be admitted. The poetry-loving public was too polite to take seats at the front. Prompted by healthy stirrings of entitlement, she removed one of the reserved signs in the first row and sat. During the next twenty minutes, as the Sheldonian filled, colleagues came by to ask after Percy and how she was coping. One, an emeritus professor of French, told her that he had been scanned and recently received the same diagnosis. They swapped notes in curiously humorous mode. Within several minutes she experienced something swelling in her spirits. It was simple pleasure, she later told her sister, in meeting people she admired and liked, who liked and respected her! 'I was crawling out of my cage,' she wrote. But she also noted, when everyone was seated and she was alone again, a 'boiling impatience' and a sense of 'life charging past me'.

As Professor Harold Kitchener brought his distinguished guest and brother-in-law out and the applause began, Vivien was reviewing her neglected projects – two essays for a collection, a conference keynote speech she should have given, a state school outreach programme she had been about to run, two abandoned PhD students and her abandoned book brought her back to her 'dismantled' personal life. The 'piles of wreckage' behind her included a two-week stay in Aleppo she and Percy had planned for this year, staying with a scholarly Arabist friend and her husband, a diplomat. At the bottom of the heap of that 'builders' rubble' was desire. Its remnant was a soft ache she felt in the early mornings. She was not, she thought, so old after all.

The applause died away as the two men took their seats. She watched the famous poet closely. She had come reluctantly to his work. In her twenties she had written on her cherished American women, Bishop, Sexton, Rich, Glück. Blundy's concerns were not hers. It was his technical flair that began to attract her attention. Then a handful of end-of-the-affair poems moved her. A celebratory lecture on Blundy given by Karl Miller and another a year later by Frank Kermode were impressive, but it was a paper by Barbara Hardy that won her over and she read Blundy again with growing respect. There was no way round it, he had a gift.

The two men sat on leather armchairs. Between them were glasses of water on a low table. After announcing that Francis Blundy needed no introduction, Kitchener went on to introduce him at length. The awards, the prizes, his themes of love, urban decay, the blessings and afflictions of modernity, his notorious refusal to bow to the queen, his scathing attack on the prime minister Tony Blair and New Labour, Blundy's championing of certain elderly, neglected poets and novelists who had refused to conform to the prescriptions of modernism. For almost fifteen minutes, Kitchener spoke with soft assurance through a half-smile, slumped in his chair, right leg crossed over his knee. Occasionally, he made a wagging movement with his free foot encased in its soft suede boot.

Throughout, Blundy sat rigid, staring straight ahead. He was a fair representation of the public's idea of a great poet – white hair swept back, a lined and sculpted face. At fifty-one, an early curse of age had turned down the corners of his mouth into 'a default expression of scorn, like Graham Sutherland's drawing of Somerset Maugham'. Blundy was a man facing into a gale which could not intimidate him. His chin was raised, and he did not blink to modify his reproachful pale blue stare. He was not listening to the speech and its pointless praise.

When Kitchener was done, the poet rose and crossed to a lectern. No formal thanks, no greeting, no ingratiating himself before his readers. In a flat tone, he announced the title of a poem – 'In the Saddle' – and spoke it from memory, glaring at his audience from left to right and back, daring those tempted to let their attention wander. It was a popular beginning. Many would have known it from their schooldays. A young girl, probably in her mid-teens, is helped onto the back of a large horse. From this vantage point, she looks down at her father, who is holding the leading rein while talking to a friend. The girl sees the 'old coin of baldness' on her father's scalp and feels a rush of delight. She is above him and no longer fears him. There is a muted suggestion that she knows he is unfaithful to her mother. The giant horse stirs impatiently. The girl runs a hand over its silky neck and the smooth polished saddle. If she is not free yet, she knows she will be soon, when the rein will fall from her father's grip and the horse will be at her command. The promise of impending liberation – from people like Francis Blundy, detractors liked to say – made the poem especially popular among schoolgirl adolescents.

Between poems, he returned to his seat and spoke loftily about his life, poetry in general and the famous poets he had known. Unlike most writers at public events, he felt no obligation to make his audience laugh. He talked about Auden, Larkin and his 'far too gifted rival', Seamus Heaney. The event was over quickly. Including Harry's speech, it lasted less than an hour and a half.

By the end of it, Vivien had made her decision. There was to be a reception afterwards in St Catherine's College. She had not been invited, but her confidence was restored. She knew she would be welcome. Within forty minutes of the final applause, she was in a noisy room, glass of wine in her fist, talking poetry with the great man. Close up, he was warmer than she had expected. She was 'pushing on an open mind'. From Blundy's point of view, it was equally simple. 'A young woman, a round-faced beauty ... knowledgeable and wise about poetry, inc.

70

mine . . . softened me up by quoting me at various points . . . Seemed determined and I was fed up and couldn't resist.'

They spent what Blundy called 'a decent night' at the Randolph Hotel. Vivien's version was warmer, but equally guarded. She wrote of a 'delightful encounter' and of being 'seduced by conversation'. He sent a friendly email after a tactful three days and hoped he might 'bump into her again'. She also let some time pass before thanking him and mentioning a 'chronically ill husband', by which she no doubt hoped to convey to Blundy her availability as well as her difficult circumstances.

The return to her 'Headington non-existence' was tough. It would be a month before Rachel could get away from her own constrained life to sit with Percy again. Vivien wrote, 'I long to scream.' She found herself snapping at Percy, then dissolving in guilt and desperate to make amends. While he sat in front of the TV one afternoon, she locked the house and took a taxi to a local-authority care home and was given a rapid tour. She was back in the house within the hour and Percy had not noticed her absence. Vivien was shocked by the cheerful but worn-out staff, the overcrowded communal room, low-grade TV on all day and 'everywhere the suffocating smell of awful cooking failing to conceal other odours'. Most residents were in a worse state than Percy. In her anguish, she wrote to Rachel, 'I will never put him away.' There were better places, country houses set in parkland, with lakes, fountains, piped classical music, but Vivien had no savings.

We do not know how the arrangements were made for the famous 'Cotswold tryst'. After their first cautious exchanges, matters progressed. We must assume there were telephone conversations, or letters that were destroyed or lost. We know that Rachel helped with advice about the five-day local-authority respite care. It was in a slightly better place, beyond the Oxford ring road in the Cowley direction. No biographer has been able to locate it. But Vivien took Percy there by bus, settled him somehow, then was collected by Francis in a taxi which took them for a long, expensive ride west to an inn somewhere in the southern Cotswolds. Some have argued for the Swan in either Swinbrook or Bibury, others the Lamb or the Ship in Burford. None of them exists now, of course, and it hardly matters. What does is that when those five days were up, Francis began his sequence of celebrated love poems, eventually published in his volume *Feasting*, and that Vivien's return to the little terraced house was even harder than before.

11

Let me repeat. Most of our history and literature students care nothing for the past and are indifferent to the accretions of poetry and fiction that are our beautiful inheritance. They sign up to the humanities because they lack mathematical or technical talent. We are the poor cousins and we don't get the smartest bunch. Our offices are dilapidated. Many of them leak. Our salaries are fixed at one half of the rate for our scientific colleagues. We console ourselves that we are more in touch than they are with the bottomless ignorance of the generational zeitgeist. But as our dean Torsten Schmidt points out in his welcoming speech to the new intake of students every year, they have before them on their computers a mountain range of unexplored material. Every song, lie, casual thought, opera performance, death threat, punk-band riot – all of it, more than 120 years of the collective human mind rescued for our perusal. The view, he will say, keeping with the alpine imagery, extends from the microbiology of the flora to the peaks on the curved horizon.

At this early stage, the students are not convinced. They cannot believe that pre-Inundation people of a mere century ago were at all like themselves. Those ancients were ignorant, squalid and destructive louts. As one of the brighter students pointed out, surely they could have done something other than grow their economies and wage wars. Behind this, though never stated, is the notion that they deserved the mega-deaths they brought upon themselves. Most of our kids are well into their second year before they begin to accept that the men, women and children of the medium to distant past were once as real to themselves as we are. Until then, the students make little distinction between the tenth and twentieth centuries, between the Thirty Years War and the Third Sino-American War. Or between Mark Antony and Mark Twain. Young people today dismiss the past for not having yet devised the pharmaceuticals they enjoy, though they could never tell you how they work. As was noted long ago, we are all innocent children in the tall forest of our clever inventions.

What brings our students round to the beginning of a mature understanding of history and an appreciation of what the past has imagined is – simply – *detail*. The everyday life of, say, a mid-twenty-first-century junior doctor as told by her digital traffic, recording her week: dropping her young children at nursery, dealing with intractable illnesses, difficult patients, useless or gifted colleagues, low pay, constant pressure, keeping watch on troubling political developments, meeting friends, loving or ceasing to love her husband, paying bills, streaming new music, planning a holiday, worrying about a pain, ordering the shopping – and so on, a picture made up of countless points of different colours, like a landscape by Seurat, whose work we display and explain, can arouse even the dullest of our students into an acceptance of shared humanity across an immensity of time. If we replace the doctor with an eighteen-year-old and her cascade of confusion, frets and joys, we might have even greater success. But not always. Some students do not like to see their own reflections. We've built up half a dozen case studies over the years. Four of our subjects were obscure, two were globally famous in the forgotten youth culture of the late twentieth century. What they have in common are the tracks they left behind of the minutiae of daily existence. Before the code was written for the Web, and then for email and social media, not even Samuel Pepys came close to the blizzard of humdrum diurnal doings to be found in our six cases.

Once these details have worked their magic on the students and they sense a past inhabited by real individuals, they can begin to take an interest in what those people imagined onto the page or screen. Then, in due course, how some were better at imagining than others. And so, literary studies, growing out of a historical sense, and deploying the old-fashioned tools of comparison and analysis, can begin. And then – the hoped-for final stage, an appreciation of the imagination leaping clear of time-bound circumstance into the bright air of timeless aesthetic pleasure and human relevance. That, at least, is the theory. Sometimes it works.

Teaching the 90–30 seminars to our groups of postgraduates has been our greatest reward. Our forty years were the best and worst of times, to misquote Charles Dickens. 'The spring of hope . . . the winter of despair.' I prefer teaching the post-2015 period, when social media were beginning to be drawn into the currency of private lives, when waves of fantastical or malevolent or silly rumours began to shape the nature not only of politics but of human understanding. Fascinating! It was as if credulous medieval masses had burst through into modernity, rushing into the wrong theatre and onto the wrong stage set. In the stampede, grisly government secrets were spilled, childhoods despoiled, honourable reputations trampled down and loud-mouthed fools elevated. Meanwhile, good poetry was written, and in 2016 the novelist Mabel Fisk was born to chaotic neglectful parents in the English town of Stockport. At last civilisation had delivered an imaginative genius to equal Shakespeare's. In 2023 first intimations of a cure for Alzheimer's and related diseases were published by a Cambridge research team. Far too late for Percy Greene.

12

A literary work, like a small child, may take a long time to achieve a fully independent life. Or it might have no life at all. We know from Blundy's journal entries and emails to Harry Kitchener that the poet was pleased by his reading of 'A Corona for Vivien' and remained proud of his achievement. He wrote, 'CfV – it works' and underlined the words twice. If he committed the poem to memory, we have no evidence that he wrote it out after he had destroyed all previous versions. Many scholars before me have been to Snowdonia to look for a draft or references to one and there's no trace. It seems Francis kept to his plan. Vivien was to have the only copy. Francis responded warmly to Harry's ecstatic praise and the matter of the biography was dropped.

In the mid-1990s, Harry and Jane bought a cottage in northwest Scotland, close to the coastal village of Glenuig, not far from Loch Moidart. They went frequently and loved it there, so much so that when he died of a heart attack in 2016, Harry's papers went to the University of the Highlands and Islands in Inverness. A couple of years later, the university opened an annexe in Fort William, and the Kitchener archive moved there. In 2039, just three years before the Inundation, Harry's papers were moved yet again to the new University of Ardnamurchan, safely perched in the heights around Mount Roshven, only a few miles from the old but submerged Glenuig cottage. Nothing of Harry's that was in electronic form is in his archive and his papers are not accessible online. Scottish scholars in the humanities showed no interest in H. Kitchener, an English second-homer who never, in prose or poetry, expressed any engagement in Scotland's affairs, its history, landscape or literature. Even as the Corona's fame spread, no serious scholar troubled to visit the archive. Then the Inundation and social chaos isolated the UoA in the far north-west. For southern Blundy scholars, the journey became too hazardous.

I assumed there was a quantity of valuable material in the Kitchener papers, possibly even a draft of the Corona. If it were as close as Snowdonia or even the Pennines, I would have gone long ago to the Ardnamurchan peninsula. But from our place to UoA is 600 miles. A passport is necessary and can take months. Forty years ago there was a direct ferry to the north by way of the open seas, but that no longer runs. The so-called inland route involves many unpredictable changes of vessel along the way and is a long and expensive expedition. Once you gain the Lake District Archipelago, there are treacherous shallows, powerful tides and rumours of lethal whirlpools. It is said that predatory gangs come shooting out from any of the countless hidden inlets on powered skiffs to deprive you of your goods and perhaps your head. There is no safety until the rough Sea of the Central Belt is reached. But once that is crossed and the comforts of New Glasgow are behind you, the same dangers repeat, especially as the boat skirts wild Rannoch Island. In all, not a journey for a desk-bound academic. When I said that to Rose, she told me the dangers were overstated and the journey would be good for me. It became a running joke. She accused me of cowardice. I accused her of wanting me dead.

But here I must pause to reflect on a subject of deep sentiment, of a familiar feeling I can no longer suppress. Typing the words 'the Lake District' . . . In my teens I became absorbed in the poetry of Wordsworth, the notebooks of his sister Dorothy and their youthful friendship with Coleridge. I was in love with simple Dove Cottage. They became mine, those 900 square miles of mountains and lakes, those 'rocks, and stones, and trees'. Submerged long ago, they remain a familiar terrain, boundlessly free, one that I can almost convince myself

I remember. It comes without warning, like a slap – nostalgia, though that can hardly be the word for a place I never saw. But it strikes, deep in my chest, a curious pleasure-pain of longing, delight, sadness. I think those who love our accumulated centuries of literature feel this most.

And it's not only the Lakes. Simply writing those place names –magical Swindon! – brings on a sweet melancholy. Oh, to have been there, when strawberries and oranges came in winter as a matter of course. Even to set down a date – 2010! To have been alive then in those resourceful raucous times, when the sea stood off at a respectful distance, when you could walk in any direction as far as you liked and keep your feet dry. When you might see and hear the real Francis Blundy in proud Huddersfield – 1994, in the town hall. This longing for what was never known and is lost needs its word, something beyond nostalgia, which pines for what was once known. It's not quite an affliction, but nor is it a resource. That pleasure-pain is emotionally disruptive, it wrecks concentration. I happen to know one of its most exquisitely evoked descriptions. I read it many years ago as a research student and it has never left me.

I was twenty-two years old and had not yet settled on a subject for my doctorate. I had been chosen to read a paper to a seminar on the art of biography. Browsing through the stacks, I came across a book by the writer Richard Holmes. I knew of him as an eminent biographer in the late twentieth and early twenty-first centuries, during a golden age of biography. But I did not know this early book, *Footsteps: Adventures of a Romantic Biographer*.

I eased the hundred-year-old hardback from its shelf in the manner I'd been taught. So many books have been lost. The cover showed a painting by Hans Thoma. I looked him up. A nineteenth- and early twentieth-century painter of idyllic pastoral scenes who was untouched by modern movements in art and favoured – though hardly Thoma's fault – by Adolf Hitler. This book's cover showed *The Wanderer*. A gentleman with shoulder bag, straw hat and walking stick is strolling along a rising stony track near a stream. Both sides of his route have been cleared and the trees have a bedraggled, etiolated look, a foretaste of the deforestation to come.

I read the book at my carrel in two days. Among its many treasures is an account of a journey on foot the eighteen-year-old Holmes took in the Cévennes, southern France, tracking the same route taken by his hero, his 'friend', Robert Louis Stevenson a hundred years before. *Travels with a Donkey in the Cévennes* was Holmes's bible. He stopped in the same villages as Stevenson, tried to keep to his exact route on the old country tracks and slept like him in the open, '*à la belle étoile*'. As he walked, he constantly referred to his copy of Stevenson's book. In the early 1960s, the last remnants of the ancient French peasantry hung on in the rural fastness of La France Profonde. Holmes chatted to local people along the way, pitting his schoolboy French against the twangy southern accent, aware that Stevenson's French was near perfect. Both men covered the 220 kilometres in twelve days. At every point, Holmes was conscious of Stevenson's progress, whether he was ahead that day or behind. Most often, he struggled to catch up with his hero's rapid pace. And always, Holmes was intensely aware of his presence, his humour and resilience, his way of seeing and recording, and even the details of his equipment, including his eighty-page notebook. It was partly a twelve-day tutorial in the craft of writing.

One evening, after walking through a heavy storm, Holmes crossed a bridge over the River Allier to enter the village of Langogne. It appeared to him a cheerful place, with its eleventh-century church and medieval market. But Holmes, footsore and exhausted, was gripped by a feverish idea that would not let him go, a blend of hallucination and hope: Stevenson would soon be arriving. The young man retraced his steps to the bridge and stood there a long while as darkness began to fall. He removed his hat in preparation for a formal greeting. Passers-by gave him odd looks. Bats started swooping over the river. Then he saw, fifty yards downstream, picked out against the fading gleam of the western sky, the old ruined bridge into town, the one his dear Stevenson would have crossed. Holmes was bereft, close to tears. 'There was no way of following him, no way of meeting him. His bridge was down. It was beyond my reach over time, and this ruin was the true, sad sign.'

This is the feeling I'm attempting to describe. The waiting figure on the modern bridge is me. The collapsed bridge downstream and the man crossing it a hundred years before represent the past from which I too am excluded, the past that from here seems whole and precious, when many of humanity's problems could have been solved. When too few understood how sublime their natural and man-made worlds were. Professionally, I've spent a lifetime getting on intimate terms with people I can never meet, people who really existed and are therefore far more alive to me than characters in a novel. I have tried to embrace what is 'beyond my reach in time'. For example, I think I might have loved Vivien Blundy. Perhaps she is the one I would be waiting for as light fell and the bats dipped over the river. I might have married her. I have come to admire and love her agile, inward mind, her honesty, her learning, her tender care for Percy, even as she longed to be free. Holmes too could have been my dear friend, just as Stevenson could have been his. That fervent longing and melancholy on the new bridge is what I feel when I read of their carefree treks across a glorious but demanding terrain, my true sad sign of a lost world that I have come to know too well. The Cévennes region is now one more archipelago, with steep wooded massifs rising from silent islands, perhaps beautiful, in its way, if you did not know what it once had been. For many years, since the war with France, travelling there has been hazardous, given the strength of local feeling. Even if that were not the case, I could never go. It would make me forlorn to think of the youthful shades of Stevenson and Holmes, those bright and hardy spirits, striding the country tracks somewhere below my boat's prow.

But to return to Blundy's Corona and its journey towards an independent life; the long-term goal is to discern the difference, the chasm that divides the poem as it really was from what it became in the culture. A hopeless task, perhaps. We start with shreds. A Kitchener-to-Blundy email on Christmas Day 2014 extends the thoughts of his October handwritten letter.

> I'm torn between thinking of it as, above all, a crown you set on Vivien's head in honour of a long love; or as a celebration of nature's glories, not only a lament for what we have mindlessly killed, but a passionate reminder of what is still there and must be loved; or a prolonged, sad bugle call to bring us back to ourselves and our approaching end, which we should face calmly and with gratitude for our luck in having existed at all. As you read that night, I thought the valedictory tone was predominant and it moved me. Now, I'm not so sure.

It is not clear if Harry had possession of the poem at the time of writing. Like Vivien and Francis, he had a good memory for poetry, and he may have taken notes at the reading. If he had asked Francis or Vivien to see the poem or make a copy – and he would have longed to read it – then the request was made in person or over the phone. There is nothing in her papers or his, in emails, letters or journal entries, that touch on such a request. In December, when he wrote to Blundy, he had only thirteen months to live, the last four of which were spent in the cottage at Glenuig. Jane Kitchener's anguished messages of grief suggest that being so far removed from the best medical care may have shortened his life. In January 2015, Harry wrote to the *Times Literary Supplement*, and perhaps this could be said to be the beginning of the Corona's odyssey, which was to take longer than Odysseus' twenty years and is not concluded yet. The pretext for the letter was a review-article about the art and changing fashions of reading poetry aloud. Harry's letter gave a brief sketch of Blundy's reading of 'an unpublished poem, a sonnet sequence, to a gathering of family and friends'. He initiated in passing the association with Keats and Wordsworth's 'immortal dinner'.

This privileged listener was convinced on the night, and remains so, of the poem's greatness. Its bold reach will establish it as Francis Blundy's monument. It will be seen as a priceless gift, an astonishing work of warmth, understanding of nature's fabric, and of technical mastery. All of us were moved, and when the last joyous lines had been read, no one could speak. On that evening last October, as momentous in its way as Haydon's famous supper of 1817, reading in solitude and silence could not have evoked in us such powerful feelings. As Jim Craigmore notes in his article, no poet today reads with such restrained power and emotional insight as Blundy. The art of reciting poetry needs to be taken more seriously by our younger generation of apologetically mumbling bards.

There was no follow-up to the letter, no stir of impatience to read the poem. Among those who would have cared, Kitchener's assumption that it would be published must have become general. The Corona would be out soon enough, included in Blundy's next collection, and meanwhile literary life slogged on. Fifteen months passed. Someone wrote on an obscure blog an unsigned piece on the Immortal Dinner, and quoted from the *TLS* letter '. . . as momentous in its way . . .' For the first time, the words 'Second Immortal Dinner' were used. The contributor's name has not been discovered. Vivien and Francis's email inboxes show four enquiries about the poem. Neither replied, perhaps by agreement between them, perhaps separately for very different reasons. By that time, Harry was dead. Jane Kitchener was not known to the literary world. She stayed up north and after finding some useable clay on a hike, founded the Smirisary Pottery, a local success. Another year passed and at last a young journalist, recently employed on *The Times* and keen to make an impression, started digging. Again, Vivien and Francis refused to talk to him, or even reply. The piece came out under the headline, 'Francis Blundy's Precious Gift'.

The poem was ready to be launched – but not quite yet. By

this time, Harriet Page was the mother of three, a small child, a toddler and a baby, and still living with Chris on Observatory Street. Her career in freelance journalism was, understandably, on the slide. Now she stirred. She gave an 'I was at the Second Immortal Dinner' interview for a follow-up piece by the *Times* journalist. Out of that came, eventually, a commission from a rival paper, the *Guardian*, for a full-length piece, and Harriet rose to it superbly.

Memory is a sponge. It soaks up material from other times, other places and leaks it all over the moment in question. Its unreliability was one of the discoveries of twentieth-century psychology. That did not stop people from relying on their own or from believing in the recollections of others, if it suited. Harriet's memory absorbed her circumstances and her convictions. She had faded from the Blundy circle, but not from any falling-out. She adored her children, was immersed in their care, no longer had any decent clothes, and had found that motherhood had drained her of ambition and self-confidence in the world outside the home. She had no time or energy to 'keep up', to read books or newspapers – if she tried, she was asleep within minutes. The prospect of a smart, opinionated evening at the Barn was intimidating. She would have nothing to say, and Francis could have no understanding of her kind of life. She would be a disappointment to Vivien, who had such hopes for her future. She would not have wanted to face Vivien's perceptive questions.

Outside of her intense, constrained existence, Harriet had one interest that consumed and angered her. It could never send her to sleep, and its urgency sometimes overwhelmed her. The Derangement – not that she would have known the term. For all the international conferences, and the promises of politicians, the madness continued. She belonged to two organisations and sometimes managed to write short pieces for their magazines or websites. When she could get Chris to have the children – he worked hard – she attended meetings of the Oxford local branch, and she went on marches. Other people's indifference to the issue infuriated her. The poem, or rather, her memory of the poem, was the sponge that soaked up her concerns – the future that her children and all children must inherit. The reading of the Corona was now three years behind her. Accurate recollection of a densely written poem, heard not read, had faded for all who were there. Conviction and perhaps parental fatigue helped to make that recollection especially porous for Harriet. Another factor could have been her rekindled journalistic ambition. A national newspaper was giving her space for a long piece, and she had a message.

The children tended to wake at different times through the night. She was still breastfeeding her eight-month-old baby. Invigorated, 'on a strange high', working through the night at the kitchen table, she snatched her writing sessions during the periods when all three were asleep. In the morning, Chris stayed home with the children while she worked upstairs in the bedroom, hunching low over a laptop, which she balanced on the unmade bed. When she was done, she printed out her copy downstairs, fed the baby, went back up to scrawl her corrections and second thoughts, typed them in, printed out, corrected again, typed in – and filed. She had turned in the requested 2,500 words in a day and a half. The features editor emailed back within twenty minutes, delighted, even excited. Harriet was in an elated state. Lack of sleep must have played a part. She 'hugged and kissed my husband and did a belly dance in the kitchen while Todd and Jack laughed and shrieked'.

She knew it was the best piece she had ever written. It is unlikely that she knew Francis had fallen seriously ill around this time. She drew on her earlier profile of him. The October 2014 gathering she dramatised as being 'tense with expectation', which the rest of the company may not have remembered. When the great poet began to read from a roll of vellum, they fell under a spell and no one could move. It was hard even to breathe. Their thoughts were no longer their own. The words, the images, the unearthly music of their ruthless truth, bore the listeners away, as if in a dream. Harriet enlisted Francis to her cause. His poem was a *j'accuse* of those who would, in her words, 'shrivel nature by slow roasting'. It exalted love – for people, for the living world – and promised love's victory over destructive forces who cared nothing for earth's beauty and whose gods were money and power. *Amor vincit omnia*. Harriet described the 'wondrous moment' when the poet presented the poem to his wife. But the sensational core of the article, its journalistic hook, were its concluding questions, which other newspapers, broadcasters, social media and bloggers began to pursue: where was the poem and why, after three years, had it not been published? Why had Blundy not spoken of it? Who else had read it? Had someone offered money to suppress a masterpiece?

13

Even if Vivien never read her birthday present, never even untied the scroll, everything I've learned about her suggests that she did not destroy the poem. At the least, by having it intact, her options remained open. More to the point, she loved Blundy's poetry, she admired the Corona even as it troubled her, and she did not possess the necessary arrogance or stupidity to deny history its chance to form a judgement. She may have preferred not to be its dedicatee, but she accepted that 'time would neutralise the association'. She had a passion for poetry in general and would never destroy a major work to satisfy a personal animus or because she was disappointed in her marriage. Apart from the diary entries, we have her emails. She wrote to her sister that the thought of the poem, 'just its green ribbon', brought on 'a peculiar form of turmoil'. In milder terms she wrote five days after the reading that the poem was 'beautiful but hard to think about'. A week later, off the subject, 'We should have adopted. He was against. A child would have knocked him flying off his pedestal.'

In early November she recorded in her journal a few trips to London to see Peter. 'Francis wants to talk about the poem. He wants praise. There's much to like and there are some lines I can quote back to him, but I'm not being completely honest because my own feelings are in a mess. Anyway, after each exchange he seems satisfied, but then he comes back for more.' Vivien supposed she could not blame him. 'He put so much into the poem. I'm under pressure to be grateful, and I suppose I am.' Perhaps she was fortunate that Francis was in his study for 'almost every waking hour with his keyboard clattering'. We know that he was writing his essay 'Wings and Shackles', about the role of form in poetry as liberation and constraint. There is nothing in Blundy's papers about unhappiness in the household. That was not his kind of subject. Instead, he records a feeling of relief to have finished with the strictures of the corona form. 'Time for some free verse. Or call it by its real name, prose with line breaks.'

Vivien wrote in her journal a short paragraph that has received over the years a fair amount of scholarly attention. We cannot know whether this was a draft of a letter that was lost or never sent, or a note towards a conversation that might or might not have happened.

> I came into your life after a lecture as an admirer, a fan. I promoted myself to secretary, but we never got beyond that. I gave up my career and that was my decision. I've been happy to cook your meals, write and post your letters, wash your socks, discuss your work. I entered your life. You never entered mine. Your poem reminds me to ask – is this all about to change?

Vivien had asked the sort of question that many women posed who, like her, came of age in the 1970s. She was forty years late. 'I'm a certain kind of female academic. In the domestic politics of women's space versus male entitlement, I'm a late developer. I'm also a natural housewife, a compulsive tidier!' Despite her hopes, life went on as before. Francis worked, Vivien read, gardened and continued to serve her husband. 'What's the alternative?' she asked herself. 'Ask him to cook?' Her visits to London increased, though there is no record of the meetings with Peter. In early December she moved her clothes and toiletries into the guest room and, without discussion, she and Francis began to sleep separately. It suited them both. As we age, she might have told friends, unbroken sleep unravels to become an intermittent affair. Francis and Vivien needed at different times to be reading or listening to the radio in the small hours. At almost 6,000 square feet, the Barn allowed much privacy and was comfortable and warm in winter. It was too inconvenient to go elsewhere.

The empty tranquillity of their lives was broken in February 2016 by the sudden, shocking news of Harry Kitchener's fatal heart attack. Jane's emails from Scotland to Vivien in that period were distraught and the two friends grew closer. At that point, Harry's papers were at the University of the Highlands and Islands in Inverness, soon to move to its annexe in Fort William. If Vivien or Francis had allowed him to take a copy of the Corona, it would have gone with the rest. He was buried in the Glenuig cemetery and six months later there was a memorial service in Oxford. It angered Vivien when Francis said he did not intend to go. Too upsetting. She tried to persuade him. He should be there for his sister's sake, and for the brother-in-law who was also his close friend, the man who had most eloquently promoted his work. She went alone. After the service and speeches in St Mary's Church, she and Jane spent two days together. There is no record of what they discussed.

The following year, days after Francis had been given the diagnosis of the illness that would kill him, Harriet's *Guardian* piece appeared. Francis was already in pain, and he was furious. Francis's agent and the publisher's publicist were inundated with requests for interviews and demands for answers. Where was the Corona poem? Then there appeared an anonymous blog that went viral. It informed the world that one of the oil giants had paid Blundy $100,000 for the rights to his poem and it would never be seen. Francis asked Vivien if she would object to the poem's publication. She told him she did indeed object. There was a shouting row, she said to Jane, but she recorded nothing in her journal. Two days passed and she discovered that the drawers in her desk had been turned over. She said nothing.

Because Francis Blundy would not feed the frenzy with an interview or comment, it began to ease after several days. His pancreatic cancer took twelve weeks from diagnosis to death. Since he had been reluctant to see a doctor and submit to tests, it must have been working on him months before. Vivien confirmed for herself that the outcomes were poor for this disease. She was 'immobilised by despair'. As he began to fade and shrink before her, following a round of chemotherapy which he did not intend to repeat, he worked all the harder and barely ate. He was eager to see friends, including his agent and publisher, but he would not have Harriet Page in the house. He spent time alone with nephew Peter. Vivien rallied and distracted herself by cooking for everyone. Francis would watch his visitors eat while he sipped a white wine and said very little, except on a couple of occasions to speak calmly about death. He was not complaining. He was sixty-seven and had gone 'a decent stretch' and was lucky to have lived the life of a published poet and to have found love with Vivien. He was looking at her when he said this. 'I couldn't meet his eye, I felt so ashamed,' she wrote to Jane.

Soon, the necessary morphine, in mounting doses, obliterated his capacity for work. He did not mention the Corona to Vivien again. That she would not allow it to be published to please Francis and refute the conspiracists might suggest that she had already given the scroll to Harry or someone else. Or her heart was untypically hard. During his last three weeks he was, she wrote, 'a muffled consciousness, hardly himself, shockingly thin'. He sometimes rambled in a low murmur, returning often to an old slight from 2013 when he was not invited to speak at Heaney's funeral. Then he appeared to rally and lay propped up in bed, correcting what would be his three last poems. Jane was on her way down from Scotland by the night train from Fort William to be with her brother and to comfort Vivien. She was due into Euston at eight and would reach the Barn before midday. When Vivien looked in on him at 9 a.m., Francis was asleep. At ten she looked in again and he was dead. He lay on his back, arms raised above his head as if in surrender. At last. Thankfully, his eyes were closed. She liked to think he had bestowed truth on that old white lie of the obituary pages – 'peacefully in his sleep'.

This statement was from a respected anti-censorship organisation: 'If the late Francis Blundy took cash from a fossil-fuel lobbyist in exchange for his silence on the climate emergency, it would be a bad day for freedom of expression in this country.' And here was the head of a large publishing group: 'We don't know if he was bought out by Big Oil, but if he was, I'd never read a word of his again.' If, and more ifs. A thin tissue of hypotheticals barely protected Blundy's posthumous reputation. But there was scepticism too. An economist writing in the *Financial Times* offered some common sense: 'The notion that the oil industry would care a hoot what a poet, however eminent, has to say about global heating is fatuous beyond belief.' But for a while the idea hung in the air like a bad smell. Three years later, in 2020, an Italian scholar wrote, 'That Blundy took money for silence was an internet meme that had no basis in fact. It was lodged in the public mind immediately after H. Page's article appeared in the *Guardian*. The mystery is why Vivien Blundy did not speak out in defence of her husband. She had a copy of the poem. She could have told the world what was in it and why it had not been published.'

This was reasonably put. In those dying days, when the media gale hit the Barn, the publicist advised Vivien to pull the plug on the house router. She was glad to. Francis was suffering and had to be protected. She told him the internet was down, but he did not seem to care. He was working on his poems or dozing on morphine. Vivien wrote emails on her phone and sent them by a weak signal from a hillock in the field above the garden. The drawbridge was up. Everything in the Barn was centred on Francis and his declining strength, and on his visitors, and everyone's distress. The oil-bribe rumour began to seem irrelevant. For an educated readership who loved Blundy's work, the story was just another piece of shameless disinformation. For those who believed the tale, it added to the

90

poem's lustre. If it was worth paying a large sum to suppress, it must be an extraordinary, powerful work. When had poetry ever mattered so much?

As for Vivien, here was the surprise. Within a year of Francis's death, after the funeral, after the big memorial service in Southwark Cathedral, the television documentary and the updating of his *Collected Poems*, she arranged to let the Barn out. On her last day there, with all furniture gone, the rooms stripped bare and the tenants due to move in later that month, she and Peter dug a hole in the garden to bury the dog, a terrier called Jack that had died two days before. The grave was next to Jack's mother, Kip. Vivien moved to Scotland to live with Jane Kitchener, and they stayed there together in the Glenuig cottage for the rest of their lives. Peter visited her a few times and Rachel went regularly over the years. Vivien was happy to be absorbed into a new milieu and landscape. She ignored all enquiries from academics or the press. With Jane she explored the wilderness of Moidart, the Rough Bounds. Between them, she and Jane held all, or nearly all, the Blundy secrets. When Vivien died in 2038, her papers went to the Bodleian in Oxford to join the Francis Blundy archive. Three years earlier, Jane had died. What happened to her private papers is not known.

I return to the loud week that followed Harriet Page's article. The poet was sealed off from the world, but it did not take the media long to track down the other guests at the Second Immortal Dinner. John Bale and Tony Spufford would not comment, nor would Graham Sheldrake. Chris Page referred everyone to his wife, and she was laid low with guilt at what her article had inflicted on a dying man. She would not talk.

Only Mary Sheldrake was prepared to give an account. She had recently published a novel in the new style that she had promised herself and it had not gone down well with critics or readers. The flat and colourless tone they expected and loved was missing. The clichés remained, but they were not enough. Her approach had changed radically, and she and her publisher had forgotten to change the readership. Mary guessed she would have to revert. She may have thought that until then, she should keep up a presence in the press. She told interviewers she remembered every minute of the evening and that she had been 'transfigured' by it. She agreed, the poem that Francis read described the natural world beautifully and if we were to value what we have, and do whatever it took not to lose it, then to that extent, it certainly could be seen as 'a climate-change poem', though she would not have thought to use that term. When she was asked if she could remember hearing Blundy talk about the issue, she paused before saying that she knew he had strong opinions about it. I admire her tact.

14

Something extraordinary and wondrous happened and it was here, *now*, not in 2010 or '14 but in our muted present. On a hot day in June, Rose and I went swimming after our last classes of the day. It was early evening and the air was warm and creamy on the skin. A smell of baked earth and herbs rose from under our bare feet as we crossed the grassy slope that gave on to the sandy bay below the faculty accommodation towers. We passed the lifeguard station and its single eucalyptus tree. The beach, a wide horseshoe of fine pinkish yellowish sand, was deserted but for a bunch of students playing volleyball half a mile away at the far end where the chalk cliffs begin. We stripped off and walked into the sea hand in hand. Usually, I lower myself in inch by inch. This evening the calm water gave a welcoming caress, and when it was deep enough, I collapsed into its embrace. We swam a couple of hundred metres from the shore, out across the sea grasses, gliding through translucent water, over the occasional sea turtle, to where we knew a sandbank rose without breaking the surface. The incoming tide was at its midway point, and we were standing in water chest-deep.

Face to face and close, we rested our hands on each other's shoulders. We were grinning like imbeciles. It was as if, she said later, we suddenly remembered that we weren't just minds, we had bodies too. We kissed and then, overcome by delight and desire, and for the first time in years, we made love. We stood in a rising sea, still breathing hard from our swim. Small pebbles and submarine grasses tickled our soles and ankles, and the smooth tidal wavelets made all the movement we needed, lifting us by inches and setting us down gently in a steady rhythm. The transition from seedy seminar rooms to this sensual paradise was preposterous. To see clearly a familiar face – ex-lover, long-term colleague – and in a quiet revelation understand her to be beautiful, was a transfiguration. I felt younger, healthier and more attractive than I could possibly hope to be at the age of forty-four. Some rapturous form of inner swagger assured me that I was worthy of the moment. The sea that had once obliterated cities was now our placid friend. We had tamed it. Rose's face, her intense vertiginous regard, her wet hair curling in spiky loops below her ear, her firm shoulders and arms, her breasts part-submerged, her loveliness and intelligence appeared as one essential human element. I was gripped by an impulse to tell her that I loved her, but a lifetime's various mishaps made me cautious of uttering those contractual three words, easily uttered and near impossible to unsay. I blamed myself for my caution and bad faith. Then she spoke the words for me, eerily, on one note, like plainsong. I had no choice but to say them too, and I did not want a choice. But how strange, even awkward, it was to say for the first time 'I love you' to an old friend.

It was done, we had crossed a line and made a promise, one that we would have found difficult to define. We would not always be standing here in a rhapsodic state, arms looped around the other's neck, deep in warm clear seawater in beautiful evening sunlight with no one around. We sensed we had said something that implied a future, one that we would share and was bound to be more crowded and less ecstatic.

In acknowledgement that we were holding that time off a little longer, we swam further out, perhaps another hundred metres, keeping time with our strokes. We did not say much, preferring to remain with the echoes, the aftershocks of our declaration. Its stark subject-verb-object simplicity couldn't be matched or improved. We stopped to tread water and rest. This far out, the water looked black, and six inches below the surface it was icy. There was now a deeper swell, with an obscure threat of danger in the freshening wind. We would no longer be visible to anyone on the shore. Our peopled world and all its obligations now seemed more homely. We set off to return to it and, still in silence, made a wide arc across the bay, moving faster now on the tide that surged towards the shore and our pile of clothes.

Her apartment was larger than mine. Over the next month, when I was not marking exam papers, I moved my stuff across. Everything went back to how it had been before, and everything was different. I informed the university accommodation office that I was terminating my rental agreement. Rose and I told each other we had never been happier in our adult lives. We were tender, passionate, sweet. We marvelled at how we could have been so stupid not to have found our love years before, when we lived together. Back then it was a perfunctory arrangement, an almost professional affair, until it became, after fifteen months, oppressive to us both, and I had moved out.

Once the exam papers were handed back and the examiners' meetings were over, the long summer break would be ours. We decided to stay put, working on our projects, swimming and reading for pleasure on the beach of our south-facing bay, which would be empty once the students had left. Rose was forming some ideas for a paper she wanted to write. She was as happy as I was to stay here together on a deserted campus.

Lately, she had been mentioning again the Kitchener archive in Scotland. It was the one collection I needed to investigate, she insisted. I merely repeated myself. The Moidart library would of course be of great help to me, but getting there was too dangerous. I was more risk-averse now than in my twenties and thirties. I was not prepared to offer up my life to a bunch of Lake District thugs in electric canoes.

The summer of 2120 was a delight after the cold, wet winds and storms of the months before. Rose and I embarked on our idyll and it was just we had hoped – we swam, hiked, read, worked and loved. We had never felt fitter or more capable and energetic. We woke early during the long heatwave to swim before breakfast which we ate on her apartment's narrow balcony. It overlooked a bicycle park and a high-rise identical to hers, but it was at least shaded in the mornings. We worked or read until lunch. Rose needed the library, so I had the dining table to myself.

She was putting notes together for a monograph in which she would describe a crisis in realism in fiction between 2015 and 2030. The Derangement was a vast and complex subject, it was 'existentially transformative' and bred Metaphysical Gloom. The conventions of fictional realism, with its close attention to the mundane, the personal and the assumed continuity of everyday life, were inadequate. New forms were needed to frame the physical and moral consequences of a global catastrophe and certain writers were struggling to find them. The subject was a little too theoretical for my taste, but I was sure she would write a fine essay and I was impatient to read her first draft.

As for me, I had decided that before finding Blundy's poem and and revealing it to the world I should prepare the ground with a historical essay. For more than a hundred years, it had been accepted practice in the humanities to address not the matter under discussion, but the *idea* of the matter, how it was represented in the minds of others, and how that spectre flitted and danced across the decades. Long ago, as an undergraduate, I was required to adopt this approach. I was against it, even at the age of nineteen. I would tell my tutor that I wanted to write about a particular poem, not its reputation. Surely, it should be taken for granted that whatever I thought about the poem *was* an idea of the poem. I was not sufficiently informed or confident at that stage to make a good argument. I was easily swatted aside as a naïve empiricist. The only existence a literary work could have was in the minds of those who had read it – or, it should have been added, of those who had heard about it. My tutor tapped out the syllables on my sternum with, I remember, a long white finger: *there is nothing else.*

So here I was, twenty-five years later, a man in love, setting out with a fat bundle of notes to write about the thoughts and aspirations of a few generations concerning Francis Blundy's 'A Corona for Vivien'. The poem on the page did not yet exist. It had lived and still lived only in countless minds. There was nothing else. The thing itself might turn up one day in the attic of some ancient dwelling. There was a one-in-fifty chance it lay waiting in Harry Kitchener's archive but I would have to accept that for now I was writing not about a poem, but about its shadow – and I was aggrieved. Rose was sympathetic. We were on our beach in the shade of the eucalyptus tree, eating a picnic lunch after a swim. The Corona was an exceptional case, she said, soothingly, and an important one, a vital cultural artefact. She reminded me that I had once described it as 'a repository of dreams', and on another occasion as 'a mirror for the ages and all their anxieties'. My job, she told me, was to describe the dreams and the anxieties, not the poem.

I wondered about her inheritance, whether it was large enough to liberate us from low-paid teaching. It pained her to talk about it. In an account she never looked at, she said, was a 'mid-five-figure sum'. 50,000 naira? She turned away and I knew not to ask. We were generally helpful with each other's work. But we had a running dispute that predated our discovery of love. Rose thought I was subject to distorted notions of the period in which we specialised. I romanticised the late twentieth and early twenty-first centuries. I foolishly convinced myself that I was living in the wrong era. I exaggerated the vitality and beauty of the past and ignored its squalor and cruelty and morbid greed. If I was transported back there, I would loathe it. The stupidity and waste would suffocate me or make me insane. So would the nastiness of social media, then run for profit rather than as a public service. What, she demanded, of the self-serving short-sightedness or plain folly or mendacity or viciousness of political leaders – take your pick – and the quiescence or craven idiocy or terror of their populations? What of the people's careless love of autocrats? How could we overlook or forgive the desolation those times bequeathed, the poisons they left in the oceans, the forests they stole, the soils and rivers they ruined and the Derangement they acknowledged but would not prevent? It was all scorched earth, all blithe contempt for the generations to follow. The world I hankered after was a privileged corner – Gloucestershire! The big world beyond was sinking. How could I go on about the James Webb telescope?

I reminded her of a biological truth established during her despised twentieth century. The smaller the island, the less diverse its species. In this country, we lived on islands, and we were lucky that ours was thirty-eight miles long. Others were far smaller. As in biology, so with culture. We all thought the same things. We were almost all the same pale brown colour. We lacked diversity! There was no tension of ideas or ways of life, or of understanding life, no opposition to the moribund orthodoxies we lived by, nothing radically new or interesting to challenge us or prompt discoveries. If we weren't crushed by the past, we were terrified by it. Our finest achievement was not to be at war. It was not enough to tell ourselves that our seas were cleaner, with life beginning to return, and that our islands in good light looked lush and pretty. That was not down to virtue. It was the result of civilisation's collapse. Whenever humans got out of the way, the rest of the living world edged back and flourished. As for our precious universities, the kids we taught were inert, the culture fed them pap, and we were the elderly scolds, repeating the orthodoxies, the sacred canons, every year, just as we might have in the fifteenth century.

I conceded that much that Rose said about our special period was true. Its talent for self-destruction was unrivalled. It had been ready to take the future down with it. But that was not the entire picture. I knew she loved the literature of those days as much as I did. Sure, the golden age, the Mabel Fisk period, was a few decades ahead. Our period of interest was a bronze age, perhaps not even that. But those people tried hard. The times were copious, like rivers in spate. Its teeming hordes of novelists, poets and dramatists formed a giant army massed against its readers, who were never quite sure of what was *good*. So the arguments were insecure and loud, and that was fine, a democracy of contesting tastes, a chaos of unconformity. I treasured the crazy music and fads and troubled movies and serious science, serious history, serious biography. My list was long – the suspension bridges, the orchestras, street parties and a thousand forms of music festivals, and people's gardening and cooking, their need for holidays, extreme sports, historical enactments, gay-pride carnivals, the risks they took with AI, the sense of humour, the safe airplanes, the passion for pointless sports. A hundred thousand at a football match! An astronaut playing golf on the moon! Did she know about the cheese-rolling competitions? Four billion people watching the—

'Enough, Tom.'

'Rose, have you any idea how delicious and varied the food was back then?'

'That would depend on where you lived and what you could afford.'

I told her again. The best thinkers of the twentieth and twenty-first centuries were troubled by a world in love with war and its technologies, and they wrote well about it. As for us, all that kept us from each other's throats was seawater and a shortage of metals to make decent weapons.

We have been around this too often. We haven't raised our voices – we are island people. But I suppose we came to influence each other a little. I've come to appreciate that our period of study might be described as a sewer. I might not want to live in it, but I wanted her to accept that sections were majestic feats of design and engineering mastery.

After nine days, I had set down 3,500 words of introduction to what I was calling my 'reputation essay'. In it I promised to explore the ghost of a poem that lived in people's thoughts, but

I could not help myself, I insisted that the poem existed. Rose read my pages.

A day later she told me what she thought. 'Thomas Metcalfe, you've checked all last messages, wills, Letters of Wishes of first- generation survivors and of their survivors. You've studied Vivien's papers and what's left of Blundy's agent's and publisher's archives. You've read the contemporary press, masses of internet material, masses of scholarly stuff.'

All true. I had been down those rabbit holes, as had many others. We had looked into the last wishes of Vivien, Rachel, Peter, Peter's wife Jessica and their children Basil and Kirsten, Jane and Harry Kitchener and their children Susanne and Ralph, Harriet and Chris Page and their children Todd, Laura and Jack. Rose's advice was simple. Stop driving yourself nuts. I had searched, others had searched. The poem was no more. Accept it. The essential business was the biography of a nonexistent work whose reputation endured. Such was the power of literature – and there was my subject. I did not attempt to argue. However, I still could not abandon my secret hopes, which were founded on one reasonable assumption and one possibility. Vivien's love of poetry was too fierce to let her consign the poem to oblivion. It was somewhere and I would find it. The Corona might be in a document box in the stacks of a small library 500 metres up a mountain in the north-west of Scotland. Only cowardice stood in my way.

Rose and I were married in August in a modest five-minute ceremony in front of the university administration office's mainframe.

15

On the suggestion of my wife and my old tutor's stabbing finger, I became the biographer of the reputation of an unread poem. Perhaps I was never anything else. Here is a summary. The Corona was recited by its author at a dinner 107 years ago in October 2014. From then until 2021, an important year in my research, the following happened. Harry Kitchener wrote a letter in which he referred to the first 'immortal dinner' and announced a masterpiece. In 2016, he died. A year later, an unattributed blog quoted him and spoke of the 'Second Immortal Dinner'. I have shown that there was nothing immortal about it. The company mostly daydreamed tipsily while Blundy read. An article by 'Jane Smith' spoke of 'Blundy's "precious gift"'. Harriet Page's 2017 *Guardian* article saw the poem through her own Derangement concerns and asked why it had not been published. Francis Blundy died soon after. Rumours spread on social media of fossil-fuel interests paying him to suppress his poem. The conspiracies were dismissed in mainstream quarters. Vivien Blundy was upset by what she thought was a misleading portrayal of her marriage to the poet and was determined to keep the Corona out of circulation.

2021 was the notable year in the Corona odyssey. My discovery was accidental. A year ago, our students were developing a distorted and negative notion of the past as it related to our 90–30 seminars. It was mostly due to Rose's influence, for she was forceful and persuasive in class. I believed the students needed to find out for themselves that people of those times were not all greedy fools. Not only climate scientists, but millions, even hundreds of millions of ordinary people understood the processes of the Derangement. I persuaded Rose to let me set our students a project on the opposition to fossil-fuel interests.

The kids' contempt for the past could be challenged by the activities of long-ago young protesters. People just like themselves with a serious mission. Since this was my idea, I marked the projects. The work was above average, decently presented with photographs, videos, charts and diagrams. The essays were semi-literate but adequate by the low standards imposed from above – it would not help our funding if too many students were to fail. The kids were doing their best with what they knew. One shy young woman, Michelle, who had never spoken up in the seminars, had written about an international Derangement conference in Glasgow in 2021. Interspersed through her essay were photographs of protest marches. My attention happened to settle on a photograph of a teenage boy. He held up a placard in a forest of placards. BLUNDY SPOKE TRUE. I zoomed in on the face. Of course, it told me nothing.

Here was evidence of the Corona drifting free of the page, the scroll, and trickling through the interstices of the internet and through to the Derangement movement. I began searching for Blundy's name in the activist sites. Within seconds I had this from an American e-zine, *Joshua Tree*. The dateline was August 2020. 'Blundy's poem, suppressed by Dark Oil, was a masterpiece, reputedly the greatest work ever achieved on the need to change our ways through love.' I found 107 mentions of Blundy's name between 2018 and 2020. Then 678 between 2021 and 2025. The sites were obscure, needing password access. The German site *Final People*, which encouraged sabotage, was encrypted and required extra software that was hard to locate, but I succeeded. In 2030, a Danish e-zine in several languages published its first issue. Its name was *Blundy*. Across many of these outlets, the oil conspiracy theory was routinely cited, merely to emphasise the importance of the poem. Some early mentions of Blundy came during the 2020 coronavirus pandemic, when attempts were made to link the poem to a

102

disease. By 2035 it was possible to buy a T-shirt with the poet's face printed on it in black and white.

'Blundy corona' also took me to relationship sites. Here the connection was to 'deep love', the marriage or love affair that lasts forty or fifty years. How the lover loved only his lass, how the ravages of the decades could not breach the calm of the inner keep. A glance in one of the many Blundy biographies would have shown that his marriage lasted thirteen years, until his death. That was not relevant. People in the developed world were living longer. The old were getting older. Seventy, even eighty years of marriage was becoming possible, a perfect encapsulation of hell to some, to others a noble goal. To a wide online community, the Corona was the revered manifesto, the long poem to celebrate a long love. 'We are a Blundy couple of sixty-one years . . .' one posting began. The poet's name and his poem were evoked with minimal knowledge of the source. A parallel might be 'Shangri-la', used as a synonym for a paradise on earth with no awareness of its origins in a largely forgotten bestselling novel of the 1930s.

Many reasons have been given for the decline of the climate-change movement in the twenty-first century. I would propose Derangement itself. The planet, with almost 200 jostling nations, was already tense. Some historians have marked the beginning of the new dark age with the Russian invasion of Ukraine in 2022, and that is where quite a few history books begin or end. I would propose the first climate war in 2036, one in a sequence, between two nuclear states, India and Pakistan, traditional enemies. One issue was water, once plentiful in the form of Himalayan glacier-fed ice-melt. Now, as long predicted, drying up. The two states were prepared to obliterate one another. The world, as the cliché ran, held its breath, and it is not easy to organise or attend mass protests in favour of decarbonising civilisation or write books about it when you are holding your breath. While the slaughter began in the traditional way, with infantry, artillery and drone units fully engaged, the missiles and their launchers stood ready. Nationalist and religious fury merged in both states. Merciful Allah on one side, diverse gods, some with elephant trunks, on the other, inflamed and blessed their separate constituencies. The tension lasted months. The armies clashed, there were gains here, losses there, and then, prompted by hair-trigger artificial intelligence choosing the pre-emptive option, missiles were launched, two from each side. They were of 'limited' yield, but with over a million killed instantly, they were enough to cause each side to draw back in horror and diplomatic peace missions to rush in to take advantage of the lull.

Meanwhile, two other crises were developing to the west and east. Against such catastrophe and general global frailty, people clung to notions of survival, of making bunkers, of fleeing cities and of writing peace plans. When Saudi Arabia joined cause with Israel to invade Iran and deny it possession of nuclear weapons, they discovered that it already had some. In that chaos, six 'battlefield' nuclear weapons were exploded over the heads of the respective armies. Again, AI on both sides, hungrily and blindly seeking advantage, decided that attack was the best form of defence. It was not known how many tens of thousands died. In the Taiwan Straits, there was an exchange of fire between Chinese and US navies. A year passed before the notorious sinking of an American aircraft carrier and the death of 2,500 sailors. Little hope now of encouraging governments around the world to resist Derangement. Francis Blundy, by way of his Corona, ceased to be the high priest of altered climate or undying love and became instead the prophet of the biosphere.

As the world economy broke apart and nature rose against us, ideas of progress or even change slowly vanished. Survival was the thing. People wanted to cling to what they could rescue. In our times, we have grown used to nothing much being different across the generations. We are approaching the stasis of pre-modern days, when children could expect to live the lives of their parents and grandparents. Our relative isolation has enforced a form of peace, which some like me take to be stagnation. We cannot imagine how it was a hundred years ago, to experience the vertigo of accelerating change imposed by new technologies, by novel belief systems and by wars. People were blinded by the pace of events. They could not think clearly, even when there rose out of adversity some obvious benefits. It was repugnant to accept that the savagery of war had offered the possibility of a reprieve, a chance to correct the errors of the past. Nuclear explosions in the deserts of the Middle East and the hard-baked earth of the subcontinent disgorged into the upper atmosphere gigatons of dust and sand, much of it fine gypsum that lingered and filtered the sun's harsh light. Over the graves of millions, the earth began to cool. What came now was not the nuclear winter that scientists had once predicted, for this was not an all-out global exchange. In five years, average global temperatures dropped by almost two degrees and did not rise for many years. There were other small wars distracting attention. Acknowledgement of a 'climate opportunity' came slowly to a dazed world.

This was because of a catastrophic distraction, the Inundation of 2042. The long-predicted war between Russia and the West began with yet another pre-emptive strike, this one aimed most likely at US military installations in New Mexico. Faulty engineering caused the missile to drop 4,000 miles short. The outsized hydrogen bomb hurled seventy-metre-high waves towards Europe, West Africa and North America. Too deadly to be the accident the Russian authorities claimed? That question was never resolved. There were only a few hours of warning. The survivors were those who trusted their governments sufficiently to act, had transport and were not trapped in traffic jams and knew the routes to higher ground. Three-quarters of the Atlantic-facing populations were not so lucky or well resourced. Even cities on sheltered coasts were swamped. Lagos, London, Rotterdam, Hamburg and most of Paris did not emerge from under the counter-surges that raced up estuaries, or from the savage storms that followed. In revenge assaults, Russia lost

Petersburg before international diplomacy prevailed. The list of vanished cities is long. More than 200 million died. Britain became an archipelago, its population halved. However, none of the twenty-first century's nuclear exchanges led to total war and humanity's extinction. There was our morsel of consolation. We were not so irrational after all.

Against all expectations, within twenty years of the Inundation, the post-nuclear global cooling was encouraging a new spirit of optimism. The trauma and mourning were beginning to fade. Initiatives to decarbonise were returning, boosted by a collapse in industrial production and global trade. Public demands to save vanishing flora and fauna, sometimes unrealistic or sentimental, were growing. By then, the destruction of the biosphere was beyond the worst of earlier fears. Unrestrained corporations, reluctant governments, poverty and armed struggle made the early twenty-first century look species-rich. Now, old romantic yearnings for thriving nature – or biophilia, a term once made current by the great biologist E. O. Wilson – were unstoppable. By the time of the Inundation the knowledge base had mostly been digitalised and distributed. Thousands of years of cultural expression were swept away, but multiple copies survived in zeros and ones. Scientific insight was regaining confidence. Rapidly reconstructed institutes headed for the highest ground in case of future waves. With old dreams revived came renewed interest in the lost ecology of animals and plants within the fifteen sonnets of the Corona. The Second Immortal Dinner of 2014 seemed as remote as the court of King Alfred. To those who loved poetry, it was irresistible to put the poem, or their idea of the poem, to contemporary use. It was a hymn to the glories of nature.

It is a wonder that a poem, let alone an unread poem, could have such a vigorous life in the culture – and its story still had decades to run before the present day. In the late twenty-first century, even as wars broke out in the Pacific (China against South Korea, Malaysia, the Philippines and others), vanished poem and vanished opportunities coalesced into a numinous

106

passion for what could not be had, a sweet nostalgia that did not need a resolution. This was demonstrated in the various poetry competitions to reimagine and write Blundy's poem. There was little public interest in the winner. When Mabel Fisk wrote fifteen sonnets in corona form to recreate Blundy's work, her adoring critics dismissed the result. A novelist, however important, had no business flaunting herself in the clothes of a great poet.

The Corona was more beautiful for not being known. Like the play of light and shadow on the walls of Plato's cave, it presented to posterity the pure form, the ideal of all poetry. Any upstart version was a relegation to the abject humdrum real. My guess is that if ever the one true scroll were to be found, the excitement would not spread far beyond academia. Compressed diction, challenging imagery, the 'artful braiding within its pentameters of iambs and trochees' – H. Kitchener – and all the other demands of serious poetry would ensure the Corona's death before a larger public.

The imagined lords it over the actual – no paradox or mystery there. Many religious believers do not want their God depicted or described. Happiness is ours if we do not have to learn how our electronic machines work. The characters we cherish in fiction do not exist. As individuals or nations we embellish our own histories to make ourselves seem better than we are. Living out our lives within unexamined or contradictory assumptions, we inhabit a fog of dreams and seem to need them.

I write here of global tragedies purely in the context of Blundy's Corona. That period of 'Climate Opportunity' and ecological longing lasted no more than thirty years. The long-delayed Third Sino-American War broke out as the inevitable overspill of the Pacific chaos. Though 'contained' by improved AI to conventional exchanges, many famous cities were turned to ashes. Worldwide disease, famine, drought, unprecedented mass migrations – no one had time for poetry or any other cultural endeavour. Survival was the only dream, which many did not fulfil. Between then and now, our numbers fell from nine to four billion, but still, in our calmer, or moribund, twenty-second century, 'A Corona for Vivien' remains precious for those who care, a talisman to the survivors and a promise of a better future. A poem has served history well by remaining a blank sheet.

16

Not long after I moved back in with Rose, I saw a cloud of butterflies. Apparently, this eruption of colour and erratic motion happens every year and I'd never noticed. On an afternoon stroll I saw a dog leap up and snap a tortoiseshell out of the air. I was shocked and wondered if an early symptom of ageing was fretting about and caring for the natural world. To honour the victim I taught myself some common names: meadow brown, ringlet, gatekeeper. I read about the butterfly's brief life cycle and learned that right across the archipelago there are as many as eight species. But in Francis and Vivien's time, I discovered, there were fifty-seven resident species, and I was reminded again of our diminished world. When I went with Rose in the early evening across the wild grasses to the beach, scores of pale moths called plumes rose from under our feet. It saddened me to read that many other June moths that Vivien would have known were extinct. My subject, my fixation, has settled on me a peculiar form of discontent. It is a constant background matter, a low hum, a one-note melody, a malady of yearning. Our clean sea, its turtles and schools of dolphins, its vast beds of gently undulating sea grasses are never enough when I know that Vivien and her contemporaries swam in seas whose depths contained cod, mackerel, hake, shad and sprat, pollard and three-bearded rockling, and scores of other extinct fish whose muscular names are known only to a few. Here is my Robert Louis Stevenson coming over the wrong bridge. I have one foot in the past, perhaps two. I live there, in 2014 or 2025, not here.

It may have been in a mood of self-punishment that I once took a virtual tour of an Oxford bookshop, the one Vivien had her back to as she was about to cross the street to hear Francis Blundy read. The year the shop was showing off its goods was 2018. I saw from the digital time stamp that I was the first to look at this clip in eighty-three years. Why would anyone take the trouble? To feel bad. I made myself feel worse by thinking of the Vale of Oxford Sea, and the bookshop, the Sheldonian, the Bodleian Library and Broad Street, silent in the watery dusk many feet below the surface as their limestone structures softly crumbled. But what treasures as the camera in a shaky hand showed me the shelves and packed tables. All recently published! I wandered through the shop in the company of what I imagined to be a young and earnest assistant. The history section should shame us. That season's books outstripped a decade of our efforts. Serious and hefty, with richly coloured covers, general and abstruse topics, and likewise in the sections devoted to biography, science books for the general reader and the immediately outdated volumes on who we are or were, and where we were going. All wrong, of course, but enticing, with their gleam of intellectual boldness. The books in that shop can be summoned in an instant to our screens, but oh, to have wandered the aisles, thrilled to be riding the crest of newness, interest and abundance. At our middle-ranking university as at our best, we crouch in the shadow of the thought-rich past of a century ago. Its ringlets and three-bearded rockling are but dreams. I would like to shout from the twelfth-floor window of my and Rose's apartment, We too are thought-rich, we too live in an open society! But our core concern is with cheery updates on heroic salvage crews bringing up the next 10,000 barnacle-encrusted vehicles for the steel mills. We celebrate our skilled engineers for creating simple new phones out of complex old ones.

Rose studies the same period and it does not sap her pleasure in our sleepy ahistorical times. She says that dolphins and turtles are an improvement on the jellyfish swarms and 3,000-mile-long algae blooms of the mid-twenty-first century. She points to our immaculate bay fringed by green slopes below the residential towers. Isn't it beautiful? I agree. Empty or not, the sea from a distance right to the sharp horizon looks unchanged across the centuries. But I remind her of the shifting baseline effect. As natural beauty declines over the years, so too, unnoticed, do standards of beauty. I would have loved to be at Vivien's side when she stepped out of the Barn on a sunny spring morning in 2008. She celebrated the glories of the landscape in an email to her sister. But an Edwardian lady, time-travelling forward a hundred years to stroll with Vivien, would be horrified to see banks of nettles along the roadsides in place of wildflowers, by the absence of river meadows, hedgerows, elms and cuckoo song. The roar of eight-lane motorways and the grotesque stride of giant pylons and their power lines would appear as elements of a nightmare.

The 'peasant poet' John Clare – subject of Vivien's doctorate – was one of the few nature poets who knew about nature. If he too were to make the hundred-year journey from the early nineteenth century to 1908 and tour the country with the same Edwardian lady, he would be shocked in his turn. Trees felled, pastures and their wildflowers vanishing under the plough, precious fenland drained, steam engines belching filth, roads and overcrowded cities congested with horse manure, open country enclosed for private ownership – an ancient way of life and its animals and birds discarded for profit. In pre-industrial times the baseline shifted more slowly. A Roman centurion traversing a thousand years to the European landmass of the thirteenth century would be surprised to find that more than three-quarters of its forests had been felled. He wouldn't care.

In one of our exchanges Rose said, 'It's not all about hedgehogs or whatever else has gone. It took an agricultural and an industrial revolution to start to make a difference to human well-being. So there's a cost and we're happier than Vivien Blundy's lot.'

'Not me.'

'Because you have a personal problem with happiness. Tom, it's not the absent mackerel.'

I let that pass and said that three-quarters of species had vanished and I *minded*. Those creatures and plants were our companions. Without them our loneliness deepened.

'OK,' she said, 'I'll put it another way. If you were an ecologist working on restoring lost species, your discontent would be going somewhere, it would mean something. But you're an academic like me, a bystander. You're making yourself unhappy for nothing.'

'I'm not a bystander. I'm restoring a great environmental poem to the canon.'

'You don't know that it was great. And was it that important, Tom, or is it just your obsession? Anyway it's gone the way of the – what was that fast bird?'

'The swift.'

'And you told me once that Blundy couldn't tell a buttercup from a dandelion.'

'Irrelevant. The Corona is out there.'

'Tom, it's gone!'

We'd had the conversation so often it had acquired a ritual quality. All she wanted was for me to be happy. I conceded that I complained too often about our fallen world. It had always been falling and we had to make a life. If she thought the poem did not exist, then I would find it, publish it and prove her wrong. She told me she would be amazed and delighted to be wrong.

'They'll have to make you a professor.'

'You too, Rose, if you'll write the introduction.'

In fact, during that period, late summer of 2120, I was content with my work. I had abandoned hunches and theories and was relying on serendipity, making random trawls through my material with low expectation of finding anything significant, but taking pleasure in other times, other minds and in the constancy of human nature set against radically shifting circumstances. They touched me, these ancient everyday texts between Vivien

112

and Francis, hypnotically unpunctuated and never intended for rereading: 'doorway of laundrette where you?' and the instant response: 'almost there no umbrella'. This was Francis and Vivien trying to locate each other in a rainstorm for a secret rendezvous in the market town of Thame in Oxfordshire in 2002.

In 2009 Francis underwent a routine colonoscopy and was amazed to watch on a screen as a camera went gliding through his 'coral pink entrails'. He was enchanted by a drug called fentanyl. While still in the recovery room, sipping tea, he made notes towards a poem about the experience and finished it a day later. He showed it to Harry Kitchener, who advised him to put the poem – three quatrains – in a drawer. Blundy emailed, 'I agree. Now that fabulous stuff has worn off I know the poem is, in every sense, crap. But Harry, everyone should have a colonoscopy *every day*.' The poem and notes are not in the archive.

More on my trawls. In 1997, Percy sent his first email. 'I hope this goes off ok. I might be pressing the wrong buttons. But anyway, this comes first – I love you.' Vivien, already an adept, wrote back, 'It came through! Well done darling and welcome. No more licking stamps. I love you too.' In 1999 there was an email from a consultant neurologist, himself an amateur violinist who, by coincidence, had bought an instrument from Percy. 'Your scans are here. Nothing to worry about. Phone me please tomorrow morning between 7 and 8.'

I went shopping in 2012 with Vivien. She drove from the Barn to Oxford to buy herself 'a beautiful, handmade pleated skirt' at half price in a shop called Annabelinda. Vivien wrote to Rachel, 'There was champagne. Everyone was merry and sad all at once. There were tears. This lovely shop is closing the day after tomorrow, after forty-one years!'

In 1997 a customer wrote to Percy, 'After all that (and thank you!) it had its first outing, Beethoven, Razumovsky 3, at the Holywell music room. Mr Greene, it is so warm, so lively, so sensually playable. It was all I could do not to sing along with the gorgeous creature in my hands. You could have charged someone richer than me twice as much. You're a god!'

Two men losing their minds over Vivien: in 1996 a breath-less handwritten letter from Percy to Vivien (my copy from her papers). 'What happened? I can't stop thinking about it, feeling about it, reliving it. Couldn't work this morning. So wonder-ful, unbelievable, to arrive at this new place with you. Again please. Tonight?' Then 2002, a postcard and its envelope, from Francis to Vivien, my copy from the Blundy archive – 'I can't stop thinking about you. I'm going nuts. Where is this taking us? I must see you.'

There were earlier lovers, including a lawyer called Roder-ick, and before him a graduate student, Ted. Vivien kept only one passionate letter from each. Blundy was prone to fits of retrospective jealousy and she had to be careful. But during her marriage to Francis, she risked keeping Percy's letters and scrawled notes. I stared for a while at a photograph of Vivien in her twenties. Her hair cut in a bob, white blouse and short white skirt, three fat books under her arm. She stood on a col-lege lawn, a river at her back, probably the Cherwell. There was liveliness and daring in her look, an appetite for fun in the way she shifted her weight and jauntily cocked her hip.

In the long hot afternoons at the dining table in the flat while Rose was at the library, I would tip back in my chair and day-dream. Vivien was bold, her desires were strong. Was she more beautiful than Rose? No. Was she cleverer? Probably not. But she was the lead character in the story I was trying to uncover. She was the one I was closest to. Blundy fascinated me, but he repelled me. Harry Kitchener was too self-regarding. Percy was sympathetic but he was cursed, and his world did not include the Corona. Vivien knew where the poem, my poem, was. We are side by side on that lawn. There are silent punts on the river. We exchange a squeeze of hands as she begins to tell me what she did with my poem.

It was a terrible idea to have once said to Rose that I could imagine myself falling in love with Vivien and marrying her. We, that is, Rose and I, had been married only a few weeks. It was a tactless remark, and she was in a mood to take it badly. I

114

tried to backtrack, but I made matters worse. It took a day and much contrition to smooth things out and return us to where we had been moments before I spoke. But during the following year, whenever matters were not quite bonny between us, which was rare enough, she would recall tartly that I would rather be with Vivien Blundy. No matter that she was dead these past eighty years, I had revealed that among ideal wives, Rose was not my first choice. So whenever I spoke about my research, I avoided uttering Vivien's name. The effect was to make her a living presence, a neighbour, working in the same department as ours, an ex-lover of mine, the number-one lover. Vivien was vivid in my afternoon daydreams. I, not Francis, drove to Thame in heavy rain, light-headed with expectation. Rose's feelings were not unreasonable.

But Rose and I were happy and I should not exaggerate our difficulties. Or, rather, mine. We were more than happy – often ecstatic, irreversibly changed and charged, as we told each other, by that swim out to the sandbar. Well into the first week of November we swam daily. Rose was bringing her paper to a conclusion and was excited by what she had so far. It was rich with good ideas and apt quotations. She convinced me that in its infancy, the Derangement could not have been addressed by fictional realism. It was inadequate to the scale of the problem. I was content too, drifting through the vastness of my material, putting aside selections for later consideration and hopeful, after deciding to take guidance from NAI, the national AI service, that the machine would propose useful paths. I was already set on a return to Snowdonia. Beyond work and sensual pleasures, Rose and I were harmonious, companionable, we stimulated each other with good ideas, we read to each other and we laughed a lot. We even talked about having children, but didn't reach a conclusion. At weekends, we cooked for our friends. Months went by without Vivien's name coming up, and when it did at last, gentle breezes soon dispersed the little cloud.

17

Our students are permitted limited access to NAI. To prevent over-dependence, they must sit before an approved desktop. They also need to wait five days before they get their next shot. The kids mostly want advice on relationships, parents, music, fashion and money. They murmur their confessions and questions and get an immediate response. The Machine, as they like to call it, knows when it is being asked to write a student essay and will terminate the session. In written form, guidance can run to half a dozen single-spaced pages and is, I think, sensible and robust, though I know that others disagree. The tone is comradely. A response to an anxious question from a nineteen-year-old might begin, 'I believe she's trying to tell you something here and I'd say it's time for you to be more reflective and analytical about your own behaviour. Remember the trouble you were in last year.'

NAI knows about a respondent's life in intimate detail and its memory, of course, is long. The kids like that. They feel important, known and cared for. They are proud of an accumulating dossier that tells of their escapades, successes, disasters and growth. NAI is a friendly aunt, concerned, critical and worldly. The young make confessions to her they would not dare make to close friends or parents. Dossiers can swell by more than 200 pages a year. The kids boast to each other of admonitions as well as praise they've received. They enter early adult life as heroes in an epic of trivia and passion. Young newlyweds can destroy a marriage by swapping files, but many insist on it. People continue their consultations through life and seem reassured that neither the state nor commercial entities have access to the material. But confess to a crime and NAI will turn you in.

Most of us in the Humanities Department are wary of taking personal problems to a lifeless piece of software, however sophisticated. Our privileged allotment is every other day. Over in Science and Tech they have unlimited access. The scientists we know are more inclined to take their marriage or career problems to NAI. Along our corridor we tend to approach it as a research tool. I've made use of her during my Blundy research and received useful notes on background reading and social contexts. NAI lets me know who's doing what in my field, who might be trespassing on my territory and who is following an interesting lead.

By early December 2120, serendipity was leading me nowhere and my work was stalled. I had the curious experience of knowing too much, of being burdened by the weight of my material. I had lost direction and was oppressed. In the small hours, I indulged mutinous thoughts: abandon the entire project, work instead on a pre-digital figure like George Crabbe, another among my favourite nature poets. What deliverance, to be immersed in a still-unthreatened natural world, to have only the poetry and correspondence to sift, to reimagine the poet through the admiration of his friend and supporter Edmund Burke, and his devoted readers William Wordsworth, Jane Austen and Walter Scott. What liberation, to be relieved of the three million internet mentions of Francis Blundy in his lifetime, the 219,000 messages that were written to him and by him and the near-infinite references since. I longed to escape and breathe that dank and salty air of muddy foreshores with their rotting wooden hulls, the marshes and sluggish tidal rivers, to hear the mournful call of the bittern, to meet the poor inhabitants of this low-lying coast that Crabbe observed so closely and which was one of the first east-facing zones after London to be claimed by the sea.

Rose was forthright. 'Idiot! Don't you dare give up. Talk to NAI.'

I resisted, then one afternoon, with little else to do, I sketched out some questions for this beloved program that some in the Philosophy Department believe has attained consciousness. Nonsense, the hard tech people have told me. Pure projection. NAI is no better than the systems of the 2030s. Lack of progress hasn't been down to know-how. Our various forms of disaster and chaos have blocked the development of better machines and software. No gallium and germanium or even copper in the Surrey Hills!

I asked NAI to go back to the two years before and the immediate period after the Second Immortal Dinner and speculate freely for me about the network of private relations around Blundy, and to suggest where I might take my investigations next. Most of what came back was familiar and of no use. NAI wanted me to go to the Kitchener archive in Scotland. I suffered my usual irritation at being first-named by a computer.

'Tom, you resemble that fabled fellow who loses his watch one night and confines his search to the pavement under the street lamp. In the days after the birthday reading, Harry Kitchener would have been desperate to have sight of the poem. Something must have passed between him and Vivien. The absence of any email exchanges between them is interesting. Deletions? There is nothing in her journal. After the Corona reading she writes that she was spending a lot of time in London with her nephew Peter. In one week, she went three times, but wrote no accounts of their meetings. Are you sure this was where she went? Was your Vivien without blemish? Perhaps you're too fond of her. Don't let a spot of seasickness get in your way. Take another look at her Bodleian papers.'

As winter drew in, I was diverted by a related project. Rose suggested that we could draw our students into the history of the rise and fall and partial rise of AI. NAI was integral to their personal and social existence. It was their confessional, their mirror, the focal point of their self-esteem. We could exploit this engagement to counter their solipsistic resistance to the past. There was once great anxiety about machine

118

intelligence – never resolved so much as forgotten. The students could return to those old debates and understand why AI had to be wrenched away from private companies. We would set writing assignments, 400 words maximum. Nothing too taxing.

Rose said, 'A hundred-year overview of their love object. How can they resist?'

I could think of at least four reasons not to take this on. More work, more bureaucracy, more marking, reluctant students. But that night as we made love my reasons melted away. Afterwards, I agreed. She had given way on my pet project. I owed her this one. She wanted to roll three seminar groups together, which would mean applying for a larger room, not a simple affair for a sleepy administration reflexively hostile to any slight change in the schedule. We visited software experts in their spacious quarters suspended within a lustrous concrete shell. We were in awe of these brisk scientists, but they put us at our ease. It helped to be reminded that most of them didn't know how to write longhand and had never read a poem. I thought they seemed to be in awe of us. Rose thought that was their way of being polite.

We assembled images of social and military chaos to grip our young audience. The colossal US aircraft carrier ablaze in the Taiwan Straits, listing as it sank, with sailors leaping from the deck; video of the annihilation from the air of an AI research centre ten miles from Beijing; a colossal open-cast mine in northern Europe – a failed attempt, one of many, to locate rare earth deposits.

We sent out a note to the students, reminding them that attending was not an option but a course requirement. On a Thursday at 2 p.m. Rose and I sat side by side facing a horseshoe of fifty-eight students. Since this was her idea, she gave the introductory speech. As she began, I scanned the faces. The kids were silent, attentive, but they seemed tense and unusually still. Rose's tone was relaxed and warm. The essay projects would be short, she reassured them. Their long experience with NAI would mean they came to the course with inside knowledge,

119

genuine expertise in dealing daily with a seemingly conscious mind. She digressed to offer some thoughts on the value of historical thinking and the dangers to any society that loses its memory. The same was true for individuals. She was a practised speaker and was untroubled as she paused to look about and gauge the silence in the room. In effect, to dominate it.

'We're all fine so far?'

No one spoke, but there was a muted stirring and rustling among the students which she pretended to take for an answer.

In ten minutes she gave a condensed history of computing, starting with the Antikythera Mechanism built around 200 BCE, one of the first analogue computers, with elaborate cogs and dials. It was pulled out of the sea in 1901 and took many years to understand and reconstruct. Its likely use was to predict eclipses and other astronomical events. She moved on to the calculating machines of Babbage and Lovelace, then to Turing and then the sixty-year 'cold' period of AI as it floundered for lack of theoretical underpinning. The students remained quiet, but I sensed that something was up. I saw one young man leave and made a note of his name. Rose also saw him go but she pressed on, untroubled. There came the discovery, she said, that it was not the human brain that needs to be imitated to create an artificial intelligence. Instead, the brain's product, the internet, could be mined for the appearance of conscious thought. Later, quantum computing and software breakthroughs led to a return to discarded neural networks. But then, global chaos interrupted progress.

She turned to me. 'Now Tom is going to say a few words about the road to freedom.'

She had cued me correctly. NAI was a good instance. When does a useful tool become a necessity, and then our master? What first appears as liberation can end up as enslavement. Did the students want their NAI to be conscious and more intelligent than they were, so that their decisions in life would be sound and their dependency complete?

'You can decide. This will be another of our group discussions.'

I was talking into the same thick silence Rose had managed to ignore. Now, someone in the front row of the horseshoe was standing. I had seen him around the place but didn't know him. I was aware of his strange face and that he had a name formed of two first names. David Paul, Christopher Raymond or some such. Rose had told me he was exceptionally bright for a humanities student. I was about to tell him that there would be time later for questions.

'Apologies for the interruption, Tom. My name is Kevin Howard and I'm a graduate student. I've been chosen to give a short message from the group.'

I remembered. It was the mouth, a rosebud, singular and perfect, and all the brighter for being set in a pale face as smooth as a child's. He was well under average height. I was so taken by his appearance, by its vulnerability, that I was reluctant to close the young man down.

He was looking at his notes. 'Rose said she wants us to consider the hold commercial interests once had over the internet. That's our point. Every day we're being told about the Inundation, the dark ages, the idiocy of those times, the warming they ignored and all that, their stupid wars, the animals they killed, how skin colour meant so much. On and on. The morons of long ago. And then of course, their neon strips, hamburgers and clubbing. Back when our island was a paradise a thousand miles long and you could go for a walk and see, what d'you call them – hedgehogs!'

There was laughter. Howard was staring at me. No denying he had presence, a defiant self-confidence. Burdened by a look of such radiant innocence, he was not going to be taken for a precocious little boy.

'We're saying, no more, thank you very much! Enough of what you think we've lost. Enough of some war a computer program started a hundred years ago. Or thousands of seamen

121

jumping off a sinking ship and getting eaten by sharks. We want to talk about *now*, what we actually *have*, not what we don't have, what we can hope for, about who's doing all the thinking now, not *then*.'

There was something else I hadn't noticed. My attention had been entirely fixed on Howard. As he was talking to us, the students were leaving in choreographed protest, one by one at intervals of several seconds.

'So, well, look, I've been asked to say this. We're tired of your anger and nostalgia. This is where we live. We've got more future than you and that's what we want to talk about. So, very sorry Rose, very sorry Tom. We're not interested in the value of historical thinking and the screwed-up past and we won't be attending your course.'

I thought he sounded regretful. He sat and waited while the remaining few students left the room. Then he stood and, head down, hurried away, leaving us sitting side by side facing the empty chairs, unable to look at each other or speak.

18

I left South Downs Harbour at eight in the morning. The ferry made it across to Ball Hill Quay in a heavy early-autumn mist. I took an electric bike across and was in Port Marlborough by midday. The mist had only partially lifted and seemed to soothe the usual quayside frenzy. Boats were waiting for the incoming tide. Parts of the straits had silted up and dredgers, like other heavy industrial equipment, were difficult to procure. High tide was the only way out for the bigger vessels. I waited in a pub making notes and nursing a herbal tea laced with a local rum made of beet sugar. After ninety minutes I went to find the Snowdonia ferry. It took me a while. I discovered it moored on the far side of a giant twin-masted barge. My boat was driven by four small electric motors and once I was on board, I learned that we would need to wait two hours after high tide for the batteries to be charged. The current overnight had been weak. I paid extra for a cramped bunkroom and slept.

I've had the same dream in various forms over the years, unsurprising, given my preoccupations. When I woke, it often raised my spirits. The common element was the poem. I have dreamed it on parchment and heard it recited, but this time it was on the printed page, in a book that someone passed to me. By the usual dream logic, I took it for granted to have it in my hands. I read the first two lines – clear, intense, rich in imagery and layered meanings. It seemed simple to commit them to memory. Of course, when I woke, they faded, but an impression of their beauty lingered throughout the day.

I was cheerful as I put on my shoes and went up onto

the ferry's passenger deck. The afternoon was still. The mist had been replaced by low cloud and everything – the sky, the smooth channel, the last of Marlborough Island's coast – was in the same shade of grey. It was too cold to stay out long. I went back in to find a place on the cramped wooden benches and abandoned myself to the liquid sound of half a dozen murmured conversations.

Next to me was a man of about my age, and from the look of the scratched leather satchel on the floor by his feet, I guessed he was also heading to the Bodleian. We added our own quiet exchange to the mix. Lars Corbel was a professor of history at UC, the University of the Chilterns, and his special subject was North America. I said I had heard that fewer big boats were making the crossing to Rockwell now. He nodded and told me that things were worse than people imagined. The Nigerian empire had its own reasons to keep on cutting the Atlantic seabed cables. They alone had the submarines to do it. Very little news was getting out of North America. Corbel had friends who spent time there and were lucky to have made it back safely a year ago. They told him that the old warlordism continued but it was no longer correct to speak of 'armed groups'. Many had merged. Now large armies were fighting each other. Peace was fragmentary – a ceasefire might be negotiated in the northwest, while fighting flared in the Midwest. During periods of peace, the armies either taxed or plundered the civilian population. Each faction claimed to be the legitimate inheritor of the spirit of the once great nation, the greatest in the world. All fighters claimed to be true patriots. Every warrior loved his country with a passion and was prepared to die for it. Empires, Corbel said sadly, declined in pain. Take China. A thirty-year-old experiment in democracy was falling apart under pressure from a violent populist revolution wanting war with Nigeria.

He had written a paper comparing the situation in America to that of Europe from the time of Charlemagne in AD 800 to the early nineteenth century, when the highest prestige and divine right were associated with the precious mantle of the Holy

Roman Empire. The professor's conclusion was presented as an optimistic one, though the time frame seemed damning to me. In the end, after a thousand years, the lure of the ancient past, the weight of a dead hand, became irrelevant. After Napoleon imposed his will following his victory at Austerlitz in 1805, no one cared much for the Holy Roman Empire. The wars in America would exhaust themselves one day, new ideas would replace the American worship of the old dispensation. It might take centuries, but it would happen.

I suggested that unlike the American case, the Holy Roman Empire had conferred a degree of stability on Europe.

Corbel nodded impatiently. 'Yes, yes. That could happen one day in North America too. But what interests me is the persistence then collapse of an idea.'

He politely asked about my own work, and I told him. He said he had sometimes wondered if the Corona had ever existed. I assured him that it once had and that I was determined to find it. Corbel said that long ago he'd had a passion for Blundy's poetry, but it had been many years since he had read him. He quoted the opening lines from 'In the Saddle'. We were getting on well.

The conversation moved on to a subject that had always interested me – the strange stability of the English language. We considered the orthodox notion that the internet, having survived so long, had imposed a lasting homogeneity.

Corbel said, 'There's an old saying that I like to repeat to my students. In human psychology, anything worth studying has multiple causes. So, if the English language happened now to be dynamic, we could just as plausibly claim that the internet was the cause. I'm not saying it had nothing to do with this stability, but we could add in the nostalgia for the old times that still infects the educated classes. Then include the Inundation, when the way we spoke and wrote froze. Now, cultural timidity stifles innovation in all kinds of areas.'

'I'm with you on those,' I said. I was thinking of Kevin Howard at Corbel's mention of nostalgia. 'And I like your multiple causes. So here's another, one that you should appreciate. Over a hundred years ago it was the United States that had the cultural energy to drive change in English usage. In my research I've come across many historical anglophone writers who complained about the Americanisation of the language. That can no longer happen.'

'Back then,' Lars said, 'there were all kinds of English on every continent driving change. Now people don't move around much. Too dangerous. We don't have intimate contact.'

I said, 'America tears itself apart, and on our archipelago we're as peaceful and dull as a Hampshire parsonage in a Jane Austen novel. Perhaps we're a bit like the England of 1370, reeling from the Black Death but just beginning to recover.'

'Here's one more cause for the list,' Lars said. 'Since our dark ages ended, our populations have grown older. It was always the young who experimented with language.'

We talked of history and literature into the evening and the hours passed quickly. I liked Corbel. His mind was quick and open. He was generous in conversation, he listened as easily as he talked and he had a sense of humour, of fun. Later, we dozed uncomfortably through the night in the sitting position along with three dozen other passengers. The bunk I had paid for was now occupied by one of the crew. I did not feel brave enough to wake the man and tell him to go elsewhere.

It was not only conversation that shortened the journey. At dawn the captain came by to tell us that a following wind and a useful swell had powered us along and we would arrive at the quay beyond Maentwrog-under-Sea an hour early. Corbel and I cycled to the Bodleian funicular station. This was my fourth trip and I had not yet lost my fascination with the mechanism that would raise us to the library. At the top station, a large tank fixed under a carriage was filled with water from a stream. As tank and carriage descended on a looped chain down a railway track, their combined weight pulled our carriage and its empty tank up along a parallel track. When the journey was complete, the tank at the bottom was emptied, the tank at the top filled, and the process was repeated.

We had the handsome oak cabin to ourselves. As we rose to our destination a thousand feet above the sea, I challenged Lars to derive a lesson for humanity from the funicular's ingenious machinery. He pointed through the window at the track up ahead. We were about to pass the descending carriage.

'An optimist's charter: we see our same old mistakes coming at us again, but their weight will see us to the top.'

We parted at the library reception and went to our rooms to catch up on sleep. At four o'clock I ate a lunch of bread, protein cake and mint tea, all that the library canteen could provide at that inconvenient time. I learned that the archivist Donald Drummond was unwell. It was a relief not to have another conversation about the phone numbers in Vivien's journal.

A scholarly project extending over years involves much drudgery and boredom, easily forgotten when the entire undertaking is over. Only amnesia permits the folly of a fresh undertaking. I suffered as I stood in the doorway of the room I had booked. I needed it for its long boardroom table where I could set out the Blundy archive. Stacked on the floor were 135 identical sealed boxes, each one numbered and coded. So familiar. Twelve were Vivien's, a misleading figure, for her life was at least as interesting as his. Seven of her boxes were dedicated to her Blundy years. Her academic work, drafts of papers and books, and research notes for her doctorate on John Clare were missing. She may have destroyed them in an act of self-obliteration when she gave up teaching to become her husband's secretary. Or she never thought of herself as someone whose life and papers would be archived.

I surveyed the room from the doorway, reluctant to step back into the tangled lines of other people's lives that I had foolishly made my own. I had been doing this too long. The Corona, even its long-dead author, even his entire era had no business squatting across so many of my best years. I was almost forty-five, a time when maturity and accumulated knowledge intersect with the last of youth's lingering strength and quickness of mind. I should be doing something of my own. Something useful, for others. The loudmouths over in the Science and Technology building may have been right, the humanities were a waste of mental breath, of paper and ink, of entire lives. I sometimes compared myself and my colleagues along our corridor to medieval monks. But they at least were preserving a body of precious ancient knowledge that would one day stand against the violent tyranny of Christian thought. Whereas we were a diminishing band whose field, from Chaucer to Fisk, no one read but us. A thousand-year enterprise was turning to dust. It was history. History was history. Our students were right, the past was what they had to leave behind.

A fit of pointlessness gripped me and I could not move. I was a parasite, an intruder on the intentions and achievements of people who lived in another world more than a hundred years ago. They would not care for or about me if I'd lived then or if they had lived now. If I met them, I probably wouldn't like them. I wouldn't like the way they thought they lived on a historical summit with a privileged all-round view, when in fact they were 'crouching', as Blundy's beloved Larkin had it, 'below extinction's alp'. I pretended otherwise, but I would never grasp how different they were from me. They were as shaped and trapped by their times, their material circumstances, their expectations as I was by mine. We were flies confined in separate bottles. When Francis Blundy was fifteen, in 1965, it would have been possible for him to have a conversation with someone born in 1885. Blundy's contemporaries often declared that they could not comprehend the Victorians. If so, I had no chance of understanding Francis or Vivien. I could not describe them. Or judge them. Or believe they had relevance.

I forced myself into the room and sat down heavily on the nearest chair. The boxes were stacked three high around three walls. No point sifting through one when I would never find time to sift through them all. My notes already filled boxes of my own, piled up in a cupboard in our apartment. Our? I didn't want to think about it, or of Rose. Not now. It was not going well between us. I had to do something, so I turned to the screen in front of me and tapped out on the loose, worn and yellowing keys the password that would take me into the Blundy files. The machine mirrored my paralysis. It was no more powerful and probably not much different in design from the late-twentieth-century computer Vivien used to type the email that now appeared on my screen. I must have pressed a box reference number without looking.

3 May 2003, 15:09
My darling,

It's been eighteen days. I'm miserable. I'm going mad. I've just spent one of the worst nights of my life. At 3 a.m., Percy was shouting or screaming in his bedroom. I came out of deep sleep into a panic and rushed into his room. He had crapped in his bed. It was getting light when I finished cleaning everything up. How I loathed the human body, his, mine, everyone's. We're foul. All the time, he was trying to help and making it worse, spreading shit everywhere. When I'd got him showered and his bed ready, he said he wanted to get up, it was daytime and he had 'things to do'. I lost my temper. I screamed at him to get into bed but he wouldn't. I was desperate to sleep after being awake with him the night before, and the night before that. But I don't dare leave him to go downstairs by himself.

So we got up. He wanted fish fingers. I said we didn't have that kind of food and it wasn't right for breakfast anyway. But he kept on. I shouted at him again and he started crying and wailing. A police car stopped outside. Two officers were at the door, a woman and a man. A neighbour had phoned. The police were OK. When they left, I wished they'd taken Percy with them. That thought stirred up my guilt and we went out for fish fingers. Once they were cooked, he wouldn't eat them and had forgotten that he'd ever wanted them.

He begs me every day not to put him in a home, or in a hotel, as he calls it. He must have overheard something. He cries. I can't possibly send him away but I can't go on either. That home, the one that was almost bearable, gave the place away to someone else and I was relieved – it settled the matter. All the other council places are too grim and are also full. I couldn't do it to him anyway. I couldn't live with the knowledge of him a few streets away pining for me. I need to see you. Rachel is ill again so there's no chance of my getting away. Write today, phone, whatever. But don't come, not today.

I love you,
Vivien

––––––––––––

28 May 2003, 15:31
My darling,

What I realise is this: he's already dead. His body keeps going, sort of, but the man I married has left. When he's up and about, dressed in the clothes he always wore, and he looks sort of thoughtful, I think this is one of those weird remissions, a 'retrieval of lucidity' we once talked about. But as soon as he says something, the dream collapses. I know that if he had one of these retrieval moments it would frighten me.

So look, I don't like to repeat myself, but I worry about how this is for you. You've got yourself involved with a woman in a nightmare that you're having to share, when you could be as free as you like. Our times together amaze me. A late afternoon, an evening and part of a morning are like a whole existence on some gorgeous faraway planet. But our last meeting was eleven days ago, twenty minutes in the lane, and we don't know about the next. It would nearly kill me I suppose, but if you have to go, this is the time, now, before we go even deeper – after which it would kill me if you decided on the rational thing.

I love you,
Vivien

---

28 May 2003, 19:34
Dearest,

In haste from a shabby little dressing room, about to go on stage with Craig Raine.
    The most erotic two words I've ever read are your 'even deeper'.
    Must get them out of mind. I have to give a talk.
    Upwards to the deeper! We can do it.

My love,
Francis

---

7 July 2003, 03:17
My darling,

I hate him. No, I hate what he's been forced to become. I can't handle his awful bulk, his dependence, and I hate the way his disease is sucking the life out of me. He barely knows who I am, but he wants things from me all day and never leaves me alone. I hate the pathetic anger fits and the stupid questions he keeps repeating. I can't remember what it was like to love him and I hate Alzheimer's for wrecking our memories of love. I hate my life. You're better off without me. Just go.

7 July 2003, 09:53
Dearest,

I'll be there tomorrow, 2 p.m. Come out the back, into the lane. He'll be OK for ten minutes.

Keep the faith,
Francis

I had read these exchanges and taken notes two years before and remembered them. There was no hint of what was discussed in the lane the next day, but soon after, Francis sent the name of a private care home ten miles from Oxford and Vivien made an appointment. He was playing a constructive role, though it was clearly in his interests to have Percy out the way and Vivien freed from twenty-four-hour care. On the day, Percy refused to go and Vivien cancelled. Francis must have offered to help financially. But he had written earlier to say he was broke because of the Barn conversion.

'He was a wonderful man once,' she wrote to Francis, possibly atoning for her 'I hate him' outburst.

Last night, when he was asleep, I went into the garden for some fresh air. There was the darkened locked-up shed, the workshop where he'll never work again. I remembered the time I went in there to clean it up. Not long before our four nights together. I unwrapped the Vieuxtemps Guarneri violin he was working on. It looked finished to me, ancient and

132

worn round those lovely dark raised edges as if generations
had played on it. It felt so light in my hands. It was beautiful.
To hold it was to remember what a brilliant craftsman he was
(don't be jealous again), how capable and kind and loving a
man, and what a tragedy this is – for him, not me.

It was useful to be reminded of the burden on Vivien of the
sorrow of Percy's illness in the time before his death. I read
all their emails of that time. Neither Francis nor Vivien could
afford a private care home set in parkland with fountains etc.,
and yet he was telling her to make an appointment.

After Percy died, Vivien sank in grief and the affair seemed
to be over. Francis went to the United States to teach and their
parting must have been bitter, for the emails cease for many
months.

But my purpose in being here again was to look at post-
Dinner exchanges between Vivien and Harry Kitchener. I had
to know if she or Francis let him see the Corona or make a copy.
Old questions, but it was easy to miss a clue buried among so
much material. October 2014 onwards was catalogued from box
110 in the Blundy archive, and from box 8 in Vivien's. I lifted
the two boxes onto the table and removed their tight-fitting lids
and the perforated container of preserving chemicals.

It was as though I had stepped into a crowded room, or
was watching a play for the hundredth time. Here were all the
characters, the Blundy friends – John Bale, the vet, the botanist Tony Spufford, Graham Sheldrake, referred to by Francis as
'the fainéant', the do-nothing, and his wife Mary Sheldrake,
the lauded novelist that time forgot, and Harriet and Chris
Page worrying about their baby, Jane Kitchener the potter and
Harry Kitchener. Once they were people whose lives, friendships, loves and possessions were self-evidently real, while
behind them and ahead, the past and future were populated by
shades. Now they were the shades, ghostly traces, their lives
reduced to words, confined for decades in the dark, buried
under packs of absorbent crystals, inside boxes stacked on

the bolted basement shelving of a mountaintop library. Back among them again, my mood improved. But I wondered sometimes if writing about them would be an act of betrayal. They needed me, and in return for my care, I needed them to whisper their secrets. Their journal entries and emails were not enough. Sifting through the remains of Francis and Vivien's last years, together then apart, would at best give me only a small fraction of the truth. I needed them to tell me what was really happening between them.

Over the next two days I read through everything between October 2014 and October 2016 and found nothing, or nothing new. I read all the messages from Vivien and Francis to Harry and he to them. I searched for Harry's name in everything that passed between Francis and Vivien. I did not neglect any of the social media available to them. If Harry arranged with Vivien or Francis to read or possess a copy of the poem, it must have been by telephone or in a meeting. Between Vivien and Harry, the messages, never that frequent, cease for a while after the Dinner. That was not surprising. Her irritation with Francis may have spilled over – the last thing she would have wanted was to have anything to do with her husband's editor. In that time, she travelled frequently to London, but it was Peter she saw rather than Harry and Jane.

In the afternoon dusk of approaching winter, I walked along the cliffs beyond the funicular station. It was not only Corona business that had brought me here. I wanted to be alone. The unusual student walkout, the collapse of our course and the embarrassment it caused us in our dealings with the administration, which regarded us now as fools and failures – all of it had brought on a coolness between Rose and me. It was not mutual blame so much as shame and wariness. We had failed at this, and we might disappoint each other again. We would not have brought down such ignominy on ourselves had we not been so close, had we been living apart and more objective with each other. Disruption of any kind by students was an astonishing event and everyone was talking about it. The clamour amazed us. Hilarity, ridicule, contempt. That Rose and I were left staring at empty chairs was entertaining. The spokesman, Kevin Howard, became a local hero. His little speech, described as an 'evisceration', had been recorded somehow and a transcript circulated. The entrenched enemies of the humanities joined in. Our 'History of AI' course was yet one more example of a pointless project. The students were being failed by an outdated and exhausted mode of thought that was typical of the humanities in general. The various subjects had no proper theoretical underpinning. Their confident assertions were not subjected to conventional methods of proof. Published essays were not peer-reviewed. The best portion of the Humanities funding would be better spent in the Science departments.

Rose and I could no longer discuss the mess we had made and the damage we had caused. We could barely look at each other. When I told her that I was leaving for the Bodleian, she did not conceal her relief. So I took my walks after work along the clifftop path and wondered about our future. I made no progress. Surely, we could not end our marriage because of a failed course. That we were thinking of it suggested our bond was frail. That we blamed each other suggested the same. But I was in the right – this course was her idea, not mine. When I asked myself if I loved her, I felt nothing at all, neither for nor against her. That was an answer in itself. Then I should fight for our marriage and go on living with her. I mentally shrugged. If I moved out, I would be offered a 'studio' apartment, one small room and a shared bathroom along a corridor. Fine by me. Stay or leave, I didn't care.

One evening, after dinner in the Bodleian canteen, I spent time with Lars Corbel. He was more engaged politically than I was. He was exercised by the state of the various Citizens Committees that ran the country at local and national levels. According to him, there was corruption and malign influence in the selection process for the committees. He was astonished by my political innocence. For all the calamities and change, Corbel said, our system was unchanged in 130 years.

The same top two per cent, highly educated, highly trained, hard-working, met their spouses at elite institutions, ensured the best schooling and health care for their progeny to whom they passed on their capital and ensured their group's continuation. They were cut off from the rest of us and were large and varied enough as a faction that they didn't even think of themselves in those terms. They had taken over the high ground of the Pennine Chain, transforming it into a massive and wealthy suburb. They were barely aware of how they controlled almost everything. In the name of 'fairness' they had selected a preponderance of early school-leavers to serve on the Citizens Committees. Those with minimal education were more easily influenced by subtle input. 'Ordinary' people were predisposed towards hearsay, prejudice, ill-placed anger and an absence of objectivity. They were easily steered. Lars said that if there had to be a selection process, he would want it to go the other way. Education to a high level should be a minimum requirement to sit on a Citizens Committee. There were still enough freethinkers around to ask the awkward questions. The elite promoted and hid behind the wisdom of the common people. But early school-leavers made disastrous decisions.

'Like what?'

'Legalising cigarettes.'

'Nicotine? Really?'

'It'll be law next year. Where have you been, Thomas! It's grown under glass in the lawless south-west. The bureaucracy hasn't the resources to fight smugglers and dealers, and the Treasury needs the tax revenue. The committee was a pushover.'

'How do you know about this influence?'

'It's common knowledge!'

A conspiracy. Lars had a cranky side.

I said, 'Have you tried it?'

'Tobacco? You inhale it once and you're addicted. Then you die of cancer.'

'Why would an early school-leaver vote for it?'

Lars glared at me. 'The administration gets the results it wants.'

I didn't ask him how he knew this because I guessed the answer would be some variant of 'common knowledge'. I would have liked to challenge him on the Citizens Committees, but I didn't have the background and I hadn't been following events. I never do. It was my old problem. I preferred the past. I moved Lars on to the safer ground. We talked happily about Milton's *Comus*.

Next morning Lars was due to leave. I waited for him in the reception hall. A librarian I did not recognise approached me with an envelope in her hand. She told me it was a note from her colleague Donald Drummond and apologised for not passing it on sooner. I stuffed it in a pocket of my coat. It would be an apology for his absence. I wished illness on no one, but I had been happier without him. At that moment, Lars appeared and I walked with him to the funicular. We stood to one side to watch the carriage water tank being filled from a pond fed by a small waterfall. I didn't refer to our conversation of the night before. I'd had enough of being told I was politically naïve. I preferred a brief and pleasant farewell. Before he boarded, we swapped contacts and shook hands. I waited to wave as he receded down the mountainside, then I went back to work.

I suspected that I would be going through the motions. I had no hopes for fresh discoveries, but after an hour I opened box 98 of the Blundy archive and found a passage in a notebook from 2001, probably jottings of his towards a poem, though not one I recognised. Nothing relevant to my immediate research but it spoke to me and I took a picture.

Loss in general. Something pure. If you find that thing at last (which you probably won't) it will not live up to your hopes. Always beyond reach, is the principle. This is how religions begin, with pursuit of the ineffable, and continue, as their gods become lost gods. Where is Thor? Where is Jupiter? Or God?

(See Norman Cohn's *Pursuit of the Millennium*. The prediction and the longing are for God's return.) If you love the natural world, you will think of loss. Paradise Lost. Expulsion inevitable. Childhood is the lost estate. Children at their happiest enact for adult onlookers a tragic foretelling – the estate will not last. Loss is the fabric of existence. All bad things are lost too. All torturers, all diseases. Lost civilisations, lost causes, lost symphonies, computer files, Edens, umbrellas, loves, landscapes, keys, wallets, pens, cats, innocence, sorrows, talent, parents, wits, reading glasses – a ceaseless parade of receding carnival floats.

Half an hour before lunch, I decided I could do no more. I'd had enough. There was nothing between Vivien and Harry beyond sparse and uninteresting emails. NAI's proposal was a dud. I decided to leave a day early. I would have tried to phone Rose to let her know, but I knew that any conversation between us would be awkward. I packed at speed, made my closing arrangements with the librarian in my section and by two o'clock was making my own descent to the afternoon ferry.

We had a lucky escape as we made our way southwards along the Welsh coast. After five hours and only slow progress against a headwind, the skipper came to tell the passengers that there was a storm on its way and we might have to put in somewhere for safety. The sea was choppy rather than rough and no one was seasick as we dozed through the night on the hard benches. By the time the storm broke the next morning, we were already a few miles into the relative safety of the old Severn Estuary and soon we were passing between the piers and eerie ruined towers of an old suspension bridge. Then we turned east and later passed the Cotswold Hills to our left. We were not in the moorings at Port Marlborough until six that evening. All the bikes were out on hire. I had to choose between walking the twenty miles across Marlborough Island to Ball Hill Quay or waiting for a bike to be returned. I was tired from the journey and decided to wait. It was a lucky call, for I was on a bike by seven thirty and was on the last ferry to South Downs Harbour at ten.

It was one in the morning as I walked the last couple of miles to the campus into a strong wind. I was cold and exhausted. Rose was likely to be in bed. My plan was to sleep on the sofa in the living room rather than wake her. When I was at last outside our apartment door and reaching into my backpack for my key, I had an intimation that something was not right. Nothing extraordinary in that. I was coming into a tense situation. I indulged a wild fantasy that she might have killed herself and her body had been lying on the floor undiscovered for days. All my fault. I turned the key softly. There was a single lamp on by a low table close to the sofa. On that table was an empty bottle and two glasses with the dregs of red wine. The sofa resembled an unmade bed. Two cushions that belonged with it were on the floor. The bedroom door was closed. As I advanced into the room and the apartment door clicked shut behind me, I heard Rose's muffled voice. 'Shit.' The sibilant sounded loud in the night. Then, the creak of the bed. Seconds later the door opened, and she was before me in her dressing gown, my wife, unkempt and beautiful, tenderly closing the bedroom door on her lover.

In the circumstances, any opening remark was going to sound stupid. She said in a flat tone, 'You're back early.'

It was spoken like an accusation. After a silence I said, 'You have a visitor.'

She went forward to pick up the cushions and take the wine glasses and bottle to the kitchen sink, removing evidence, making everything OK. Or a step in that direction. She came towards me and stopped and used both hands to settle her hair, ruffled by the rut I had interrupted.

'Tom, I'm sorry.'

I waited.

'We can talk in the morning. You could sleep over at—'

'Get him out.'

139

'No.'

'Then I'll do it.'

As I went towards the door, she stepped in front of me. 'All right. All right. I don't want violence.'

'There won't be if he leaves now.'

She went in, closing the door noisily behind her. I tossed my backpack onto the floor and sat. I heard voices, mostly hers interspersed with a monosyllabic male's. Even in my worked-up state, I could not suppress my curiosity. There was a Jane Austen specialist on our corridor said to be active among faculty women in the residence blocks. Another possibility: when Rose and I had gone to one of the Science buildings for our course research, there was a big blond fellow, an AI coder. Rose had spent a long time with him. He would tear me to pieces in seconds.

The door opened and my wife came out first.

'He's going, OK?' She made a downward pushing gesture with her hands to mime or promote a lowering of tension. Some hope. Her lover followed her out. I knew him instantly and was amazed. Kevin Howard of the kissable mouth and spotless complexion. I stood. It could have been taken for a mark of respect. Perhaps it was. What an achievement! His best friend, even his mother, would have thought that a woman like Rose was beyond his grade. There was a time when Rose would have thought so too. He would not meet my eye as he hurried towards the door. Rose took care to keep herself between us. As soon as he was gone, she went past me, also careful not to look in my direction, and locked herself in the bedroom. Silence settled over the apartment. I took off my coat and shoes, found a blanket in a cupboard and lay supine on the sofa, waiting for my heart to calm and sleep to come.

19

The man I shared a bathroom with was an authority on the thirteenth-century papal court of Innocent III, its reforms, crusades and spiritual sway over Christian princes across Europe. When I bumped into Cyril Baker on the landing for a chat, he soon turned the conversation to that court. He spoke with an air of baffled wonder at its complexity and intrigues. He wanted to lend me some books about it, one of which was by him. Not to have lived in that time, he told me once, was his only enduring regret in an otherwise happy life.

Cyril was an obsessive tender of our bathroom's porcelain and its tiled floor. He wiped down the walls, the chrome taps and shower head and used bleach on the lavatory after each use. When he was done, he took his towel and washbag back to his room, leaving no trace. I was no slob, but I felt obliged to raise my game. After sharing with others at the Bodleian, I was sympathetic to the notion of an aseptic communal space, burnished clean of a stranger's presence. I wanted to be alone, purged of mess, connection, entanglements and reproaches, especially my own or Rose's. The indifference I experienced on the Snowdonian heights had hardened into the saintly detachment of a hermit. I was beyond liking or disliking anything or anyone. My monkish cell of a room suited me. Lidded boxes of clothes, books and notes were piled along the walls, almost to the ceiling. More boxes than the Francis and Vivien archive. What was not there of my entire life was held digitally elsewhere, suspended, just as I was.

My one tether was the project. I made no advances or

141

discoveries and wrote nothing. Immersion was all I needed. To swim through the gloom of the irrecoverable past, among the familiar sunken wrecks and their scattered debris, was enough. Rereading was the thing. With no aim in mind, I went through hundreds of Percy Greene's emails of the 1990s onwards. Specifications and costings for violins, loving messages to Vivien, arrangements for evenings, weekends and for what he intended to cook for her. He knew his way round Italian cuisine, he liked 'the hearty country wines of the Midi', he was fussy about knives and brought his own to her flat on the top floor of a north Oxford house. In his twenties he had played rugby as a second-row forward with a serious amateur team until he tore a ligament in his knee. He was an experienced hiker and scrambler, could fix things, knew basic wiring and plumbing. Among Vivien's friends, Percy the craftsman and handyman was a rarity and welcomed, just as Chris Page was in the Blundy household. Percy carried out emergency repairs for them sometimes. Vivien's circle consisted of academics married, mostly, to other academics. Percy had left school at sixteen. Reading and talking about books made him restless. To relax from the painstaking construction of violins he played a five-string banjo for a traditional jazz band, the Hotfeet, that performed Jelly Roll Morton numbers at weekends in an east Oxford pub. He played, it was said, in the languid but precise style of Johnny St Cyr and, as if by instinct, knew his way round the more unusual augmented chords. His solos, especially the one for 'Doctor Jazz', were big favourites with a knowing crowd.

The pub was on the Cowley Road, well off Vivien's usual beat. She was taken there in 1993 on a warm Sunday lunchtime by a husband and wife, professors of Arabic and Spanish respectively. Jazz, and in particular traditional New Orleans jazz, had never interested Vivien, but sitting with her friends, drinking halves of bitter, sometimes chatting, sometimes listening, she became entranced by the merrily whirling counterpoint of trumpet, trombone and clarinet, the elephantine tread of the euphonium and most of all by the syncopated choppy clinking

142

sound of the banjo. She was a half-competent pianist and she knew enough to be impressed to hear him strike four different but related chords to each bar. She watched the banjoist's left hand flash up and down the frets, she admired the flickering muscle in his bare forearm and, naturally, she studied his face, 'that most erotic of parts, second only to the mind. Ah, is this the almost middle-aged woman's first flight from the body?'

Her journals record and seem to predict her course towards him. He never glanced at his hands. His attention was on the audience, though 'sometimes he bestows a grateful nod and half-smile on one of the other players'. It was a 'big, generous wholesome face'. His expression was 'bold and friendly'. There was 'a challenge in his look which seems to say I hope you're having as much fun as me'. He became aware of her gaze and briefly met her eye and smiled without parting his lips. Meanwhile, 'his fingers go on playing as though they have nothing to do with him, though occasionally he cocks his head to listen'. The next Sunday she went to the pub alone and approached him at the bar during the break between sets.

He saw her coming and before she could speak, he said, 'You again. That's nice.'

He bought her a drink, they chatted and she came to hear the band the next four Sundays before, as she wrote, 'our first date, and I'm nervous'. After it, she told herself, 'Beware. Good sex can be your undoing.' Elsewhere: 'that such a big man can be so kind, so delicate in bed!' She was in love, she told her journal. He wrote to her, 'I want to write I love you a thousand times but I have a bus to catch so this will have to do.' The postmark shows 17 October. She noted that he took her to see his workshop, a damp basement in Jericho, Oxford. 'A weird yellow mushroom is growing on the wall which he refuses to remove. Too close to the canal. No place for a master luthier.' She found him a place in Summertown on Oxford's north side, a ground-floor flat in an Edwardian terraced house and paid the rent out of her lecturer's salary. Three months later, in one day Percy received late payment for one violin and sold

143

another. He paid her back. That night they 'feasted, drank and decided to get married. I think it was my decision. P too dazed and happy to disagree.' The next day Vivien wrote, 'If I was a bank manager of love, I would estimate that P's principal asset is kindness. Big and kind. What luck!'

Until his cognitive decline, history knows nothing of Percy Greene's faults. A close friend, the trumpeter of the Hotfeet and a doctor, said at Percy's funeral, 'Whatever natural substances occasionally surge through our brains to make us delighted and delightful, the endorphins, the serotonin etc., Percy had quantities all and every day to supply a small town. His daily allowance would be for us a lifetime's high point. Call it virtue or genetic luck, we were privileged to be around him.' These were the faintly humorous exaggerations felt obligatory at funerals. Vivien was closer to the truth when she wrote, three weeks after the wedding, 'what's so lovely is that basically, in a quiet way, he's simply glad he exists. Whatever the difficulty, the baseline isn't disturbed. Then that line becomes mine too.'

In the brief years before the illness hit, Vivien exulted in their love and in Percy's temperament that, as she saw it, made their union so delightful. In volume four, when they were well established in the Headington house, she wrote:

Books bore him. Gluing violin bits together doesn't interest me. So a marvellous space is opened up for everything else. We must have walked all the footpaths between here and the south Cotswold Hills. He can tell at a glance every bird, moth and butterfly. He was excited to see in one afternoon a swallowtail and a Duke of Burgundy. I know the names of wildflowers. We trade! He loves music in all its forms and he widens my tastes beyond Bach etc. I read to him. He loves it, especially when it's poetry. But he wants to hear it, not read it. Last month he mentioned his taste for red socks. I read him that too-famous poem, 'The Red Wheelbarrow'. He wanted it again. He got it because he loves *things*, how they feel and look, how they work, what they do to us or for us. He could *see* that wheelbarrow, its redness, the white of the chickens. I quoted Williams's line from another poem, whose title I've forgotten: 'no ideas but in things'. It's become his catch-phrase. After breakfast he sometimes murmurs those words as he kisses me and heads off to his shed for the day's work.

Three years later she returned to this passage and scribbled in the margin, 'In love, we forgot that we too were things that could get broken or lost.' Nowhere in the journals are there doubts or complaints about the marriage until the burden of nursing her husband began to crush her. His death in 2003 and the coroner's court proceedings were reported in the two local papers, with mentions of the slow response time of the ambulance service. The cuttings were among Vivien's papers but over time they disintegrated. Probably handled by too many researchers. About eighty years ago, a curator replaced them with downloaded printouts, along with an explanatory note. The matter came before the coroner because of doubts whether Percy died from injuries to the brain or because of a loss of blood and the delayed ambulance. According to one press item, Percy was certified dead on arrival at the John Radcliffe Hospital. He had been suffering a loss of motor control and stumbled and fell down a flight of stairs. After hearing expert medical evidence, the coroner concluded that since Percy was a big man, the impact on the hallway's tiled floor would have been severe. Likely he was already dying as Vivien came running from the kitchen.

She sank into herself and corresponded with no one, except her sister, Rachel. The occasional journal entries are mostly bitter self-reproach. She should have been kinder, more patient and sweeter to Percy, should have managed some detachment in looking after him, should have remembered their love as it had been, should have acted sooner on the health visitor's advice and made a bedroom for him downstairs in the living room. Her liaison with Francis might have been another cause for guilt but she does not address it. After seven months, there is a brief email message from him, presumably in response to a phone call: 'OK, we'll talk tonight.' A resumption of the affair or a consolatory conversation – there is no record.

Vivien asked her sister if she would come and help her clear Percy's workshop of its contents and sell off his tools on the internet. Despite poor health, Rachel came immediately. Percy's two banjos fetched a high price. The sisters cleared the house of the rest of his possessions. 'The dressing gown hanging in the bathroom contains his shape. It's agony to see it there . . . The leather strap of his watch is curled round the form of his wrist. It all must go . . . The Red Cross came last week to collect but it's made no difference. Only added to the unrelenting din of his absence.'

During this period, the Blundy journals are focussed even more than usual on work, on poems in progress and notes towards some seminars and lectures he was giving at Princeton. Proof of Vivien and Francis together again is the holiday they took in May 2004. She was positive enough to buy herself a first digital camera. There is no record of their travel arrangements. Her photo library shows them in southern Europe, in a location which others long ago identified as the Greek island of Amorgos. It was reached by an eight-hour ferry journey. Chances were reduced of meeting anyone they knew. The best or closest of the photographs, possibly taken by a waiter, shows them sitting side by side, but not touching. No holding hands, no friendly arm around a shoulder. Vivien smiles bravely. The poet looks tense.

I remembered where I was, stood up, yawning, and glanced around me, at my cell. My life had shrunk, my career was in poor shape. On publication, my introduction to my 'biography' of a lost poem had aroused little interest. My marriage was over. In Rose I had lost my best friend, best colleague, best lover, and I had hit a bedrock of indifference. A fiend had come in the night to take an ice-cream scoop to my brain and made off with my darkest emotional flavours, fury, humiliation, self-pity, desolation. If they all came back at once, they would wreck me. Any day now, I told myself, I would start to feel. Watch out. But two months passed without change. I taught the same classes, including for the thirteenth time the Wyatt sonnet, to first-year students, 'They flee from me that sometime did me seek'. I did it as if in my sleep, explaining rhyme royal and reading out their various attempts to parse the poem – 'Those girls used to screw me, now they cool me' and so on. After two shouting rows, I was courteous and cool to Rose whenever work threw us together. Neither of us wanted to talk. In our first set-to, much the louder, I did not need to lay out an accusation. I merely had to say his name. In our bed! Sensibly, she went on the attack. I was emotionally dead, detached, closed off to her, careless of her needs. My indifference caused her betrayal. I was unhappy to find myself in the wrong century. Did I have any idea how infectious unhappiness could be? The only person I cared for was Vivien Blundy. Touché!

It was too late for supper in the refectory. I ate an apple and remembered Blundy's poem about the Covent Garden apple juggler. When Francis died in 2017, his obituaries had long been in place in newspaper offices. The more popular media, loath to be discussing poetry, fell back on the enduring story of the poet meeting Queen Elizabeth II in 1988. Instead of bowing or giving even a cursory bend of the neck, he smiled pleasantly and gave a formal but friendly greeting. He treated her as an equal, was the judgement of outraged commentary. Asked about it afterwards, he said to reporters, 'On monarchy and inherited power I'm with John Locke, our greatest philosopher.' He liked to quote, 'Regal and Supreme Power is properly and truly his, who can by any Means seize upon it.' He was dismissive when others pointed out that Locke's quarrel was with absolute, not constitutional monarchs. In the serious papers the missing Corona was at that stage no more than an interesting footnote. One obituarist wrote that Blundy was our finest poet since Tennyson. Others mentioned Donne and, of course, Eliot. On the poet's character, there was much made of the worn trope, 'not suffering fools gladly'. Harriet Page would have been pleased to be quoted and see her 'awkward genius with a heart of gold' reiterated. One writer jokily wondered why Blundy had so few wives. 'A poet of his stature should have five or six weddings behind him by his mid-sixties.' The rumour that he was privately gay and had an affair with an Oxford vet was dismissed. Blundy was happy, the consensus ran, to indulge a life of serial monogamy but 'his late marriage to Vivien brought him not only love but the calm domestic setting of the famous Barn in Gloucestershire during his last dozen years. In this time, he published some of his greatest and most popular work, including the cycle of love poems inspired by some days with Vivien in a Cotswold hotel.'

Reading through these articles again only pushed Francis and Vivien further from view. The absence of genuine detail had a wintry effect. The subject hardened into a public posture, like a pigeon-stained statue of a forgotten general. I prefer Francis omitting to wish his wife a happy birthday, then heading to his study to make the final preparations of his vellum gift and eating an apple along the way. But that fruit was my supposition.

In the months after his death, it was too soon to say of Francis Blundy that he was vain, opinionated, self-important, careless of others, ungenerous, mean-spirited, dependent and entitled and a great poet. In his personal pantheon, his bust would be up there on a stone shelf with John Locke's. His present to Vivien was more about himself than her, which was why he needed to perform it to the company on that evening in October 2014.

If apples served the poet well in three poems, they were not enough for me. It was almost ten and I was hungry. A half-hour's walk away was a pub that served food as an afterthought to its tasteless beer. I looked outside. Another November snowfall and the wind looked strong, but I decided to go. If I walked fast, I should be in time for something dull but filling. There was no space in my room for a cupboard and the administration had not provided hooks for outdoor clothes. I rummaged

148

in my boxes until I found my warmer coat, which I had not worn since my last Bodleian trip. I couldn't find a hat or gloves and I was in a hurry.

Outside, the snow was six inches deep from the last fall and the wind was bitter. I hunched into it and rammed my hands into the pockets of my coat. In the right there was a folded piece of paper. Old notes, I thought as I pulled it clear. It was a crumpled unopened envelope with my name on it typed in capitals. I slowed, struggling to remember, and then I had it, Donald Drummond and his note of apology handed to me by his colleague. I walked on.

The remaining item on the pub's menu was a leek and potato soup with bread and a square of greasy protein cake. Monday night and the place was almost empty. I had forgotten to bring a book, but it would have made little difference because the light was poor. It was no different in daytime. Glass was expensive and windows were generally built small. For something to do, I took out Drummond's letter and could just make out the typing, which covered a whole page. Sure enough, it was a long apology for his absence due to flu. But he had been wanting to talk to me about an important matter. He had his brother's family to stay. It included a quiet and gifted girl of fourteen. Donald got along with her very well. She often came into his study to chat. She had a lovely manner, was exceptionally gifted at maths, in fact, something of a genius. Her name was Dolly and she . . . I gave the exasperated gasp of the childless and put the letter down. Whose children, nieces, nephews and grandchildren were not geniuses?

The publican himself brought my meal, setting it down hard on the table. He didn't like university types in his bar. It was the kids who caused the trouble, but he made no distinction. Vegetable flavour had been artfully purged from the soup. Only more salt could rescue it. I fetched it myself from a stained tray by the door to the men's lavatory. I morosely resumed my supper. After I had finished, I was reluctant to move from my warm seat. I picked up the letter.

I had some notes on my desk and she asked me what I'd been up to. As soon as I mentioned that we'd been trying to solve a puzzle she was interested. I told her about those phone numbers in Vivien Blundy's last journal and how they were not in any contemporary directory. Dolly was intrigued and wanted to see. I wrote the numbers out for her and she took them over to a chair in the corner of my study. I went on answering the emails that had piled up during my illness. A half-hour later, she came over and told me what she thought. After some false starts, she guessed these were *not* phone numbers, in which case the zeros in the first position were irrelevant. She took them out and wrote out the digits in a string – and straight away knew what they were. She set them out in the standard format. When she showed me, I gave a yelp. Tom, it's a decimal map reference!

I called up an old map and entered the numbers. Blundy's property! Within a couple of centimetres of accuracy, the point was near a corner of the dairy. Empty ground. Something must be buried there. My first thought will also be yours. Please be assured, I'm going to do nothing about it. This is yours by right. You must get yourself there, 51. 769[XXXX]. 2.09[XXXX] and take a look. But you do owe me this – I want you to tell me immediately what you find. You'll need to keep the find in a safe place with expert curating resources. The Bodleian will be at your service. And you must please send Dolly a reward – a bar of real chocolate (if you can find one!). I hope you can sleep. I know I can't.

I sat immobilised by powerful and contrary feelings. Excitement, naturally, and exultation, and impatience to start my preparations for a journey. But the letter was two months old. Drummond could have reasonably given up on me and have gone to see for himself. It was suspicious that he had failed to send me a follow-up message. He could be there now, hauling up a sack from a hole in the ground by torchlight the treasure that was, as he had conceded, rightfully mine. Or he was at his desk, readying the Corona for publication, with his accompanying monograph in which I would be kindly footnoted. I had to get the numbers into my computer and see for myself. I snatched the letter and envelope, stood up too quickly, sending my chair crashing backwards against the floorboards. I picked it up and strode to the door. The publican shouted after me to come back and pay for my meal and beer. I did so, and then I ran through the snow for the first half-mile. For no reason. It was too late to phone the Bodleian. I did not have Drummond's home number. I faced a night without sleep.

I slowed and in my rare state felt amazement at my stupidity: if the numbers were not in any directory, then of course they were not phone numbers. Dolly knew to take that first simple step and put me to shame. How wrong I had been about Donald Drummond, a truly decent man – unless his hands were closing around my poem. And that lovely clever Dolly. I would write her an emphatic letter of thanks – and include ten bars of real chocolate if such stuff still made it across the oceans.

Soon, I was nearing the faculty residential blocks. Their stacked lights illuminated snowflakes in windblown downward spirals. What came next was inevitable and I had to stop to consider. There was only one person in the world I wanted to tell, one person who would fully grasp the magnitude of this development, bring the right degree of scepticism and – better face it – possess the funds to mount a proper expedition. In an instant my indifference dissolved. Yes, I loved her and of course, I had known it all the time. I looked up, blinking against the thickening snowfall. I knew which window in which high building was hers. Blessed place! The lights in her apartment were off and the eloquent Mr Howard, active or post-coitally asleep, was in my bed.

20

I passed a part of that snowy night writing an apologetic note to Drummond. I lied about the cause of my delay and told him I was mounting an expedition and promised that he would be the first to know what I found. I intended to call the library later that morning to make sure he hadn't set off to see for himself.

I got up at dawn, made coffee, and spread out a map on the floor. The gigantic waves of 2042 had smashed into the west-facing coast of Britain and also rolled inland by way of the Severn Estuary to form an inland sea that eventually included the Vale of Oxford. After many years of heavy rain and rising sea levels, it surged and forced its way further north and west into the valleys of the southern Cotswold Hills to form a series of islands and numerous islets. Most of those were abandoned a long time ago – too cut off, too small and steep to farm, and there was an acute shortage of labour.

For the fifth time, I validated the map reference online. There it was, right by the old dairy. X marked the spot. I called up an ancient map, Ordnance Survey, 1:25,000 and experienced famil-iar wonderment at those beautiful miles of open countryside, the spidery trails of footpaths, some of them a thousand years old, magnificent copses once intended as cover for foxes, and hillsides too steep, even for grazing. Half asleep at my desk, I sent myself across that landscape, mile after mile, across well-tended fields and past farmhouses of local limestone, built in the vernacular style, and down hollow ways, where mossy walls of the same stone and gnarled tree roots enclosed the path.

On the 1:1,250 Official Land Registry site plan, the Barn was shown after its conversion, which was when various small out-houses were demolished. The boundaries of the ten-acre plot did not change after Blundy made his purchase. Vivien's map reference pointed to a spot three metres from the north-east corner of the old dairy, as Drummond had said. I knew from her accounts that across a wide lawn was a wooden gate in a hawthorn hedge that gave on to a path that descended through pastures to cross the stream by a footbridge. I had walked that way many times in my thoughts, always with Vivien at my side. We lingered on the footbridge, hoping to catch sight of small brown trout shooting through the broken shade.

I called up a current map, barely twenty years old, based on Nigerian satellite imagery, which showed the site of the Barn to be on one of the smaller islands, steep-sided, tree-covered, roughly three miles by two. I could not see an obvious landing point. I would need a boat with an experienced captain who could thread his way through the islands and avoid the shallows. I guessed such sailors were few and not cheap. Difficult. To approach Rose, ease matters between us and ask favours while Kevin Howard was in her life would be further humiliation. I had a higher goal, but I cared for my self-respect. I lacked the courage to abase myself. I knew no one else with spare money. The Blundy Society might contribute but then my secret would be out.

I dozed off and woke at eleven, forty-five minutes before my first seminar of the day. In a hurry, I tried the Bodleian but could not get a line. I was due to teach Mabel Fisk's *The Hammer*, an early novella about first love. A masterpiece. The setting was Glasgow. An eighteen-year-old lad, son of an Italian waiter, works in a quick-change tyre franchise. A lass his age comes by one day with a flat tyre on her open-top sports car, a recent birthday present. They fall in love. She's from a wealthy bohemian family – her mother is an artist, the father is a well-known jazz pianist who takes an immediate dislike to his daughter's boyfriend. He's too low-class for her. On the evening of a big concert, the young man vengefully removes a wooden piece – the hammer – from the jazz player's piano. The E above middle C won't play and he has to improvise around it. The novel ends sadly, with the young couple going their separate ways, but not before a hilarious and moving speech from the boy's father, the waiter. Many of Fisk's later themes of love, revenge, class and integrity are condensed within this simple coming-of-age tale, one of the loveliest literary achievements of the late twenty-first century. Only a master could evoke such laughter and tears. Only Shakespeare could have conjured such a finale as the antic figure of the Glaswegian waiter with his Scots-Italian accent. After a lyrical remonstration, he bestows forgiveness on the small cast of characters. So warm and wise and funny.

I was only a few minutes late for the session. In the two weeks allotted, almost half the kids had done some of the reading, well above the norm, though none had managed the full ninety-six pages. My students found it near impossible to read a whole book and form a judgement, even an adverse one. I did most of the talking, pushing myself to coax responses from minds that were flattened and timorous, indifferent to the entire enterprise of literature. But I was inured to their ways and not cast down.

Afterwards, I walked to the refectory in mellow state after my immersion in the prose of the mighty Fisk. I had read some passages to my students, wanting them to hear what I heard and rouse them into a passion for her work. From the looks of two or three, it might have succeeded. I was watching out for Rose. Hoping and dreading. She usually went across at this time for lunch. I had no plan beyond seeing her and letting something happen. I was almost at the building's entrance when she stepped out. She was close behind a loud group, but she was not part of it. I assumed what I hoped was an open expression, more inquisitive than friendly. Hers, I thought, was wry. She stepped back and held the door open for me. I went past her and turned.

She said, 'Eating?'

'Yes.'

'Why don't you invite me?'

'Come and eat.'

'I'll watch you.'

The faculty dining room was too small for the size of the teaching staff and there was always a din. We found a table, smeared and littered with the remains of abandoned lunches. We cleared up and sat. She asked me how I was. I said I was fine. We had to raise our voices.

'How's Kevin?'

'I told you.'

'What?'

'When we last spoke. It's over.'

I shook my head. I knew this wasn't right.

'You wouldn't listen. Anyway. September. It was a two-night thing.'

'I know of at least three.'

She was irritated. I had to remember my purpose.

'Whatever. Two, three. I kicked him out.'

I wished I'd been more familiar with the old TV soap operas. I would have been ready with the right lines. But what I did next might have been well within the tradition. Or I surpassed it. I shrugged, took out Drummond's letter and handed it across. As she read, I watched her face closely. I had to keep stern. Unforgiving, but ready to fold.

She looked up. 'This is amazing.'

'It's interesting.'

'Are you mad? Tom, this is stupendous. Of course. It's just the sort of daft thing Vivien would do. Bury it and leave it to fate. The librarian is right. It has to be the poem.'

I shrugged again. 'It might be.'

A nearby table was erupting at a joke. Rose was having to shout. 'Tom, what's wrong with you? Look at the date. Two months ago. Some genius child has given you the place on the map. You can't just sit on this. You've got to go!'

I looked at her and smiled and held her gaze. I too was a genius. I said, 'Come with me.'

That afternoon, between seminars, I got through at last to the Bodleian. At first, the news I had dreaded, then relief. Mr Drummond had been away from work for several weeks. He had been ill again and was making a slow recovery. He was expected back within the month. Hardly decent to rejoice in another's ill health, but I couldn't help myself. The treasure was safe. I sent a second message to wish him a good recovery. After classes, I went to Rose's apartment. Or was it ours? The route back to reunion was not smooth, for that evening we had another row in which I rose to operatic heights about trust and marriage and how she had torn ours apart. We made up by eight, in time for dinner. I kept up the pretence that going to the site of the Barn was her idea. I was the laggard who wanted persuading. But we would need a boat with a shallow draught, I told her, and a skilled captain who knew the area. It would be expensive. Was she ready for that? She smiled and reached across the table for my hand. I squeezed hers, but we were not ready for declarations of love. That night, we parted with a chaste but friendly kiss, and I slept across the way in my cell.

We met again in the department the next morning. If her manner was different, I realised within minutes, it was because she was her old self. Her behaviour yesterday – the enthusiasm for my quest, the affection – was an element of her version of con-trition. Now, that was behind her. As we settled on a torn sofa in a recess by the herb tea vending machine, she started by warning me that if Vivien had not taken expert advice on preservation, her document would be at best a stain of dried mould. If the material was stored in a wooden box, there would be nothing. Rose set out her conditions. The captain we hired would be paid half before we set out, the rest after bringing us back safely. She had checked the Land Registry. The site belonged to the military. If we were told to leave, we would leave. She warned me against confrontational behaviour. Even the lowest-ranking soldier had powers of arrest. The earliest date we could set off was mid-March when the university closed for the 'reading break', treated by students and faculty alike as a holiday. We would still be on winter hours and to extend our digging time we'd need powerful lamps of the kind builders used. Not easy to find. Rose had a friend living near Port Marlborough, an artist, a nature-sculptor, who kept a little sailing boat and had friends down at the harbour. They might know the right captain.

Rose's proposals were sound and I agreed to them all. To get my way and her funding, I had to let her take over my adventure. A fair deal. She had been the transgressor, now I was the suitor, waiting on her forgiveness while pretending not to. Even that strange reversal did not bother me much. Our expedition was launched. But Rose, working through her list, had saved the most important item until last.

'How do we find it? There's no GPS.'

She was right, the system had failed months ago. The old low-orbit satellites were dropping earthwards, burning up in the atmosphere. The handful of people who knew how to replace them were busy on other projects and, as usual, materials were scarce.

'It's simple,' I said. 'We take bearings on two landmarks and where the lines cross—'

'Tom, you've seen the map. We'll be in a forest. There are no landmarks.'

I was struggling. I said, 'OK. We'll mark the site on the Nigerian map. The captain will know where he's landed. We can get a compass bearing to walk by. We can pace the distance to Blundy's barn. My stride is about a metre.'

'We'll be on our hands and knees in the undergrowth.'

I had vague notions of a sextant and a chronometer, but I thought they needed stars or the midday sun or the horizon of the open seas.

'Then I don't know,' I said finally. 'We could speak to someone in Earth Sciences.'

And so our meeting ended. She went off to teach an Aphra

Behn seminar, and I went back to my cell to start on a grant pro- posal for our department's Auden week. We parted without a kiss.

Preparations for the voyage held us together, and there was not much else between us. But in early December I spent an afternoon in her bed. It was not an explosive embrace of joyous reconciliation, more a cautious or exploratory exchange. We knew each other too well to fail to give immediate pleasure, but there was sadness in that half-hour, I thought. It seemed merely collegiate, even contractual. We were on a job together and the niceties must be observed. Afterwards, as we lay side by side, and as if to compound the sadness, Rose told me how it had ended with Kevin Howard. It was morning. They faced each other over the table in her flat drinking coffee. He had been silent for a minute or two, propping his head on his hand and staring into his cup. Then he made a fateful announcement. He loved her and always would, wanted to live with her, marry her, have children with her.

'I should have cut him off. Every word was a hook in my skin. He said he imagined three pregnancies close together. He wasn't asking, he was telling, as if his plans laid some kind of obligation on me. I said as kindly as possible that I didn't want any of that. He didn't hear me, and he started over again. Children, marriage, love forever, complete fusion of minds. Finally, I couldn't take any more. I said, "Kevin, just leave." He looked baffled. I opened the door and stood by it, waiting, and watched him walk out. How, after a couple of nights, could he feel so entitled? Three times over! I heard him shouting some- thing along the corridor to the lifts. I felt guilty. And I suppose the best cure for guilt is anger.'

I said, 'He's just a kid. So, Rose, what the hell were you doing? Trying to get yourself sacked?'

Bad questions. She turned away and, fortunately, did not reply. If she had, the starting bell would have sounded for another row. Later I thought about her story. I couldn't deny

158

some satisfaction in my rival, my disruptor, dispensing of himself so conveniently. But Rose's account had softened me, a little, just a little, towards Kevin Howard. A young man, clever, strangely pretty, inexperienced, falls crazily in love. He sees, as in a vision, the bright terminus beyond which his loneliness need not proceed. Rose's tender arms were around him last night. This is where their lovemaking has brought them, and he knows she'll understand. He blurts it out, three children so close in age that they and their toys are constant happy playmates. He is the willing prisoner of an ecstatic solipsism. But Rose brings ruin with her alien antipathies and withdraws her love. Banishment! He takes his sorrow along the airless corridor to the lift that will carry him down into an indifferent world. According to John Milton's *Paradise Lost*, Adam, expelled by God from Paradise, departed hand in hand with his Eve. Not so Kevin Howard.

Rose's story felt familiar, clammily close. I was Percy falling for Vivien, then driven from her love by disease. Or Vivien in love with Blundy's poems, then discovering the man. Or Francis himself, so in love with his fifteen sonnets that he could not judge them. Or Rose, risking our happiness for nothing much. All blended into me, in love with non-existent Vivien. Our myopic little company. How hard to see straight when we felt so much.

In recounting the disappearance of Howard from her life, Rose may have been warning me. I was not to oppress her with demands for children. We had spoken before about having a baby. She was not exactly against it, I was not exactly for it. We were busy. The decision could wait. I was weeks from turning forty-five and now I was more interested. But we did not even have a marriage. Had I forgiven her? Not quite. But I wanted to be with her. Did she want me? I didn't know, and she didn't either. It was going to be hard. Nothing could be discussed until we returned from the Barn – and only if we were successful. We were not good at joint failure.

Rose spent Christmas with friends in the Chiltern Hills. I

passed it mostly alone, with an occasional evening drink in the company of my neighbour, Cyril Baker. I was content, rereading Fisk's last novel and looking at maps and making lists of provisions for our journey. In January, Rose's nature-sculptor friend found us a captain with a shallow-draught boat, but our teaching duties prevented us from meeting and negotiating a fee. We did not know how to judge captains or boats or their value or how long our trip would be. We did not know what would be available when we shopped for equipment on the quayside. No one in Earth Sciences could improve on my idea for locating the Barn.

The reading break began and those who liked books stopped reading. After a smooth passage over the Weald Sea, we arrived mid-morning at Ball Hill Quay. The day was anti-cyclonic, crisp and clear, worth feeling the cold for. At the hiring station there were no electric models available, so we took oak-frame pedal bikes. It was delightful to make the familiar journey side by side, chatting as we rolled along the chalky lanes. There was one hill where I had to dismount and walk up – our age difference was beginning to tell. Rose rode to the top and waited.

'It's only approaching death,' I said when I reached her. She laughed gaily.

The Marlborough quay was as loud and chaotic as I'd ever seen it. We stood near a wood fire where a row of upturned barrels served as tables and we ate freshly baked eel pies. There was a four-man pipe band playing fifty metres away. Too close, too loud. The world seemed crowded. When the Blundys were alive, there were far more people, but Francis and Vivien managed a more spacious existence. It was while we were resting by the barrels that I noticed something different about Rose and realised that I had seen this a couple of times before. It happened as we finished our pies. I caught her staring at me oddly, as if weighing me up for the first time. When our eyes met, she smiled warmly – just as she had before.

'What's up?'

She shrugged. 'Nothing. Just looking.'

She had been told that our boat, *Salty*, was moored along-side a 150-foot twin-masted barge named *Grace*. It took a long time to locate this large boat, and when we did, *Salty* was not there. After another search and some well-intentioned wrong directions from a sailor, we found her, moored on a muddy tributary. It looked to us like an old fishing boat, of the kind we knew from children's books. There was no sign of the captain. We waited and soon began to feel the cold. We left a note and went shopping and found it easier than we expected, for at one end of the quay was a three-storey chandlery and hardware store. Perhaps the shopping lists of all novice adventurers are too long. Fork, spade, saw, trowel, rope, string, large backpacks, water bottles, sleeping bags, compass, ration packs, an extra map and a tent – all appeared reasonable. We also bought wax, cleats, a mousetrap, a whistle, nails, clothes pegs and twenty other items we would never use. Electrical goods were hard to find and expensive. We compromised with rusty miners' headlamps. We filled the packs. I took the fork, spade and saw, and we humped our loads back to the boat. On the way I saw a wooden shack advertising spices, coconuts and other rare foods. I left Rose guarding my heap and came out waving a 200-gram bar of dark chocolate for Dolly. We calculated later that it cost me the equivalent of three hours of teaching.

Knowing I was bound to be wrong, I had imagined the kind of person who would be our captain. Tall, angular, brooding. Or large, bearded, jolly. A pipe smoker. I was right. The captain coming towards us was slim, compact and had short dark hair. She introduced herself as Jo Mideksa as she took Rose's pack and my fork and spade. We followed her on board across a springy gangplank. We dumped our stuff on deck and sat in the cramped space of the wheelhouse while Mideksa went to the galley below to make tea. As it grew dark, we agreed on her rate. She knew the island but had never been on it. The military owned it, but no soldiers had been seen there, as far as she knew. A man called Hunter had lived in a cabin on the north shore for a few years and then vanished. A long time ago a scientist of some kind had tried to put wolves on the island, but it was not large enough to sustain them. Jo thought that March was a good time of year to walk into the interior. It was light until six and the undergrowth would be sparse. She showed us on the map where she intended to put us ashore. Together we calculated from Dolly's map reference our destination on the same map and its distance from the landing point. We would need to walk 1,810 metres keeping eight degrees to the west of due north. Jo warned us that holding to a straight line across wooded knolls and gullies would be hard. As we progressed inland, we should improvise waymarks to guide us back to the boat. She intended to moor a couple of hundred metres offshore so she could watch a stretch of coastline and would expect us back within three days. She said there had never been a phone signal in the Cotswold Islands. When she was a teenager working this boat with her father, it was possible to rent walkie-talkies, but she hadn't seen one in years.

Salty had one electric motor, three back-up batteries and a mainsail. Jo hoped to use the prevailing wind to bring us round to the old course of the Severn Estuary and pick up the incoming tide to waft the boat north-east towards the islands. Once there, we would depend on the motor to thread a looping course to our destination. Our island was not named on any of the maps. Jo thought she would recognise it. She used to fish with her father off its southern tip and sell the catch on the nearest quay, about fourteen miles away. We would need to cast off at 5 a.m. so an early night would be useful, but first she would cook us a meal. While she got busy in the galley, we brought in our stuff, stored some in the wheelhouse, and the rest we carried to the cabin below, squeezing past Jo to get there. We unrolled stowed mattresses and made up three beds on narrow wooden lockers which formed three sides of a rectangle.

Knee to knee, we ate a vegetable stew in the wheelhouse. Jo had not asked our business on an obscure island and we thought we owed her an explanation. At the name of Blundy she smiled and quoted, as so many could, from 'In the Saddle'. She knew about the lost poem and would have come with us,

162

she said, but she would be worried that her boat would be stolen.

Later, we talked ancestors. Back in the mid-twentieth century, Jo's family had come to Britain from Ethiopia.

'First they married in, then they married out, then in, then after the Inundation, out, out, out. Like breathing your last breath!'

My composition, as far as I knew, was Pakistani and Scottish white and various others. Rose gave hers as English white, Malian, Pashtun plus unknowns. When she was three years old, Jo lost her mother, and her father brought her up. He did not like talking about the past so Jo had only the vaguest idea of her own make-up. After Ethiopia, she assumed British white and thought that one of the Caribbean islands was in the mix. We agreed that we were, all three, chapters in the accidents of long-dead strangers' lives. Then our captain suggested that Rose and I tidy up the galley while she checked on the boat.

Two hours later, I lay in total darkness listening to the steady breathing of the other two. That I was at right angles to my wife, feet to feet, was unhelpfully suggestive of our unresolved problems. Tomorrow's journey and what we might have forgotten on our jaunt also kept me awake. So did our conversation in the wheelhouse. It reminded me of a book I had read a few months before. It was a sixty-year-old social history of Britain, something of a classic. An entire chapter was devoted to sunbathing. From the 1970s onwards, millions of white British travelled south in summer by cheap flights to spend hours each day spreadeagled by swimming pools and on beaches beneath a ferocious sun. The purpose was to turn white skin brown, which was considered a healthy and attractive look. That this idea coexisted with white racism was, the author suggested, one of the fascinating enigmas of social history. Even when medical science established the cancerous and ageing effects of excess exposure to sunlight, the practice continued well into the twenty-first century. With the tragedies of the Derangement, the Inundation and much else, the population plummeted. As systems broke down, international trade and travel became difficult. Chaos spread and the population continued to decline. Against all demographic predictions, inter-racial marriage increased to the extent that within a mere three or four generations, the descendants of many whites have realised the old sunbathers' dream. However disastrous our condition, one much-quoted commentator insisted, 'out of adversity, we are honey, we are golden'. A wider gene pool improved general health, though radiation from the wars pushed in the opposite direction. Completely white people have become a substantial minority. It is shameful that they experience discrimination. Same old story. We are not so sweet or golden after all.

I fell asleep sometime after three. At five the captain was shaking us awake. We were already moving. Acorn coffee was on the stove, eggs were in the pan and Jo wanted help with *Salty*'s sail.

21

It was dusk when we anchored off the island. We were out in the channel, a quarter of a mile offshore, in the hope of catching a breeze to turn the wind turbine and charge the batteries. In the gloaming, we heard the sad ululating cry of a loon calling across the glassy water to its mate, who called back. According to Jo, these ducks moved in ten years ago. There was not much to see of our island beyond the outline of a black mass of trees rising then dipping in two long curves. Away to our left, vivid against the remains of the sunset, was the unsubmerged portion of a church spire. We had seen many along our journey, marking the sites of lost villages. They had outlasted the office and apartment towers of Francis Blundy's time. The islands we had passed on the way seemed to pretend that they knew nothing of what was once here, and I was almost persuaded. Hard to admit, but it was beautiful here.

Jo and Rose went below and I remained on deck for a while, wondering at the dread I felt. The dark shape of the island seemed to carry across the still water an accusation of trespass. It was reckless to invade this dream buried in a century-long sleep. I was here to disturb phantoms. The land belonged to Francis, to Vivien and all who once visited them. The island was a tomb and I would be breaking in to steal its treasure. That these literary ghosts were my own creations, conjured from library archives, made them more forbidding. So familiar, and absent. It was my own madness we were about to break open.

I considered all the gear we would have to drag through

the trees tomorrow, the tent and sleeping bags and bottled tap water and a cooking stove that might not work – and I hated all of it. Like Francis Blundy, I was a creature of indoor spaces. It was the business of other people, of our frail civilisation, to keep me sheltered and warm, hydrated and fed. We all had our specialisations, our own particular talents. The others could rely on me for mine – for what? Retrieving a lost poem and unhinging myself in the process.

The next morning, under a watery sun, the island looked more approachable. After acorn coffee, bread and jam in the wheelhouse, Rose and I packed. With much discussion about what to leave behind, it took two hours. Jo laughed when she lifted my pack. She fetched some ancient scales. Fifty-nine pounds. The fork and spade we would use like walking sticks. We pulled up the anchor, and since there was no wind, Jo used the motor to steer us towards a spit of bare limestone rock where we were to scramble ashore. At less than a slow walking pace we slid silently across clear water barely two metres deep. We saw shoals of small grey and orange fish, freshwater turtles and water snakes among fronds of pale green seagrass growing from what looked like limestone brash. We passed over a straight line of dressed stone, probably the remains of a drystone wall. The island, like most of the others, was a dense mess of competing oaks and birches and leaning dead trunks, right to the water's edge. The undergrowth was mostly nettles and brambles, collapsed and soon to regenerate. Jo had been right, getting through in summer would have been tough. She put the motor in reverse, cut it and let us drift alongside the rock. Rose climbed ashore with a mooring rope, and I passed the packs across. It was well after midday as Jo backed the boat away and called out her good-luck wishes. She would anchor at the same spot in the channel and wait.

Pack on my shoulders, spade in hand, I followed Rose along the spit. Ahead was a steep bank that stretched away to left and right, as far as we could see. No going round it. Until we got to its base it looked vertical. I took our coiled rope, paying it out behind me as I climbed up, using the base of trees as footholds. Rose attached a pack and once I was at the top I hauled it up. Twice she had to climb up and free it where it wedged between trees. An hour passed before we were both at the top with all our gear, catching our breath. From here we saw Jo's boat already at anchor. We figured we had advanced thirty metres along our line towards what we were calling Dolly's spot. Before we set off, we built a waymark of dead branches.

We checked the compass constantly for our 352 degrees bearing. Our method for keeping on course was simple. Rose walked ahead as far as she could while remaining visible. I kept the compass open on our course, and when she turned to look back at me, I waved her into a position which she would keep while I caught up with her, pacing out what I guessed to be metres. I kept a tally in a notebook. This was slow progress. The loads we carried were set to break our backs. The spindly trees grew close together, in places as dense as a bamboo thicket. Within ten metres, Rose would disappear as if behind a screen. After 291 metres by my reckoning, we were on a steep descent at the bottom of which was a grassy bog. It was not possible to cross it in one-metre paces and we had to guess its width. Our feet were sodden. Later, an immense patch of high bramble blocked our route. We walked 210 metres to the east to get round it. We thought we could walk the same distance west, but the brambles were not formed in a convenient rectangle. I drew a map of our corrected course. Rose was certain it was wrong. Discussing that and making a compromise, which put us both in error, took up half an hour.

We had gone 600 metres when I saw that she was limping badly. Or, as she put it, well. Our backs, deskbound academics' backs, ached from our loads, so we stopped for a late lunch. Bread, protein cake, water. As I was helping Rose with a plaster for her heel, something went into my eye – an insect, or a fragment of a leaf. Her careful intervention to extract the speck took up more time. Still, it was a tender moment. The light was beginning to dim as we passed the 1,000-metre mark, and we should have set up camp. But we continued and to our relief the final stretch, along the top of a hill, was easier and we reached what we decided was near the Barn as darkness fell. We were not quite in a clearing, but the trees were sparser and for a few minutes we were cheerful. Neither of us had ever erected a tent before our rehearsal on the grass outside the apartment building in the week before we left. But that was in daylight. By the narrow beams of our headlamps, it took us an hour and a half. The process and its petty reversals made us irritable with each other. That souring of mood had not faded by the time we struggled, fully clothed and with cold wet feet, into our sleeping bags, too tired and disheartened to bother with the stove and supper.

After I had dozed uncomfortably for a while, Rose woke me to complain that I was snoring. She went back to sleep immediately. I lay on my back, watching swirls and shifting swags of purples, greys and black on my retina, and listening to the rustle of animals close to the tent. I thought of the biologist who had tried to introduce wolves onto the island. He may have been successful after all. I opened my eyes. Perhaps his mistake was to have left too soon. Ours was to have brought our food into the tent. Its fabric was against my arm in the narrow space. Easily bitten off. I moved towards the centre and now I felt Rose's familiar warmth and her breath on my other arm. In the dark, my desire was sharp, like a needling pain. It was more than three months since we had made love. I recalled the vague disappointment, which we could not discuss. Hard now to bring back how it once had been, how it felt from the inside, sensually, emotionally, the wildness, that spontaneous intimacy we had conjured between us. I longed for its return. Without it I'd be condemned to go on pursuing it for the rest of my life. On the fading of that self-pitying thought, I fell asleep.

When I emerged from the tent at seven, Rose was crouched over the camping stove making chicory coffee, a rare treat. We were pleasant with each other as we ate bread and protein cake again, and last summer's mushy apples. They had a bad effect on Rose because later, when we were dressed and ready, she went off into the bushes to be sick. After I had fetched water for her and was waiting for her to recover, I became alive to the extraordinary fact: I was perched on a damp log in the Blundys' garden. The gentle slope of the ground told me that the house would have been off to my left. The gate on to the footpath that led down to the stream would be more than a hundred metres to my right. I imagined an indignant Vivien, fresh from her breakfast, striding out from the Barn to shoo the bedraggled travellers off her lawn. I bestowed on her, from old films, the level well-enunciated tones of the twenty-century English elite. As I stand, I explain that we have come from the future, academics with a special interest in the poetry of your husband. That does not go down well, and she does not let me finish. We must leave immediately, she tells us. It would not help to confide what I feel about her, or that I have read her journals and know the dates and circumstances of her and her husband's deaths. The grubby intruders must go and take their mess with them, including the fork and spade.

Rose had been resting in the tent and was now ready. We discussed our ailments. My back hurt, my eye was fine, her heel was bearable but her wrist was sore from carrying the fork. I was starting to suggest she wore my gloves for the journey back when I broke off. My view was through the slender white trunks of birch trees towards what I thought was a portion of a steep green hill in the distance. Then I leaned to one side and as my perspective shifted, I understood what I was seeing. It was a portion of a wall covered with moss. Rose saw it too and stood. We walked towards it slowly, as if to delay disappointment. We used sticks to beat aside last summer's tangle of collapsed fern, bramble and nettles. The wall of Cotswold stone stood about three metres high and formed a large rectangle with one wide gap where the double entrance had been. Beneath the foliage were the rotting remains of roof beams. There were no roof tiles. They could have been taken long ago for other buildings. Birch and smaller plants had colonised the building's interior. It

169

was a big space. Underfoot were broken bricks that must have formed the interior walls. Somewhere within it, Vivien had sat at the desk and dreamed of the book she would never write. Now, outside her study, dense moss was converting the remaining limestone wall to a more complex vegetable existence.

'I'm sure it's the dairy,' Rose said. 'And over there is the right corner.'

We went round the outside of the building to look. From the Land Registry's 1:1,250 site plan we had calculated that Dolly's spot was four metres from the corner of the dairy, along the line of its eastern edge. I thought Rose was right – beneath my hand was a portion of that corner. But I knew how hope distorts judgement. I used our compass to confirm how lucky we were to have found this remnant. We knew the dairy from photographs and phone-videos. A fine building of trimmed stone, stone-tile roof, cream window frames and pale blue doors. There was a weathervane on top with a playful cut-out of coach and horses and a highwayman. Harry Kitchener thought it was a more interesting building than the Barn itself.

I held one end of the tape against the corner while Rose measured out four metres. Our intended spot was two metres into a bramble patch. We had nothing so useful as the secateurs Vivien used to snip her roses for table decoration, but we had bought in Port Marlborough a rusty machete and a pair of leather gloves. I went back to the tent to fetch them. On the way I took time to look for the Barn and found only broken bricks and overgrown cement traces of the foundations. The building must have been demolished. Perhaps the military had used it for target practice. Back at the site we took turns at slashing away at the bramble patch. We wanted a cleared circle three metres across. The growth was tough and prickly stems flew up in our faces. The machete was blunt. I tried sharpening it on a boulder. We needed granite, but here there was only soft limestone. We kept working as it started to rain. It took us until lunchtime, four hours, to clear the digging circle. We sat shivering in the tent, barely speaking as we ate another round of bread and protein cake. There was nothing hot to drink. We had left the stove out in the rain and it would not start.

The downpour ceased and we started work by marking out east–west and north–south lines across our cleared patch. At my first thrust dead centre where the lines crossed, the spade barely penetrated the ground. There were more roots than soil forming a lattice of bramble, tree roots and the wiry suckers of nettles. The machete was useless. The saw was unwieldy, but it was all we had. We were on all fours in the mud, working at awkward angles. Further down were thicker tree roots. We loosened the earth beneath them with the fork, then scooped out handfuls to make space for the saw. It was sometimes possible to use the spade to lever a root up so that the other could saw it. After two hours our hole was only thirty centimetres deep. Rose suggested driving down a stick as a probe. If it met resistance, it might give us hope. But nothing was easy. The wood lying around us was rotten. It began to rain again. We sawed off a branch of scrub oak, hacked it clear of twigs, made a pointed end and hammered it into the ground with the flat of the spade. We hit something solid. Another two hours of digging, scooping and sawing uncovered a bed of limestone. It was impossible to dislodge, and it was slow work breaking it up. We were not thinking straight. It did not occur to us that nothing could have been hidden underneath.

It was late afternoon and we were cold, dirty, tired and disheartened by our incompetence. We left our tools on the ground and went to the tent. As I was untying the flap with mud-caked hands, I had a sudden thought, an impulse of curiosity, despite my exhaustion. I told Rose I was going to explore further down the slope. She was already halfway in the tent.

'Fine. But I need to lie down.'

I went through the woods, down along the line of its descent. I looked out for remnants of the Barn's boundary, once a hawthorn hedge. Nothing now of course, no wooden gate onto a footpath through open pasture. I kept on down the slope. Now there were more oaks than birches. Where the ground began to level, I heard it before I saw it between the trees. I went closer and stood amazed. It was wider than I remembered from photographs. But the same stream, holding a tenuous line between present and past. I forced a way through the undergrowth and crouched down on the bank to wash my hands and face.

To understand my joy at the discovery, a stranger would have needed to share my obsession. My surprise and delight were misplaced. A hundred years was nothing in the life of a river. They might shift their course, but they lasted a very long time. The original drainage line of the River Thames was almost sixty million years old. A mere 20,000 years ago, it was a tributary of the Rhône. It could have lasted another ten million years if it had not disappeared under the sea. As I sat by the stream, those facts meant nothing. From a vanished wooden footbridge near here, Vivien started out on her walks. When I was a child, I used to imagine that the past existed somewhere other than in people's heads. All that happiness and sorrow, those jokes, battles, holidays and people could not simply disappear. Surely, the past lingered in a hidden dimension by its place of origin. The walls of a room were altered, I suspected, by everything that had happened between them. I knew the sensible grown-up response – the present vanished forever into the gaping mouth of the greedy past. Vivien existed only in the minds of those who thought about her. But my research had revived childish dreams. Different water flowed here, past different bank vegetation, with different creatures living in the stream and different air flowing above it. But it was the same stream, and she was here once, looking at it, just as I was looking at it now. That our presence here, screened from each other by time, constituted a separate reality, was at the core of my obsession, and perhaps the obsession of all dedicated historians, biographers and archaeologists. Vivien's contemporary, the young Richard Holmes, tramped across the Cévennes in Stevenson's footsteps. For Holmes, the writer he admired and pursued was a colleague and a friend, a living presence worth waiting for on a bridge, the wrong bridge, as dusk fell. For my neighbour, Cyril Baker, with whom I shared a bathroom, the court of Innocent III was a teeming reality. A million historical movies, novels and serious histories expressed our yearning to keep the past with us. Kind or cruel, it haunted us, and its ghosts, unlike most, were real.

I went back to the tent to tell Rose about my find. She was lying on her sleeping bag. She was excited by the news and wanted to see the stream for herself. As she pulled on her boots, she told me about a passage in Vivien's journal describing how the stream had flooded the surrounding meadow, and in a later entry, how the water turned a polluted milky green. As we walked down through the woods, I reminded Rose that Vivien accused Francis of being indifferent to the sighting of a king-fisher flying upstream.

Rose said, 'When you get your hands on the poem, you'll forgive Blundy everything.'

She too washed her hands and face in the stream. She also drank from it. I would never do that. A rotting animal could be lying half-submerged upstream. Radioactivity was another consideration. We went back to the tent. We were happier. Only now did we realise that if Vivien wanted the Corona to be found, she would not have heaved a slab of limestone over it. Tomorrow we would keep to the plan and dig the next hole further along the east–west line. We agreed on everything, our moods matched and we were walking hand in hand.

After a bad half-hour, I had the stove working again. We warmed up a can of vegetable soup and ate it with slices of protein cake sliding about on its surface. Later, we lay in our sleeping bags, in absolute darkness, exhausted, though it was barely eight thirty. We gossiped about department colleagues for a while, then were silent. I reached for her hand. She took mine, gave a squeeze, a stroke with her thumb, then withdrew. I understood a 'no' or 'not yet'. The expedition had given us good cover for not confronting our situation. My thoughts were now clear. I wanted us to continue. Rose's brief scene with

Kevin Howard still lay between us, quietly suppurating. I was baffled as well as angry. To probe would be heard as accusation and bring on another row when we were already on a cliff edge. But I had my theories. A taste of youth, a jolt to recall me from my obsessions, the thrill of the illicit – consensual sex with graduate students was no longer a sackable offence, but it was still frowned on by the older professors who might cook up some other charge and throw her out. I knew the kind of fight Rose and I would have – my emotional illiteracy against her flagrant betrayal. Each believing an apology was owed. Usual stuff. Could we engage with such banality? I had rehearsed a muscular notion: only by being together, sharing difficulties as we had yesterday and today and solving them, could we act out, rather than analyse, our best path into the future. A typical evasion, I could hear her say, but her silence was evasion too. A hand squeeze and a thumb's brief caress in the dark kept my hopes alive while seeming to forbid discussion. There was our route, eight degrees east of south, a non-talking cure or the slow poison of silence. Nothing induces sleep so handily as a looped thought. I was soon oblivious.

A metre or a metre-fifty along our east–west line? Back at the site in the bright early morning, we tossed a coin. The head of our republic's president, Mary Tyndall, gleamed in the wet grass: one metre fifty. We soon hit the same network of roots. This time, we accepted the work would be slow and we knew what to do. We were forty centimetres deep when we drove down our probe. It sank unobstructed sixty-five centimetres before hitting an obstruction. We stopped for lunch – bread and the last of the protein cake – and then kept on with sawing and digging. We had lost the sun to a bank of dark cloud. That, and the brevity of the late-winter twilight depressed us. We should have been out of our sleeping bags in the morning while it was still dark.

Around half-past four, the edge of the spade caught something so hard that it sent an electric pain through my elbow. Another rock. I dug clear limestone brash and clay. What we saw rarely, if ever, occurs in nature. We were looking at the outlines of a right angle. When we leaned in to look closer, our heads blocked our light. We had forgotten to bring the headlamps from the tent. As we cleared the soil away, we could make out the corner of some kind of container, and a hint between the dirt of dulled metal. We froze. We looked at each other but said nothing. It was not a moment of exultation. It was awe. One thing to have a hypothesis about some numbers in a notebook, another to dig down on that lead and find a steel box, put there by someone we felt we knew. Vivien had wanted us, strangers from an unknowable future, to find what she had buried. We took turns to touch the cold metal of that grubby corner embedded at a tilt in the floor of our excavation.

The president's head had served us well. The container extended under the earth, away from the dairy. If the tossed coin had shown tails, we would have missed it. Digging it clear would take time and the rational option was to start in the morning. But we were not feeling rational. I fetched the lamps, more water and our last chunk of bread from the tent. On the way back, I could not help myself, I broke into a run, like a child on its way to a spectacular treat. It took us an hour and a half to get our treasure clear. We burrowed into the side of our pit, above our find, and then dug round it with care. At seven thirty, as it started to rain hard, we lifted the steel container onto the grass. We used our bare hands to clear away most of the remaining sticky mess of clay, earth and limestone crumbs. It was a smooth case, like a piece of luggage without a handle. It was secured by two clasps which were encrusted with a white foamy substance which felt as hard as coral. Like the professionals we were not, we recorded dimensions in a notebook. Sixty-five by forty, and twenty centimetres deep. We guessed its weight. I thought two kilos, Rose four. She took off her coat and wrapped it round the case, I carried the lamps and water bottles, and we retreated through the downpour to our camp.

Our dirt-smeared steel treasure lay between the sleeping

bags in the squalid disorder of the tent. It had a sinister appearance, like a piece of advanced technology of unknown purpose, dispatched across light years by another civilisation. As we shivered in our bags, hoping to dry out before we slept, there was nothing to do but stare at our prize by the light of one lamp and try to forget how hungry we were. But sleep was not possible alongside a sealed box whose radioactive contents were stimulating every nerve end in my body. Nine hours until sunrise. We should have brought a bottle of local poitín in anticipation of success. For a while we talked through the expedition and our initial doubts, of our growing feeling of triumph, and of various mishaps that we now recast as comedy. We celebrated 'Vivien's stream', how finding it and washing in it had boosted us. We would open the case in the documents room of the university library with the help of a technician. Vivien must have called on expert help, for the container was unlike anything we had ever seen. Then, mid-sentence, Rose trailed off significantly. I thought she was about to change the subject and say something hopeful about our future. But her breathing settled into its familiar steady tread. I turned off the lamp.

For the third successive night, I was alone in the dark. How was I to sleep when the Corona, most precious document in the world, lay between my wife and me like a small child come in the night to share our bed? Like many people, when I lay sleepless in the dark, my thoughts sometimes drifted towards death. A history of the years that lay between us and the Blundys could easily confine itself to the stories of those who died before their time. So numerous they formed mountains behind us, the accumulated victims of global heating, nuclear battles, drowned cities, ruined economies, shattered ecologies, untamed viruses. The kids I taught thought no more of those victims than Vivien's students troubled themselves too much with the dead of medieval famines and plagues or the slaughtered of the Napoleonic Wars or the victims of the twentieth-century Holocaust. Vivien and Francis had the massed dead right at their backs. They grew up in the aftermath of civilised Europe's long civil war, 1914 to 1945, when scores of millions died. During the Blundys' lifetime, there were enforced famines, invasions, genocide, drought and savage local wars. They could see what was coming next. When 2.4 degrees above pre-industrial levels was recorded, early in the twenty-second century, no one was surprised. And this despite the cooling effect of previous nuclear exchanges. Like us, the Blundys had good reason to think they might be living at the end of time. And this was what we had in common: even if we occasionally thought of history's victims, we went on loving, playing, cooking, surviving somehow, attending or, Vivien, Rose and I, teaching classes, on Shakespeare, Jane Austen, Mabel Fisk and the rest. Francis liked to quote T. S. Eliot's 'Teach us to care and not to care'. Sonorous lines, but empty, for no one ever needed that lesson. We can't care. We are trapped between the dead and the unborn, the past ghosts and the future ghosts, and they matter less. Whether Jack and Jill can pull their marriage together trumps what happened at Thermopylae. There would always be the eccentrics who cannot get their heads out of the past. I included myself and my colleagues along the department corridor who knew all that could ever be known about their sixteenth-century subjects. But we had no choice. Our ultimate loyalties must be to the loud and ruthless present.

I was aware of my heartbeat growing heavier as if someone or something outside the tent was walking towards me. Foolish fears. I thought again of Adam Smith's 'there is a great deal of ruin in a nation'. A nation is so large and full of things and ideas that it takes a lot of determined folly to ruin it all. So with the planet. We wrecked much of it, but not everything. Here was the other story, not of the dead but of the descendants of the survivors, whose three-word history was bleakly simple: *we scraped through*. Devastated cities came back to life or were established elsewhere, just as they always had been. Significant parts of the knowledge base were preserved. Many institutions crawled through the gaps between catastrophes. People lived at poverty level, but they lived. When the rising curve of global temperatures met the descending curve of population numbers and industrial activity, nature seized the moment and pushed up through the ruins. Constant destruction, constant reinvention. Sail through the clear waters of the Cotswold Islands and be delighted by what's starting to come back.

We might one day lose our internet, or be reduced much further to become subsistence peasants, or dissolve into widely separated bands of hunter-gatherers eking a hard life from a degraded biosphere. But I doubted it. There were knowledge centres across the habitable world. Ours was in the Pennines. It contained indestructible illustrated handbooks of simple step-by-step instructions. How to make high-temperature fire; how to melt sand with lime and soda to make glass; how to grind and polish a lens; how to build a simple microscope and look through it to develop a germ theory of disease. Literacy will have to survive, at least for some. There were other handbooks on crop rotation, childcare, pulleys, printing, soap, human rights, electricity, how to make painkiller out of willow bark, how to combine copper with tin to make bronze, and hundreds of other basics that took thousands of years to develop. Then, so informed, we will start cutting down the trees again, digging for iron ore and eating the mammals and fish that flourished in our absence. Round we go. Each time we fail, or calamities overwhelm us, we will come back from a slightly higher place. Rising and falling, we would continue to scrape through. Like one of nature's rhythms, spring and autumn, when the earth breathes in then exhales carbon dioxide. With civilisation barely 10,000 years old, an eyeblink of time, we hardly know our cycles yet. My optimism says that with each one, we will adapt and improve. Slow progress, and how soothing and deceptive, to avert the gaze from individual suffering and think in the inhuman long term. In 500 years there might still be a Literature Department somewhere on the planet. In 5,000? Five million?

We were up at sunrise and packed with surprising efficiency.

The case fitted into a backpack as we had hoped. Like siblings competing over a new toy, we both wanted to carry it, but I could not deny Rose. We packed the tent away and left it with the stove in the undergrowth. It was comforting to pretend to each other that we might come back. We brought the sleeping bags in case we could not find our boat. I went to the site and filled in our two pits. I drove the fork into the softened ground as a marker for whoever might want to come after us. I left the spade leaning against a tree. Back at the camp, I paused to make a mental farewell to the Blundys' garden, to the imagined smooth lawns and richly tangled flower beds by the barn where the poet worked, the gate to the path meandering down the valley to the footbridge. It no longer had such power over me.

With the compass showing us our route, 172 degrees, we set off and covered the ground easily with lighter packs and our hands free. But we did not see our waymarks, nor did we remember passing a large tree blackened by a lightning strike. The boggy stretch did not appear. We made another detour around brambles, but this patch was far bigger. It was hard holding a course through overgrown forest. When Rose was walking in front of me, I could not take my eyes off her bulging backpack. Tiredness exaggerated my exhilaration. I was walking on air, not watching where I was putting my feet as we came down a slope. I tripped on a root, fell hard and gashed my knee. Cleaning up the wound with dirty hands took a long time. Now I was walking with a limp and every step hurt. Though our progress was slower, we still made it to the cliff above the shore by early afternoon. The return was two hours quicker than the outward journey.

But no sign of Jo's boat, for we were facing across a different bay, narrower, with longer headlands reaching into the channel, blocking our view along the coast. So, east or west, left or right? We turned east because the way looked easier, but there was a gully to descend and climb, then another, but even when we made it onto the neck of the headland, we could not see the water below. We descended to get a better look and soon we had gone too far down to think of climbing back up. It was a long scramble to the shore. On some sections we slid on our backsides, clinging to trees to break our speed.

East was the lucky choice. Still twenty metres above the shore, we parted some branches and saw *Salty* a mile away, anchored off the next headland. An hour later we were climbing onto the rocky outcrop where Jo had set us down. Three blasts of the whistle brought her on deck. Within twenty minutes we were on deck too, embracing like old friends. We took out our find to show her. It touched us, the way she punched the air and hooted. There were two bottles of a local apple brandy waiting and a vegetable stew. The bunk room through the galley appeared palatial. Its stowaway table of polished wood spoke of a rich civilisation. There was a narrow shower-stall that gave a thin trickle of lukewarm water. We had left on board a set of clean clothes. While Rose took the first shower, I cleaned the steel container. Then it was my turn, and though by then the water was running cold, it was a fine thing to step out, shivering but free of dirt and encrusted blood, and into the towel that Rose held open for me.

From outside in the dusk we heard again the echoing sound of a loon and its mate's reply from far away. The stew – turnips, carrots, potatoes – and our success brought Rose and me to a state of bliss. We raised our cups in a toast, brandy for the captain and me, herb tea for Rose. I lifted the case onto the table.

'Look,' I said. 'Forget professional procedures. We should open it now. There'll never be a better moment.'

Rose agreed. Jo fetched a screwdriver and hammer. The white substance around the clasps was lime deposit. A few gentle taps and it fell away. In a mock ceremony, Rose and I stood side by side holding the clasps.

'Ready?' Jo said. 'Then . . . open!'

Nothing happened. The lid needed to be prised open with the screwdriver. It came up with a squeak and a musty smell filled the cabin. What we saw was a disappointment. Another

case fitted snugly inside the first. It was made of tough continuously welded plastic. No going back now. We had to cut
it open. Jo brought out every cutting tool she had on board.
Again, another discussion. The idea was to make an incision
with a sharpened chisel, then use a bolt-cutter to slice open the
sides. But chisel and hammer made no impression. We used
a hand-drill to make a line of holes, which we joined up and
enlarged with a keyhole saw. The blades of the bolt-cutter were
too big, and we took turns with the saw again. That done, the
cutter could gain purchase. But this plastic was tough. Each
cut needed two of us on the bolt-cutter's long handles. Getting
round four sides took an hour.

We sat back and Jo poured herself and me another drink
and topped up Rose's tea. We were too tired this time for cere-
monies. As we lifted the top half of the case clear, a shower of
crystals poured across the table. No one spoke. We were looking at two packages embedded in moulded foam. One was
tapered and almost as long as the container and perhaps thirty
or forty centimetres across at the wider end. The other was rectangular, about twenty by thirty. Both were thickly wrapped in
a semi-transparent material. The larger object was surprisingly
light. Through the wrapping I made out something dark in the
centre, like a chrysalis, a creature waiting to be born. As I turned
the object in my hands, light was refracted through the plastic
and caused the thing inside to appear to move, to writhe. I had
watched too many horror films in my early teens. I discerned
a curving line of a deep brown colour and, at the narrow end,
something black with short protruding arms. Of course.

I said in a whisper, 'A violin. Percy's violin.'

His copy of a Vieuxtemps Guarneri. Only Rose could know
the meaning and weight of this. Her eyes shone with unspilled
tears. I placed the package back within the moulded foam. The
other piece was rectangular, and I guessed it held a document
in a standard format. It felt comfortable and familiar in my
hands. I cut the protective layers away. There were more crystals within each fold, and I let them cascade to the floor. I had

181

been standing a long time and my injured leg was throbbing. I sat down. I felt the heat of Rose's scrutiny. I had in my hands a heavy folder. Trembling, I opened it out and felt the paper's unusual thickness, saw the first page and gasped, turned to the middle, then to the last page. I could not bear to read it.

I looked up and into Rose's eyes. I too was emotional. I tried to keep my voice steady, and I failed. 'It's not . . . It isn't poetry. It's prose.'

I passed the folder to her and she began to read from the beginning. Then she too turned to the middle and read.

There was silence, broken by the rustle of a page turn and the faintest creak of the boat's timbers. From much further away this time, we heard the falling cry of the loon, a melancholy farewell sound but no answering call. A couple of minutes passed before Rose reached across the table and put her hand on my arm and said quietly, 'It's going to be all right.' Then she took my hand and guided it onto her belly, onto a faint swell I had not noticed before, and while our captain looked on, smiling, Rose added, 'And we are too.'

PART TWO

I was late for my train. As I stood by my taxi fumbling for the fare – and this rural driver insisted on writing out a receipt – I saw across a picket fence the platform and passengers boarding. I heard the carriage doors slamming. I ran onto the platform of this village Victorian station as my train was pulling out. I stood to catch my breath and watched it go. I had been to visit an old friend, Martha MacLeish, a specialist in modern French literature who had been ill for months with a rare form of blood cancer. The clumsy photograph I took with a disposable camera sits on my desk as I write. She sits up in bed, books and papers scattered about her. Martha's smile is determined. She had just been told by her doctor that she might live a year, possibly less. We had been holding out hopes for a cure, and sadness for her, for us both, must have made more vivid what I saw next by the summer evening's orange light. The platform was deserted but for one figure at the far end watching the last carriage recede. Not much in itself, but this was a very small child, a boy of three years, I guessed. He was minute against the scale of the long platform and parallel railway tracks converging on the mouth of a distant tunnel. I looked around. There was no one. I went towards the boy cautiously, not wanting to frighten him. I knew what I was walking towards, the ghost I lived with, and I even wondered if I should turn round and leave. I felt the day's heat coming off the stone slabs beneath my feet. Stupidly, I felt relief that the child was not a girl. He remained staring in the direction of the departed train.

I stopped a few yards away and called in a friendly voice, 'Hello. Are you all right? What are doing here all alone?'

He turned. Dangling from one hand was a limp soft toy. He wore T-shirt, jeans and trainers. Even without the immediate circumstances, I would have thought it was a sad and watchful face. Blond hair, pale skin that had not been touched by our recent heatwave. My questions made no sense to him. Or he didn't know the answers. He was wary as he scanned my face. He may have already received that first knock to innocence and been warned off talking to strangers. My assumption was that a parent, or whoever, had been lifting an awkward pushchair onto the train when it started to move. I assumed a panicked parent would be making calls to the railway company or police and looking to get straight back on the next train.

At last, the boy lifted his drooping and well-fingered companion closer to his chest. It was a green lizard with red spikes along its spine. 'I'm waiting for my mummy.'

In that English way, I automatically registered the fully enunciated 't' and was already placing him in a social order. I disliked myself for it. I went closer. 'Did she go on that train?'

Again, to him the question did not make sense. After a few seconds he said, 'I'm waiting for her.'

At a sound I turned. At the far end of the platform, a few passengers were gathering for the next train. They were looking in our direction. I said, 'What's your name?'

'Christopher.'

'Shall I wait with you, Christopher?'

As I spoke, I was taking my phone from my shoulder bag. I flipped it open, pressed triple nine and asked for the police. I thought the word might alarm the boy, so I turned away from him as I said it. A voice came on and I explained the situation and where I was. While I was speaking, I saw a man walking towards me at a confident pace. I broke off and said, 'Hang on, I think someone's coming to collect him.'

What a relief. The little drama was over.

As the man came up, he said, 'Ah, so you found him. Thank

you.' He was a chunky-looking fellow with a broad face. Mid-thirties, I thought, quite well dressed, with a fawn linen jacket over a crisp white shirt, well-cut jeans and polished loafers.

'I was just phoning the police.'

'No need.'

He went close to the boy and crouched down to speak to him. 'Are you OK? Ready to come home?'

The child's expression did not change. He repeated, 'I'm waiting for my mummy.'

'She says come over and get you.'

There was something about the way this was said, its speed, its grammar, that caused my relief to give way to the first soft whisper of anxiety.

'She's waiting. Let's go.'

As gently as I could, I said to Christopher, 'Do you know this man?' But the boy did not answer. He did not know what he knew.

I said, 'Wait a minute. Do you know his name?'

The man stood between the child and me and came close. His arms were crossed. I thought he was about to be violent, and my legs went weak.

'Course I do.'

'Would you mind saying it, you know, to put my mind at rest?'

'We're grateful for your help, Miss, but don't insult me.'

My voice came out as a croak. 'If you know him, tell me his name.'

For an answer, he stepped back and picked up the boy, who stared straight ahead. By keeping us both out of his sightline he banished us and the situation. What was happening to him was so remote from his comprehension that he was beyond fear for now.

I was nothing but fear.

'Let's go, laddy.'

I tried to stand in his path, but the man walked straight at me and brushed me aside. I said loudly, 'You can't just take him.'

'Watch me.'

He walked off at speed. I ran to catch up, overtook him, turned and tried to block his way again.

'You've got to stop.'

I don't think he even looked my way as he stepped round me. I reached in my bag for my little cardboard camera. It was slippery in my hand. I ran again, passed the man, and now I was skipping backwards in front of him, shouting – I've forgotten what I was shouting – and trying to keep his face and the child's face on the tiny smeared screen. I had used up my last shots on Martha. We were among the passengers, about a dozen watching us. I shouted at them too, something like, 'He's taking this child and doesn't know him. Not even his name. Stop him, help me!'

But no one stirred. Here was a man and his little boy, pursued by a hysterical woman, perhaps an ex-wife or a discarded lover. A domestic, as the police say. And if it wasn't that, why get in a fight with a handy-looking fellow when you weren't sure which side to be on?

Then we were out of the station, on the edge of the car park. A couple of the passengers followed us out to watch but essentially, there was no one to help. Suddenly, the man came at me and, holding the boy steady on one arm, tried to seize my wrist.

'I'll have that,' he said, meaning my camera. 'Or I'll break your neck.'

He almost had my hand – our fingers brushed – but I lurched sideways and ran from him towards the nearest car and flung the camera under it. It was, by luck, a large low saloon. To get under it, he would have needed to set Christopher down and crawl in on his belly. Instead, he came after me. I ran round the car. He reversed direction and I did too. My shoulder bag contained books and Martha's most recent essay and was heavy, but I was wearing tennis shoes and I was nimbler than he was. As the boy bounced about in the man's arms, he began to laugh. Here was a game of chase he recognised, the first familiar element in an unintelligible half-hour. Childish laughter seemed to bring my pursuer to his senses. Whether he took the boy or left him, the camera and what he thought was its record were more important than breaking my neck. He put Christopher down, told him not to move, got down on his knees and eased himself under the car until only his backside and legs showed. In theory, while he was so vulnerable, I could have stomped on his legs or kicked between them. But I've no gift for violence. The thought of it makes me go weak, and besides, at that moment everything changed.

As I took Christopher's hand, intending to hurry back into the station to be among the indifferent crowd, a police car drew up, two constables got out, ignored me, dragged the fellow from under the car by his ankles, prised my camera from his fist and made an arrest. It unfolded as fantasy, as desperate hope dissolving into a vivid dream that turned out to be real. But it was less magical than that. Not long after I had made my emergency call, one of the passengers at the other end of the platform had also called the police. Minutes later, two others had phoned. Those witnesses had not been as indifferent as I had thought.

A second police car arrived to collect my man. Soon after that, a social worker arrived, a sensible woman who made an instant bond with Christopher and took him away. By that time, I was dictating then signing a statement for the first policeman. When I finished, his colleague came over and said he had just heard that the mother was picked up on Swindon station, fifteen minutes down the line. She had a history of depression and self-harm and had abandoned her child once before. She was in a bad state but able to confirm that she had asked no one to collect him.

I arrived in Oxford at dusk. It was one of those rare evenings one dreams about in winter, when the air seems viscous with warmth, scents and fading light together melting onto the skin as a balm and soaking into the senses. It was an easy decision to walk home from the station rather than take a bus. Within minutes I was crossing Hythe Bridge. On an impulse I turned

189

down the footpath that led in a few yards to the beginning of the Oxford Canal.

I rested on the low wall that separates the canal from the Castle Mill Stream. I was watching a lean hippie-ish man of about my age, still with the ponytail of his youth, watering the potted geraniums on his houseboat. He gave me a friendly nod. He didn't mind being observed. Hanging by the stern was a paraffin lamp. There was a homely gleam from the cabin. Another life. It looked so simple from where I sat. I could ask to join him and from somewhere along our slow journey north, perhaps where this minor canal met the Grand Union, write my letter of resignation to the college and never be seen again. What would I be running from? I did not want to think about it. As I stood, I felt light on my feet, exhilarated at the prospect of flight, as if everything had already been arranged. The air that slipped so easily into my lungs made it possible. I realised that I was in shock and that I was bound to crash. For now, I thought I should abandon myself to the experience. I picked up my bag and walked back onto the bridge, intent on describing myself in a fantastical third person. She was a Victorian waif, as thin as air, floating up Beaumont Street, along St Giles, onwards up the Banbury Road, on her way to a dusty basement office in Park Town, where an ancient lawyer would divulge in grave tones the terms of her vast inherited fortune from an unknown benefactor.

By the time I arrived at my flat on Linton Road I was coming down. I turned on all the lights and, in the kitchen, as I filled a tall glass with cold water, noticed that my hands were trembling. My mind was trembling too. I opened a window in the sitting room and lay on the sofa. Was I too hot, too cold? Neither. I was alone. No one to talk to. No one cared. Nonsense! My husband was out for the evening at a reunion in an east Oxford pub with fellow musicians. My lover would be back from New York tomorrow in the late afternoon. At the thought of how I was betraying a kindly decent man, my emotions stood ready to be opened easily, like a drawer that slides out at a touch.

Here, nestled neatly like soup spoons were familiar items of self-excoriation: I was false, cruel, a deceiving faithless woman whose everyday lies served to keep herself sexually amused. I didn't think it was like that at all, but I was trying to upset myself. After so much pity, fear, anger and relief compressed into forty minutes, something had to come out and only crying would restore me. I needed tears to help me avoid the nightmare that lay just beyond the periphery of mental vision. Guilt about my affair with Harry was a hard and hot feeling that did not mix with sorrow, and Martha's situation was too close, too frightening to be exploited as an emotional emetic. Instead, and because he was now safe, I enlisted the abandoned little boy on the platform, helpless and understanding nothing, and that did it. I indulged a fit of weeping, and what release it was. A poor thing without his mother, so determined to wait for her, believing she would come back to him from out of the tunnel, along the same track. And poor me, whose blameless neck could have been snapped in two. Poor world that bore evil in the form of such a man. I wept and minutes later I was done. Feeling better, I sat up. Unbearable to consider what he wanted, what he might have done. The kindest thing one might say was that he was the slave of a compulsion he did not choose. He too wanted to keep himself sexually amused. That rogue thought did it. Horrified at the connection, I stood up and dismissed it. I was cured of emotional blockage. I went back to the kitchen for more water and, leaning on the counter, decided to make a sandwich. While I was cutting the bread, I began to think about the next day's teaching.

The principal business would be George Eliot's *Middlemarch*, three tutorials and a lecture in the afternoon. I had given the lecture last year and had already rewritten it. I needed to look again at the student essays. But before all that, I took out Martha's introduction to her scholarly edition of the non-fiction of Albert Camus. She had composed her monograph propped up in bed, a drip hanging from a tripod at her side. She managed a few hundred words a day, without recourse to a library. Respectfully, her Parisian publisher had not hesitated to hold up publication. Martha had written in French of course, so I had to go slowly, though I could just about get by without a dictionary. She concentrated on a lecture Camus gave in 1957 in Uppsala, Sweden, shortly after receiving the Nobel Prize – 'The Artist and his Times'. In it, Camus approved of an observation by Gide. *'L'art vit de contrainte et meurt de liberté.'* Art lives by constraint and dies from freedom, by which was meant the constraint the artist imposes on himself. For Gide as for Camus, grammatically at least, artists were men. I hesitated. Perhaps Camus was rejecting literary experiment. Further down the page Martha quoted his rejoinder: *'L'art le plus libre, et le plus révolté, sera ainsi le plus Classique.'* The freest art and the most revolutionary will therefore be the most ... classical? Meaning, written in a form and a prose long established in the tradition and therefore immediately understood. Or 'classical' meaning such writing would endure and would become, over time and through many appreciative readings, a classic. I decided on the former. Camus wrote his lecture when Europe was recovering from a cataclysmic war, when the world was trying to grasp the possibility of nuclear extinction, and when many of his contemporaries kept righteous faith with a dream of utopia in the Soviet Union, which he regarded as morally bankrupt, dangerous and cruel. In troubled times, Camus insisted, the best writing should be the most immediate in its clarity. Surely, Camus' writing conformed to that ideal. I wrote Martha a long appreciative letter and wished I'd had the skill to have written in French. For her troubled times, in classical French.

A half-hour later, not long before midnight, I was on George Eliot duties when Percy came in. I could tell that he was just a little drunk, but alcohol only made him kinder and funnier and more cheerful. I shoved the essay aside and listened to the story of his evening. He and his jazz-band mates were soon recognised at their table in the pub. After a din of foot-stamping, they went on stage. They did three numbers on borrowed instruments, with the euphonium player on double bass, and 'brought the house down'.

Percy broke off to ask about Martha. I said there was bad news and I would explain later. First, I wanted to tell him the story of Christopher. Usefully drained of feeling, I told it ruthlessly, as if to punish myself with details, though I felt nothing. I wanted to convey to Percy every perception, move, spoken and shouted word, all the moods and their transitions, the blank incomprehension of the child, the man's ugly ferocity, the dreamlike appearance of the police, their grip on his ankles, on his black socks as they extracted him from under the car 'like a rotten tooth', and how his white shirt was besmirched by a puddle of engine oil. Besmirched! I had never uttered the word before in my life. Percy followed closely, cocking his head, as if he'd gone a little deaf, and he grimaced sometimes as if I was punishing him with my details, not myself. But oh, that big black-bearded good-natured face, creased with concern. I *was* hurting him, if only he knew it.

When I had done, he laid his hand, his heavy paw, on my arm and squeezed. His eyes were bright. 'Many people would have preferred to believe the guy to stay out of trouble.' He shook his head. 'What courage, Vivien.'

'The police have got my camera.'

'We'll get it back.'

Later, in bed, it was a joy to be making love and be amazed again by the almost comic union of his bulk and his tenderness. But afterwards, as he slept, I lay on my side, facing away from him, and lingered on the prospect of being with Harry tomorrow evening. I had to see him. There was nothing I could do about it. Or about myself.

*

My father was an airline pilot. That may sound dashing and unconventional, even daring to some, but it was none of those to my sister Rachel and me. He was everything passengers would want in their captain as they settled in their seats and listened to his reasonable reassuring voice. Meticulous, upright, unyielding. He knew how to fly a transatlantic jet and he knew what was right. He was born in 1929 and I suppose he was a man of his time. He did not place much value on the education of his daughters, though he laid it heavily on our younger brother, pushing him hard with expensive extra tuition to get him into a private school with high academic standards. Rachel and I could not remember a single instance when our father took either of us aside for a conversation about anything. Mostly, he ignored us, or told us off. Poor Sam did not flourish at Winchester, which threw him out after two years. Not that we cared, for we had suffered through childhood from making way for our brother in all things and learning from the pilot that we should be helping our mother with the ironing or in the kitchen with the washing-up, while he and his son watched cricket on the TV. We took for granted, as did our mother, Sam's right at meals to larger portions than ours, even though he was smaller, and that his anecdotes mattered more than those we tried to tell, and that when he was speaking, or prattling, which he did often, our father would hush us with a glance. Poor Sam. No one could go through such a childhood and not become – at least until misfortune knocked it out of him – an arrogant entitled little prig.

What redeemed our father were his frequent absences. During them, lodged in a house of females, our brother shrank enough to make life tolerable. Meanwhile, a state education served Rachel and me well. We got scholarships to the kind of universities that Sam was intended for. We were high on books, movies, plays and art museums. Nothing was expected of us, and we disappointed no one. Unlike Sam, who was spooked by failure throughout his twenties. The world beyond our front gate did not fall silent when he wanted to speak his thoughts. It handed him smaller portions. Once he was done with his drearily conventional crises of drinking and drugging, he came out the other end as gay and a far nicer person. It makes me squirm with regret and guilt that after our mother died, in our thirties, we three abandoned our father, Sam through bitterness, Rachel and I out of indifference. He lived alone. We saw him occasionally for a birthday or a Christmas, but never at the same time. We would say to each other, 'Your turn!' When he died, I had not spoken to him in four months. He never told us he was ill. Guilt was his parting gift.

We girls did not come through without permanent stains. Rachel's were easy to spot. The first time I met her husband, I came close to a fit of giggles. She had married our father! Same impoverished emotional range, same gift for rectitude and disapproval and, in low light, a shared look. Like our mother, Rachel stuck with her husband, never challenged him, and got seriously ill, but unlike her, lived on. My case, my stains, the ones on the surface, were also comic. Of course, a taste, though not exclusive, for older men. Still seeking my father's unattainable approval? I've come to despise those just-so therapy stories. There can never be any proof. Instead, you choose the story that fits neatly or gives most comfort. Another stain: after a childhood and teenage indoctrination in dishwashing, baking, tidying, vacuuming and ironing my father's and brother's shirts, I was left with a compulsion that I would overcome only once, with shocking consequences. Those few months apart, I never had the will. If I saw disorder, I moved helplessly towards it and set it right. Until that was done, there was a nagging presence in my thoughts, a feeling of incompleteness. I was troubled if Percy's washed but unironed shirts were left too long or if the sofa cushions were unplumped or the dishwasher unloaded. Where there was order, there was mental space and calm. I could not read a book while in the same room as an unmade bed. I liked cooking, but I knew that I didn't have a choice about it. It would shame me to list the lovers I skivvied for and how quickly they assumed it as their due.

Which brings me to the deeper stain. Too many of those teenage boys and men were shits. Again, I could do nothing about myself, not at first. I had to get involved. In the early stages of an affair, something emotionally insufficient, ungenerous or disparaging in a lover would draw me in. I went towards him as I would a pile of dirty dishes. I was not one of those women who were on the lookout for a man to 'rescue'. Nor was I a masochist. It was just . . . difficult to explain. Even as I loathed it, I was motivated by the squalid bedsit, the white sheets gone grey, and lying between them, the neglectful partner. As I came to see it, my past cried out, thank you for neglecting me!

The converse was predictable. On occasions, the loveliest, kindest and most sensitive of men would fall for me. I turned them away and they would be crushed into silent despair or baffled pleading. I liked them but found them cloying. I was ashamed of my lack of sexual interest. I could hardly say, look, sorry, but you're too nice, too attentive and your company is too agreeable, so leave me alone. More considerate to put myself out of range.

So, my father was not dead. He lived in my head, walking my neuronal battlements in 'solemn march', like King Hamlet's ghost, not demanding revenge but projecting into my social world a misogynist's sulphurous contempt and all the manly indifference I could hope for. It should be obvious that I passed through the therapy mill. I took it from all angles, from every creed. We also spent long hours together, Rachel and I, talking about our childhood. What comfort, to be witnesses to each other's past. I eventually believed that I knew myself well enough to challenge the ghost and drive him out. But I should have known better. Self-knowledge is not the same as a cure.

Many years passed. The catastrophe descended and I'll come to it later. I became an academic and as I passed my mid-thirties, I was still on my old path, deep in an affair with an unavailable man. Harry Kitchener was married, emotionally stunted, self-absorbed. What could be better? At the same time, in an act of defiance of everything that I was and despite my deeper stain, I accepted the love of the wonderful caring Percy Greene, an esteemed violin maker, a weekend banjo player, the perfect lifelong friend, and I agreed to marry him.

Eventually, I dismissed Harry Kitchener. Percy and I moved

out of the Linton Road flat and set up home in Headington, on a side street off the main road. We were delighted with each other. No pretence on my part. We were happy and everything looked good for the future. Percy built a stout shed in the garden for a workshop. Two good commissions for a violin and a viola came in during the early months. My book on the poet John Clare was out and had some good notices in obscure places. The house was small, far too small for Percy, and the stairs were unnaturally steep but we did not care. Rachel came to stay and brought along her first child, Peter, then a six-year-old, and we loved him. We cooked meals for friends in the half-built kitchen. Man and wife, we began long rambles across Oxford-shire. Percy knocked together a bed out of old oak planks. The night it was done, we made love on it. I was enjoying my teach-ing. We lived mostly on my salary and we had enough to get by. Happy lives, with everything so fresh.

But sometimes, when alone, I thought of Harry and wondered if marriage had been a mistake. He was a man of the world and we had parted on reasonable terms. I wondered if he would leave Jane, his wife, one day soon. I assumed he was in a new affair and that troubled me. I needed proof. He had been peeved when I announced my marriage plans. I had laughed at such outrageous double standards, and he took my point. Now it was my turn to be unreasonable. I was happy with Percy, but I needed Harry. He commuted by train to London three days a week to his office at Turnbull's, the publisher. The rest of the week he worked at home in Jericho. Our paths were unlikely to cross.

In 1998, communication had not advanced much in a hundred years. The telephone was still the latest thing in general use. Email was beginning to spread, and I had been signed up for three years but Harry, like most of his generation, was holding out. The very subject made him irritable. He had never missed this so-called emailing in the past, so why should he bother with it now? Capitalism, I once reminded him, invents furiously and persuades us of new needs. We were at the dawn of the digital age. According to Harry, this was the sort of 'piffle' that excited mediocrities. In college, my older colleagues had proof that word processing would kill literature. I was afraid of phoning Harry in case Jane picked up. I did not want to phone him at work. He was not associated with any Oxford college and had no anonymous pigeonhole in a porters' lodge. If I wanted to be in touch with him, I would have to use the ancient Penny Post.

I sent a bland postcard and took care to include Jane in the salutation, but no Percy in the sign-off. Belatedly, I thanked them for their wedding present, a non-stick wok, and hoped to see them one day soon. The absent reference to marital contentment was my signal to Harry, but I also guessed, correctly as it turned out, that he wouldn't get round to reading the card.

What would I have said at the time had I been asked to set my psychoanalytic determinism aside and list this man's attributes? As a lover, well, he was ten years older than me, and though he was not tender like Percy, he had a quality of emotionless and knowing detachment that thrilled . . . that resonated deeply with . . . no, forget all that. He turned me inside out, for whatever reason. Generally, there was a glow about him. He was tall, very striking, wonderful face, with some resemblance to Stephen Spender, spoke beautifully, had read everything and remembered it all, was witty and, once you managed to get his attention, he was a good listener.

His brother-in-law was the famous poet Francis Blundy, second only to Seamus Heaney, according to some, to others, second to none. Harry Kitchener was a poet too, by general agreement no good at all, too in love with obscure and untranslated classical tags and allusions. In time, I realised that even as he was proud of the association and promoted his work, he was envious of Blundy's fame and determined one day to rise above him. As poetry editor at Turnbull's, Harry was shaping the tastes of a generation. He was that rarity in Oxford, a well-known literary type who would have nothing to do with the university. It somehow leaked out that he had declined to be a fellow of All Souls. It was of more interest to some of those colleagues that over the years, Harry had turned down dining rights in Merton, Christ Church and Magdalen among other colleges, including ours. Harry's one contact with the university was to have played 'real' or royal tennis many years ago on the court across the lane from Merton. He once said it was the best two hours of his life. Here was another attribute – he was a good tennis player, competing in his twenties at county level, and he remained formidable into his forties.

Three months after I sent my card, we made contact, and it was not quite by accident. I was invited to give a lecture on John Clare at Columbia University in New York. It was the first time Percy and I were to be apart in our marriage and we made a fuss about it, shedding tears during our long embrace at the Headington stop for the Heathrow coach. My lecture was part of a well-endowed series and a big occasion, especially for me. I had spoken at NYU and Hunter colleges before, but this time there was to be an honorarium of $1,000. There was an audience of 500, the questions at the end were sympathetic and knowing, I was loudly applauded and ended the day immensely pleased with myself.

The next morning at breakfast in my hotel I read in the *New York Times* that this was the week of an annual international book fair. I did not need to think about it. I took a cab west, to a vast exhibition hall by the Hudson River. Even though I had a map of the fair's exhibitors, it took me half an hour, threading through dense voluble crowds, to locate the Turnbull's stall. I must have walked past a million books, most of them new. Finally, there he was, his back to me, stooping politely to listen to a sharp-faced diminutive woman whose face I thought I recognised. I waited by a display of the beautifully designed standardised hardback editions of seventeenth-century poets, one of Turnbull's and Harry's great commercial and critical successes. My heart was thudding. What was I getting into? To calm myself, I tried to predict what his first words would be when he saw me. I got it wrong, of course. The woman went away, Harry turned, smiled, but without surprise, and spoke as if we had not been apart nine months but had been chatting five minutes before.

'That was good last night. No, Vivien, it was *very* good.' And he quoted, ' "Thou'st heard the knave, abusing those in power." '

I continued, ' "Bawl freedom loud and then oppress the free." So you came! Why didn't you say hello?'

'Too many fans. Couldn't get near you.'

He smiled to confirm that this was not true. 'Besides, I hoped you'd come by. I've got us a table at the Odeon. Near my hotel.'

He stepped aside to a lobby to make a call. I guessed he was cancelling his lunch date, whoever she was, or making the booking. I didn't care. The word 'hotel' had settled our fates. We could have skipped the restaurant, as far as I was concerned. Instead, we drank a bottle and a half of overpowerful Californian red, and then he wanted to 'show you my room and offer you a coffee'. Such euphemisms in our liberated times. Simply, we resumed.

Later, as I was leaving his place to go back uptown and get dressed for a formal dinner at Columbia, Harry stroked my cheek. 'Adulterous Mrs Greene, the king of Saudi Arabia has kindly asked if he might have you buried to your neck in desert sand and have rocks thrown at your head.'

'But not at adulterous you.'

He kissed me. 'So unfair.'

In the afternoon of my last full day, I walked up Lexington Avenue on the Upper East Side, feeling good about Harry, about my lecture and the hospitality of my hosts. I was on the lookout for a present I would take back for Percy. Guilt is an accommodating emotion. It can sit comfortably alongside happier feelings, asking only to be softened or eradicated by a kind act. When I saw a bookshop, I went in by force of habit. It was a small independent store that appeared cramped, but it stretched back a long way. The shelves were of an unfamiliar orange-tinted wood exuding a pleasant scent, and finely constructed, with carved fluting on the uprights. The mosaic of colourful book spines in packed receding rows excited me. I occasionally fantasised about an enchanted life on a couch, doing nothing but reading. Reading and sex, perfect bedfellows. I went to the biography section to find my own book, as first-time authors do, and stared hard at the place it should have been.

I began an aimless browsing around the store. My mood was beginning to dip. Almost every book whose title I read, I wanted to read and knew I never would. The cumulative effect of seeing the results of so much labour, researching, composing, revising, doubting, defending then hoping, was spreading an ache of weariness through my limbs. Lingering jet lag, surely. By my body's uncertain clock, I had been up since 3 a.m. A silly slogan repeated itself in my thoughts: too many books is like too much chocolate. The bookshop air that had seemed so fragrant was now insufficient and stifling. I thought I could fall asleep on my feet. I wanted to leave but I did not have the will. They seemed in league, these busy ambitious authors, striving to teach, frighten or entertain me. To lie down on the floor was tempting. I would not have minded the creaking bare oak boards. People could step over me for all I cared. But I kept upright and arrived at a table, a restored kitchen table, of new hardback history books. It was an act of self-punishment to read the titles. An illustrated history of silk, of the 1944 Battle of Hürtgen Forest, of the valve flute, of the thirteen Chinese dynasties, of children's furniture, of mental disorders. The past was as monstrously heaped and oppressive as the books about it. I was too weak to face it or them. There was too much of everything.

This odd turn may have been a premature encounter with ageing. I was only thirty-eight. Or it was pique at the absence of my John Clare, my own little squeak for attention. Or it was jet lag. I saw a sign for a coffee bar downstairs and there I shared a table with a young man, bearded, pale long face, rimless specs, threadbare sports jacket, an image of the closeted scholar. But he taught PE in a nearby high school, and we passed a soothing fifteen minutes explaining ourselves. Meeting this warm soft-spoken American with a direct manner revived me and I went back upstairs to resume my search for a present.

I was a long time in the music section before I found on a bottom shelf the perfect obscure thing for my husband, a biography of the eighteenth-century Guarneri del Gesù, apparently one of the finest violin makers or 'luthiers' of all time. The book had contemporary diagrams of early modern violin construction. Such a scholarly edition was for a specialised market and cost $70. That would obliterate the guilt.

But not entirely. When I arrived home in the early evening after my day flight, Percy greeted me on the threshold with a bottle of champagne in his hand. He was wearing a chef's apron. All afternoon he had been preparing a feast. First, my one hot moment of shame as we looked into each other's eyes, then our tears of joy as we embraced and kissed by our freshly painted front door.

*

I started Tuesday evening classes in Italian. I spoke a little already, so my lack of progress would not be noticeable. I assumed that Jane Kitchener did not know that Harry rented a one-room flat at the top of the Banbury Road, within earshot of the ring road. When I asked him how long he'd had it, he laughed. I didn't ask again. On his urging, tough though it was, I attended the first two classes, and after those, managed one every four or five weeks. The community centre in Summertown was a fifteen-minute walk to Harry's place further north. After the lesson, some of my classmates would head for dinner at a Chinese restaurant close by. 'We' would attempt to speak only Italian. I went once. Those meals and the lessons I did not attend were sufficient cover. Occasionally, when Percy was away for a conference or driving to Newcastle or Edinburgh to deliver a violin, Harry and I marked up a whole night together. I encouraged Percy to get his band together again, for they sometimes played in pubs outside town. He shouldn't let marriage stand in the way of doing the things he loved, I would selflessly insist. Around the same time, I persuaded Harry to invest in a mobile phone. The TMI was what he called his, the Tool of Marital Infidelity. What I loved about our evenings included not only the sex, the secrecy, the obscure hide-away and the suppers Harry and I cooked there. They also included books.

I felt, though I could never say, that I had made a sacrifice in marrying a man who had no taste for reading, who would rather fix the plumbing than talk about literature, even though he liked it when I read short poems to him. By an unspoken accord, we used to talk about everything that existed that was not gluing violins together and not books. But a world minus the glued violin is larger than a world without books. It would have challenged Percy's generous nature to think that I had lost more mental freedom in our marriage than he had. But of course I had. A significant portion of all possible worlds, real or imagined, is touched on or explored in the earth's total accumulation of books. Violins, completed or not, refer mostly to themselves. This seemed too obvious to state. We were delighted to acknowledge what we each had gained, but Percy and I never discussed what I had lost. In him I had a partner and a playmate, but I also wanted a thought-mate. I never found such a person in college. By convention, high table was devoted to small talk. The American critic Edmund Wilson's journal reveals how disappointed he was by college dinners at high table, where serious discussion was politely avoided. He was visiting England in the 1950s. After Cambridge and Oxford, he was intellectually liberated to be staying in London with the writers Karl and Jane Miller.

Like Wilson, I needed liberation and thought I was owed someone like Harry. I needed our rambling, sometimes hilarious post-coital cocktails of literary argument, celebration and gossip. His cleverness made me clever. It was rare, but it pleased me when I knew a poem, a book or an author new to him. Tuesdays, late evenings, walking slowly south along the Banbury Road, watching out for a Headington bus, I fairly vibrated with well-being. Easy then, to convince myself that by becoming whole, I was doing our marriage a favour. I could honour and adore my husband with even greater abandon. In the hailstorm of lies I told Percy, I persuaded myself I was virtuous. Truly, I was clever.

But not as clever as the vengeful gods as they perfected my shackles and looked for an opportunity to slip them round my ankles. There are dire developments in life whose earliest signs can be known only in retrospect. Then we might say, I wish I had known! But in my case, it would have made no difference. It began, according to me but not the doctors, at breakfast on a Saturday morning in the early summer of 1999. We were drinking coffee in the back garden. Percy raised a subject that we had been through a few times before. He approached it delicately, with no pressure, he said, but he wanted to be clear. It was the large matter of whether we would have a child. He would love to be a father, he said, but he would respect my decision. Previously, I'd said that I was too old at thirty-nine. I was concerned for my career and the books I wanted to write. I did not add that a baby, in its ruthless way, would demand an end to my Tuesday trysts.

None of this was on my mind that sunny morning. I had decided it was time to tell my husband a shameful secret that only my sister Rachel knew, along with a few people I hadn't heard from in many years. I've kept journals at different times and I have never been able to set down this story until now. The boy left at the station was also forbidden. Nightmares of abandonment have pursued me. I could not confess to my journal, but I could tell Percy. I see him now, his folded arms resting on the garden table, forgiveness already in his look. Whatever he was about to hear, he would embrace it, understand it and love me.

When a young person leaves home after an oppressive upbringing (parents, religion, poverty, in any combination) there might follow a period of destructive rebellion. It can be brief, before the passing years impose some order, or it can last a lifetime. Every case is different, and mine was curious. I worked hard at school, got the scholarship, escaped from home, but remained a diligent student with only the occasional lost weekend, calmed down before finals and came away with a good degree. I moved into a shared house in Clerkenwell with three women medical students and found a job in an estate agent's office. The work was dull, but I typed fast and I was valued and soon I was promoted and on a commission. These were the early Thatcher years, and there was crazy greed in the air and a house-price boom. My hours were not strict. My housemates were wild drinkers and everywhere there were pink and blue Ecstasy tablets for the asking. My first seemed like permission, a ticket to do whatever I liked, and for reasons I have tried to explain, I had a string of awful boyfriends. This, not my student years, was my time of breakout. Then, breakdown.

Within six months I was pregnant. The father walked away. If my parents had known, they would have urged me to have an abortion. Sensible, given my circumstances. But coming from them, it would have sounded to me like more of the dead-hand oppression I was in flight from. In the shared house there was a tiny unused room next to mine and with Rachel's help I cleared it out, decorated it and made a nursery. The housemates were helpful too. My sister was living a sensible life, training to be an executive in an Arab Gulf airline. She lent me money. The baby was born in mid-December at St Bart's Hospital, a beautiful little girl I named Diana after the huntress. She had a blazing blue-eyed gaze and curly wisps of blonde hair. Everybody adored her and my medical friends fought over the chance to look after her. For six months I stayed at home and was happy. The Clerkenwell house became the centre for gatherings, or parties, weekdays and weekends. I went out a few evenings while one of my housemates babysat. One night I took Ecstasy. I was slipping back into my old routine.

That same week there was a bigger than usual party in the house. About thirty people. I brought Diana down around nine and all the women and some of the men cooed over her. Around midnight I looked in on her and she was fine. I was going back to work in two days and taking Diana with me in her push-chair. I don't remember how the rest unfolded. I suppose the celebratory atmosphere was part of what drove me to become dreadfully drunk. The music was still loud around two thirty when I went to bed. I hardly dare write this down. *I forgot about Diana*. I did not go into her room. The fact of her existence did not penetrate my disgusting state. I abandoned her. I sat on the edge of my bed unlacing my shoes and the next time I was conscious it was ten in the morning and I was still fully dressed. Hungover, I stumbled into her room. She was lying on her belly in her cot, face down in a puddle of vomit.

At the inquest, the coroner was deeply sympathetic about my loss and took pains not to mention my drunkenness. Sitting in court, I felt my shame even more intensely. Rachel told me that it was helpful the press did not cover the hearing, but I was beyond thoughts of help. Silence fell like fog and smothered my existence. I became deaf. Or rather, when people spoke to me, I heard their words, but I didn't hear their meaning. I didn't move, I didn't eat or speak. Rachel went to the funeral in my place. The only time I left the house was when I went with her and the medical students to an obscure corner of Spa Fields. We intended to dig a hole with a garden trowel to bury the pale blue teddy that Diana always cuddled at bedtimes. It was a hopeless occasion – heavy rain, a cold June wind blowing and the ground too stony to dig. The idea had been to read some poems aloud, but we couldn't stand it. I collapsed in grief and at my insistence we brought the teddy back with us. I never saw or heard again from my medical friends. The next morning my sister took me home to our parents.

She insisted that they had to be told. I sensed their reproach in every kind word. To be treated as the focus of their attention was an unfamiliar experience. I regressed to a sour teenager and hated them for all their care, but they kept at it. Eighteen months later, I applied to my university to do postgraduate work and I was accepted for a DPhil. My oppressive parents raided their savings for my upkeep. I took it as my due and I never properly thanked them. In another age, I might have taken myself off to a silent nunnery. Oxford would have to do. All my undergraduate friends had left, and I was glad. I made no new friends and lived alone while I researched and wrote about the poetry and sad life of brilliant John Clare. I knew I did not deserve to have another child.

This, in shortened form, was what I told Percy that beautiful early-summer morning in our Headington garden. When I had finished he was silent for a while, for which I was grateful. The memories of two decades ago had brought me to a tearful state. Percy waited, and at last he spoke through a long sigh. 'It's a terrible terrible story. You were young and crazy. You made the worst possible mistake. But you can't go on punishing yourself for the rest of your life. Having a baby could be wonderful for us both. And redemption. But if you don't want one, for all your other reasons, well, I'm with you, whatever you decide.'

With that he got up and embraced me and kissed the top of my head, then walked the few yards to his homemade workshop. I sat in a daze. His response was what I had hoped for, and I don't think I ever loved him more. Perhaps it was time to think differently about having a child. I thought again about that tiny boy at the end of the platform and the mother who abandoned him. By denying a life, I could be a version of her. Time to choose. I went to the bottom of the garden, through the gate to the lane that ran along the backs of the houses and led into an enormous dreary field. I walked for an hour, then doubled back, making a route between the lane's huge puddles that never seemed to dry out. By the time I reached our garden I had made my decision. I was not going to break in on Percy's work with such momentous news. I would wait until he came into the house for lunch and meanwhile look at some lecture notes. But it was hard to concentrate. Flashes of deep excitement and a sensation of floating scattered my thoughts. Telling my secret had lifted something dark or had shrunk it and turned it into a seed of hope. Diana, in another form.

Percy worked a half-day on Saturdays. He came into the house, as usual, just before one o'clock. I assumed his work had gone well. He looked cheerful as he stopped in front of the table where I was trying to read and asked if I wanted a sandwich. Cheese, tomato, lettuce and pickle.

I nodded.

'Coming up!'

I said, 'After our conversation, I went for a stroll.'

'Yes?' He had moved away and was going towards the kitchen counter.

My heart had picked up speed, the way it does when I'm about to give someone close a present I know they will love. I couldn't stop smiling. 'I think you're right.'

'Yes?' He said this with his back to me.

'About self-punishment.'

He was placing a fresh loaf on the bread board and taking a bread knife out of a drawer. He said quietly, 'Um . . .'

'And redemption.'

Now he turned and came back towards me, the knife still in his hand. 'Sorry darling. I'm lost.' He said it warmly, as if indulging a child.

I stared at him. He sometimes went adrift in the intricacies of violin construction. I kept the irritation out of my voice. The beauty and importance of the moment was too precious to spoil. 'I'm talking about our conversation this morning, when I told you—'

'But Vivien—'

'—the whole story. And I've decided, Percy. I would love us to—'

'I don't know what you're talking about.'

We stared at each other. He sat down opposite me and rested the knife on the table. I was scanning his features for some hint of an inappropriate joke. All I saw was bafflement.

Finally, I said, 'You don't remember our conversation?'

'No.'

'In the garden.'

208

'No.'

'Percy. This morning.'

He was shaking his head, and I was beginning to feel frightened. 'What have you been doing this morning?'

'I went . . . I went . . .' He looked around the room in search of an answer.

'Did you mow the lawn, go to the shops? Did you read a newspaper?'

He put his face in his hands. 'I'm trying to think. Don't keep asking me.'

But he could think of nothing. I waited, then I patted his hand and went to the phone. I had a colleague at college, not a doctor, but a professor of neuroscience who long ago had accumulated clinical experience in psychiatry. There was a chance I would find him at home. His wife answered and went to fetch him. He was on his way to tennis, he said, but he had a couple of minutes. I was conscious of Percy watching me closely as I described what had happened.

He was reassuring. It sounded like a TGA, a transient global amnesia. It might last a few hours, during which Percy would not be able to lay down new memories. Not that uncommon. Weird to experience, unsettling to witness, then it lifts. No consequences, no treatment necessary.

'But he should have a scan. I'll phone a friend at the John Radcliffe on Monday. Meanwhile relax! He'll be fine.'

When I turned back to Percy and started to tell him what my friend had said, he spoke over me in the same cheery tone. 'I thought of making myself a sandwich. Cheese, tomato, lettuce and pickle. Want one?'

'All right.'

'Coming up.'

But after a moment he wandered to the other end of the room and moodily stared through the French windows at the garden. Then he roused himself and told me again in the same eerily cheerful voice that he was going to make a sandwich, listed the ingredients and asked if I wanted one too.

When I said I did, he called out, 'Coming up!'

He made no sandwiches that afternoon. I made them. When I gave Percy his, he took the plate with a grunt of surprise. We ate in silence. Afterwards, he went to the shed and later, when he returned to the house, the lotus-eating spell was over. He had found his current project on the workbench. Everything he had intended to do had been done to his own high standards, but he had no memory of doing it. Or of anything else. 'There's a hole in my life,' he kept saying in wonder.

Two months later we were at a consultation to be told the results of Percy's scans. The neurologist pointed with his pencil at a screen where smears of grey and black converged. They meant nothing to us, but the drift was clear. My college friend had been right and there appeared to be no neural damage that could have caused the amnesia, and no visible consequences. We were about to thank the doctor and leave when he raised a hand to delay us. He brought up another scan, hardly different from the one we had been looking at. Again, he tapped the screen with his pencil. There was some enlargement here of the ventricles, he told us, and a possible degree of shrinking in one area of the hippocampus. Nothing to worry about now, but another scan in six months would be advisable, and some cognitive tests beforehand. Percy and I were keen to get away from the cramped office and its general air of unhealthy interest in mental dysfunction. The shelves around us were filled with books whose spines declared 10,000 ways a brain could go wrong. We stood, said our thanks and agreed to make a date with the secretary.

My elated optimism never returned, and the question of a baby was dropped. Not even that, for we never got that far. I could not bear to tell Percy the story of Diana again. The luminous idea of having a child had been dimmed by a moment of frightening mental failure. It was difficult to admit it, but the episode challenged my faith in Percy's strength, his reliability and competence. He was my rock and now a crack had appeared. It could not be wise to make myself vulnerable by having a baby if Percy was to be vulnerable too. The conventional medical view was that transient global amnesia was without consequences. I could not believe this, especially now that a doctor wanted Percy to be scanned again. I explained this to Harry one evening. He listened patiently He agreed that I was right to be concerned for Percy's mental health.

For some reason Percy missed his appointment for the scan and cognitive tests and had to wait a further three months. The diagnosis when it finally came was no surprise. A box-ticking cognitive test backed it up. Our neurologist insisted that what I called the lotus episode was coincidental and had nothing to do with his Alzheimer's. I did not believe him. But it hardly mattered. By then, the long decline had already begun. Percy's forgetfulness was its most obvious feature, until irritability and then anger crept in. It was all bad and it was all slow, and my own brain's protective amnesia eased me from one stage to the next.

During the year after the second scan, Percy remained fully aware of what was happening to him and knew that there was no way out. Or that there was only one exit and he could either take it now or let the disease take it for him later. He was depressed, as anyone would be. He told me that our lives together were ruined, that our future had been snatched from us. I would remind him of the marvellous hike we had planned for the next day and the friends who would be visiting, of the plain fact of our love and how we would stay close and live for the present. But he was right. The future looked appalling. We had a few fake rational conversations about suicide – the timing, the method, the need to protect me from suspicion of murder. I say fake because I knew that I would never help him, and he would never do it. I had been told that there would come a time when he would unknowingly cross an invisible frontier and no longer have what they called insight into his condition. Suicide would be forgotten.

We did see our friends and Percy was merry in their company, and our big hikes across Oxfordshire, Wiltshire, Somerset

211

and Gloucestershire were a success. We stayed in old inns and looked round ancient churches and in warmer weather swam in rivers. He often told me how much he loved me. I read him short poems. The shorter the better, he would say. Emily Dickinson suited him well. At home, we cooked together from intricate recipes. He found that red wine was unpleasant and he developed a taste for white. He listened to old Beatles records. He took pleasure in young Peter's visits. They made a special bond and had ludicrous intimate conversations.

Folded into these pleasures was the long retreat. By stages, his violin work dropped away and was no longer mentioned. When he was confused, he became irascible. He began to resent it whenever I went out. However often and clearly I explained where I was going, for what reason and when I would return, he would be angry when I came home and would accuse me of going off without warning, of deceiving him. That hurt, because those evenings when I was not at my Italian lessons, he was right. The pleasures we had at the beginning were no longer possible. There should have been something both dark and grand, even dramatic, in witnessing the person you love cast off, piece by piece, all the elements of their being in relentless disintegration. But the day-to-day reality of the process was its banality. Percy's consciousness was a closing door. He became simple, boring, repetitious, unlovely. By all usual standards, he was grossly unfair, sometimes abusive, then weak, then demanding. But those standards were what he had also cast off. I lived by the irregular clock of his moods. Worst of all, he forgot he loved me. I was the presence who looked after him, fetched things, tried to explain, reassure, comfort. Now and then he had trouble with my name. After some effort it would come, but he had forgotten who we once were. I tried to keep it alive, but it was a lost cause. I went to look around a state-run care home and that was when I remembered how much I loved him and that I could never leave him in such a place. I decided to take extended leave from teaching so that I could look after him properly.

The days of insight, suicide conversations and river swimming, lumpy mattresses in old pubs and declarations of love were two years behind us. Percy had crossed his frontier and I crossed it with him. His journey was mine. There were many milestones of deterioration ahead of us and most decayed in memory as soon as they were passed. But one remained fresh. It was a September afternoon. I was in the garden clearing up the dying summer's growth. My best resource apart from Rachel's respite visits was Percy's newly developed taste for daytime television. There was nowhere in the house where I could escape its gaudy clatter but that was a small price. At least I could be on my own in the garden knowing that he would not be moving from his armchair. I was lifting withered plants, shaking the earth from their roots and tossing them into a wheelbarrow. I went indoors for a glass of water in the kitchen and checked on Percy. He was in a state of high excitement. His game show or whatever had been interrupted. The screen showed a jet passenger plane flying into and slicing through a tall building I immediately recognised. Then a cut, and a second plane hit the adjacent tower. And now, another jump in time, a long-lens view across the East River and the second building sinking into itself as though in slow motion. I stood frozen in horror. There were hundreds, if not thousands of people in that building. We were watching their deaths. Then we were back in Manhattan. A colossal cumulus of dust rose up and surged through side streets and people fled before it. And now we were watching the first tower go down, and again, the second tower. I could not speak. But at each new shock, at the two impacts, the twin collapses, Percy punched the air and shouted 'Wow!' And 'Brilliant!' And 'Again!' He turned to me, his face flushed and contorted with joy. He was scanning my expression, wanting me to share his elation.

'Don't you like it?' he shouted.

I left the room and went back into the garden. I assumed that people were sharing the anxiety that what had happened in New York was about to happen everywhere. I called Harry on my Nokia. Like me, he had seen it late and we exchanged shocked impressions. Everyone was doing the same that afternoon. I wanted to see him, but there was no chance. He was in London for work. I called my sister and then my friends and repeated the conversation – it was important and reassuring. I could hear from inside the house Percy's happy cries as the footage was shown yet again. By remaining in the garden, I was keeping away from his infantile insufficiency, the high wall of stupidity that the disease had built round him. Shocked reporters were speaking into microphones, the urgent drumbeat music announced that this was news, global news, and history must surely bend to a new direction. But Percy understood nothing. His grisly joy made the catastrophe appear even more horrific. Irrationally, I felt shamed by him. While others embraced loved ones for mutual comfort, my husband squawked with delight, like a toddler out of control or, for all I knew, like the mastermind of the attack, watching from a mountain hideout. Yes, yes, I knew that his brain was dying, his mind shrivelling. But the habits of ordinary personal exchange die a slower death. Until I made the effort and intervened, my automatic responses to Percy were moral, not clinical. In the instant, I could not help judging him by what he said or did, as I would anyone else. Then I would be furious with myself that I could momentarily forget that he was ill in a special way. Not with a fever or cancer or a tricky heartbeat, but through a transformation into a lesser being of – dare I name them? – lower intelligence, few interests, diminished sympathies, a man unable to act coherently in the social world and with an enfeebled grasp of the actual.

On three occasions, before it became too difficult, I went with Percy to a support group run by the city council in a room in the town hall by Carfax. He did not speak but sat calmly and seemed to be following the discussion. The atmosphere was kindly, and I learned a few useful tips and spoke up a couple of times. There were around fifteen of us carers, two-thirds of whom were men. I could not agree with the lady who described the husband by her side, with some maternal fondness, as 'adorably childlike'. A child is in a constant state of becoming. Its curiosity is instinctive and its world is expanding. I said nothing and smiled supportively like the rest. I gathered from the group that Percy had deteriorated at the same rate as the others. The carers confirmed what I had begun to suspect. Alzheimer's patients can reach a plateau. For a long while their symptoms do not worsen. For a year or two or even three, they are trapped in their condition and make no advance towards their final release.

Stasis or decline, it was a vile prospect and I counted more and more on Harry to keep me sane. At the beginning, it had been easy enough to drop the pretence of the Italian lessons and leave Percy on his own. When that became impossible, I depended on my sister's overnight visits at weekends. We did not talk about it but she knew what I was up to. She and Peter were happy to spend time with Percy and allow me a break. I knew she was glad to get away from her needling, bossy husband, Michael. He had never approved of her career as an airline executive and now motherhood had taken its place. My few hours at the top of the Banbury Road swelled in importance. Sometimes, Rachel had to cancel because of her own health, or Percy's needs were too pressing and I would have to let Harry down on the day. He was always understanding. As my visits became irregular, I came to resemble the cloying lover I used to run from. I was attentive, I brought him little gifts, I insisted on more than my share of the cooking. I became sensitive to any perceived slight. That he was so kindly whenever I had to cancel made me suspicious. My changed and somewhat neurotic behaviour was getting in the way of our pleasures. Our amused and ironic exchanges faltered. I suspected he was being careful not to upset me. Even as I saw all this, I could do nothing about it. It made me more desperate not to lose him. If I did, I thought I would go mad.

The network of gossip within and between the colleges was a finely wrought construct. On the phone with a colleague one morning, I heard the latest. Harry Kitchener's marriage was in trouble. He had a lover and Jane was throwing him out – not for the first time. In another call, a friend confirmed what I already feared. This lover was not me. She was a young editor at Turnbull's. Everyone there had known about it for a year. Two days later my mobile rang. Certain it was him, I fumbled with the buttons and by mistake cancelled the call. When it rang again, Harry said he was in the lane by my back gate and wanted to see me. Percy was watching TV. I ran down the garden like a fool, as if I was rushing towards good news. Rumours are not always true. Harry had brought his car up the lane and was standing by its open door. Jaunty piano music was playing on its radio and that annoyed me. He didn't waste time on greetings though, oddly, he was smiling at me. He had come, he said, to tell me what we both knew.

'It's this, dear heart. We've run our course. Pressures on me, bigger ones on you. I thought I'd get it out before you said it to me.'

This was supposed to be disarming. I said, 'Please turn off the radio.' My only concern was to keep face.

He reached into the car. 'Begone, Fatso Waller.'

The sudden silence did not help me. I said, 'I haven't been myself lately.'

To concede like this was to risk throwing away the one lively element of my reduced life. But I kept an expressionless look. Perhaps it appeared stony.

He was standing behind his open car door with his arms resting along its top, still smiling, as if he was enjoying a pleasant chat over a five-bar gate. 'Agreed. But let's not forget. It was a lot of fun for a very long time.'

My lower lip was starting to quiver. I sucked it in and managed to say, 'Yes, it was.' Dignity was all.

'And we got away with it.'

'I suppose.'

He stepped round the door and approached me 'So ... dearest, "since there's no help, come let us kiss and part".'

The old quotation game. I could not suppress a puny dry

216

laugh, which I thought might push me over the edge into tears. I said in a flat tone, ' "Passion speechless lies." '

'Never once caught you out,' he murmured just before we kissed lightly on the lips.

'I should get back to Percy.'

He nodded and turned towards his car, and I went back through the gate, determined not to watch him drive away.

*

This laconic dismissal coincided with a shift in Percy's condition. He was still crossing his plateau and it was not so much decline as a subtle intensification of his symptoms, of what was there already. His repeated questions and remarks were more frequent and expressionless, as though he too were bored by them. When he followed me about the house, he stood closer, his great bulk a reminder of how constricted my days were. The upsets and tantrums were not more frequent, but they were louder. He wanted to hold my hand. At first, I was touched but he insisted at inconvenient moments, like when I was cooking or making the beds. When I pulled my hand free, he was tearful. These minor upsets made me irritable and I tried hard not to show it. Instead, I turned on myself. I had good material for self-loathing and I should not have needed a demented husband to bring me to it.

I was outraged by the way I had stood there, sweet and decent sort, mousey and passive, obliging with my nervous laughter while Kitchener preened. So determined not to play the victim that I became one. I let him dump me unchallenged. Long ago he had moved on to his young editor, retaining me until it was inconvenient. How smooth he had been this last year in his deceit. That I had been cheating on Percy I set aside. That cheating had been my and Harry's daily bread I did not need to consider. In the lane I suggested I'd been poor company. All my fault! I let him kiss me. I played along with his stupid Drayton quote. I should have called him out on his

217

ludicrous oily manner. I kept myself awake at night refining the terse remarks that would have cut him down. At the very least, when Harry claimed that 'we got away with it', why could I not have said, 'I hear that Jane has chucked you out'?

Our conversation out the back lasted barely two minutes and was such a humiliation that I couldn't let it go. I squirmed at the memory of standing on the edge, the shore, of a puddle in house slippers and lumpy corduroy skirt, while he lounged by his car in pressed suit and starched white shirt playing the dandy, on his way to Turnbull's, wearing the tie I had given him a month ago. After all that had passed between us, how dare he toss me aside in seconds. It was a relief to direct my anger away from myself. I loathed him. Next stage, I wanted to *do* something about it. As the weeks passed that resolve did not fade. It swelled. I was learning something about myself. I had a capacity for bitterness that surprised me but kept me from self-pity or depression. I considered what I would do in the real world, a parting shot that might extinguish his insulting smiles from my thoughts.

The solution came by post in the form of a handwritten note from a friend, Shelley, I used to work with, arranging literary events. She was inviting me to an evening at the Sheldonian. The poet Francis Blundy would be reading his work and talking about it with his brother-in-law and friend, the editor, critic and poet Harold Kitchener. I had once met Blundy at a conference. I remembered a combative five-minute conversation about poetry in translation. I had two weeks to prepare, time enough to arrange a respite visit from Rachel and Peter.

Percy's need for sleep at the end of the day was growing. Perhaps his plateau was gently tilting downwards. Into the late evenings I read Blundy's work with pleasure. I still had the knack of committing lines to memory without effort. I read up on his private life, many affairs, a messy divorce, and the poets he valued or dismissed. Hard to explain or excuse the happiness I felt in those days of preparation. I wondered if I was becoming someone else. I had never experienced such impatience for revenge. Having a purpose, however base, made it almost tolerable, my life with a man whose brain was infested by 'amyloid plaques' and 'tau aggregates', whatever they were. It was glorious to leave those microscopic assailants behind. In the early evening of the big day, I waved goodbye to my husband, sister and nephew as I got into the taxi I was taking to Broad Street. I had a toothbrush and fresh underwear in my shoulder bag.

I arrived in good time. A long queue was already forming in the courtyard. I went straight to the front and walked in. I knew Shelley's assistants from public lectures I had arranged in the past. I was shown into the auditorium and had my pick of viewpoints. I chose an aisle seat four rows back, dead centre, to be in Kitchener and Blundy's sightlines. Ten minutes later they let people in. It was going to be a packed house and the place filled rapidly. I spotted a few colleagues, but if they saw me, they pretended not to. I understood and felt for them. They knew that Percy's condition could only worsen. They would have to lower their spirits with polite enquiries, and such con-versations are hard to terminate. I was relieved not to be talking about the business I most wanted to forget for an evening. I sat snugly in my isolation as the din of conversation rose around me. Impossible to explain to anyone the elation I felt at being out of the house, away from my caring role, at a cultural event in which I was to play a part. I might have looked like one more member of the audience, but I was an agent, an angel of justice. For the first time in over two years, my little cup of self-worth, once habitually full, was overflowing.

Shelley came on stage to make housekeeping announce-ments that included fire exits, future events and thanks to sponsors. She did her best with feeble jokes at which the audi-ence tittered generously. Her halting speech was earnest and decent. Mr Blundy would not be signing books afterwards. Instead, there would be signed copies on the bookshop's table. All the better, I thought.

At the organiser's cue, the two men strode out to loud

applause and cheers. All that I once admired in Harry, I now loathed. His height and stoop, his fraying grey hair, the affected vaguely ironic way he waited for his guest to sit before he lowered himself into his chair with a mock grimace. From there, he launched into his introduction of overheated sloppy praise. I alone knew how jealous he was of his brother-in-law's enthronement as a national treasure. We were in bed together once when Harry read me his parody of Blundy's style that he dared not publish. The target was a spoof of a supposedly typical dissection of some small human moment. I told him it was funny, bang to rights and so on. I had no choice when we were about to make love. But Harry's poem was too bitter, too vehement to be a decent parody. I remembered a line by Dwight Macdonald to the effect that the good parodist does not go hunting with a machine gun. Unspoken admiration, not contempt, was a more effective motive. In Harry's case, envy blackened the page.

He rambled on in his louche dishonest way while I continued to look at his face, his eyes. He appeared not to see me, even though I had edged my chair sideways several inches into the aisle. When Kitchener finished and Blundy stood to go to the lectern, the place went wild. Very un-Sheldonian. Not since Mark Twain received his honorary degree here in 1907 had there been such a friendly eruption. The younger half of the audience would have been made to study Blundy's poetry at school, and now took a more benign view than they probably did at the time. Like many famous people, he seemed smaller than his publicity photographs, and better, I thought, more sculpted about the face and grand in the way an eagle is grand. Sitting or standing relaxed, he looked as if he had filled his lungs with air, ready for a confrontation. He was compact and muscular. You would not have wanted to try out one of your newfangled fashionable opinions in his presence. He started by thanking Harry, his 'loyal friend', and said he was pleased to be back in the Sheldonian. The last time he came it was to listen to Philip Larkin who, it turned out, had not been invited or scheduled.

On being told this at the door, young Blundy had left in disappointment, in no mood for a lecture on the military strategies of General Philippe Leclerc. 'I must have misheard the night before. I might have been drunk.' There was laughter and the beginnings of applause.

He said he would start with a poem he had recently completed. Then he waited for a half-minute until he had complete silence, and it was in this frozen hiatus that he caught my eye. It happened in a slow-motion double-take. The line of his leisurely pale grey gaze passed through mine, and two seconds later flicked back. I thought I saw a barely perceptible nod as we exchanged a look, as if he was already agreeing to or deciding on something. Pure fantasy. I was gratified by the glance but no more than that. Blundy was merely instrumental to my scheme.

He was famous for knowing his work by heart, but this one he read from a sheet of paper he took from the inside pocket of his jacket. It was an end-of-the-affair poem, a sonnet that held to the Shakespearean form, rhyme scheme and final couplet included. It was densely written and on first hearing it was difficult to follow. Surely, a tribute to the master. Its central conceit was that an affair or marriage that ends resembles a whole life. He and his lover do well to stop short of blundering senility. After a small-hours brawl they decide on 'mutual euthanasia', though they 'forgot to slaughter the regret'. Now it is too late to go back, for that life is done. Regret is all they have. The poem was too grammatically convoluted to strike the right melancholy tone. But I was not sure. When he was done, Blundy stood to attention, glaring at his listeners as if he could force from them total comprehension, slavish appreciation. The audience knew not to clap. Or they did not dare. He was like the concert pianist who remains motionless over the keyboard, hands still poised, after the final chord has died away. Blundy exhaled loudly through his nostrils and began to introduce the next poem. He was a frightening bastard, I thought.

He read two more poems, both familiar to me from recent

reading, and then he sat with Kitchener for a short conversation. Harry's questions were as convoluted as Blundy's sonnet but stripped of verbiage and attitude they amounted to the usual stuff. How did a poem begin to form? What were the respective roles of memory and invention? When and how did Blundy know a poem was finished? Who were his first readers? There was weariness in Blundy's curtailed responses. He had been questioned too many times. Kitchener appeared to weary him too. The man who had championed the Blundy opus in two critical books was a useful idiot. Harry had found a fine place for himself in the literary culture, shaping the Turnbull's poetry list and praising a man he envied and personally disliked. Grandly, the poet did not answer the last question about first readers. Instead, he went back to the lectern and, without introduction, recited another poem. We all knew this one, 'In the Saddle', and I knew the poems that followed, but even as I admired them, I had doubts. I read more poetry than most. Some of Blundy's was long and required sustained and focussed attention. Not seeing the words of a poem on the page were to me a form of blindness. I was a reader, not a listener. The audience appeared rapt. When literary heroes hold forth, the atmosphere gets churchy, but I wondered if many in the Sheldonian were daydreaming like me, thinking about what they would be doing next. I was imagining a paper plate of finger food at the reception. Then I would be ready to make my move.

An hour and twenty minutes passed before Kitchener announced that there was just time for a few questions from the audience. The silence was tight. No one wanted to risk asking something daft. At last, from the front row, an elderly lady with a bent back spoke up and asked Blundy what he thought of Tennyson.

He said, 'What do *you* think?'

She straightened as she said proudly, 'I believe he was a genius, one of our greatest poets and nothing will convince me otherwise.'

Blundy clapped his hands and laughed. It was not an act. 'I'm so glad. I agree with you completely. "We are not now that strength which in old days / Moved earth and heaven."'

Famous lines from my favourite Tennyson poem, and generously spoken. The applause rose as Blundy stepped away from the lectern to go and shake the woman's hand and start a conversation with her. He had brought the event to a close, stealing that customary privilege from Kitchener. It had ended well.

I was among the vice chancellor's guests as we filed down the narrow stairs to the basement reception room. There were more than eighty of us in the wide room, not so select a company as I had expected. In the roar of raised voices I had the impression of general release. School is out. No more poems. I felt that way too. Francis Blundy was facing a horseshoe of respectful male students. I saw Harry Kitchener at one end of the long drinks table, talking to a historian I knew. I went to the other end, took a glass and moved to make sure I was in Kitchener's sightline. I looked around, hoping to spot waiting staff with trays, or paper cones of miniature fish and chips. A woman, a Russian-literature specialist from my college, came by and asked after Percy. It turned into a cheerful exchange. Her husband had died a few years back of motor neurone disease. Of course, there was emptiness and grief, she said, but only at first. On the far side was freedom after the heavy duties of care. In summer, a year after her bereavement, she and friends rented a dhow with a local captain and three-man crew and spent six weeks dawdling through the Dardanelles, stopping to explore islands. There were barbecues on deserted beaches. After a swim by moonlight, she had, at the age of sixty-seven, tried marijuana for the first time and loved it. I told her I would feel guilty even thinking about such pleasures. She laughed and said that she could see that I meant it. But I was still young, she told me, and there were adventures waiting for me.

She lifted my spirits. I stood patiently through the vice chancellor's welcoming speech and the great poet's measured response. I made my way through the throng towards him. Yes, I would rent my dhow right now.

The students were determined to keep hold of Blundy, but as soon as he saw me he said, 'Aha. Gentlemen, if you'll excuse us.'

He watched them as they dispersed. 'Nice kids. Read more than I had at their age.' Then he turned to me and when I shook his hand and told him my name he said, 'Ah, John Clare.'

Encouraged, I said, 'I won't tell you how brilliant that was because you'll have heard it enough. Instead—'

He cut me off by spreading his palms and shaking his head.

I had been about to flatter him with a technical question.

'Look, Vivien. Have dinner with me.'

There it was – done. Or half done. I said, 'What about the vice chancellor?'

'I bailed out last week. Anyway, he needs to get to Heathrow. Just say yes.'

'Yes.'

'We'll go now, if you don't mind. I've had enough here.'

'Shouldn't you say goodbye to Harry Kitchener?'

He nodded. 'But don't get caught up.'

We made a wide arc around the edge of the room to avoid his fans. As I followed him, I recalculated. His first poem, the sonnet, suggested that he was between affairs and available. Getting out of long book-signings and post-reading dinners with local worthies and organisers was routine. I was as instrumental in his scheme as he was in mine. I was at least forty minutes ahead of schedule. It was going too well and I should have been suspicious, not of the poet, but of fate. Someone in the crowd put a hand on his elbow to detain him but he kept going. For all my shifting about, I was still not certain that Kitchener had seen me. If he hadn't, all the better now.

He had moved only a few feet from the drinks table. I did not know the elderly couple he was talking to. As we approached the group, I kept close to Blundy's side to make matters clear. I had my reward. Harry saw us and before he could prevent it, his mouth opened just enough to part his lips, then he recovered and forced them into a smile of pleasant welcome.

'Maestro. They ate from your palm.'

'You were solid as a brick, Harry. As always. We're about to head off, so . . .'

'Let me introduce you. This is Charles and Edna Grosvenor, who might be lending the Ashmolean a Willem Kalf.'

'Ah, the Golden Age,' Blundy said as we shook hands with them. 'Will there ever be another and will we know it?' And then he added, 'And this is my friend, Vivien Greene.'

I found myself saying, 'Nice to meet you,' as I shook my ex-lover's hand. It was limp in mine, and cool and sticky. Strong emotion? I hoped so. I let Blundy do the rest. He merely raised a hand, made a farewell nod in the direction of the Grosvenors and put an arm round my shoulder to steer me away. More beseeching hands snatched at his arm as we went back along the edge of the crowd. Blundy was brisk. 'Misha, sorry, have to rush. Let me know how it goes.' There were similar brush-offs until at last we emerged onto Broad Street in relative solitude.

*

On the short walk to the Randolph, he took or made three quick phone calls. Mildly offended, I kept my distance. After the third, he stopped and muttered as he bent over his phone, 'I'm turning this bloody thing off.' In the end I did it for him and at the same time tried to show him how. He would not have it. 'That stuff is torture to me.' Then he began an exasperated account of time wasted doing events like the one he had just left. Prompted by phone technology, he was talking himself into a bad humour.

'Boring travel, hard work, no pay. They think they're doing you a favour, paying for your hotel.'

'Why do it then?'

'I'm not. Two more and I'm stopping.'

This was when he told me, just as we came to the hotel entrance, that he had found a buyer for his London house and

225

was doing up a place in the country, fifty miles west of Oxford. 'A new life!' As he talked, we headed not to the dining room but up the stairs, to his room on the first floor. I said nothing and followed him in. His hosts had at least spent money on his accommodation. We were in a comfortable suite with a lurid floral carpet. On a polished round table were flowers, a bottle of wine, a jar of stuffed olives, mixed salted nuts, a bowl of fruit and a welcome note in copperplate on a card from the management. I sat on a deep sofa with the nuts while Blundy opened the olives and drew the cork and described his rural retreat. A barn of unbelievable dimensions. All around, a rural paradise. His architect was a genius. When the balloon glass was in my hand, he picked up the hotel phone and asked for room service. Was Dover sole OK, he asked me over his shoulder. That done, we clinked glasses. Anticipating his new life and ordering dinner had improved his mood, and mine improved with it. Now that I had delivered the blow to Harry, I was wondering if I had to go much further. Dinner yes, for I had not eaten since breakfast. But I had seen the pretentious four-poster bed and its mock-medieval drapes, I had listened to the prickly poet's resentments and expensive barn-conversion plans, and I was wondering how I might painlessly slip away after the fish and tiramisu.

But the evening changed direction, as it was bound to. Courteously, my host sat across from me on a hard chair and asked me about myself. I explained that I was on extended leave from teaching to look after my husband. Blundy's mother had also suffered from Alzheimer's, and though his sister Jane and her first husband had done most of what he called the daily stuff, the heavy lifting, he had been very involved. A protracted nightmare, we agreed, and an open question whether it was worse to be the patient or the loving carer. We compared experiences of the mood storms, the disorientation, the pathetic disintegration of a personality. I lamented my constricted and ever-shrinking world. Percy and I were in the same prison, suffering in different cells. Blundy said that was his sister's experience too. He described how his mother on two occasions became lucid again, completely herself, asking concerned questions about the family, whose names she recalled without difficulty. Then, after a few minutes, she sank away from them again. She was, he said, like a drowning woman breaking the surface to gulp the air for the last time. I said that if Percy had a moment like that, it would frighten me. It would be like a haunting. Blundy disagreed. He had been there for the second bout of lucidity. It came two days before she died. His mother drew him and Jane towards her and knew exactly who they were. She thanked them and whispered goodbye. It was a miracle, it was joyous. If it should happen to me, I was bound to treasure it, he insisted. Neurologically it was a mystery. Those memories were clearly there but inaccessible to the sufferers. Some researchers thought the phenomenon might offer a clue to useful therapies. I recalled Percy's lost morning and said I could not help thinking of it as his first symptom, though medical science said otherwise. Blundy thought we all experienced some version of Percy's amnesia. Nearly all of life is forgotten.

Our dinner arrived and we shifted to a table at the other end of the suite. We moved on to dementia and madness in general. I said that in my early twenties I believed there was a redemptive and creative element to madness. At that time I was close to the tragedies of the children of older friends, gifted teenagers who became schizophrenic, delusional, paranoid – frightening and self-destructive states that inflicted misery on their respective families. That cured me of romantic notions about creativity and insanity, even as I became interested in John Clare's work. His most famous poem was written in the Northampton insane asylum. Blundy, like his brother-in-law and like me, was a prolific quoter. He murmured the sad hypnotic lines: 'I am! yet what I am who cares, or knows? / My friends forsake me like a memory lost. / I am the self-consumer of my woes'. I said that there was no point pretending Clare was a misunderstood depressive. In later life he was seriously delusional. He claimed he was Shakespeare. But I accepted that he and a few others, including Van Gogh, were exceptions to the rule that psychotic states were terrifying disorders and generally nothing good or wise came out them.

Blundy said that when he was nineteen, he was severely disappointed in love. He took himself off to a borrowed cottage on the north Norfolk coast. He had never taken drugs before but had come into possession of five tabs of LSD. Each one, he had been told, was a 'major trip' and it was advisable to start with a quarter or an eighth. In a dark state, he swallowed all five and within an hour 'I entered hell', and it got worse and lasted not just hours but more than a year. Even then, he was not completely free. Sometimes, without warning, the experience would burst in on him and he would return to a state of terror. After that first hour, everything he looked at – the clouds he saw through a window, the ceiling beams, the dark fireplace – bore a message for him personally of infinite malice. A bush at the window gestured accusations in the wind and blamed him for not killing himself. His hands became independent of his will. He knew that if he let them creep up his chest, as they kept trying to do, they would surely strangle him. He did not dare go outside for help. Obscenely gesturing trees were waiting for him. He was huddled on the living-room floor, his hands clamped between his knees, trembling and mute with fear when a knock sounded on the front door. He heard it open, then heavy steps. A giant lizard with green and blue markings and bloody mouth came right into the room, walking unsteadily on hind legs. It turned on him a look of loathing and swore at him in a language he did not understand. It was clear that he was about to be eaten alive. He screamed continuously until the creature retreated. Now, it too waited for him in the garden. He learned later it was the cleaning lady from the village.

The lizard made me laugh and I could not stop. It was not nerves. I was having fun. Fortunately, he was laughing too. I was in danger of wetting myself, so I stood and went in the direction of his pointing finger to find the bathroom. There I recovered and splashed my face in cold water. When I looked in the mirror I was pleased to see how young I looked. I felt young too. I reckoned that I had not laughed in two years.

When I returned to my seat, Blundy said, 'For eighteen months I was in therapy. I took a year out of my degree course. Mentally, I was badly shaken up. But at least this ridiculous humiliating episode taught me what madness is, what a psychotic paranoid delusion is. The entire universe of objects and people are threatening you with hateful messages. Everything makes horrible sense. You see patterns of dark significance where there are no patterns, no significance, no darkness. You shrink before the world. No good art can come of that. So I bless sanity, and I don't care about the definitions. We know sanity when we can think about and act coherently in the real world, the one that we share. To hell with relativism.'

Staff came in to clear the plates and set out the dessert. I noticed how little we had been drinking. After more than ninety minutes of conversation, the bottle was two-thirds full.

When the waiters had left, I said, 'But you can be sane and bad.'

'Surely. Rational people can do a lot of damage.'

'It's a narrow band. More like a tightrope. Easy to fall off.'

Blundy poured himself some wine at last but put barely an inch into his empty glass, then he passed the bottle to me. As if playing a defensive game of chess, I poured a similar measure.

He said, 'I'm not sure about that, Vivien. There are many ways to be sane.' We were silent for a minute. 'But I like your tightrope. Good or great art might come when the artist thinks he's about to fall, or when he's had an encounter with madness but still knows what's real. Like Blake.'

'Like Sylvia Plath.'

He paused again. I thought he was about to disagree, but he said, 'In the second half of the twentieth century there was no better volume of poetry than *Ariel*. She had her deep disturbances, but only a rational mind could find her kind of poetry to communicate them, the beauty and the terror, the violence . . .'

'Not all dark,' I said. ' "Love set you going like a fat gold watch." ' Following his lead, I forced myself to first-name him. It did not sound right. 'Francis, were your very devout parents insane?'

'Good question.'

We ate the sugary dessert while he thought, and this was where the conversation turned and we talked into the night about our families, that deep well, the shifting story which, even as the years pass, still needs to be rewritten. We had been around the subject many times together, Rachel and I. We summoned our indictments, anger and remorse. Our brother – spoiled brat, druggie disaster, redeemed and living happily with a talented agreeable man – came in for it too. The day might come when, simply to be free, we might dump our gripes in favour of misty celebration of our parents. I already acknowledged that they had rescued me. I was expert at talking about my family, but I was waiting for the poet to go first.

So it began. He explained that his parents were decent people, loving and attentive and, strict Anglicanism apart, his childhood was happy, though constricted by post-war austerity. By his early teens he was out of sympathy with his parents' beliefs. He refused confirmation classes and stopped going to church. There were arguments and distress, particularly for his mother. In the end, what kept the peace was her certainty that as he matured, he would return to the fold. By sixteen he knew he was never coming back. He wanted to be an existentialist and then a socialist and anti-imperialist, and later, a beatnik and then, briefly, a scientist, and finally a freethinking poet. It was harder for Jane. She was two years younger and close to her mother. Her late-teen breakout cost them both dear. Was religion a form of mass delusion or even a mild psychosis? Long ago he used to think so but not now. Too many decent intelligent and fully functioning people were believers. Instead, he thought it might be a deeply embedded inclination within human nature, sustained over hundreds of generations, to find supernatural explanations for natural phenomena. But, 'Now, at last, thunder is not an angry god.'

He was quoting from an early poem. I knew roughly the line that followed but did not want to get it wrong. Here was a new turn – I was anxious for his approval. At least I knew the title. I said, 'Galileo.'

He almost smiled. 'Now it's your turn.'

I let myself go. The high-flying father who thought daughters were not worth educating, the complicit mother who tuned her attitudes and feelings to his, the brother compelled to failure by the pilot's expectations, us girls liberated by neglect into a decent education, but pursued by an emptiness and hunger that we had spent years trying to define. I spoke of my family with an intimacy I had only ever shared with Rachel. I even borrowed some of her lines and spoke for us both. Unprompted, I pushed on into my late teens and my taste for uncaring boyfriends. I set out my theory that it was my father's indifference that I was pursuing. After university came the men, equally terrible in the blur of my estate-agent job and mindless partying. As I described the shared house I began to slow and to hear a drone, a dullness in my voice. I was no longer the expert.

Blundy interrupted. 'If there's something you don't want to tell me, then leave it.'

His tone and look were carefully neutral, but I read into both a degree of acceptance that set me free. I told him the worst story of my life. I laid it out as I had for Percy that morning in the garden. But no tears. I wanted to get it right, and though breathing while speaking was difficult, I thought I brought clarity to my disgrace. I did not hold back from describing my drinking or Diana's face in a pool of sick or how upset I was by the coroner's kindness. I was not the first to discover that it can be easier to tell an intimate secret to a stranger. I pushed on. Rachel's rescue of me, the long retreat at my childhood home, my stony ingratitude towards my parents, the desperate application to do postgraduate work at Oxford where I buried my sorrow in John Clare's.

A waiter came with a tray of coffee. Blundy suggested that I took mine to the sofa while he signed for our meal. Behind me, the dishes were being cleared and loaded onto a trolley. I felt agreeably emptied out. The waiter left. Blundy came to sit beside me and I assumed that now, having exchanged so much, our night must begin. I was resigned rather than actively hungry. I imagined a comic cockney voice saying, ''Ere we go.' Sure enough, Blundy reached for my hand.

'The concierge is calling a taxi for you.' Perhaps he saw in my expression a hint of surprise, for he added, 'We'll meet and talk more. I think we have to.'

I nodded and said, 'I think so too.'

We sat side by side in formal exchange of phone numbers, emails and addresses. The concierge phoned to say that my taxi was waiting. Blundy walked me to the head of the stairs. We did not kiss. He took my hand again and gave a squeeze which I returned, and that was enough.

It was two fifteen when I let myself into the house and removed my shoes. Carrying my bag with its dry toothbrush and fresh underwear, I went stealthily up the steep flight of stairs, avoiding the three treads that creaked. If Percy had woken, he would have made demands and bent my evening out of shape. But it was not easy to sleep. I smiled in the dark at the story of the poor cleaning lady, wearing lipstick I assumed, confronting a screaming lad curled up on the carpet.

I had been an unfaithful wife – again. More seriously this time. If Blundy and I had had a night of wild sex, I could not have betrayed Percy more. I had told another man my most important story, my core of shame, the story that my husband could not retain. I came as close to Blundy as I was to my sister. I had laughed tonight and I had talked and listened in a way I had forgotten was possible. There was another thought, more complicated than the rest. It concerned a failure that should have bothered me more. I had set out to punish Harry Kitchener and discovered in the process something unpleasant in my ingrained passion for revenge. I regretted that but, more importantly, I had allowed myself to become ensnared. There was nothing I could do about it. I had been seduced by

232

conversation, like Desdemona when she listened to Othello 'with a greedy ear'. After Kitchener, Blundy was in another league, a higher and more complex species of human. The mind, as I had already noted, was our most erotic feature. I needed Blundy's mind, just as I had, at other times, needed sex. I longed to turn it on again, this flow between us, the emotional immediacy, the simplicity. I wanted his attentiveness and insight. I had to see him again. Even today, the convention persisted that I should wait for him to contact me, not me him. He might not. He was busily famous, likely to move on. At that possibility, anxiety squeezed my heart and I did not sleep for another two hours.

*

Harry Kitchener's furious letter came later than I expected, almost two weeks after the Sheldonian event. By then, too much had happened, and it gave me little satisfaction. He accused me of 'petty vindictiveness that surprised and disappointed me'. He reminded me that we were consenting adults who had agreed that our affair was over. 'Our responsibilities in this are equal.' Watching me at my 'silly manoeuvres' that night made him ashamed to have been associated with me. What rendered the letter ineffective was the stilted prose. Harry without his sheen of nonchalant irony became a whining supplicant. He did not have the courage to own up to being hurt. His single typed sheet was like a relic of a teenage past, the sort of thing a once-feisty girl might come across years later in an attic shoebox of ardent letters from forgotten boyfriends. I returned the letter to its envelope and slipped it into the book I was reading.

Or trying to read. Thirty pages in a week. In the days that followed the Randolph Hotel evening, my domestic situation became yet more difficult. As if suspecting something, Percy gave up his early nights and was now rarely asleep before midnight. No corner of the day was my own, unless there was an afternoon TV programme that did not upset or excite him. After three days, a friendly email came from Francis Blundy.

233

He wanted to know when and where we could meet. It took much coaxing to get Rachel back. She had been in hospital. Heroically, she agreed to come for one night, but she could not get to Headington until eight.

Same hotel, and a small room now that Francis was paying. This time, conversation was the birdsong that preceded sex. Home again the next morning I thought I might be in love. I told Rachel everything over the phone. When I said I was feeling 'unhinged' looking after Percy, she suggested that I put him into respite care for a few days. I was sickened by the idea, but I arranged to visit again a local place that catered for dementia patients as well as for the vulnerable old. I had no choice but to take my husband along. I told him we were going to look at a hotel. He believed me, but he was reluctant to come. The care home was divided into two 'wings' and we were shown the dementia section first by a friendly Filipina carer who was sweet to Percy. He did not respond.

She knew her charges well. The main room was dominated by a television showing a documentary featuring reindeer. Facing it, in battered high-backed chairs were a dozen residents, some of whom were dozing. We went to the vacant room that could be Percy's. It was eight dilapidated feet by ten. A small window faced onto a wall and a parked car. In the main part for elderly residents of sounder mind, we were shown around by a young woman from Poland, equally friendly and capable. Same big TV with reindeer, and thirty or so watching. On a cork noticeboard was the programme for the week – bingo twice, a singalong, a conjurer. The couple of residents I spoke to, both men, seemed to think I was an official of some kind and were nervously deferential. Silently, I sounded out the depths of my intellectual snobbery. Old people were dim, timid and culturally impoverished, tolerant of condescension and in awe of authority. This was what dragged the country down. Many here would have fought in the last war and seen danger, death and heroism beyond my generation's imagining. Some might have suffered through childhood in the Great Depression. They should be standing on their dignity. I did not ask if there was a little library apart from one pine shelf of severely foxed pulp fiction. I knew the answer. I would rather Percy were dead than leave him here. I could not consign him to that poky room, the singalong and bingo, even for three days. Even for love of a poet.

On the bus home I wondered at the good-natured under-paid staff working in this dreary underfunded place. My selfishness would not allow me to make a sacrifice like theirs. I tried to remember the last time I did anyone a favour. I was that bad. Instead, I asked favours, like phoning my little sister and begging, wheedling and bullying her to come for three or four days at half-term. She refused outright, then guilt crept up on her and she said she would think about it. I suspected she was intrigued by my affair with a famous writer and wanted it to blossom. Her life of childcare, sporadic illnesses, abandoned career and a martinet of a husband must have made my dimin-ished existence appear exotic. While she was making up her mind, Francis wrote to say he had heard of a promising place that had recently opened. So Percy and I took a bus to the east-ern edge of Oxford. We found a Victorian primary school, long abandoned, with smashed windows and wide scorch marks on the brickwork. Rubbish and junk were strewn across the play-ground. A faded sign announced that after refurbishment, a new 'care facility serving the community' would be opening in June 2000, almost two years ago. On the bus ride back, Percy said plaintively, 'I hate hotels. I want to go home.'

With changes of minds and dates along the way, it was fixed – in three weeks, Rachel would come with Peter and stay for four nights. A long time to wait, otherwise a perfect arrangement. Percy and our nephew got along well, and Alz-heimer's had brought them even closer. My mood improved. I had ahead of me, its distance shrinking by the hour, my island of discovery, four unbroken days with Francis.

We were not completely denied each other. Apart from a stream of emails, in which I was disloyally expressive about my frustrations with Percy, we had clandestine meetings at the back of my house. Francis made frequent trips from London to the southern Cotswolds to check on his barn conversion. His route brought him minutes from my house. As he approached the Headington roundabout, he would phone me from his car. If I was occupied with Percy, he would swing right in the Cheltenham direction. If Percy was inert before the TV, he would come straight on into Headington, turn into the gravel lane and park near our back gate, on the exact spot Harry chose when he came to dump me. Francis and I would sit in his car, embrace and talk. We spoke longingly of the four days to come. We were like teenagers in love, though we did not attempt to make love on the back seat. He wanted to show me his barn. There was also a dairy, built in 1804 and not in use for a hundred years. I would see the magnificent setting and meet the architect. I never lingered in the car more than twenty minutes and our partings were tender. 'The time has come,' he would say sometimes in homage to Joyce's 'The Dead', 'for me to set out on my journey westward.' Once, as we hugged, it thrilled me to see that his eyes gleamed with tears. I stood by my gate, watching and waving as he reversed his car through the puddles to make a three-point turn. He would blow me kisses through his open window as he pulled away. Then I would go indoors to resume my role of guardian and nurse.

But now I was animated and cheerful. I had a hazy sense of a new future, of a door opening just a crack, and through it I foresaw the suffering and tragedy that Percy and I must endure before that future was realised. Too bleak to dwell on. I had to live for the present and be a loving wife to Percy, more positive, inventive, and above all kinder. If guilt was driving me, it did not matter. I straightened out the house, especially the living room and Percy's bedroom. I sat with him and we discussed the television he wanted to see. He could not find the programmes or remember their names or when they were on. It was the children's stuff he liked, certain cartoons and *Blue Peter* and 'things about animals'. I wrote out a schedule of times and

236

channels so that each day I could get him to the right place. That made more time for myself, but I sat with him for half an hour every afternoon watching a children's show and talking about it with him. It had to be done immediately. Within minutes his grasp and recollection of what he had just seen began to fade.

A bout of organisation brought me one afternoon to the shed. Whenever I passed it in the garden, I had blocked it out. Too sad a reminder of another life. Now, I could face it and unlocked the door for the first time in eighteen months. I had brought with me a vacuum cleaner and a bucket of cleaning materials. I had no good reason to be spring cleaning here. Percy would never work again, but it helped to pretend that he might. When he returned after a miraculous remission, he would be so pleased to see his studio in good order. Looking after his special place was another way of caring for him. And it was simply too depressing to let it rot.

There were many dead spiders, their bound prey suspended among the ruined webs, there were dust balls, and a fruity smell of neglect. On the workbench, a coffee mug and, at its bottom, a dried disc of mould. The poor yellowish light was at one with the neglect. An overhead bulb did not dissolve the gloom. The problem was the cobwebby windows, stained on the outside by polluted raindrops. The last tool Percy had in his hands, a fine chisel, was lying across the bench. Next to it was a mound of velvet cloth. I unwrapped it and found the replica violin he had been working on. It was without its strings or a bridge. It looked beautiful, ancient. Its sensuous human shape was picked out around its perimeter by a dark raised edge.

As I held the violin in my hands, my good intentions began to collapse. The man who made this gorgeous instrument had vanished. While I stood in his workshop with my stupid array of cloths, cleaning fluids and rubber gloves, another man was slumped in a chair staring dumbly at a cartoon that would barely distract a five-year-old. Despair swelled in me and my grip on the violin tightened. It was senseless, beyond irrational, but I let

237

myself blame Percy for wrecking our lives. Soon, my unpaid leave of absence from the university would be up for review. My academic career was on the edge of collapse. We had no significant savings left. We would live meagrely off the state. Our daily round was nothing but crushing repetition. It was fixed that everything must get worse – slowly and with only one end. It was his brain, not mine, that was ruining us. Our lives were wasted. His violin stood for the life we once had. I was suddenly furious. From nowhere, its name came back to me. I held the Guarneri by its narrow black neck and lifted it high, ready to use all my strength to crash it down against the workbench. Just then, I saw hanging from a peg the apron and goggles that little Peter used to wear when Percy brought him into his workshop and found things for him to do. He was so kind to the boy, so sweetly protective, always ready to take him seriously in their long chats. Even now, Percy was lovely with him. He would have been a wonderful father. Remembering what he once was pulled me back from self-pitying rage. I set the violin down, paused to calm myself, then wrapped it in its velvet cloth. I became tearful with remorse as I stepped outside and started to clean the windows – self-pity in a harmless form. I checked on Percy, then came back to the shed to dust and tidy the shelves and workbench and vacuum the floor.

I had started keeping a journal soon after seeing my future husband playing in his jazz band in the Cowley pub. My entries were never regular, and I often had to force myself to write them. I tried to keep going because, like Francis, I believed that most of life is oblivion. To rescue fragments of the past would be to claim a bigger existence. I had made other attempts in my teens, twenties and thirties, and each time had given up after a year or two because I was too busy or too tired or because my life was too repetitive. This time, I was determined to hold on until old age defeated me. Like most people who talk in private to themselves on the page, my loyalties were to the truth as I understood it at the time. If I had to present myself in a poor light, I did not care. I had read several published journals over the years. Among my favourites were Samuel Pepys, of course, and a politician, Alan Clark. Neither was afraid of letting the world know they could be calculating liars, greedy, selfish, vain and disagreeable. I aspired to their high standards, and I failed. I began to worry about the future of my journals after I was dead. I did not want Peter as an adult to know how weak I was. At the end of my life, I might not have the strength of mind to destroy an extended record of myself. But if I was going to destroy it, no point writing it. Subtly, my journals were becoming the report of a better self. I would have denied it, but over time the entries ceased to be private. I had a reader in mind.

When I spoke to Rachel that evening, I described coming across the violin and 'becoming upset'. Not untrue, but not the truth. My dear sister was tender and sympathetic. Before going to bed that night I told my journal the same story. I was teaching myself to lie by omission. Most useful, for behind and ahead of me were acts that were too shocking to own.

*

Percy was in deep unhinged conversation with Peter, and Rachel was watching television. I was able to leave the house by the front door without fuss. Francis was waiting for me in his car. We kissed and as he pulled away from the kerb, I put my hand on his knee.

'Do that and I won't be able to think straight.'

I laughed and kept it there. And he was right, for when we got to Headington High Street, he turned towards the centre of Oxford instead of making for the inner ring road a short distance away. He had a second chance moments later and could have turned at the filter towards Marston, but he kept on. I said nothing. He had made this journey many times. We crossed Folly Bridge and stopped behind a long line of traffic. There were a dozen policemen ahead of us, two on horses. Streaming past us, heading in the same direction, were the city's young, mostly students, some with placards. I remembered. A cabinet minister with responsibilities for the environment would be talking at the Union that evening. A big climate-change

239

demonstration was planned. St Giles and the surrounding streets would be closed. On banners and posters I saw black capitals on red background – OIL IS GREED and BEWARE SEA LEVELS. Every minute of my four days was precious to me, and I was annoyed with them all, until Francis took over. His knuckles were white as he gripped the wheel. He was a better hater than me. He thumped the wheel with a fist.

'Fucking loony-left dupes. Ignorant credulous scum. God-damnit! We can't even turn round.'

For obscure reasons of their own, the police had closed off the other side of the road. The traffic was stalled ahead of us and piling up behind. We were trapped. Blundy's outburst obliterated my own irritation. I muttered, 'Well, I suppose the kids might have a point.'

He turned on me and shouted. 'I can't believe you've fallen for this fucking claptrap. You idiot! You, an educated—'

That did it. Life with a demented husband had worn my tol-erance low. I unfastened my seat belt and put my hand on the door release. 'Enough. I'll walk back.' I pushed the door open a few inches and took my bag. I could not believe that I was about to get out. He clutched at my arm.

'I'm sorry, I'm really sorry. That was rude. Appalling. I apol-ogise. Please, please don't get out.'

I said, 'I didn't know you could be a screaming hysteric.' Even talking to him was a concession. But I did not push the door further. My teenage self would have known how delicious it would be to get out. I had a streak of stubborn sulkiness back then. But misery would follow, and much untangling, accord-ing to the grown woman who knew that Francis could coax her back. I hovered between these selves.

'I beg you to accept my apology. It was disgusting behav-iour. I've thought of nothing else but this time together. We got stuck here and I exploded. Humiliating. Disgusting. Honestly, it will never happen again.'

I took my hand off the door, but I did not close it. 'All this swearing makes you sound like an old man out of control.'

My voice belonged to a prim stranger. When it suited me, I liked swearing. I looked through the windscreen. The police were letting cars through one at a time at longish intervals. I pulled the door shut.

He murmured, 'No more swearing, I promise.'

We sat in silence, waiting for the bad moment to dissolve. He knew it was too soon to reach for my hand, and I was glad of that. It took us fifteen minutes to reach the front of the line. We were not permitted to turn right and loop round to our route north then west. Instead, we were sent up the High Street. When Francis had to stop to let a surge of demonstrators cross the road, he remained silent. I was familiar with his kind of views. I occasionally read the *Telegraph*, *Spectator* and *Wall Street Journal* among others. Francis was hardly alone. I assumed something nasty in the climate was coming our way, but slowly, and it did not occupy me much. I felt vaguely grateful that others were protesting on my behalf. Further on we were sent on a long clockwise turn around the city centre, past the ice rink, where Percy used to take Peter, across Hythe Bridge where I dreamed once of heading north on a barge. We passed Worcester College where, as a student, I was found in bed with a disagreeable rugby player, now high up in railway management. Then, past the Phoenix cinema, where I once watched the same Éric Rohmer film three nights in a row.

All these landmarks in a city from which I had been isolated. They seemed drearily familiar and again, as we headed westwards at last, crossing open country at speed, I indulged dreams of leaving when, of course, I had to stay. But I was leaving now, and here was my dhow. Setting out in it with a man I thought I might love, a man who thumped the steering wheel in fury while shouting at me, thereby fulfilling my preferred form of partner. No escape from myself, whichever compass point I fled to. If I stayed and one day resumed my career, I would not only be teaching, I would be fighting again, in committees. We had fought off the construction of a giant mosque on land part-owned by the college, just as we would have opposed a

241

giant cathedral, but we failed against a business-studies building. Biotech was blurring the boundaries between commerce and academia, kids were deserting literature and history to get rich in finance, underqualified foreign students were admitted as cash cows, and we, the old guard, argued against it all and defended our shrinking corner of the humanities, not yet as underfunded as other places, but demoralised, uncertain, our old centrality to the culture gone, our various subjects sunk in the postmodern turmoil of their separate civil wars over 'theory', or race or gender or social exclusion – battles that were mostly generational and unnaturally fierce. It was time to leave.

Ten miles out of the city, the atmosphere between Francis and me neutralised. We talked of harmless matters and collaborated in persuading our four days back into their proper shape. Our destination was a useful subject and he spoke of the project with excitement. I asked obliging questions. The architect and foreman would be there to walk him round the site and talk through latest developments and problems. There were already cost overruns, but he had planned for those. What was in prospect, he explained, was a radical shift in his life. He was exchanging a town house in Islington for a rural idyll, one existence for another. He had been amazed by how much his London place was worth. A charming woman from a village close by would be a part-time housekeeper, and chauffeur once he had taken the decision to give up driving. Her husband would be occasional gardener and handyman. Bookshelves were being constructed in a workshop near Witney and were going to be beautiful, the views of the valley from the master bedroom would be stunning and his study, already taking shape, was unlike any he had ever had. As he went on, I had the sense, vague at first, that Francis was talking of a future in which I was implicated. He referred again to an outbuilding, the dairy, in which he thought I would take a special interest. He did not wish to say more about it now. It was absurd, for he knew my circumstances, but it was also amusing, even a touch erotic, and I played along and said I couldn't wait to see it.

Some miles from Stroud, we turned down a narrow road with passing places, and two miles later we took a narrower farm track cut into the steep side of a valley of mature beech trees. Thirty feet below us was a meadow of buttercups, and a stream with a wooden footbridge, and before us the head of the valley rose to a natural plateau in the centre of which was the big barn, its roof covered in plastic sheeting and surrounded by scaffolding. Several cars and vans were parked close by. Our track dipped down to cross the stream and rose again to the site.

In a portable cabin, where plans and diagrams were spread on a table among chocolate-bar wrappers and empty mugs containing used tea bags, I was introduced to the architect Simon, the foreman Vicenc, and a couple of the trades. I was given a yellow jacket and hard hat to wear and heavy boots that had been ordered specially in my size. After some routine jokes about health and safety regulations, we went on the tour. The barn, two centuries old, was enormous. Partition walls were already in place. I was advised to be careful stepping over power cables, copper pipes and bags of cement as I was shown round various rooms in the making and asked if I could stretch my imagination to grasp the beauty of it. I could. I kept saying, 'How lovely.' A long corridor opened out at one end into the poet's sunlit study. In the huge open space that would be the kitchen, dining and living room, an immense limestone fireplace was under construction.

Discussions began and Francis was required to make decisions. I did not think he cared for or much understood the technical details, but he was anxious to show that he was in charge. Simon and Vicenc steered their client to the correct or convenient choices. I left them and wandered away from the barn and crossed to a hedge where there was an old gate, beyond which the ground dropped gently towards the stream, almost a river, that wound across the rich green and yellow meadow. Francis had told me it ran uninterrupted by hedges and fences for at least a mile. John Clare, who lamented the

243

enclosure of land, would have exulted in it. I had assumed that Francis, as new and proud owner, had been exaggerating the attractions of his acquisition, but it was an enchanting location. Most valleys like this had traffic running through them. It was a secluded place suspended beyond time, a secret that had to be kept. Standing there, somewhat rapt, I began to think of Francis in different terms, as a capable man of interesting tastes, one who could take control of his fate and steer it towards an enviable unusual result. Where most would be content with a terraced house, he had taken possession of this plot at the top of a gem of an isolated valley and was ready to make a new life on his own terms. He dominated people with his own style of reasoned kindness. There was no scheming. He did not even know he was doing it. He was logical and he cared. It was obvious to him that the one he cared for should do as he suggested. I thought of him then, not as a poet – that was a side issue – but as someone determined to have what he wanted, and I felt a little afraid, and at the same time exhilarated, a mix I had not experienced since my early twenties.

I heard him calling me and went back across a muddy and rutted terrain which, Simon had explained, would be an immense lawn framed by flower beds. I had forgotten about the dairy. It was on the far side of the barn and Francis was outside it now, waiting for me. It was a dilapidated building of weathered honey-coloured stone, in contrast to the barn's darker brick and timber. A set of high double doors, wide enough for two cows to step indoors side by side, was rotting and the hinges were partly torn from their timber frame. Perched on the roof line was a crumbling dovecote.

Francis was in a high state. 'What do you think?' he shouted twice over, when I was still a way off. 'Wouldn't it be perfect?'

For what, for whom? I did not ask. When we went inside, he steered me around, gripping my elbow, for fear I might run off. There was not much to see. The old milking stalls were still in place, but the building had been used as a beef-cattle shed by the last owners. With extravagant sweeps of an arm, Francis set out his plan. A big study here with woodburning stove, small bedroom on this side for those nights of working late, a good bathroom right where we were standing, this window enlarged for the view, a separate lavatory over to the left, a counter for making coffee, a butler sink, a fridge. Perfect, was it not? I said it was perfect.

We stayed on site two hours. Before leaving, I would have liked to take the path down the valley to the footbridge, but Francis insisted that we had a long drive ahead and he was already feeling tired. Three hours later we were parking in a street of flat-fronted dove-grey terraced houses of, I guessed, the early nineteenth century. Francis's place was the sort of tasteful book-crammed environment I was familiar with from the homes of north Oxford colleagues. In a knocked-through sitting room on the ground floor, above an outsized fireplace, hanging at a careless tilt, was a long-ago gift, a Howard Hodgkin painting that overflowed onto its frame. Elsewhere in that room was a baby grand, an ancient gramophone with a brass horn, and two giant chesterfields facing each other across a long oak coffee table piled with books and periodicals. I lay on one of the sofas with a cup of strong tea, reading a recent copy of *Areté* while Francis snoozed upstairs. It was an unexpected way to begin an idyll, but I was content. Precious, to have time alone to read or browse, or kick off my shoes, lie back and stare at the brown stains on the ceiling and think of nothing much. I felt at home in this scruffy serious room.

I woke to the sound of footsteps on the stairs and was struggling into a sitting position as Francis entered. He was in fresh white shirt and grey flannel trousers with sharp creases. His face was pink from his shower. He had a drink in his hand, and billowing under his chin was a paisley cravat, a modest item of male display I had not seen in years and it made me smile. My bag was upstairs, he said, and a bath was drawn. He would be waiting here for me and we could discuss dinner. For half an hour I lay below the rising steam, staring up at another stained ceiling. From downstairs I heard a familiar Satie piece played clumsily, with many pauses and faltering repetitions. I hoped it was not for my benefit. I had not bought new clothes in a long while, and as I went downstairs I felt mousey and vaguely undefended – a feeling I get wearing the wrong stuff. Francis sprang out of his chair when I entered and offered to 'build' me a drink and told me how well I looked.

'You are a gent,' I said. 'A negroni please. That was you at the piano.'

While he mixed my cocktail, he told me how he had wanted piano lessons all his life but at every stage, from when he was twenty, he thought he was too late, too old to start. Eighteen months ago, just after his fiftieth birthday, he got down to it. Six months ago he had taken his Grade One exam. He found himself in an anteroom with other students, waiting to be called in. In silence, they sat on identical dining chairs, probably from a job lot.

'I was the only one there whose feet reached all the way to the ground. The others, little girls from the same school, with bunches, pigtails and white ribbons, nervously swung their legs while they waited. And I couldn't. But we all passed! Afterwards, very excited, we compared notes, as one does, and told our stories, where we went wrong with "Frère Jacques" or with the scales and how we thought we were bound to fail. Vivien, those kids treated me as one of their own. I never felt so flattered and happy.'

I listened to this story as the icy negroni warmed my throat and chest and suspected that there might be no going back. How far removed he was from that intimidating spectre at the Sheldonian. What man had ever run me a bath and offered to construct for me a luxurious study in a pastoral paradise? It aroused me to think I had no choice. I went to where he sat, took his head between my hands and kissed it. Then I found his lips. Our operetta of an idyll began with our making love on the chesterfield. I worried that the curtains were not drawn and we could be seen from the street. But the high back of the sofa sheltered us. It was as if this was something we did every evening, for later we gathered up our clothes from the floor and dressed in a routine sort of way while we discussed where we would eat. Like a couple married for thirty years. He suggested an Italian place where he was known – a few minutes' walk away, five tables crammed into a busy kitchen. There we ate parmigiana and a green salad, and this was where I learned for certain what I had suspected. Francis was planning the life we would lead together. The building site became the Barn. For the first time I heard the word capitalised as he conjured our work-places, my dairy, his study, the books and poems we would write, the garden we would tend, the friends we would invite. It was delightful nonsense. I had to interrupt.

'Francis. You know I can't.'

But that too was, as builders say, all taken for. He allowed for a change of subject by reaching for my hand across the table and remaining silent for several seconds.

'I understand. But we know that your situation can't last.'

I waited.

'You know better than I do. It's a progressive disease. Soon you won't be able to manage. That means some kind of care home. Or something. After that there's the only end, as Larkin put it. It will be very very hard for you. I want you to know that on the far side, there's a life.'

But Francis knew there was no care home. I felt suddenly sick. Too much olive oil in the aubergines. I drank deeply from my water glass and said, 'I can't think that far ahead.'

'No need. But I can. That is, if you'd like me to.'

'I don't know. I need to think. It feels . . . callous, having a plan while he's still . . . it's bad faith.'

'I understand.'

'I need to think.'

He said gravely, 'Take your time.'

We went back to his place, undressed in his bedroom and made love again before we slept. I was intrigued to find in Francis the lover a tender submissiveness – such a contrast to his fully clothed and commanding social self. He wanted me to take the initiative, which was not in the pattern of my usual choice of man. I was hesitant, then I adapted without much effort and felt happy and free. The pattern was set for the next four days – reading, talking, sleeping, loving and restaurants – my kind of Elysium – until it was time for me to go home.

*

I am writing these words in longhand at a wooden table in our back garden. The view below me includes Glenuig Bay, a pub and its car park, and away to my right, steep hills rising towards Mount Roshven. Early May, a slight breeze, no midges yet, and at my back, indoors, Jane Kitchener is preparing sandwiches for our muddy tramp through Smirisary to Port Achadh an Aonaich, a sandy beach favoured by kayakers. I have yet to pronounce its name correctly. The local people are friendly towards us. None of this 'it takes forty years to be almost accepted'. Besides, a few around here, including our electrician and our roofer, are English too. I heard by a roundabout manner that we are known as 'the two widows'. No contesting that. Our departed husbands preoccupy us, but we are businesslike about it, or them, and our lives of elective exile are pleasant enough.

My journals are on a shelf above a writing desk in our cottage sitting room, but I'm happier to be free of them and exercising my memory. Working hard at it, as in a mental gym, making the effort and prising open a scene, opens others along the way. It gets easier the more I try. In addition, guilt and remorse are useful aids to memory. I use the journals mostly to remind myself of the sequence of events, on which memory is notoriously weak. The past, jumbled in the mind, survives in its own special tense, a form of ahistorical present. A journal, whatever its quality, fixes events like beads on a string.

*

Returning from my four nights in London to my earthbound existence was easier this time. I was helped, paradoxically, by an immediate crisis. No time for lamenting fate, mine or Percy's. The evening before I got back, he and Peter were happily playing a board game. It came out of nowhere, a sudden frightening lunge, and Percy slapped the boy hard about the face. I saw it for myself the next day, a tender red patch on Peter's cheek. He would not go near his uncle. Rachel was desperate to leave. Percy was sulking in his bedroom. He had forgotten the incident, but its shadow darkened his mood. He knew something was up and that he was to blame. I wasted much time attempting to get him to come down and apologise. I had in mind how much I would be needing Rachel and Peter in future. But Percy lay on his back on the bed, forearm covering his eyes, refusing to move or speak. Rachel's suitcase was already in her car. Usually, we passed an hour together before she set off. This time, she was curt. She'd had enough, she had problems of her own. When I spoke cheerily to Peter, he turned away. I was lumped with Percy into the single source of pain and humiliation.

After they had left, it took up much of the evening, coaxing Percy downstairs to watch some old recordings of children's TV that I kept for times like these. Slowly, his mood improved. While he watched a programme about a petting zoo, I made supper. My attempts to get him to talk about his attack on his nephew went nowhere. It was gone. Instead, we sang some songs and looked through a photo album together and talked about the pictures, or I talked about them, our adventures in the past. Here was Percy, backpack in one hand, car keys in the other, outside an inn by the Evenlode River. Here I was on a woodland path by a patch of bluebells. Here was a smiling Percy presenting a recently completed violin to a happy customer. To each photograph, Percy made an appreciative humming sound of assent. Our doctor had told me that this was an effective way of keeping the memory from decaying. It was hopeless, but I persisted. There was nothing else to do in the hours before bedtime.

When at last Percy was asleep I read three emails from Francis but was too tired to write more than, 'Some pressure here.

Will write in the morning.' I hesitated over the usual last three words. I had just kissed Percy goodnight. The betrayal, my outrageous infidelity, was too fresh for my exhausted spirits. But omitting our habitual sign-off would demand an explanation. So I wrote the sentence anyway. 'I love you.'

After those Islington days, everything stood still for Francis and me. There were various unconnected factors. I could not get away to be with him. My sister and Peter, or my sister alone, were no longer available. That slap apart, Rachel had marital difficulties and she had breast cancer. Peter was frightened of his uncle. Work on the Barn slowed after foreman Vicenc returned to Estonia to care for his ill mother. It was hard to replace him. There were tensions between Francis and the architect Simon over a miscalculation of the strength of a steel joist. The house sale in Islington foundered and the process had to begin again with a new buyer. Percy was no longer crossing the plateau of his illness towards another stage. He had set up home on the heights and was not budging, not declining. There was nothing progressive about his condition. This was who he was, sometimes angry, sometimes childlike, always demanding, occasionally loveable. I remained determined to keep him at home. I could manage, just about. Francis and I emailed every day and continued to meet at least twice a week in the lane out the back as he detoured from his Barn business on outward and return journeys.

Brazenly, I tried incorporating Francis into my domestic life and on four occasions he came into the house. He was introduced as a colleague from college, not that Percy could have held that or any other of my lies in mind for long. Francis brought presents each time, including a pocket screen loaded with Disney cartoons. Percy loved it but did not remember for long how he came by it. He remained suspicious of Francis, then rude, and on the final visit a touch aggressive, so we gave up. Our erotic horizon shrank to kisses in the car, but mostly we held hands and talked. Perhaps it was good for us. I liked to think we came to know each other better than many lovers

250

do. Our sessions were always short, for I could not leave Percy alone for long. We did not waste time. Our conversations were urgent and to the point. Francis talked about the love poems he had written in the weeks after our Islington time. He read them to me in the car and left various drafts. I made suggestions, some of which, to my surprise, he accepted. He spoke about the oppression of fame, the constant demands on his time, the good causes that would not let him go, the careless promises he made that 'come back to bite me'. Retreating to the quiet valley would be his way out. He expected his work to move into new territory and he was impatient to begin. He talked often of how it would be when we lived together at the Barn. There would be herbs growing in earthenware pots outside the kitchen. We would have poultry and eat fresh eggs for breakfast. I always felt guilt, but I could not help myself, I joined in and told him how I would love to be feeding the hens each morning. These exchanges were a delightful form of escapism.

I told Francis about my plans for a book I'd had in mind for years. It would be a well-illustrated life of Thomas Aiken-head, the last person to be executed for blasphemy in Britain. He was a highly gifted twenty-year-old Scot, whose eloquent and heartfelt apologies for questioning the existence of God could not save him from the granite authority of the Presby-terian Kirk – and, in 1697, the gallows. His case gratified some, outraged others. My book would explore the religious and intellectual turmoil of the late seventeenth century. Francis was encouraging, though he had never heard of Aikenhead. The converted dairy, Francis said, would be just the place to write such a book.

This period of stasis between us lasted months. But there were other developments. The Islington house was sold, but for less than Francis had expected. The proceeds of sale went to settle the Barn debts. Francis was broke. When my unpaid sabbatical ended, I resigned from my college. Someone fresh, not a series of part-timers, should be hired to take on my load. The man who had tried to take away the little boy on the station platform was found guilty of a separate offence and his picture was in the national press. When I had seen him last, he was being driven to a police cell. The following day he was returned to prison for breaking the terms of his parole. For the new offence he was sent down for a further six years. I took Percy to see the neurologist, who thought his patient was 'doing just fine' apart from being less steady in his movements. He had developed a tentative gait, as though he could not trust the ground under his feet. Apart from that, little change.

Whatever it was that began to shift came on slowly and at first I thought low spirits were distorting my judgement. I began to think that Francis was having a change of heart. My anxieties would come on in the small hours when I should have been sleeping in preparation for Percy's early-morning starts. The emails Francis sent were shorter, less inventive. He was subdued in our meetings in the lane, his tone was flatter. He had cancelled twice. He kissed me only at our hellos and goodbyes. He was behaving as I would if I were seeing someone else. With these thoughts, our project, our life beyond the unnameable ceased to be a pleasant fantasy. It became a lifeline, sensible, necessary, profoundly desirable.

I intended to confront him but once he was beside me in the car, I couldn't do it. I was frightened of having my suspicions confirmed, and if I was wrong, I risked angering him or even driving him away. But one afternoon, while Percy was absorbed in a TV drama about sheepdogs and the rain was coming down heavily, swelling the clay puddles and hammering on the car's roof, Francis told me without prompting. He laid matters out in the correct order. First, he loved me. Second, he knew my situation was truly awful. Third, everything was stalled between us and it was hard for him too. So, yes, he was having a fling, more than one, and he thought it was right that I should know. I could not stop nodding at each of these items. I was neither wretched nor furious. I was making calculations. A fling that could not threaten our love was merely a first stage.

It could be an accurate description of a changing situation. One of those flings could blossom and meanwhile I was nailed in place, unable to oppose the process or give anything to the relationship. But all I said was, 'I see.'

We listened to the thunderous rain. I assumed he was waiting for me to say more, but I was wrong. He was preparing to pronounce what at first sounded like the inevitable notice of termination. He raised his voice against the downpour.

'Vivien, you must have thought this through as well. We don't dare talk about it. We thought your sister would be on hand. Now she isn't. You tell me that Percy's crossing a plateau. What happens when he gets to the far side and goes into serious decline? How are you going to manage?'

'I've told you. Health visitors, three times a day. It's a free service. I can get help with nights too. He needs to stay in familiar surroundings.'

'He could live for years. Dorothy Wordsworth was nuts for twenty before she died. Are we going to keep doing this for twenty years? Meeting in my car?'

I said, 'If you want to move on, then do it. I'm not going to argue about it.'

'I'm not moving on. I love you. We're in love. We're staring at an amazing existence together in a beautiful place. Inches away from paradise, but we can't touch it. It's clear to me and it should be to you.'

'Meaning?'

He paused and looked away. 'He has to go into care.'

That again. I spoke as if to a child. 'You know I've been back. He came with me. I'm not putting him in there. Or any place like it.'

'As you've said.'

'I don't have the money for private care. I can hardly pay the mortgage here. And you're broke.'

'Exactly.'

The rain was easing off and I was able to lower my voice. 'So what's your point?'

'It's this.' He too lowered his voice, but to a fraction above a whisper and repeated slowly, 'We have to act.'

He spread his hands as he said this. Seconds passed before I understood him. When I did, I laughed like an inept actor in a terrible amateur play. Looking into his eyes, I saw he was serious. I felt a chill in my legs rising and spreading into my gut. A bad smell, my own, appropriately sulphurous, filled the small space.

I said, 'Ridiculous. Disgusting. No.' And again, 'Francis, no!'

'You won't have to do anything, I promise you.'

I laughed again. I was so nervous, so horrified that I didn't know if I could stop.

He added, 'Face it. Percy has a lot of suffering ahead of him.'

For the second time, mid-conversation with Francis in his car, I felt for the door release. Getting away from him was all I could think of.

He put a hand on my forearm to restrain me. 'I want you to listen to what I'm saying. It's either-or. We act, or we part, however much it hurts. I can't tolerate any more of this, and I promise you, if you agree, all the risks will be mine.'

When I got out of his car, I did not pause to close the door behind me. I hurried through our gate, bolted it and ran across the garden, past Percy's shed and into the house.

*

Around 4 a.m., during a long night of insomnia, I sat up in bed and wrote an email to my sister. Not to my real sister, who was ill, but to the phantom sister of my turbulent thoughts.

Dear Rachel,
Three days ago, Francis Blundy kindly offered to murder Percy, promising no risk to myself, so that we can go and live together out at his country place. Sensible plan? Any thoughts?

I did not put her name in the address field for fear of my finger accidentally touching the send button. Now I could see in summary, in typed letters rather than in my thoughts, how bizarre, how extreme the idea was. My sardonic or jokey tone was self-protection. I did not want those words too long on my screen in case some form of electronic palimpsest developed that I could never erase. Lady Macbeth's damned spot. Over and over, my eyes travelled along the lines and back to the beginning. The more I read, the more implicated I became. The message was now stupid and dull and . . . I struggled for the word. Less frightening? No. *Normalised.* My typed words drew me into a simple pain-saving arrangement, a form of rational extralegal euthanasia. I could not go to the police. I was already party to murderous intent. Too late to phone them now and I never would.

I positioned the cursor by the final full stop, kept my forefinger on the back button and erased the message word by word. As soon as my email vanished, my thoughts swayed dizzily. I wanted the message back. It had steadied me, it concentrated the issue, it reminded me of what was wrong, and therefore, of what was right. Staring into the screen I saw, or imagined I saw, the faintest impression of the word 'sensible'. I did not dare type the email again. Computers were routinely hacked, by governments as well as by fraudsters. Besides, for some reason, I could not recall the vaguely comic way I had set the matter out for my sister.

I moved heavily through the week, unable to think of much else, stunned by lack of sleep, more irritable than usual with Percy. I did not write to Francis, nor did I hear from him. He was waiting for my decision. Even to withhold it in writing, I supposed, would implicate me. As far as I knew, there were complex definitions around the legal concept of conspiracy. I had to be careful. But like an idiot, I missed him. Months of talking in his car had brought him closer to me. He was my best friend, best confidant, the brother I never had in Sam. I could have written and blandly suggested that we meet up. I resisted because I was also frightened of him, of his ability to talk me into something crazed and loathsome. I developed a theory that his 'we have to act' was an expression of sexual frustration. If only we could have made love. I had discovered in him that surprising element of sexual surrender, submissiveness even, an element that he would never acknowledge. No need, as long as we were physically close and it was an unspoken secret between us. I recalled reading that Hemingway in later life had sexual fantasies of being a little girl in a frilly white frock. He was dressed that way as a small child. Hunting rifle or deep-sea fishing rod in hand, his urge was to be in command. Likewise, Francis, behind the wheel of his car, fully clothed and safely distanced from the erotic, unthinkingly assumed power over me. If we could have spent time in bed, some form of balance could be reinstated. Together we might be reasonable. It crossed my mind that if we ever lived together without sex, he would crush me.

But Rachel, who had been about to come over at last and relieve me, was in hospital again. Peter had written an affectionate note in extravagant copperplate and seemed to have forgotten the slap. He would come as soon as his mother was feeling better. Among my academic friends there was no one I could trust to be with Percy for the night. His musician friends had dropped away. We were alone together, but not in the same way as before. Even as I rejected it, Francis's proposal lay between Percy and me, almost invisible, like a polished sheet of glass. I felt horror and guilt, then sudden tenderness like an electric charge, or occasionally, an eerie sense of distance from him as if he was already *gone* – I could use no other word – and he was appearing before me like a vivid memory. I had to turn away and compose myself.

The dull rhythm of these days was interrupted by a sad outing, but it was social at least and involved a journey. My dear friend Martha MacLeish, the brilliant scholar of contemporary French literature, died peacefully at home. She had held out longer than her doctors had predicted and during that time, bedridden, often in pain, had written some fine monographs and completed her translations of lesser-known essays by Simone de Beauvoir. I had often been out to see her before Percy became ill, and we had talked for hours and even laughed at some old stories. Now he and I were making the journey together, bus to Oxford station, local train to Martha's village, taxi to the village church. I needed to reassure Percy several times that we were not going to look at a hotel. Apart from that, he was content to stare out the window.

Many academic colleagues were there, gathered in knots among the graves, waiting to go in. It touched me that at least half the congregation was French. We were an irreligious crowd, but conventional in our acceptance of what must be gone through. It often happened when a faithless friend died without leaving instructions, church rituals were the default, and the godless living were relieved. We lustily sang the improbable words of the familiar hymns and listened to the likeable vicar evoke the everlasting bliss of the afterlife which Martha was beginning now. How we would have loved it to be true. But it was soothing to hear someone appear to believe that it was waiting for us all. Percy was unusually well behaved. He sat and stood in time with everyone else, sang the hymns and even knew some of the words. Those memories were laid down long ago and not yet lost. Martha's family had asked four of us to address the congregation. I was first to mount the carved oak pulpit. I spoke of her courage, her impish sense of humour and her brilliant scholarship. While the others, including a poised twelve-year-old granddaughter, gave their speeches, my thoughts wandered.

Each time I passed through that rural station on my way to Martha's house, difficult memories of Christopher had returned. It was not the fear that came back, nor did I think much about the sudden improbable appearance of the police. It was the moment of my arrival and my first sight of the boy at the end of the platform, near the red sign that warned

257

passengers off the concrete slope that descended to the tracks. In memory, the landscape was vast, towering above his minute form as he stared, with his back to me, at the distant tunnel through which his mother had vanished. He craved the return of the love of his life. He could have no grasp of how lost and helpless she herself was in the face of real and imagined problems. What I felt now in church and whenever I had passed through that station was a longing to comfort the abandoned boy, draw him onto my lap, hold him in my arms and ask his forgiveness. Squashed into the front row of pews with friendly strangers, no one knew that my tears were not for Martha but for my lost girl who would have been my lifelong friend, in her early twenties now, at the dawn of her exciting adult life. The boy on the platform was her sad emissary, her brother come to make me reckon again for what I did.

Two days after the funeral, there was a development that in my haunted state seemed like an extension of my punishment. In his sleep Percy crapped copiously in his bed. Cleaning him up and sorting out the bedding took more than half the night. By 4 a.m. he was determined to be up and dressed and eating a cooked breakfast. He wanted to phone someone, though he was not sure who. He insisted on going out for a walk. He wanted all three at once and was distressed in his confusion. After that, his sleep routines went to pieces and mine, already fragile, went with them. Gradually, a new pattern set in. He was asleep by seven or eight in the evening, then awake and ready to be up and dressed between two and three in the night. On one occasion, I was about to get up with him, then fell asleep to be woken later by the police bringing him home. Another time, local search and rescue volunteers brought him back. With two or three hours' sleep a night, I entered a dream state in which it was sometimes an effort to grasp what was real. Hallucinated objects, people and landscapes drifted on the edge of vision. Snatches of dreams invaded my waking experience. My heart often skipped a beat, then landed with a thump that made me clutch at my chest. I could be on my feet, sleeping for seconds at a time. It was easier for me to give in to every demand Percy made. When he shook me awake at 3 a.m. to tell me that he wanted to go out for a walk, it was less stressful to get up and go with him and avoid making tea at 5 a.m. for the search and rescue team.

It was foolish of me to resume emails to Francis, bleak descriptions that were also self-pitying complaints, pleas for help, expressions of despair. His replies were loving. At least we were back in touch. When he asked me to book an appointment at a particular private care home twenty miles away, I assumed he had come into some money, and I complied. I could not ask Rachel for help because she was undergoing radical surgery. I sent her fruit and flowers and goodwill messages. It was not clear to me if Percy was finally descending from his plateau and was in free fall, or if this was a temporary dip in a level terrain. None of it mattered. All I needed to do was keep going. Certain everyday duties helped. We still went out together to the shops. The kitchen had to be tidied, the cooking and laundry seen to. I thought I could fall in with Percy's new sleep pattern. But by the early evening I was jaggedly alert, beyond sleep, incapable of anything apart from writing to Francis again.

I could not recall how long this ghostly period lasted. In memory it squatted across months, and this is where the journals have helped. There were few entries, but the dates are clear. It was forty-three days. The differences blurred between an intention and the memory of a completed act, between imagining and knowing, hoping and having, and finally, I suppose, between right and wrong. The date for the care-home visit came, but Percy refused to go near 'another hotel'. I did not have the strength of purpose to persuade or force him. I phoned the place to apologise and the kindly voice of the receptionist made me tearful. When I told Francis that we had missed the appointment, he did not seem to care.

A week later, at around ten in the evening, I was in the kitchen, sitting at the hinged Formica-topped table I kept there for tea and coffee equipment. Percy was asleep. I had been upstairs half an hour before to check on him. I was not reading or even thinking. I was in my customary daze, too hot in the head to go to bed, too worn out to write another email or start on the dishes and pans piled by the sink. If I had heard the back garden gate opening, I would not have stirred. My indifference was profound. But when I heard tapping on a pane of the French windows, I was startled and turned and saw in the dark the faint sketch of a face. Francis was wearing leather gloves and a black wide-brimmed hat I had never seen before. When I let him in, we did not embrace. He looked unwell. There was a hint of blueish green about his pallor. Perhaps he hadn't shaved. He was carrying a cloth shoulder bag. It was odd, but I was not surprised to see him.

I said stupidly, 'What are you doing?'

'Where is he?'

'Asleep. Where are you going?'

'I want you to stay here.'

It should have been obvious where he was going and what he was about to do. I was in a state of stupefaction, of vegetative slowness. More than half a minute passed before I moved. I tried to hurry but my legs were heavy and wouldn't respond. It was as if I was wading thigh-deep in treacle. I would have had a hard time explaining myself. If my mind was such a blank, why had I stood up, why was I trying to hurry? Something was about to happen that I knew I had to prevent. No one would believe that I knew and, simultaneously, did not know, or preferred not to. Logic dissolved. I got myself out of the kitchen and as I was going along the passageway towards the stairs I heard voices. Francis was saying something to Percy, who called out my name, though not in an anxious way. As I reached the foot of the stairs, Percy was coming down them, head first, arms outstretched towards me, his mouth open in silent terror as he hurtled down the straight run. Instinctively, I leaped out of his way when I should have tried to catch him. I heard his head strike the floor and he slumped face down on the tiles. Francis hurried down behind him. Before I could move or speak, he was kneeling by Percy's head and I thought he was coming to his aid. Did I really think that? He pulled from his shoulder bag not a first-aid kit but a squat hammer, a short-handled metal mallet. And I dared to be surprised. He grabbed a handful of hair and jerked Percy's head up. I shouted Francis's name, but I didn't move. He brought the mallet down hard onto or into Percy's forehead. It was a deep muffled thump, but edged with a finer sound, a filigree of delicate rupture.

What should I have done? Locked the front door and kitchen French windows, called the police, kept Francis in the house until they arrived? Nothing crossed my mind. Not even the fact that I would be seen to be implicated and was trapped. I could only watch. Francis eased the mallet into a black plastic sack and shoved it in the bag. He bent over Percy, turning his face down in the puddle of blood that was now spreading fast in two long fingers. Francis stood with difficulty, stepped over the blood and came in front of me. He was shaking.

'He's dead. Listen. Vivien, are you listening? Look at me. You're to delete all my emails, to me, from me, yes? And from any back-up you have. You've also got my letters. Destroy them. Are you listening? Don't contact me. Give me five minutes, then phone an ambulance. Not the police. Have you got all that? Bolt the back gate and lock the kitchen door. Remember, it's going to be all right.'

He did not look as if he believed that, and he did not wait for a response. He went towards the kitchen. Something smashed on the floor. He had collided with the table and knocked over a plate. I heard the French windows open and close. I remained standing there, ten feet from where poor Percy lay. I should have gone to him, but I was a coward and did not dare, in case he was really dead. In case he was still alive. All I could think of was how I, dim subordinate, was supposed to know when five minutes were up. When were we counting from? I could make no sense of my wristwatch, which seemed to be upside down. I waited, staring at Percy on the floor, hoping to see him move, dreading that he might, trying to remember the other instructions Francis had given me. When I looked at my watch again, I thought the hands had gone backwards.

*

We did not communicate for seven months. My agony – the horror, self-loathing and despair, the crying in front of sympathetic friends and strangers – were taken by all, policemen, medics and a local journalist included, as the pitiful grief they would expect of the bereaved. No need to pretend. I hid and wept and lost weight in plain sight and was taken for the virtuous widow, the devoted wife who had given away everything, career, society, comfort for the care of her tragically afflicted husband. Some of which was true and that is where I crouched, behind the boulder of my apparent goodness. No one needed to know that what had paralysed me on the night was my disgusting ambivalence. I loved Percy and wanted him alive, and I had seen paradise in a green valley and wanted to escape the drudgery to be there with my lover. But that was not quite right. I loved Francis and the green valley, but I would never have murdered for it. My affair with him was an open secret, known to a few colleagues and, of course, to Harry Kitchener. No one thought it was relevant. No one came to the house to examine my computer and find buried in the software the traces of deleted emails to and from a famous poet. No crafty cop came to poke about in the fireplace for the black remains of Francis Blundy's letters.

Tipping forwards and falling down the stairs was a common cause of death. The elderly as well as drug-addled pop stars and drunks were at it daily. An Alzheimer's case, medically observed and noted with compromised motor skills, merely joined the queue on any first-floor landing, as though among jostling kids at the top of a playground slide. The examining pathologist in the basement of the John Radcliffe Hospital knew before he reached for his whining craniotome that the deceased's head injuries were commensurate with a heavy man tripping and, under gravity's pitiless law, colliding with

262

uneven floor tiles. As for the sickening precautions Francis took, the wide-brimmed hat to fool a CCTV camera, gloves to mask his fingerprints, his car parked two miles away outside a busy fish and chip shop, a mallet brought along in case Percy was still alive after he was thrown down the stairs, the same mallet tossed into the brown Cherwell River near the Vicky Arms, a recorded intention to place Percy in a good care home – all of it, self-dramatising nonsense. No one came looking. No one cared. The official verdict of death by misadventure was no surprise. I along with the health visitor were mildly reprimanded in court by the coroner – the second in my life – for not acting sooner to make a downstairs bedroom for Percy. Future carers take note.

I was free to writhe in self-disgust. There was nothing I could do in my torment that did not evoke sympathy and kindness in those around me. When I was alone, without that comfort, I became mad. The nights were the worst, forcing me onto an obsessive narrow track down which I ran to escape blame: Francis said we had to act. I said no, not with my lips but with my heart. My silence as I got out of his car and fled to the house was my no. He said we had to act, but I did not act. I made no plans. That was my no. I did not put a hammer in a cloth bag and step out into the night. I would never have harmed Percy. I cared for him, I loved him, gave up my life, cut up his food, took him to the doctors and made notes, tuned his TV, made his bedtimes fun, sang songs with him, changed his sheets, cleaned his shed, kept him from the care home and the bingo afternoons. In the dark I perfected my lists and my inno-cence and always arrived at the same question – when would I ever rest? In my delirium the answer was plain. Blundy, like Shakespeare's Glamis, had murdered sleep.

My sister was so kind to me. We spoke every day and she came to stay for a week to help clear the house of Percy's pos-sessions, his shirts and shoes and luthier tools. I thought it would help me and it didn't. Three months passed. I would never have guessed that continuing grief and self-hatred would force on me such a craving for sex. Widow's Fire, it's called. I came to resemble an ocean-floor mollusc of soft interior, open wide to every drifting titbit. There were some humiliating episodes before I landed back with Harry. By then, Francis had gone to Princeton to fill in for an ailing poet. Harry had turned up one early evening with a bottle of wine and a decent intent to commiserate. He was genuinely surprised by my needs, but he was a man of the world, and his willingness and emotional distance were what I needed. In the dance-like formality of a sexual embrace, I found brief respite from myself. We did not dwell on past hostilities, his callous rejection of me, my studied revenge. Some problems are best solved by moving on. I didn't ask him about his current lover. I didn't care. We resumed our pleasant banter – gossip and books, though I had not read much and mostly listened, or pretended to. He came once or twice a week. As soon as he was gone, I would forget about him and go back on my narrow track.

Grief is a dream-state. The linear markers of ordinary time and daily obligations are wrenched apart. All significant ties lead to the recent past, to a sudden absence and to a struggle with what could or should have been. There's a sameness to the days which accelerates their passing, and a sameness in the pattern of memories that makes them unbearable even as they must be visited again and again. That was my condition as I was passively borne along through a Christmas and an extended winter and a cold spring.

Finally, the poet phoned. He was calling from Holland, his teaching duties in the States were over and he suggested a holiday together in Greece. He named an island and I, walled up in my indifference, tonelessly agreed to meeting him on a quayside in Piraeus, by or on the boat that would take us to the island of Amorgos.

It took me many hours to find my passport. To me, Greece was merely a word, an agreement and a meeting point. I had been a few times and loved it, but those visits were not on my mind. I was not capable of anticipating pleasure. My object was to find out if I could bear to be in the company of Francis Blundy.

Harry, with his usual grip on double standards, was irritated when I told him. That meant nothing to me and I refused to engage with him. But I could have just as easily stayed at home. If Francis had phoned to cancel, I would not have cared.

*

I had underestimated Greece. As I wheeled my luggage from my taxi along the quay to the boat, the warmth, the din and excitement of the early season's tourist crowd, the glint between the docked ferries of a flat blue sea and a whiff from somewhere of fish frying in olive oil stirred in me a self I had forgotten. To be elsewhere! It was not true that travel was a false god and that you took your troubles with you and nothing could change. There was the unimaginable and unforeseen thrill of being away, of renewal, and remembering that the world was huge and various, and you and your concerns were small. I fairly bounced up the gangway. Francis was waiting for me at the top. We embraced lightly. He looked calm and well – and taller. Conceivably, I had shrunk. I learned from him in our first thirty minutes that the boat journey would take eight hours and he had tactfully booked single occupancy of two first-class double cabins; that an American arts foundation had given him a large sum of money in recognition of a lifetime's achievement; that the Barn and dairy were finished to the highest quality, the books were in order on the shelves, spices and wine in their racks, sheets piled in the walk-in linen cupboard and the garden soon to flourish; that he had yet to spend a night there, and everyone who saw the place was amazed. I made no response, but I watched him closely as he spoke and could not suppress or deny a faint beginning of my old feelings for him. As we walked up and down the deck, or stopped to watch passengers boarding, I delighted in the afternoon sun on my bare arms and felt capable, given life's brevity, of ruthless insistence on my small share of the world's pleasures. I had suffered and I was owed. I was giddy with the thought that I could take what I wanted, on my own terms. No one was watching but Francis,

265

and he was complicit and treacherous too. Far-off England was the cold locus of ungenerous morals and disapproval, and Oxford was its damp heartland from which I had been sprung. The boat was leaving. As we stood in the stern, leaning on the taffrail, looking out towards open sea with the sun and a warm breeze on our faces, I felt so exhilarated that I did what I had told myself I would not do, or not yet. I put my hand on his. He took it, we interlinked our fingers and we kissed.

In the dining room that evening we ate a lukewarm stew of lamb and okra. The red wine, almost black, had a sharp invigorating taste. Francis thought it was how the ancient Greeks and Romans liked it. In all that we talked about – Iraq, Rachel's illness, American universities, Oxford's expansion, British versus American poetry, Peter's brilliant school reports – we did not go near Percy's death and its aftermath. We did not even collude to avoid it. The conversation flowed past it. The matter – the murder – was buried. The many months I had passed in mourning I forgot in the excitement of a sea voyage. Francis wanted to talk about the Barn and was assuming that our life together there was assured. He had bought for the dairy an eighteenth-century oak writing desk and was certain I would love working on it. He showed me a picture on his phone. A kitchen designer based in Suffolk had built for the Barn a huge kitchen island out of elm. It reminded Francis that the house-keeper's husband had planted on the garden's boundary two elms immune to disease. And so, without acknowledging what we were doing, we sealed Percy in his tomb, or so we thought. The last time Francis and I had seen each other, he had a bag on his shoulder in which was concealed a mallet smeared with blood. A corpse was on the floor. With what ease we conspired not to return there. What an achievement.

It could not last. Later, we kissed goodnight and without discussion went to our adjacent rooms. As I saw it, we were not ready to resume our affair because we knew how monstrous our evasions had been. Soothed by gentle motion and the drone of the ship's engines, I was asleep in minutes for the first

266

time in months. I woke from a dreamless sleep in the middle of the night. Only when I heard a car's horn and a shout did I realise that the ferry had docked. We had arrived at the port of Aegiali in the early hours of the morning. As we came down the gangway in the pre-dawn gloom, we found that the hotel had sent a man with donkey and cart to take our suitcases and those of four other guests. It was a gimmick to please the tourists, I guessed, but it worked some magic on me as we walked uphill behind the cart through silent narrow alleys. There was a widening along the way, a tiny plaza with a pollarded plane tree by a whitewashed church. Here the carter stopped to chat with a very elderly man, possibly his father. The guests were obliged to wait. In that southern European way, our man, oblivious to time, seemed to forget about us. I was right behind the cart. Francis was several paces back, talking animatedly to the others. He had read up on Amorgos and knew it all, the poetry of Nikos Gatsos which he quoted, the geology, micro-climate, mythology, and the local politics of building the road that connected Aegiali with the other port, Katapola, at one end of this thin island with, as Francis explained, a fishtail-shaped coast. His listeners obliged with questions. He answered with casual authority, as if he had lived his entire life here. I did not know how he could have absorbed so much from a couple of guidebooks, and why was he so determined to impress. Or why – this was a measure of my irritable state – he was not talking to me. The joy of elsewhere fell away. I was hot from the walk, thirsty, annoyed at being made to wait, impatient to be asleep again before the sun was up. At last, the fellow called to his donkey and the cart rolled forwards. Francis talked all the way up to the hotel. I tried hard not to listen.

Now we were sharing a room, but there were twin beds, at least, narrow and hard. Above mine was a little black scorpion halfway up the wall. I wanted it eased into a tooth mug and put out the window. Francis hit it hard with the heel of his shoe, leaving a yellow stain where it had clung. It fell on my pillow. I brushed it off and turned the pillow over. Then I got ready for bed at speed, pulled the sheet over my head and pretended to be asleep, ignoring Francis when he asked sweetly if I was OK.

When I woke, my mood had not improved. The bedroom was oppressively bright, and Francis was not in his bed. I heard his voice in the garden below our open window. I was dressed and sitting on a stool adjusting a sandal when he appeared, energetic and loud, and began to tell me how he had arranged for our breakfast to be in the perfect spot in the shade of an orange tree. It was ready now. Then he caught my look.

'What's up?'

I had already decided to let him have it. No more evasion, but I wanted to sound airily sardonic. 'I'm fine. Just finding it a trifle awkward sharing a room with the man who killed my husband.'

'What?' He spat the word out, then did it again, even louder. 'What?' He couldn't help himself, he glanced towards the window. I think I did too. We could hear guests at breakfast in the garden. They could hear us. He crossed the room quickly and slammed it shut. Now we were sealed in and ready.

He stood facing me, arms crossed. 'I can't believe you mean that.'

'You're planning on spending this time not talking about it. Too bad. You're going to have to face it.'

He pulled up a painted wooden chair and sat down. His pretence of calm did not fool me. He said, 'Fine. Let's talk. About your responsibilities too. Or should we leave them out?'

'Francis, you came to my place without warning. You didn't speak to me. You just went for him.'

He was gazing at me in feigned wonder. 'You've really persuaded yourself, haven't you.'

'What was I supposed to do? Wrestle you to the ground?'

'My God. You are weak.'

'You mean I don't murder people.'

He laughed. 'No. You get me to do it.'

At this point we spoke at once. I was enraged by his lie. 'What fucking nonsense. How dare you.' And keeping up his appearance of composure, and surely struggling not to swear like me, he said something like, 'Do you want me to spell it out for you, what you did?'

'You acted on your own. You know it.'

'Do you want to see the proof?'

'What?'

'Let me speak. Then I'll listen, I promise. I put it to you in the car. You knew what I meant. Don't deny it. You didn't answer. Fine. Then what? You're sending me ten emails a day. He shat himself, he keeps me awake all night, I can't cope, I'm losing my mind. I hate him. He's sucking the life out of me. But I'm never ever putting him in a home. You told me that a thousand times. After what I said in the car, your meaning was clear. Why else write to tell me that you wished he was dead? Or that he was "already" dead? Remember? I said we had to act and here you were, agreeing with me. I said you needn't be involved and on the night you weren't. I did the hard bit and you didn't make a sound. So now, instead of cleaning up his shit on your own and waiting years for him to die, here you are on a beautiful island. But there's a price for that, Vivien. It's simple. We're in this together.'

He sat back, resting his hands on his knees, staring at me solemnly, waiting for me to speak. I had to be careful. He was a clever man and he could twist lies into truth. But he had aimed at the centre of my guilt. I should have done more to stop him. I felt sick, my heart was thudding, but I was determined to match his show of calm. At the same time, I wondered if I was going through the motions and whether my heart was really in this argument any longer. Logic could take us in another direction.

'I never asked you to come round to my place with a hammer. Oh yes, I was going through a very hard time looking after him. That's every carer's experience with Alzheimer's. What you said in the car and what you did next were your choices. All yours. He was an inconvenience and you killed him. You couldn't understand how I could love him. To make out you were only doing what you were told is desperate, it's pathetic. And you call me weak! You murdered him, Francis. You bashed in his brains! You, not me. If I hadn't met you, he'd still be alive.'

I had worked myself up to shouting and I felt a curious elation.

Francis was impassive. 'If Percy hadn't met *you*, he'd still be alive. But look, let's not waste time. Anyone could ask you why you didn't go to the police right at the start, why you let me in, why you told me where he was, why you didn't try to stop me when I went upstairs, why you didn't call the police when it was done. Forget all that. Let's agree to differ, or even say for the sake of argument that you're entirely innocent and I'm the monster. What matters is this. If I go down, so do you. Sorry, but I thought we might have a conversation like this. I kept your emails. They don't look good. To repeat – we're in this together.'

Before Francis reached his concluding proposal of black-mail, I had begun to think and feel differently. I had known for months that we were roped together. A clean break would be problematic, assuming I wanted it. If I did, I should not have been on holiday with him. If he had a hold over me, then I had one over him. Also, I was no longer young, I had no money, my career had collapsed, the thought of resuming life in Heading-ton was hateful to me. A studio and an oak writing desk were waiting, so was my book about Aikenhead. Beyond the dairy lay open spaces. I recalled my notion of the day before: ruthless insistence on my share of the world's pleasures. Francis had the glow of talent and fame about him and a million dollars from his American benefactors. In the longer term, he was likely to predecease me. The Barn would be mine. But these enticements were tributaries to a darker stream of thought. There was an element of my own personality I had only discovered late in life, thanks to Harry Kitchener's duplicity. My bitterness over Percy might persist. I might need, well, if not revenge . . . just then I did not know what I might need.

I smiled at Francis and stood, hesitated a moment, then

went across the room to the window and opened it wide. Leaning out into the warmth, I saw it straight away in the spangled shade of an orange tree already heavy with fruit, our green table bearing a pot of coffee, thick-sliced bread, early figs, yoghurt and honey in earthenware bowls. Across the garden the cicadas were starting up their hypnotic buzz and a waiter was coming with a cloth to protect our delayed breakfast from the birds. I turned to look back into the room. Francis was watching me with interest.

Resuming the conversation, I said, 'Well, in that case we had better get married.'

*

In September 2007 Francis published his twelfth book, *Feasting*. Turnbull's threw a party for him at the Wallace Collection, Marylebone. Harry, as editor, gave an amusing speech. After our four-month resumption during those dark days of bereavement, he and I were getting along nicely. The launch was a grand affair, unusual by the standards of poetry publishing – eighty guests, champagne, a jazz quintet, a sit-down dinner presented by the River Cafe. *Feasting* included the cycle of love poems that Francis wrote after our Islington idyll. One of those, funny, lyrical and erotic, found its way into a movie, a romantic comedy, one of the big hits of the autumn season. Beautifully read by Francis for a voiceover during a love scene on a train, it caught the public mood. Tens of thousands, who had never bought a volume of poetry and especially not a hardback, picked up a copy in cinema foyers across the country and propelled the book onto the bestseller lists, among the murder and SAS novels. Francis was in a strange state, torn between exhilaration at this new form of celebrity and contempt for his new readers who had never heard of him and would soon forget him. But the serious press gave him the best notices he'd ever had. Looking back, I would say that *Feasting* was the peak of his career.

I was in a strange state too. This suddenly famous poem

and the others in the cycle were about me. I knew the sequence from the typed pages Francis gave me as soon as he had finished. Eighteen months later, I was shocked to see in the bound proof that I was named and surnamed as the dedicatee in italics above the first of the nine poems. My body and my 'inward' temperament were also named. A mole on my thigh was itemised, and the rising notes of my 'lyrical' laughter, and what he called my 'tasty lisp', which I never knew I had. When I asked if it was a typo for 'lips' Francis smiled forgivingly. So it was me, it was him and me in our most private of moments, sliced open and pinned wide for public inspection, like a dissected frog in my long-ago school biology lessons. I did not complain, and later I was glad I hadn't, for this was a vanishing process. It was me when I saw the proof, then me and not me when I saw my first finished copy, until finally, diluted and disseminated in multiple thousands of printed versions of myself, I faded into the typeface, and it was no longer me at all. What remained was not even a woman but a poetic convention, the shadow of a woman on the cave walls of a man's imagination. The cycle became well known to readers of contemporary poetry and later was ravishingly set for tenor and string orchestra by Michael Berkeley. Francis and I were at the world premiere at the Maltings, Aldeburgh. We were both in tears. That was the night we were at our closest.

There exists an unregarded entanglement of memory and physical distance. Looking back at the so-called 'Second Immortal Dinner' from the remoteness of north-west Scotland, the images and sequence of events leading up to it are blurred not only by time but also by 500 miles. From up here, what happened down there years ago matters less. Jane finds the same. Our detachment has allowed us to tell each other almost everything. I have told her about my affair with her husband, Harry, now deceased. She has told me of her loathing for my husband, her brother, Francis, now deceased. We have tramped the wilderness of the Rough Bounds and talked of little else. We are both fit for our age, still good for fifteen miles. We have approved of each other's plans. Harry's archive has been moved to Fort William, where there is an annexe of the University of the Highlands and Islands. So far, no one has been to look at his papers. She has wanted my help, over time and successive visits, to smuggle his papers out and replace them with blank sheets or any old typed or handwritten pages we can find. I feel ashamed of my part in this, but I promised to be of use, and I understand her need to protect the family's privacy. Harry made a fool of her over many years and neglected his children – with some assistance from me. We've made eight visits between us in two years. We have reader's tickets to the archive, which is run to the highest standards. We fit our larceny expeditions around occasional shopping trips to Fort William. Our methods have become refined. Inconsequential stuff of Harry's is left at the top of the piles in the document boxes. Trash is smuggled in lower down. The stuff of interest is smuggled out. We go to the library separately, months apart. The archivist there is friendly towards us and doesn't know we are connected. Sometimes I have seen through the kitchen window Jane standing at the bottom of the garden in contemplation of the bonfire, the funeral pyre, she is tending. She needs to be alone.

I have told her that in a month or so, the curtain will come down on this book. It will terminate at a moment six years ago, in the Barn's dairy late at night, October 2014, with me, a glass of water in my hand, warming myself in front of the log-burning stove. Jane has been supportive of the project. I've read to her the parts of my memoir that do not intimately concern Harry or the details of Percy's death. Is it, she asked me on two occasions, a novel? Each time, I shrugged.

I've explained to her a decision I've taken that's eccentric, even ludicrous. To my relief she has been sympathetic. 'We're allowed to be eccentric,' she assured me, 'I'm afraid we've reached that age!' It had started two years before, when I was thinking again about Percy's ashes, which I've yet to scatter. Headington was not right, nor was north Oxford. I was favouring a place on one of our big walks, perhaps along the banks of the River Evenlode where we often saw kingfishers. Then I thought of the Barn itself, in the garden, near the dairy. He would have loved that protected valley and its stream. He deserved to be there. Francis would have objected, and that may have lent some appeal to the project. Out of that idea grew the thought, or the reverie, of sending Percy's Guarneri violin into the future with an explanatory page or two describing its maker and how he would have wanted the instrument to end up one day in the possession of a fine professional player.

When I described these vague fantasies in a phone call to Peter, he was immediately interested, for he'd adored his uncle. We started talking about 'time capsules', popular at the time with primary-school teachers and their pupils. As a physicist, Peter wanted to tell me about the Voyager satellites, one of which crossed the outer boundaries of the solar system after many years, 'golden' records attached to its sides with recordings of music and voices from around the planet. Peter became deeply engaged in my violin proposal. I told him that I sensed his eleven-year-old self bubbling up. He was amused, but he was also serious, and before I knew it, he had been in touch with the Bodleian about preservation methods. That was when I began reviewing the options for this document. Leaving it with Turnbull's or any other publisher with a thirty-year embargo was a risk. Once I am out of the way and new editors come in, curiosity would overwhelm contractual undertakings given to a forgotten elderly lady. Same was true for the Bodleian once the present leadership have retired. The Francis Blundy story is, for scholars at least, too interesting. I could deposit these pages with a legal firm, but I can never forget Thomas Hardy's will. He wanted to be buried in the rural backwater of Stinsford in the grave of his beloved Emma. But after he died, his body was torn open so that his heart could remain with her, while his ashes went to Westminster Abbey. Perhaps I was getting crusty as I approached my sixtieth birthday, but I trusted no one.

Then, I thought, why not put these pages in with Percy's

violin, bury them deep and leave them to fate? If my efforts here are discovered while I'm still alive, I'll take what's coming to me. It could even be a relief. It was mere fantasy, but once I had told Peter, the matter slipped out of my control. He came to Glenuig to stay for a few days. He was persuasive, irresistible. When he left, he took with him the ashes and the violin. I told him the size of paper I'm using and the likely thickness of the document but, of course, I couldn't tell him what was in it.

There have been times when I've wondered if this burial business is plain foolish. It's an old-fashioned boy's adventure. Treasure Island! There's also a shadow of sadness across it. It took me too long to realise that I had done this before, long ago, when I went with Rachel and my housemates on a stormy day in June and tried to bury little Diana's blue teddy in Spa Fields. This second burial might be more successful. Whatever it is, it's too late to call it back now. The kindly conservator at the Bodleian, Geraldine Smythe, has been in touch several times and she has told me that her department is enthusiastic and ready for me. Thanks to her, I've already taken delivery of a ream of handmade cotton-based paper from Ruscombe Paper Mills.

When I've finished and made my corrections, I'll start printing. Double-sided please, Peter says, and single-spaced. This cotton paper, I'm told, will outlast any modern equivalent in which the cellulose from wood pulp rapidly degrades. Now I have come this far and have accepted the inevitable, I enjoy thinking about our plans. Jane will drive me to the railway stop at Lochailort to catch the local train to Fort William where I'll pick up the night train to Euston, then onwards from Paddington to Oxford. The Bodleian's Librarian, the distinguished and genial Richard Ovenden, will be waiting for me in his office with lunchtime sandwiches and a glass of wine. There is bound to be much talk of Scotland. I will return to him my twelve journals which will go back into the Blundy archive. Afterwards, he will pass me on to Geraldine Smythe and I'll hand over this document for the preservation treatment. She asked me on the phone how long I expected the items to be in the ground. I told her possibly as much as thirty years. She is taking no chances and has chosen oxygen-free storage. As she has explained, my items will be placed in an airtight container. The air will be pumped out to provide an environment hostile to all life forms. A secondary container will contain silica gels to create a microclimate and keep the humidity low.

Last week, Peter sourced a stainless-steel airtight case which he'll bring to the Bodleian the day after I've arrived, and that too will be lined with various chemicals. When all is ready and the case has been sealed, we'll set off in his car to the Barn. The tenants have already received their six-month notice and the place will be empty. I must remember to record a map reference for our chosen spot in the garden. I'll disguise it somehow in my last journal. Peter will dig the hole while I show an estate agent round the Barn and dairy. If he asks, I'll tell him we are burying our Pomeranian, fresh out of the freezer. Once Peter has filled in the hole, we'll pour the ashes over the bare earth then linger there a while to recall a few things we loved about Percy. I'll read a consolatory poem by James Fenton which encourages the living to make friends with the dead. The site will grow over quickly – nettles like disturbed ground – and the property will go on the market. The proceeds will buy a new kiln for Jane and together with Francis's occasional royalties should certainly see us both to our ends. I like to run through all these arrangements last thing at night. They ease me into sleep.

*

Time and distance have obscured my memory of the order of events after Amorgos, a time of arrangements and upheavals. I had to consult my journal entries to be reminded that I cleared the Headington house of junk, mostly mine, and the place went on sale. I had no money to smarten it up and I did not want to ask Francis. I took them personally, the negative comments of viewers. The garden was a mess, Percy's shed blocked daylight from the ground floor, the heating system was worn out, the stairs were too steep. I dropped my price. About the same time, the university offered me my job back, but I was no longer interested. I wanted another life. My college, taking pity on a bereaved colleague, found me some part-time hours. I taught seventeenth-century poetry on Mondays and Victorian novels on Thursdays. The Barn was not as ready as Francis had thought. There were drainage and septic-tank problems that required the builders to come back and take up the floor. After many years, my John Clare book went into a second printing. That encouraged me to take out the Aikenhead notes. At the end of that year Francis and I were quietly married in Oxford Town Hall. I invited Rachel, Francis invited Jane and Harry – he was surprisingly relaxed about the wedding. The five of us had dinner out at Raymond Blanc's restaurant in Great Milton. I have no memory of the occasion. Jane tells me that it was merry, and she remembers being relieved that Francis paid.

We had been married four months before I moved to the Barn and took possession of the dairy. Francis was determined that we should merge our book collections. It was a kindly ambition for total union, but I had my doubts. If life became intolerable, I thought, I might have to run for it. (Sure enough, twelve years later, after Francis died, separating my books from his to take to the little cottage in Scotland was a huge and dull task. I had to pay a graduate student to help me.) The idyll Francis and I had often imagined evaded us. The day I arrived in the removal van, it was raining hard and continued to rain for weeks. The wettest May on record. When I said carelessly that climate change was to blame, Francis set off on one of his fugues and a row followed, partly settled by a bottle of wine. The rain exposed several leaks in the Barn's new roof. Francis spent time shouting down the phone at stolid Vicenc, who was on a new job seventy miles away and insisted that the 'snagging' period had ended long ago. The architect backed him up. A vile mood settled on Francis which caused me to retreat to the dairy. What a gift that place was. I had to love him for that. It didn't leak.

But now, with hours to myself and abundant silence, recent and distant events swarmed through my thoughts. They

277

brought me to a state of paralysis. I used to sit and stare across the oak desk at my beautiful studio, listening to the haunting note the wind sometimes made as it swept round a corner of the Barn. My thoughts would be empty, or the past crowded in. Snatches of Victorian novels were in the mix along with my own tutorial voice from recent teaching, unnaturally emphatic, a sing-song of fake kindness with which I tried to protect a dim or lazy student. I had leisure now to make myself tense with old sorrow. When Percy loomed, healthy or sick, or face down in the hall, the source of two rivers of blood, I would leave the desk and lie on the bed. Once, after I had propped up her blue teddy on a shelf, Diana arrived with an infant shriek and her brother Christopher was there, on the platform, understanding nothing. Then the other horror again, Francis in black hat and shoulder bag tapping at my window.

For distraction, I made changes to the room, shifting a vase, fiddling with the coffee machine, polishing a polished wooden surface. My old compulsion to domestic order. But I conjured another persona for myself, a spoiled rich brat, feather-bedded and stifled by comfort, nothing to struggle for, lethargic among the soft furnishings, talentless. And Francis? Having murdered my husband to have me to himself, he was in his study fourteen, sometimes sixteen hours a day, writing essays on four American poets, Jarrell, Lowell, Hecht and Schwartz. All men. Who cared? I would have written on four women, if only I'd had the energy and purpose. Francis's absence, his distraction when he emerged for meals, should have been my liberation into work. But that middle-aged brat could easily persuade herself she had been seduced, betrayed and deserted, like a pallid heroine in a Richardson novel.

It cannot have been so bad. My journal, as opposed to my memory, says we talked late at night, we had sex, I cooked some ambitious meals. When he was oppressed by work, I helped him with his correspondence. The following summer I began to explore the immediate countryside, usually alone, sometimes with Rachel or Peter, by then a gangly adolescent with a passion for maths and physics. When I walked alone, I longed for Percy. I missed his constant affection and curiosity about plants and creatures. Whenever I saw something interesting, I spoke to him in my thoughts about it. There were occasions when I glanced around to make sure no one could see or hear me, and I would sit on the grass and cry.

That first year at the Barn I was teaching courses at a summer school in Oxford for American students. Their enthusiasm bucked me up and in the autumn I finally made a start on the Aikenhead book. In a long opening section, I surveyed the intellectual and religious currents of the late seventeenth century. That meant spending time in London at the Royal Society, the Wellcome Trust Library and the British Library, and in Oxford at the Bodleian. I used to overnight at Rachel's and did my best to get along with her husband, Michael. He seemed to disapprove of me on principle, but what that principle was, I never dared to ask. I noticed now that each time I came home, I loved the Barn a little more. It was glorious to be back. By then we had a small milieu who also loved the place. Jane and Harry, obviously. John and Tony, vet and a botanist, a gay couple. The novelist Mary Sheldrake and her rakish husband, Graham. Later, a young journalist, Harriet Page, who wrote an approving profile of Francis, and Harriet's husband Chris, who became useful around the Barn. There were many others, but this was our core, pleasingly diverse and helpful whenever they stayed the night, cooking, washing up and sorting out the bed linen.

The Pages' appearance in our lives led to a trivial incident that has never left me and had some consequences for my private life. It concerned an adverb. After the *Feasting* fuss and Francis's new fame had faded and a year had passed, he began to suffer from status anxiety. He was forgotten in the general memory, as poets usually are. When his publisher was approached by *Vanity Fair* for a profile, Francis, who did not get on well with journalists, agreed, to everyone's surprise, especially mine. To Harriet, he was determined to be pleasant when she came out one afternoon, but he could not conceal his scepticism. He denied this, but he instinctively doubted the intellectual reach of anyone who had not been to Oxford, though he respected Cambridge scientists. Harriet was a graduate of Newcastle University. She knew his work, apparently quoted from it at the right moments and asked no foolish questions. She was also beautiful and charmingly kitted out from charity shops. If he had tender thoughts about her, she was well beyond his reach. Her manner was pleasantly professional and she told me on a later visit that she loved her husband. By the time she left, after a two-hour session with Francis and a stroll round the garden with me, he had softened towards her. He softened further when the interview came out. She gave him everything – 'the first among equals', 'the voice the nation barely deserved', 'the deepest delver into our flawed but redeemable nature' and then, in the final line, the 'g' word: 'the uncontested genius of Francis Blundy'. The photographer also served him well, despite the poet's rudeness to him and impatience. Francis was on the magazine cover, full-bleed, softly backlit in late-afternoon light, standing against a background of the valley and its stream, the solitary genius, conveying by creased brow limited forgiveness for humankind. He read the article several times and wanted to invite Harriet to lunch.

A month later, she came with her husband, Chris, and here was another social obstacle for Francis. He was relaxed giving instructions to workmen and shopkeepers, but he was uneasy when he had to be on the level with people without formal education. He did not know what terms of reference he should be using. Or it was simply contempt, or a little of both. Certain modes of pronunciation and common solecisms pained him. He could not believe in the intelligence of someone who pronounced glottal 't's, or used a 'was' for a 'were'.

Chris was a tall fellow, slender and strong-looking. Very agreeable, I thought. He had not said much at lunch, so I brought him into the conversation and asked him about his work. He was explaining how he sometimes helped out at a children's theatre, which hopefully would be getting some lottery money. Francis could stand it no more.

'Chris, I beg you. In this household, never say "hopefully".'

The young man looked from Francis to Harriet, then back to Francis. 'What was that?'

Two glottals in three words would not have helped.

'Hopefully,' Francis explained. 'It's not a word. You're murdering the language. Don't say it.'

Chris shook his head and continued telling me about his work. When the couple had left, I confronted Francis and told him he had been unpleasant and boorish.

He said, 'What's that girl doing with him? He's a fucking moron.'

'Nonsense.'

'Then he shouldn't talk like one.'

I also kept a close account of the next evening the Pages came to see us. It was six weeks later and this time we had Harry and Jane, and it was supper. It was a warm evening and we had been sitting out in the garden drinking. At table indoors the conversation turned to the aftermath of the Great Recession. In reply to a question from Harry, Chris Page said that, hopefully, business would be picking up in the line of work he had been doing lately, which was marquee tents for weddings.

Francis cut in, genuinely irritated. 'Hopefully again. Drives me mad. Chris, do the right thing. Cast it out.'

There was sudden silence. Chris put down his knife and fork, sat back and folded his arms. He spoke in grave terms, and I suspected that he had used the forbidden word deliberately and had done some work on it. 'I wasn't using the word as an adverb to mean "in a hopeful manner", you know, qualifying the nearest verb. It's a *sentence* adverb, Mr Blundy, it refers to the speaker's attitude, my attitude and—'

'Thanks, Chris. I don't need a lesson from you in sentence adverbs.'

'I think you do.'

The silence tightened. For once, Francis was too amazed to speak.

I had the impression that Chris was hamming up his soft cockney. Every 'th' was an 'f', all 't's emphatically glottal.

He repeated, 'I think you do. If you throw out poor old hopefully, to be consistent you'll have to throw out a lot of other sentence adverbs doing the same work. If I say, seriously, you're wrong, I'm not talking about the way you're wrong. I'm talking about the way I'm telling you this. And if I say, frankly, I don't like being talked down to, I mean I'm being frank. Admittedly – that is, I admit – this is your house, but please don't tell me how to speak. Bluntly, it's rude. So, if you'll get off my back, Mr Blundy, then hopefully we'll get along, which means not only that I hope we will, but I'm making a hopeful prediction.'

At this point, things could have gone very wrong. I had seen Francis spiral into a rage at far less, but Harry intruded with a loud bark of a laugh. 'Francis. You are screwed.'

And so, the tension began to ease and my husband had the good sense to concede – there was no sensible alternative – and join the laughter that was gathering round the table. He said to Chris, 'You make a good case and, *surely*, I owe you an apology.'

Chris leaned towards Francis and they clinked glasses, and from that time on, now it was clear that Chris was not to be pushed around, they got along well. Over time, he came out to solve many of the Barn's problems. He fixed the leaks on the roof, sorted out the septic tank and arranged the quadrupling of our computers' download speeds. Later, during that same evening, Jane asked Chris how he came to know so much about grammar.

'I don't know a thing. First time Francis jumped down my throat, I looked on Harriet's shelves. She pointed me towards Burchfield's *Fowler* and a bloke called Pinker. Seems like some ignorant snob years back picked on hopefully, and a mob of so-called educated speakers got intimidated and joined in and scared each other into never using the word and crapping on anyone who did. Pathetic!'

Soon after the adverbial supper, Francis left for New York to give a reading at the Y. I didn't want to go. Chris came out to do some work on a fence. On the first day, just as he was leaving, I offered him tea and cake in the dairy. He was cheerful company and we had a good time. It was my idea to take him into the bedroom. He kept saying, 'Are you sure about this?' I was sure. Perhaps he was a stand-in for Thomas Aikenhead. For an adult, Chris had astonishing childlike eyelashes, long and dark. Naked, he was a delightful surprise. I'd forgotten what young bodies were like. My lovers had aged with or ahead of me. One gets used to the cushioning blubber around older men's bellies. Long ago, when men's stomachs were taut, I didn't stop to think it was because they were young. It was simply the human form.

The fencing work took longer than Chris had expected. On the fifth day, I told him this was our last. Francis would soon be back. Chris nodded and smiled, and when he was about to leave he kissed me on the cheek and said simply, 'Thank you,' and I squeezed his arm and said, 'Thank *you*.' It was the cleanest ending to a brief affair I'd ever known. But it started something and soon I was restless. The dairy, I now understood, was the perfect place. Three weeks later, Francis went to a literary festival in Jamaica. Once he had phoned to report he had landed safely, I thought I would invite Harry out for supper. I don't know what he told Jane, but the evening went well, and I soothed my conscience with the certainty that Francis would be seizing his own pleasures in the Caribbean.

Harry and I settled into an opportunistic routine. Whenever Francis was away, and once I was sure he was at his destination, Harry would come out to our place. We still took trouble to bolt ourselves in the dairy against an unexpected return and leave open the back door for a quick escape. Harry always parked a ten-minute walk away. By this time he was in his late fifties, but as a lover he was unchanged, adept and considerate, and as detached as ever. It was, of course, pleasing that he still found me attractive. He was in discussions about writing Francis's biography and for reasons I cannot justify, this added spice to our renewed affair. I liked to tease Harry about it. Would he write about us, would we have a whole chapter to ourselves? We snatched our times together, just as we always had, and perhaps this was the only way we could flourish. We managed several years, until he became ill. The only tense moments between us came after my birthday dinner. By then matters had deteriorated between Francis and me and I was travelling to Oxford to see Harry at his old Summertown flat. I told everyone, including my journal, that I was visiting nephew Peter in London. During that time, Harry was wild about the Corona and wanted me to let him see it. He was Francis's editor and it was a reasonable request. He kept on at me. I refused many times and finally wrote him a terse letter. It went something like, 'I've made arrangements. I don't want to talk about it, and I don't want you to ask me ever again.' That note must have gone onto Jane's bonfire.

*

As of two weeks ago, the Kitchener archive at the University of the Highlands and Islands contains only junk, including playbills, obituary notices of friends, menus from black-tie book-prize feasts and letters from conveyancing solicitors. Deeper down in the boxes are pages we pulled from wastepaper baskets, anonymised and with dates scored out. There are twenty-seven boxes in the archive and it would take a scholar two or three weeks to establish that there is nothing useful there. In his lifetime Harry had no reputation in Scotland, but one day, Blundy scholars will take an interest. I was sorry for Harry's memory, for he and I had some good times. But Jane was determined to obliterate him. There must have been references to me that she saw before they went on the bonfire. I was amazed that she bore me no grudge. When I asked, she insisted that women could never resist Harry. By the weak logic of the lovelorn or from a wish to avoid conflict with me, she blamed only him. I said nothing. We remain happy companions in the

284

safe confines of the unsaid. After she found an unusual vein of clay in a hill above Smirisary, her vases, teapots and dinner plates have found a fair distribution on the Ardnamurchan peninsula.

She works in a lean-to shed at the back of the house. I like to take my morning coffee and watch her throw a pot and cradle it as it spins in her tender wet hands. She adopts an intent maternal gaze as she wills the clay into shape. But from the kitchen I sometimes hear a howl of fury as the kiln lets her down again. On our long walks we talk about our departed husbands and what our marriages tell us about ourselves. Over many years, Jane threw Harry out three times, then missed him and took him back, even when she knew he would not keep his promises. Finally, she put up with the affairs for the sake of the children and the marriage. She loved him and thought she could not live without him. After he died, she found she could, most pleasurably, and that was when her retrospective anger took hold. She had brought up the children alone, ran the household, worked long hours into the night in her studio, while Harry lived the carefree life of a single man. 'He barely knew the names of his kids.'

We discuss her thirty-five-year-old marriage as if I was not an element in her unhappy story. This is the vital suppression we collude in, although sometimes Jane will say sadly, 'Of course, you knew him almost as well as I did.'

And I'll reply with something like, 'Jane, I hardly knew him at all.'

When it's my turn to talk about my marriage, I can't afford the luxury of Jane's candour. The corrupting secret that bound Francis and me has driven me, as I walk the hills with her, into devious accounts, almost too plausible to be true. I've worked the clichés hard. How I suffered the pressures of marriage to a famous man, how living with a creative genius was a roller-coaster ride through darkness and light, failure and triumph, how my own identity was progressively eroded. Nothing to tell of my inaction when Francis came to the house in the night with his shoulder bag. Nothing to say of my Faustian bargain, of marrying Percy's murderer in exchange for an interesting and comfortable life. But Jane and I talk often of our childhoods, our parents and siblings, and find common ground in the space stolen from us and given to our brothers. That conversation becomes even livelier when sister Rachel comes to stay and joins in. Jane has no time for her brother's poetry, or any poetry. She is annoyed with herself for wasting her childhood on Francis and his needs. As for the missing 'Corona for Vivien', she is bemused. She never asks what I've done with the poem. 'They make all this fuss, but most of these people haven't even read the stuff of his they can buy in the bookshops.'

But she has warm memories of my birthday night, the moronically named Second Immortal Dinner. 'What an evening that was! What a lovely bunch of people! Did you know, the Sheldrakes had a row and spent a delicious night making up? The caterer or his waitress dropped one of my best ever bowls on the floor, then John Bale told us how he'd operated on a snake that got run over! And Fran read his poem. It went on forever. It was all I could do to stay awake! I'm not supposed to say it, Vivien, and I know he wrote it specially for you, but it was no bad thing that poem got lost, don't you think? Too bloody long!'

I have no memory of the snake or of how that bowl was broken. Almost six years have passed, and Jane and I experienced different evenings. Memory is purposefully selective. Of the inconsequential moments, Francis on a climate rant stands out for me. Bad enough back then, but the years that followed made a fool of him. I think he knew it. The Corona was a retraction he could never admit to. Because he had been working on it so intensely, he cancelled appointments and hadn't been away in three months. No chance then of seeing Harry and I missed him. The day before the dinner, I drove all the way to Ledbury where he was giving a lunchtime lecture on John Masefield, whose birthplace it was. We spent a couple of hours together in a creaky bedroom above a Tudor pub. To my surprise, Harry told me that he was 'beginning to think' that he loved me and that it was therefore impossible for him to commit to writing Francis's biography. Harry said, 'Simply too squalid, even for me.'

That room over the bar of an old pub brought back memories of my hiking jaunts with Percy and the inns where we used to lodge. On the drive back from Ledbury, I couldn't see for tears. I pulled over and submitted to the sorrow and guilt that the years had not dispelled. When I recovered, I checked myself in the rear-view mirror. I glimpsed behind me on the back seat the chocolates, flowers and a Stilton – in case Francis asked, cover for my expedition. Those items caused me to sit for a while and reflect on the sickly compulsion of my infidelities that at other times, when I was feeling more robust, presented themselves as a healthy appetite for life. Surely, I was too old for this. In the littered layby, I felt sated, and longed for a simpler life without or beyond sex. How much more I could achieve if my thoughts were free! But an hour later I was a mile from the Barn when I found the lane blocked by a fallen oak branch. A young local farmer helped me move it, and after I had thanked him and was driving on, I fantasised about him. Nothing serious, but enough to impede for several minutes a free state of mind.

The chocolates and the rest were for the dinner the following evening. It did not trouble me as much as it might have that so much fuss was being made over my fifty-fourth birthday. My duties would be peripheral. A caterer and waitress would take charge of the meal, the setting and serving, Francis would see to the wines. I would arrange the flowers, take our friends on a tour of the autumnal garden, and later pass round the chocolates. I had known for weeks that Francis was working on a birthday poem for me and was going to read it aloud at dinner. I did not look forward to that, but I was resigned to it. He had shown me the vellum on which he was going to write out a fair copy. I no longer recall how I came to know that he was intending to destroy all other drafts and notes. I suppose I was used to his eccentric ways.

287

My carelessness or indifference extended in other directions. The next day, when Harry arrived for the dinner at the Barn with Jane, it meant little to him or me that we had made love in the afternoon of the previous day. We were inured to our respective betrayals and it no longer seemed tragic or even interesting that Francis was pouring a generous gin and tonic for the brother-in-law who was cuckolding him. The passing years had worn our scruples smooth. If I'd thought about it, I would have remembered that during my and Francis's union, I'd had two lovers, whereas he had racked up at least a dozen, some of whom he would have forgotten. For him and me it would have been trivial or retrograde to declare an open relationship. Deception conferred significance. It implied that our marriage was important enough to be worth the hazard of a lie.

So many people who were not there have written about my birthday dinner and it is oddly tense to be setting down the ordinary details I can remember. It's as if I am creeping into a house to retrieve stolen goods. It was a beautiful early evening, extremely warm for October. The caterer and waitress from Stroud came and set to work, our usual gang arrived with presents and Francis managed the welcoming drinks from his big flask. I must have taken all or most of the party outside to see the late-flowering roses. I don't remember the conversations while we were in the garden or, later, indoors. Most likely it was Russia's annexation of Crimea, about which Francis was obsessed and had made himself a fierce expert. Unless we helped Ukraine push the Russians out, Europe would one day soon face a new and murderous chapter in its history, was his drift. The rest of the group probably thought he was overstating the case but would not have wanted to argue. Francis was overbearing and had facts to hand that no one could question. Besides, this was supposed to be a celebration, not a war game. I steered attention back to the roses. It was relief when Francis took Chris to inspect the sit-on lawnmower that needed repair.

As soon as the sun was down it grew cold and we sat round the fire. It must have been the prospect of reading the poem

288

that caused Francis to be so wired up about climate change. Even by his standards he was heavily aggressive in conversation. Everyone in the room had heard him on the subject before, but nothing could stop him. I wanted to kick him hard. The general embarrassment made everyone drink more. Harry especially looked unwell and ready to leave. He was drinking wine like it was beer. Later, I would be relieved that we were almost or completely drunk. Attention and memory would usefully suffer. I remember nothing about the food that was served or how expertly it was cooked, though I know we never asked that caterer back. But I remember Harry's speech before the reading. It was without notes and it was well over the top, a parody of extravagant claims for Francis's poetry. He was sending up the kind of speech he himself had made at the Sheldonian when he introduced the star. Occasionally, he met my eye and I saw his drunken glee. He continued to pile it on until Francis couldn't tolerate it and shut him up.

*

My husband was unsteady as he went round the table to take his speech from the mantelpiece. He had trouble unfastening the vellum scroll. It was so unlike him to have thought of a piece of kitsch like that. I half rose from my chair to help, but he shook his head. Then he couldn't find his glasses. They were under his napkin by his place setting. Once they had been passed along, he was ready to begin. It took me a while to settle into the poem. I think Harry's speech had put me in a satirical frame. There was a bucolic sonnet in praise of a landscape that could well have been the one around the Barn. The sonnet ended and just as I was getting ready to stand and thank him, he began another, with a repeat of the last line of the first. I vaguely knew the form of a corona. Birds, butterflies, wildflowers and a crested newt paraded by us as if on their way to Noah's ark. I recalled that Francis had taken, to my surprise, various of my old field guides from the shelves.

Francis and I, as I heard it, stroll delightedly through an

exquisite landscape. We are down by the stream, where he puts his hand in clear water and finds a little squat fish, a bullhead, hiding under a stone and shows it to me before gently returning it to its place in the stream. So improbable, I almost laughed out loud. In the third sonnet another figure appears, a farmer, I thought, or an old-fashioned peasant. But that is not it. This person is more ethereal, not even a mortal. He is a symbol, and then, in the fourth sonnet, a minor god, big and bearded and genial like Father Thames or Falstaff. He is seen through the eyes of this Francis and Vivien.

I looked around me. Half our guests had their eyes closed, almost asleep. When the waitress had called us to the table, I noticed as I came away from the fire that we had emptied five bottles of wine. We had each drunk two or even three glasses of the house gin and tonic, a hefty brew. If Francis was going to lay on the full fifteen sonnets, none of us was going to last the distance. Perhaps it would be a mere John Donne-seven. Then some of us might be awake by the end to rouse the others.

I too had let my thoughts wander. I did not doubt that the poem was beautiful. Its language was rich and pure and compact. There was now a gorgeous description of a swim in a river. We were on sonnet eight or nine when Falstaff reappears. He is indeed a figure of misrule. He is also fecund, abundant, an enchanted gardener, responsible for the landscape and everything that moves through it or is rooted there. I thought he must be the Green Man of legend, with foliate face, leaves for beard. In some incarnations he spews green shoots from his mouth. There was a stone carving of him by the porch of our local church, which had Saxon origins. Some scholars saw him as a bridge between pagan and Christian worlds.

Later, when I was in the kitchen helping the caterers and making coffee for the remaining guests round the fire, I unfurled the scroll and had some time to read the poem, picking up from where my attention had started to wander. The bearded figure is reaching for a fiddle. The lovers come closer to listen to his 'awkward melody' of broken rhythms. But suddenly he is sickening, and as he clutches his head and begins to stumble, I saw how obtuse I had been. Reading rather than listening made it clear. The luxuriant evocation of a swim downstream through a gorge, that was Percy and me in the River Wye. This green person was not a god or fertile chimera or symbol of all threatened nature. The large bearded figure was Percy. That fiddle was a violin. His sickness was Alzheimer's. As he falls to the ground, we, that is, Francis and Vivien Blundy, move in and are by his side, but not for succour. Francis picks up a rock and, with both hands crashes it down against Percy's forehead. The woman does not intervene.

A mere half-dozen years earlier, we would have counted any evening a failure that ended before midnight. Mary and Graham Sheldrake had gone to bed straight after dinner to repair their marriage, so I've learned from Jane. The rest went back round the fire to drink the coffee I had made. The party was over. The long, barely understood poem had killed it off. As we sipped, there were murmured assertions of 'wonderful . . . brilliant, Francis . . . quite extraordinary'. Only Harry and I said nothing. He kept looking in my direction. I wanted to say to him, Not now, not here! Instead, I looked away. He and Jane were the next to leave, along with Harriet and Chris. I stood to embrace them, but I let Francis go out with them to their car. I felt bad about it, for Harry did not look well. The caterer and waitress carried their crates of crockery to their van and came back to say goodbye and receive their tip. We sat yawning and barely speaking, then John and Tony got up to leave. This time I went outside to see them off. Francis and I watched their tail-lights recede, then I turned back towards the house, reluctant to be alone with him and be obliged to talk about the poem. I did not yet know what to think.

He was close behind me as we entered the house. It was a relief when he grunted goodnight and headed towards his study. I paused to listen for the rattle of his keyboard and heard nothing. I went into the kitchen and rolled up and secured the scroll and crossed the room to rake out the fire and collect the coffee cups. In my usual way, I plumped up the cushions. I was turning off the lights when I heard a sound and turned. He was there in the kitchen, obliquely illuminated by one dimmed spot over a work surface, his head and shoulders in shadow. We were a good distance apart. There was silence. He was waiting for me to speak but I was determined not to.

At last he said, 'I saw you reading it.'

'Yes.'

'And?'

I paused. 'I suppose it's beautiful.'

'But?'

I was trapped in the conversation I did not want to have. I spoke through a sigh. 'It's a fake. A beautiful fake.'

'Go on.'

'You don't understand the natural world. You can't conceive how it's threatened.'

'Yes?'

'Plunging your hands in the stream, lifting a rock to show me a fish? Strolling the lanes, picnic in a meadow, bottle of wine, easy flow of talk? Naming the butterflies! It's mockery.'

I was making myself angry. He was calm. As he came a little closer, I could see his face under the light.

He said, 'What else?'

I didn't hesitate. 'If you can't keep your mouth shut, go to a police station. But leave me out of it. The way you promised in the car. Remember? "All the risks will be mine." Instead, look what happened. You said it in Amorgos – if I go down, so will you. Why isn't blackmail in my birthday poem?'

I decided to stop. This was about to be an argument among villains. I was party to a crime and did not want myself exposed. Hardly a noble cause, and there were other matters I could not raise. I was too vulnerable and could not trust myself. I was sick with guilt. We stared at each other across the room. He stood with his arms loosely at his side, his white hair, uncut these past three months, was swept back from his enormous forehead. He reminded me of the figure I had seen and admired in

292

the Sheldonian as he commanded the audience with his fierce stare. The downlight made a shadow under his high cheekbones. His lips were faintly pursed. I could not imagine what was coming next.

His tone was sorrowful. 'I wrote you a poem about the two most important elements in your life, love and nature. Everyone knows I don't like country walks. I don't know the names of flowers and I don't give a damn. You know I can't swim, I'd never get married in a church. I dislike picnics. Trees, paths, the entire swarming world that isn't human, this is what you love, not me, so I got down to learning about it. You've said it yourself, I'm an indoor person. If I'm not writing, I'm thinking about it. Otherwise, I'm reading. That's all I do.'

I said, 'You know that's nonsense.'

'Just hear me out. To do what I do, I need to be alone. I know I've neglected you. I wanted to make amends with a poem. As for the climate stuff, if that's relevant, you know my views. This is clearly not me in the poem and therefore it's not you. It's not a portrait of our marriage, it's not about me or you. It's *for* you. It speaks for your interests and concerns, not mine. It's a gift, as simple as that.'

'It's a confession. I didn't ask to be implicated.'

He looked away. Across the silence we heard the indignant squeak of a little owl.

At last he said, 'I think about it every day. I'm haunted by what I did ... tormented by it and it can't stay out of what I write. It's driven me inwards as you've noticed. I deeply deeply regret it. Saying that comes nowhere near what I feel. The memories have hounded me, as they should. A few months later, I came into that money. I should have waited. I would have made sure Percy was in a place you and he would have been happy with. What I said when we were on Amorgos was despicable. I should have apologised long ago, but I completely forgot that conversation. All I can do is apologise now. You're wrong to think the poem puts you at any kind of risk. There's nothing there that anyone could base a case on.

'I love you dearly, Vivien. I'm sorry – to put this at its mildest – that I'm an insufficient husband. You'll have to believe me when I tell you that what you have in your hand is the only copy of the poem. I hope one day that will make it precious to you. Now I'm tired, beyond tired, drank too much as usual and need to go to bed. We'll talk more in the morning if you'd like. Goodnight. And again, happy birthday.'

Like a very old man he shuffled away from the pool of light and vanished like a ghost. I don't know why, but I called his name. He did not reappear.

I took the scroll, locked the Barn behind me and went across to the dairy. This too I locked, back and front, not against my husband or an intruder, but as if to secure myself against the evening that had passed. It surprised me that it was only eleven fifteen. I lit a fire in the woodburning stove, poured myself a drink of water and sat facing the flames. At first, soot obscured the heatproof glass, then it was burned off like an idea becoming clear. I remember thinking that first thing the next day I would make some appropriate journal entries. I was touched by what Francis had said. I went in fighting, expecting a row. He loved me – I believed that. He didn't doubt his own sincerity. But I knew him as well as he knew me. Of course he didn't devote every minute of his existence to writing, reading and thinking. No one could. He kept vowing to give it up, but he put himself about in public, in interviews, in readings at festivals from Trondheim to Sydney. He loved talking and drinking with friends, and why not? He liked good restaurants. He chased women and I was in no position to condemn him for it. If he neglected our marriage, it was not by necessity, it was a choice. What I'd just heard was a performance, a reading, nicely delivered. The effect was heightened by the lighting, a single spot. Still, he moved me. I could probably accept his apologies. I loved him once, and something of that lingered.

But I also hated him, and not only for what he did with a mallet. He was a thief. I'd not been able to say it to him because I might have choked up when I uttered Percy's name. For his poem, Francis stole my best, most precious times with Percy, inserted himself into our carefree wandering across rich landscapes, into our joy in nature and passion for naming it, into our curiosity, our delight in river-swimming, our rough picnics in meadows and woods. To give his poem force, Francis crept inside Percy's skin. If I once loved Francis to a degree, I loved and still love Percy far more. I don't know how I can forgive a poem that ritually enacts a murder by which Francis tries to replace Percy.

Despite what Francis had said, I knew that the poem could arouse suspicion. Some bright person working for the authorities could see through Francis Blundy's compacted style to our crime. The world believes that at the time of Percy's death, I was the only other person in the house. If anyone pushed him down the stairs, it had to me. I'm too cowardly to have the facts known in my lifetime, but I want them known and I've set them out here with their background. My passive compliance is a part. So is my faithless past. If there is to be a confession, it will be on my terms. No hiding in a mist of poetics, no symbolic figures, no buried meanings. What I've hoped for is the clarity Albert Camus proposed for troubled times. I should be among the last to say it, but there are occasions when prose must eclipse poetry. The verdict is clear. Francis and I deserve to be hanged, preferably from the same gallows, one straight after the other. I should go first.

I was thirsty again. I went across the room, and while I was filling my glass at the sink, I glimpsed through the window a movement on the lawn. I turned off the lights and saw by the cloudy glow of a waning gibbous moon a fox vanish into the shadow of our hedge. How fortunate that we had forgotten our long-ago dream of keeping hens.

The night was cold. Before sitting down, I put more logs on the fire, slid the air-vent knob to maximum and left the glass door open wide. I took a deep drink of water and settled back to wait for the new logs to take. At one corner of the dairy there was an accidental alignment of the brickwork or a gap in the pointing that caused a soft note to sound whenever the wind was just a little stronger than a gentle breeze. Too hard, too soft, and the whispering flute-like note would vanish. I heard it now, the unvarying pitch coming and going with the wind's rise and fall. Its familiarity soothed me. I closed my eyes and for the first time in months, or even years, I felt expansive and peaceful, released from the fractures and tensions that the random elements of my character imposed on me. In such a state of mind, I remembered my luck in being alive, in simply being. So easy, not to have existed, so easy to forget in the fine detail of daily life, and vital to recall from time to time. That was something I learned from Percy.

The scroll was lying on my lap and it was as if my fingers had motives of their own. While I had been off in a dream, they had been fiddling with the bow I had tied not long ago in the Barn. They pulled on an end of ribbon, the knot came loose and the vellum swelled and unfurled. I sat up. Of course, I knew what I wanted. I was looking at the final sonnet, the corona, the poem's crown. I conceded Francis his due, for it showed technical mastery, to take the first line of each of the preceding sonnets, put them together in strict sequence and make perfect and simple sense. The crowning sonnet anticipated the ultimate farewell and assumed the tone of a poised and solemn valediction. But it also contained a fond invitation. From Francis to me. We have loved each other for many years. According to the poem, we are growing old and do not have long to live, and what's most important for us now is to wander together through our home, this earth, and, before we part forever, remind ourselves of the beauty and delight of living things and how deeply we are bound to them. The poet called up the ghost of Darwin – 'There is grandeur in this view of life'. In our physical constitution, Francis went on, we are also bound to inanimate rocks, water and air.

The miracle, I decided that evening in 2014, was that the poet could force these ideas into existence in such flowing terms against the grain of his being, and confer the magic of the impersonal and universal that touches all great art. But the miracle was also a lie. The invitation was not merely to a stroll. It was a summons to a journey that Francis, the man, not the poet, never wanted to take, though he knew that Percy would have taken it with me. If 'A Corona for Vivien', Francis Blundy's finest poem, lived into the future it would be admired down through the generations. I was certain of that. Wrenched by time from its context, the poem would attain perfection.

But if this masterpiece passed into oblivion, no one would give it a thought and a thousand scholarly papers would never be written. A murder would be avenged – by a party to the crime – and Francis could never steal Percy from me. What would remain would be this, my plain account, which might one day be found. I rolled up the scroll, tied it and balanced it in my palm – so light, so weighty. I leaned forward and felt the stove's raw heat on my face drawing me closer. I stretched out my hand, let go, and in an instant of brightness it was done.

Glenuig
July 2020

NOTE

The Confessions of Vivien Blundy, edited and with notes by Professor Thomas Metcalfe, with an introduction by Rose Church, Gibbon Professor of History, both of the University of the South Downs, and with a preface by Dr Donald Drummond, Senior Archivist at the Bodleian Library, was published in 2125 by the University of the South Downs Press.

ACKNOWLEDGEMENTS

[2pp to come]

ABOUT THE AUTHOR

[2pp to come]